CONGO '63

CONGO '63

J. A. Dunbar

JANUS PUBLISHING COMPANY
London, England

First Published in Great Britain 2005
by Janus Publishing Company Ltd,
105-107 Gloucester Place,
London W1U 6BY

www.januspublishing.co.uk

British Library Cataloguing-in-Publication Data
A catalogue record for this book
is available from the British Library

ISBN 1 85756 611 4

Cover Design Simon Hughes
Printed and bound in Great Britain

Acknowledgements

I would like to thank my family for their support and advice. This novel would never have come about without the assistance of Sandy Dunbar, Lynne Fredlund and Chris Adams.

Introduction

During the 1960's the Belgian Congo was in a complete political, tribal and economic mess. A Belgian controlled multi-million dollar timber company, "de Bruins", had made the decision to remove as much hardwood as possible from the Congo Basin before a government could be elected and nationalise the industry. Before they could put their plan into motion a local tribe intimidated the labour force from the sawmill. Fearing for their lives, the labour force refused to enter the jungle in search of the valuable hardwood.

I was one of the fifty men recruited by de Bruins to protect their interests. Though we were ill informed and poorly equipped, we entered the terrifying world of the big trees, mud, greed, marauding tribesmen, witchcraft, murder and madness. It soon became apparent that de Bruins was interested in only one thing – stripping the jungle – and our lives were expendable.

Then, from amongst the chaos, appeared a Russian backed witch-doctor who was manipulating the tribesmen. The Russian agent's one aim was to destabilise the region. Then out of the dark world of torture an unbelievable planned attack materialised. An isolated Catholic mission station was targeted. The attack was so unbelievable and inhuman that no westerner would understand the reasoning behind it.

Our unit was tasked to remove the nuns to safety. The operation turned into raging battles with warring warriors, army deserters and the elements. This was where I found a gold pendant that would change my life and where I met the beautiful novice nun. She was ultimately to become my business partner, my friend and lover.

I passed down this savage road physically unscathed but mentally, who knows?

Chapter 1

Dirk van Wyk walked out of the plush boardroom of de Bruins enterprises, situated on the outskirts of Paris. As he shut the doors behind him it seemed to cut off the hostile stares and tense atmosphere from within. The plush maroon carpet of the lobby was soft under his feet and strangely comforting. The nervous sweat of the past hour's grilling had made his shirt stick to his body. The tremor in his hand was still there and the stomach cramps probed uncomfortably at his bowels. He needed the toilet urgently.

Dirk locked himself in a cubical, loosened the top button of his shirt and sat upon the pan. His thoughts were rushing through his mind as he tried to regain his self-control and confidence.

"Hell man, what am I doing here? Standing up to that bunch of money grabbing bastards." He whispered and wiped his face on an already soiled handkerchief. "I shouldn't have come. I should have just let the bloody sawmill go the way of the others. Man, when they saw my figures of forty-two million dollars profit I could smell the greed! They could not even think straight. The managing director, Baron von Kleef, he is all right. He is already a rich man in his own right. Yes, he understood. He had been out there to the Congo Basin to see for himself and had taken an active role in the multimillion-dollar business. But as far the others, I doubt they even know where the place is on the map!" Van Wyk buried his face in his hands, breathing hard.

A while later he sat back on the toilet. Normality was coming back slowly. The soft music drifted through the cubicles and the aroma of the lilac air freshener was strong in his nostrils, making him feel nauseous.

Damn it, he wished he'd had a camera to capture the looks on the faces of the members of the board. Their faces he would never forget, as he lay down his demands. Six months was all he wanted and possibly a further six if everything went well.

Dirk shut his eyes, breathing deeply. He knew he was well out of his depth and it was possible they would not agree. If they fired him, there was no one to replace him as manager of Villa Vista sawmill. Given the present state of the Congo, in July 1963, no white man would be prepared to take on the venture that he had proposed and the mill would close down. In many ways it was a race against time. The other possibility was that if a new government was ever elected they would push up taxes or just nationalise the timber industry.

His three white assistants remained because they trusted him. His two thousand labourers remained because many of them had nowhere else to go, with the civil war raging in the west and south. He had also told them he would talk on their behalf at the meeting with the big bosses in Paris.

His demands had been reasonable; for he liked to think of himself as a hard but fair man. Each of his labourers, after completing the six-month contract, would receive a bonus equivalent of three hundred dollars. For each of his assistants there would be a bonus of three hundred thousand dollars. Then the crunch came. The part that had made his stomach turn to jelly and want to run from the room. He had thought of reducing his demand to possibly five hundred thousand, but with a tremendous effort had spat it out. A bonus of one million dollars for himself upon completion of the six-month contract!

His approach from the beginning had been simple. The area in which the Villa Vista sawmill operated was vast and sparsely populated. From the two neighbouring sawmills which had closed down, he would employ their retrenched labour force and then poach timber from their operational areas and strip the jungle. He doubted the timber industry would ever get another chance like this. Villa Vista would run day and night. All lumber would be brought by road or river to the sawmill at Villa Vista, where it would be squared off and shipped out. There would be no messing about cutting this valuable commodity into planks. He had already made discreet enquiries and there were a number of sawmills in Europe prepared to take all the lumber he could produce at the going rate.

At that stage he had been interrupted by a damned Englishman, Reece Jones. The fool did not understand the situation out there and the risks he and his men took.

There was also another problem that had appeared a few weeks earlier. At first he had heard whispers down at the compound, and then his "boss boy" had approached him. The labour force was afraid. They were afraid to enter the jungle in search of the hardwood. They were afraid of a primitive tribe known to them as the Mongu Teng, who had ordered all other tribes from their forest.

He, van Wyk, had been in the Congo for twenty years and thought he knew it and the different tribes well, but he had never heard of them. He knew all about the local tribe, the Mongu who were one of the largest. Seventy per cent of his labour force came from this tribe and they were intelligent and good workers.

He had approached a friend and local gendarme, Perry Hough, and he too confirmed what his labour had reported. Perry had said that there was little he could do because of under-staffing. Anyway, how did one find the Mongu Teng in the two thousand square kilometres of jungle?

The members of the board had stared at him in disbelief when he had explained that the primitive and secretive Mongu Teng had now begun to disrupt the multimillion-dollar logging operation. Then he had made a further request for armed guards to be present at the sawmill as well as accompanying the logging gangs deep into the jungle, and a further group to guard the railhead some seventy kilometres downstream and to assist the local Gendarmerie.

He had pointed out his figures to the board under the heading "Security". He had already made extensive enquiries and, for a reasonable fee, fifty trained soldiers could be hired from a security firm in Johannesburg, South Africa. These men could be on site within thirty days from the day of the board's approval.

Reece Jones had tried to interrupt, shouting something about him doing his job and duty, but Baron von Kleef had put him in his place quickly and quietly and he'd been excused and asked to wait in the lobby.

Van Wyk stood before the mirror, running water into the basin. He was not pleased with what he saw. A big, sallow-skinned, middle-aged man in a crumpled grey suit, his dark brown hair was greying and starting to thin on top. He washed his hands and face in the cold water. Then he dragged a comb through his unruly hair. He stared hard at himself in the mirror and pulled a face. This would be the only chance he would ever get to lay his hands on a million dollars. If it worked out he would retire. The Congo, which had been his home for so long, was in the process of self-destructing and he doubted that Zaire, as it was now called, would settle down for a long time.

An hour later Baron von Kleef joined van Wyk in the private bar. He bought a round of drinks. "Right my boy. You have got what you want. They have given you the green light. The only one to vote against was that idiot Reece Jones. He is still mumbling about doing your duty and your job. The funds for the running costs will be transferred and I will see to it that you get the full support of all the members of the board. Here's to a new adventure." He raised his glass, smiling, and the two men toasted each other.

Dirk van Wyk's Jeep roared along the rough, muddy, rutted road. The vehicle was caked with mud and the windscreen was clean only where the windscreen wipers had wiped layer after layer of muddy water away. The jungle on either side of the road was dark and sinister. Glowing eyes of the night animals shone menacingly in the dark of the jungle and the odd night insect splattered against the filthy windscreen.

He held a can of beer in his left hand and wrestled with the steering wheel with his right. It was very close to eleven and he had only about ten kilometres to go. He hummed to himself. He was going to surprise his wife Jean. That morning she had complained of a headache and nausea and had remained at home. He hoped she did not have an attack of malaria coming on. By rights he would only be returning the following day. The round trip normally took about twenty-four hours, but Hennie de Wet had met him halfway. They had shared a few beers and sandwiches. Then together they had loaded the saw blades and teeth and literally halved the time it usually took.

At this time of the year the roads were not that bad. They were nothing like it when he had first arrived at the site chosen for Villa Vista. Some days even the bulldozer got bogged down. He had, alone and through his dogged determination, built Villa Vista into what it was. He loved it out here with the continuous challenge of being the manager. Dirk smiled. He had done a lot of improvements over the years. There were bungalows for his managers and a country club, as well as rough but reasonable accommodation for his labour, with a school and clinic nearby. He had built the mill up to being one of the major producers of timber in the region, if not in central Africa.

Once a year, Jean and he would take their annual two months' leave. They would return home to Belgium where he would attend a meeting with either Baron von Kleef or the shareholders. They would visit friends and relatives and Jean would go shopping with her sister and spend extravagantly. Then they would board the plane and return to this world for another ten months.

His house was two kilometres away from the noise and bustle of the sawmill. It nestled on the banks of the Maringa river, in park-like surroundings that had been hewn out of the virgin jungle. There was nothing like sitting with Jean in the late evening watching the hippo and crocodiles and listening to the sounds of the birds roosting for the night. It was complete peace and tranquillity and everything he had ever wanted.

As he rounded a slight bend in the road, the Jeep lurched violently to the right, skidding sideways and ploughing into a deep slime-filled furrow on the side of the road, and then came to an abrupt halt. He knew that it was a puncture. He sat and relaxed for a moment and sipped the rest of his beer. At the angle the vehicle stood it would be a major job to change the wheel.

Damn it! Things had been going so well.

About a kilometre up the road was the camp of a small film crew run by a producer of wildlife films named Reginald P. Clark. Reginald was a tall, arrogant, thirty-year-old prat, and obviously supported by a wealthy father. They had been camped out for the last three weeks, filming the underwater activities of the river. Clark claimed to have a string of films behind his name which van Wyk had never heard of.

The three white members had visited the Villa Vista country club once and made fools of themselves by demanding to bring their black assistants with them and then had set about getting very drunk indeed. That night, at the mill's country club, Clark had shown off a gold and diamond pendant, which he wore around his neck. He said it was his good luck charm. Dirk had wondered if it was real or just fake. If real, it would probably be worth a small fortune and only a fool would carry such an expensive item around with him, especially in Africa. The film crew had not been invited to the club again nor had he seen any of the crew again, other than in passing.

Dirk van Wyk had climbed from the cab, and removed his rifle from the clip between the seats, and slung his torch around his neck. He would have to walk. He dreaded the idea of asking Clark for a lift. He decided he would not ask, though it was all of ten kilometres to the house.

Dirk strolled along, for it was not that dark. The moon filtered through the trees and fireflies glowed in the chirping undergrowth. A hippo bellowed in the distance.

The film-maker's camp appeared, nestled between the big trees just off the road. The tents were glowing white in the poor light. A smoky fire glowed between the tents. Two Land Rovers stood silent, already dripping with dew. If there was a night watchman he did not see him as he passed. It was funny, he thought. The Peugeot saloon driven by Clark was not present. He wondered where the stupid chap had got to. He passed one of the junctions in the road that lead to Swart's mine just as the moon came out from behind the clouds, casting long black shadows. An owl hooted and a monkey chattered and then fell silent and Dirk trudged on.

Jean and he had designed and built the house between them. It was the house of their dreams. It stood nestled between the road, the jungle and the river. The shadows played tricks amongst the tree ferns, the exotic plants and the rockery. As he crunched up the rough driveway he felt tired but was pleased to be home. What a surprise he was going to give Jean.

He stopped in mid-stride, catching his breath. Jean's white Jeep stood in its place in the open three-car garage. His personal Jeep was there. It had rigged spotlights for hunting at night. But tonight the third spot was taken by a Peugeot saloon.

He stood there gasping for breath. A blinding madness erupted from within him. It was something that he could not contain. With a animal like scream he lunged forward, his rifle in his hands. The dogs in the house on hearing his approach had started to bark. He hit the front door at a full run. The door was of solid African teak and was locked. With a howl like a mad animal he bounced off it. He brought the rifle up to his shoulder and fired a single shot, shattering the lock. His booted foot did the rest.

The dogs howled and yapped at their master. There was a bang of a door from within and the pounding of running feet on the wooden floor, This was followed by the crash of the side door. Dirk was running. Jean appeared before him in the passage, her startled white face framed against the halo of her untidy black hair and rumpled cream night-dress.

"Dirk, no!" she screamed trying to block his path towards the side door.

"Get out! Get out!" he shouted gasping for breath. He made a huge effort to control himself. "When I get back you will be gone or I am going to kill you," he gasped, and then he brushed her aside. Then he was running blindly down the passage. A car engine started and roared off with the screech of tyres.

Dirk launched himself behind the wheel of his Jeep. Nothing mattered now. Jean would go, and Clark would die. Villa Vista would always be there with its challenges. He engaged gear and charged forward. The taillights of the Peugeot could be seen turning onto the main road. The race was on. The road was not too good, but the Jeep had a distinct advantage.

He was starting to gain on the racing Peugeot, his lights slicing through the darkness. The hunting spotlights on the roof were switched on and would blind any driver staring into his rear view mirror for too long. It was probably this that caused Clark to take the wrong road. At the junction in the road he had taken the road to Swart's mine, seventy kilometres from Villa Vista. It was seventy kilometres of hellish, winding jungle track. The mine had recently closed down. It was a road that went nowhere since the car ferry had been washed away by the flooded river.

Dirk van Wyk was a hunter and during those long hours he hunted Reginald P. Clark, knowing the man had nowhere to go. His great love for Jean had vanished into madness. Questions raced around inside his head. Why? Why had she taken such a risk? Why sleep with a man twenty years her junior? He found himself screaming obscenities into the night. "Why?" She knew how he despised the man. How and when had they got together? Surely he could not have been so blind? She had known him so well. She had been the love of his life. She had been everything. He knew one thing for sure. She would go and not be there when he returned.

The seventy kilometres between Villa Vista and Swart's mine seemed to have passed in a flash of time. First the abandoned prefabricated houses stood alongside the road, then came the steel winding gear and the tumbled-down labourers' huts. Fifty metres before him, Clark's taillights bobbed and weaved like two red eyes.

A deep calmness suddenly descended on Dirk. All thoughts of Jean were expelled from his mind. He focused entirely on the racing saloon. Around the next bend was a straight section of road. It was now time to finish the chase. He accelerated, closing the gap between the two vehicles. He thought of Clark's panic and terror and it felt so very good.

The straight section of road was before them. Dirk stood on the brakes bringing the Jeep to a skidding halt. Taking his rifle from between the seats he stepped into the road. The Jeep's headlights and hunting lights illuminated the road as if it was day.

Chapter One

Seemingly in slow motion he brought the hunting rifle to his shoulder, aimed and fired once, and then twice. The shots reverberated through the forest and the saloon slewed sideways and vanished from view into the dense undergrowth at the side of the road. Dirk van Wyk grinned and wiped the sweat from his face. He climbed into his Jeep and drove slowly to the spot where the saloon had left the road, turning the Jeep so the lights shone into the cavernous dark jungle. The two red eyes were there marking the spot where the saloon had come to a stop.

Van Wyk went forward, rifle in hand and peered through the mud-splattered rear windscreen that now sported two neatly placed bullet holes. He could make out the dark shape of Clark slumped over the steering wheel. He opened the door and Clark tumbled out onto the forest floor. Van Wyk smiled and kicked him viciously. There was no movement. There was a soft gurgle and a mass of blood belched from the dead man's mouth. Van Wyk chuckled, shaking his head as he stepped around the body. He leant into the sedan and switched off the ignition and the lights. He stood there looking around. In a few days the vehicle's tracks would be gone and in a few more it would be covered by the jungle's growth. The vehicle was already almost hidden from the road. In a short time the body would decompose and be eaten by the animals. Death in the jungle was nothing new.

A year had passed, and then another. Occasionally he had thought of Jean with complete blind hatred. He had not returned to Belgium during those years. And he had never tried to contact her, nor she him.

There had been enquiries and an investigation. Sub-Inspector Perry Hough had come around making enquiries. Hough was a friend, a hunting and drinking companion, a man who accepted the ten thousand dollars offered for his help. The film company had asked many questions. Mr Clark senior had hired investigators. Hough had sorted that side out and slowly things had returned to normal.

Dirk van Wyk peered down at the lights of Paris as the Air France Boeing lifted off the runway. He was able to relax for the first time in days. He had pulled it off. In six months he would be a millionaire. He doubted if the government or the timber industry would last another six months. He would be rich, and he would leave the place of the big trees, of disease, and warring tribesmen. He smiled to himself. The funds would be transferred, allowing soldiers to be recruited, and the troublesome primitive Mongu Teng would be kept at bay. Nothing in the world was going to stop him collecting his bonus at the end of the six months.

Chapter Two

It was one of those hot balmy Natal Midland's afternoons, the hot
berg wind blowing puffs of yellow dust, which coated everything. I sat
dreaming on the back seat of the rickety school bus. The kids were
silent for a change, probably after a week at school, which had
exhausted them. I had a weekend ahead of me. Baker had hired out
his .22 rifle to me at the exorbitant rate of three rand a day and ten
cents a bullet.

Majola, our Zulu herd boy, claimed to have seen a very fat buck,
a duiker, at the bottom of the neighbouring farm. He claimed that if
I shot it, I'd keep the hindquarters and he'd take the forequarters.
He could sell whatever remained for fifteen rand, then divide the
money and we would both score. At that time of my life four rand
fifty was a small fortune.

The bus came to a squeaking halt at the bottom of the driveway
leading to Hill Farm. I collected my bag from the cluster on the
floor, and trotted down the aisle to the front exit.

"Thanks Chilli Pip," I said to our patient and conscientious
Indian driver.

He grinned. "See you Monday Mac." He was playing with the
throttle, making the bus rock gently.

How he had got a name like that no one seemed to know. Maybe
it was the hot curry he was known to eat. I jumped down onto the
dusty driveway, and the bus pulled off in a cloud of diesel fumes and
dust. Hitching my bag over my shoulder I set off down the driveway.
Before me stretched a kilometre of dusty track, lined with battered
bluegum trees. The wind seemed to have intensified, making the

11

trees moan gently. Bits of bark that could no longer take the windy onslaught came tumbling down into my path. It was winter and the sparse African veld was brown and dry.

The farmhouse stood at the end of the driveway. It was built of grey stone with a flaking red, rusting roof. Today there was no sign of life. Majola was either in his hut or asleep behind a bush, out of the wind. I plodded along, every now and again leaving the track to check a snare. Majola and I set the snares in areas where we were likely to catch something. Doves, hares and other small creatures were our targeted prey. Today the snares were empty.

We made the snares out of anything, like fishing line, wire and bicycle brake cables. It all worked pretty well. Once we had caught a scrawny duiker and Gran had roasted the hind quarters using garlic and bacon. It had been really tasty.

A couple of cows came into view, foraging in an old maize field. Their skinny rumps were backed into the wind. Oupa had twenty cows of various descriptions. He milked them twice a day, and sent Majola to the nearby African location, called Slang Spruit (Snake Stream), to sell the milk. That was the only income from the five hundred acres. He always spoke of leasing out ground to neighbours but it never happened.

I reached the house and went around to the kitchen door. The grapevine, the only greenery for kilometres around, looked good this year. It did well under the protection of the veranda. The kitchen screen door swung to and fro, squeaking gently in the wind. Stripe, our fox-terrier, raised his head as I approached, wagged his tail twice and then went back to sleep.

I helped myself to cold, stringy chicken from the beat-up old fridge and went out onto the veranda and sat in the shade on the top step. The chicken was really tough and it took a lot of chewing. I often wondered how Oupa managed, as he had so few teeth.

Before me was the cow shed, grey and dingy with a few coloured chickens huddled against the wall out of the wind. The old Massey Ferguson tractor stood rusting silently, weeds growing through its foot plate and two flat tyres. It had been standing there for over a year. Beyond that was the pasture, brown and windswept with broken-down rusting fences leaning aimlessly every which way. Nearby was a stand of prickly pears, with Majola's hut in the middle. Just the roof could be seen from the step. A plastic fertiliser bag had hooked itself around a small peach tree and was flapping like a battle pendant of years gone by. This was my world, a picture of complete desolation.

But I had a dream. It was to build a dam, not a very big dam, but one that would be large enough to irrigate an acre or so of kukui grass, and an acre or so of vegetables. In time, I planned to expand the irrigation so that the small valley where the seeping stream appeared and disappeared in the hard clay soil would become completely productive and green. Such was my dream.

The problem was that I had no money. Oupa and Gran had nothing, just Oupa's war pension. There was no one who would give Oupa any sort of financial backing, and I often suspected that he owed money, although he never admitted this.

I had planned the whole operation with the use of the *Farmer's Weekly*, of which I was an ardent reader. If only I had three or four thousand rand, I could do it. I knew I could. Oupa would listen patiently, nodding his head in agreement, then eventually saying he was too old to start again. Majola listened to me but did not understand finance. He said it was a good idea as cows needed green grass to produce more milk. That was as far as it went.

Strange, I often thought. Oupa was only sixty-five, still big and very strong for his age and he still carried with him his Scots accent. He had arrived in South Africa soon after the Second World War. He had travelled to the gold fields where he claimed to have made a lot of money. He had then come to Natal and met and married Gran. The farm had been a good proposition, close to the market and the large African area around Pietermaritzburg. I could remember a few years back when everything was green and lush. Oupa had grown fields of cabbages, sold milk and planted acres of maize. Then we'd had our own bull and did not have to borrow a bull when one of the cows came on heat, as we had to now. The milk sales brought in enough for food and Majola's wages. The drought came and Oupa had lost heart. He drank too much and things became as they are now, with Oupa and Gran waiting for pension day.

Majola appeared in the distance, his moth-eaten jersey flapping around his lanky frame as he drove the cows before him. On seeing me he left the cows to find their own way, and came across the dusty field.

Majola was old, but how old? No one knew. He spoke of many things. He had been deep into the earth in search of gold and out to sea in fishing boats. He had hunted elephant, lion and every sort of buck and his great love for hunting he had passed on to me. His knowledge of animals, large and small, was immense. He spoke of the Umfolozi and the Tugela rivers, of tribal battles at his home at Misinga, Zululand, and he had a number of scars that he proudly displayed given half a chance. He had never been to school, could not sign his name, but in his greying old head was a great wealth of common sense and knowledge.

"No meat today," he said with a toothless grin. He was referring to our snares.

I shook my head. "Nothing," I said, in Zulu.

"Did you get the bigger gun?" He grinned with anticipation.

"Yes," I said nodding. Hopefully Majola was not wasting my time.

"Tomorrow afternoon he will be there. Haw! He is a beauty – horns like this." Majola grinned even more widely and extended his forefinger.

I knew about Majola's exaggerations, but could not prevent myself from feeling a little quiver of excitement. If I managed to shoot the buck, it would be the biggest animal I had ever shot, not that a duiker was very big. They weighed in the vicinity of about sixteen or seventeen kilograms, about the size of a large dog, but I had seen them run. They were very quick, and extremely difficult to shoot as they plunged through the bush.

"Tomorrow," said Majola looking over his shoulder. He moved off quickly. He had spotted Oupa's pickup leaving the main road and carefully negotiating the driveway. Oupa had probably had a few drinks too many. Majola recognised the possibility of having to unload the pickup and was making his escape.

Chapter Two

It was the fifteenth of the month, pension day. Gran would do her shopping and Oupa would go to the betting shop with his pocket money which Gran would have had handed out reluctantly. Invariably the two old people would be having an argument about something really trivial. Gran would not talk to Oupa for a few days, although she would make sure she got her share of the Mellowood Brandy. I often thought it funny that Gran never got drunk. On the other hand Oupa would get completely motherless and would end up sleeping on the dining room floor.

The pickup clattered up in a cloud of dust and crunched to a halt at the bottom of the steps. Oupa, with a fixed stare on his face, climbed out carefully and shouted for Majola to remove the maize meal. Gran tumbled out. I greeted her and went down the steps to help her with her shopping bags.

"I will never understand you Oupa," she snapped at no one in particular, "half a bottle, half a bottle." She climbed quickly up the steps and disappeared through the screen door. I followed at a more leisurely pace, dumped the shopping on the kitchen table and returned to the step.

Oupa grinned cheerfully and tossed me a box of pellets for my airgun. "Give them rats hell laddie. There are far too many of them in the cow shed. Majola!" he bellowed into the wind. Then he carefully made his way up the steps.

Gran had returned red-faced and was standing with her hands on her hips. "Mackay, you know damn well what the policeman said; if you get caught driving drunk again – prison! How the hell would we get to town with you inside?" She waved a ham-sized fist at the old man, who visibly winced. "Can't leave you for a moment! You knock off half a bottle in the parking lot!" She shook her head and went back through the swing door. Oupa followed slowly and appeared almost fearful to enter the house.

Majola appeared round the shed pushing a wheelbarrow. He whistled casually as he loaded up the bags of maize meal. Stripe woke up and all of a sudden decided to attack Majola, viciously snapping at his ankles, and he received a kick for his efforts. The two were great friends.

I could hear the tongue-lashing Oupa was quietly enduring. It's a wonder the two old people never came to blows. Stripe collapsed again against the cow shed wall, where the late afternoon sun still reached. Winter around Pietermaritzburg could get really cold, and at this time of the year frost could be expected.

Later, taking my airgun, I headed for the cow shed. Stripe jumped up and followed me, his tail held at a wide-awake angle. He knew about guns, sticks and spears and, all in all, he was a very knowledgeable dog. Oupa was right. Lately there seemed to be an influx of rats. What they ate I could never work out, but they gnawed the hell out of the roofing. The little maize dropped by the cows was insufficient to keep them all alive. Stripe, like a good hunting dog, knew where to look and soon there were rats fleeing in every direction.

The idea was to kill as many as possible on the ground using a light stick. One had to be quick and accurate. When we had cleared the floor, the ones that made it to the rafters I would shoot down with my airgun. I was proud of my shooting ability. I can honestly say I never missed. Stripe was quick. As the wounded quarry hit the cement floor, he made sure that it was dead with a crunch of his jaws. By then the next wounded or dead enemy was hitting the floor. It was war.

At night we would quietly return, torch taped to the barrel and the massacre would start all over again.

My life was quiet. I'd no friends, except Majola. We roamed Hill Farm and the deserted neighbouring farm. The official hunting season meant little to us. We shot or snared anything, in or out of the hunting season. Guineafowl, francolin, partridge, they all went into the pot. One day, Majola killed a puff-adder. The snake was all of a metre long. It was duly cooked and eaten. It tasted a lot like fish. Its skin and head and its fat were sold to the witchdoctor at Slang Spruit for five rand. Majola spent it on beer and didn't come home for two days.

Oupa had been fed up and threatened to fire him, forgetting that it was me who'd had to milk the cows for the two days of his absence.

It had taken me most of the morning and it was done by hand. My hands, fingers and wrists took a real hammering.

The idea of the dam was always at the back of my mind. I often sat on the edge of the little valley with my dream of green grass, a veggie plot and a couple of really good Jersey cows, as they were my favourite. A while ago I had found a six-inch pipe and spent an afternoon setting it up. The stream now passed through the pipe that would be the centre of the dam wall. I had been pleased about that. I really did not want to leave Hill Farm as there was so much I wanted to do. If I could just find some money to get me started, I was sure I could survive and make a decent living. I sat and pondered my situation. Then I decided that, if I started to move the heavy clay soil and build a wall, maybe in six months when I was due to finish school, I could have a reasonable wall and sufficient water to start planting grass. I promised myself I would start soon.

I drifted back towards the silent old house. It had never entered my head to leave the desolate place. I knew there would be compulsory military call up of nine months as soon as I left school. But it all seemed so very far away.

Majola came and collected me late on Saturday afternoon. Armed with Baker's Remington single shot, bolt action .22 rifle we set off. Stripe fell in, tail erect and in hunting mode. Nothing was going to keep him away from this adventure. We set off across the old maize field, across the boundary fence and along the strip of bush that bordered the main road. The bush was very dense, thorn trees fighting for survival against the young black wattle. The under-growth was a mess of brambles. The wind was in our favour, humming gently through the telephone lines that could be seen sticking out here and there along the main road.

Majola selected a spot between two ant hills. He tested the wind with a sprinkling of dust.

Smiling cheerfully he whispered. "He is there." He pointed directly in front of us. There was an open space twenty metres in front of me and a vague footpath leading through the bush towards the road.

"I and the dog will go round and come from the road. You will have to be quick," whispered Majola.

Crouching next to the larger of the two ant hills I watched Majola and Stripe go off towards the road. Majola carried two heavy sticks that seemed to be extensions of his arms. It was warm, too warm for comfort, but when the sun slipped behind the hills it would turn bitterly cold.

A yellow-billed kite appeared and settled on a dead tree and set about demolishing a rat it had either caught or picked up off the road. I sat and dreamt. It was unlikely Majola would find the duiker in the thicket. It was also unlikely that it would come out directly in front of me when it had a choice of a hundred other directions to flee.

"Imbabala!" shouted Majola from the thicket. I picked up the excitement in his voice. Stripe was yapping. "Imbabala!" he shouted again. I could hear something breaking small branches and moving rapidly through the thick bush. All we needed was a bushbuck. All I had was a miserable .22 rifle, that fired only one shot at a time! I also knew that bushbuck rams were extremely dangerous, accounting for the death of many a hunter. At that moment I knew I was not going to shoot. It was going to pass. The rifle felt heavy in my nervous sweaty hands.

Seconds later it broke cover and it was a shock to my system. I froze as the buck came crashing out of the thicket into my little clearing. He was huge, probably because I was crouched down making him look even bigger. The ram had long dangerous-looking horns and one seemed to have the tip missing. He was old, almost black in colour. My mind was numb and my mouth dry.

Then he saw me. I swear, on seeing me he changed direction, dropping his head ever so slightly, he charged straight at me. Parts of what happened only came back later. The buck was ten paces from my hiding place and he came at full tilt, hooves drumming on the hard baked soil. I could see his eyes like glowing embers and the numerous old scars on his head. I could see ticks on his partly laid back ears. Then he was somersaulting, his horns digging into the hard shale earth, legs coming over frantically thrashing the air. Dust and bits of dry grass were flying everywhere.

Suddenly Majola was there before me. "Mac are you all right?" he asked.

I nodded dumbly, standing rooted to the spot. I had this frightening urge to run. The buck had stopped thrashing and was lying still.

Grinning broadly, Majola drew his knife. He looked uncertainly around. "Haw, we go for a mpunzi, it turns into a nkonka. It is magic," he said seriously.

As I came back to earth, my hands, arms and legs started to shake uncontrollably. They would not stop. Majola ignored me. Stripe was still barking in the bush. Suddenly a duiker burst from the thicket and was gone lunging and weaving, leaving Stripe with his short legs, far behind.

"Agh no, there were two!" I heard myself mutter. I could not remember shooting the bushbuck as my mind had gone completely blank.

Majola had cut the animal's throat, letting it bleed and then we started to skin it. I helped him roll it onto its back. He opened the stomach cavity, then with a little effort pushed dry poles under its sides to keep it in an upside down position. Majola chatted excitedly. I did not listen as I struggled to focus on what had happened.

Majola pointed to the bullet hole in the buck's forehead. "Wonderful shot Mac," he exclaimed smiling proudly. Majola hastily made a fire with a few dry sticks and roasted the liver, which we ate. It was only then that my shakes eventually subsided.

A while later Majola left me and went off to get bags to put the meat into. It was starting to get cold and the sun was all but gone. I sat alone next to the fire, trying to recall the shooting step by step. It had happened so very quickly. Even after an hour, I still could not fill in all the missing pieces of those few moments. But deep down there was an unexplained sadness and uncertainty. Then the thought came to mind. Was the killing of the buck a sign of what awaited me in the future?

Majola returned and we loaded up our kill.

"Mac you must take the two hind legs. There is plenty of meat on them. I will take the front legs and the rest I will sell at Slang Spruit," said Majola as I helped him balance one bag on his head. Then he took one in each hand. I hoisted one over my shoulder and the other I half dragged, half carried.

They were more awkward than heavy.

"You must think of what you are going to tell Gran," said Majola with a chuckle. "Maybe the 'kheshla' will give me a lift to Slang Spruit. He is an understanding man."

I laughed aloud thinking of him involving Oupa in our adventure.

I placed the two hind legs on the kitchen table. Gran eyed me suspiciously.

"Donavan what have you and Majola been up to?" asked Gran. She then called for Oupa, who appeared at the door mumbling at being disturbed. He looked keenly at the two bloody legs.

"It's out of season. You'll end up in prison," he growled. Gran stood nodding, but there was a twinkle in Oupa's eyes, something I did not see too often these days.

"Where's Majola?" he asked looking through the door.

This was the tricky part. "He wants you to give him a lift to Slang Spruit to sell the rest of the meat, skin and hooves," I said almost cockily.

Oupa suddenly grinned. "You two hang the meat – Majola!" he bellowed.

"N'kosi," said Majola quietly from just outside the door. He had obviously been in the shadows listening to every word. His knowledge of the English language was amazing when it suited him.

"You black buggers go stupid when hunting," growled the old man.

"Put the rest of the meat in the pickup," he ordered.

"It's already there," said Majola with an impish grin.

"Right, and if anyone asks, you two found the buck run over on the road," said Oupa.

Majola was standing in the door grinning from ear to ear.

"Let's go," said Oupa and the two men disappeared into the night.

Chapter Two

Two days later Majola gave me twenty rand, this being my share of the sale. He gave me a further five to give to Oupa for the lift. It was the most money I had ever had at one given time!

A few days later I started to build my dam wall using a pick, shovel and wheelbarrow. I began to move the heavy clay soil from about twenty metres behind my wall site. It was back-breaking work and the going was extremely slow. By ten in the morning I was drenched with sweat, my hands were blistered and my back ached. Later, when I stopped and looked back at what I had done it looked like very little.

Looking round I found Majola was watching me. "Haw that's madness. It's a job for a bulldozer," he stated bluntly. "The earth swallows up the other earth, and what you move goes nowhere."

What he said seemed true, but I would keep on. It was a slim chance for me to remain on the farm and someday to make a go of the farm that Oupa had seemingly abandoned. The holidays were coming up soon, and I would move more soil then when I had time.

On Sunday after church (Oupa was a staunch Presbyterian), Gran had prepared one of the bushbuck's legs for lunch. With a healthy smattering of garlic, crispy bacon and roasted sweet potatoes, it was delicious. Neither of the old people ever mentioned shooting out of season and nor did they ask how I had obtained a gun that would fell a bushbuck. We all just enjoyed it. Thinking back, it had been one of the most satisfying Sunday dinners I had ever had.

Oupa could ramble on telling war stories, especially when he'd had too much brandy. He had been a Sergeant Major in the Black Watch and then he'd volunteered for the Commando training and, by the sound of it, he had seen a lot of action. One day, when he had drunk far too much, he had produced an old tobacco bag containing about twenty medals. The one he said he was most proud of was the Military Medal. He said it was one below the Victoria Cross and he started telling me the story of how he had won it, but fell asleep halfway through. It had something to do with D-day. He had never completed that story.

There were other funny little things about him. He was immensely proud of his Scottish heritage and at times spoke of his boyhood, and of the mist, snow, ice and cold in the far north of

Scotland, of his mining days in Johannesburg, and big money, whatever that meant.

Once a month Oupa would go to a MOTHS (Members of the Order of Tin Hats) meeting in the town. All members were soldiers from the wars. All Oupa's friends were members of MOTHS and they seemed to look after one other. Whenever his pickup broke down, one of his mates would fix it. In turn Oupa would drop off a couple of dressed chickens in payment. Whenever he needed help, it was just a phone call away.

Why was he called Oupa by me, heaven only knew. Oupa is Afrikaans for Grandfather. Oupa did not like the Afrikaners and called them Dutchmen. The Afrikaans-speaking boys and girls at my school were decent types and I got along with them well. Then why was he called Oupa? He claimed that he did not know. On the other hand I had my suspicions. Gran had grown up in the Orange Free State and I knew she spoke Afrikaans fluently and had often helped me with my Afrikaans homework. Her maiden name had been Graaf. Funnily, she always spoke English, no matter what. Another example of this type of thing was Stripe the fox-terrier. Stripe had black and white spots, so why Stripe? I found this all rather funny.

At last the school holidays had started and I worked for a few hours a day on the dam and hunted with my airgun in the afternoons. One day Majola told me about a big snake that he had found. He called it the king of snakes. The snake was worth a lot dead. That was if we could kill it and sell it to witchdoctor Zondi at Slang Spruit. He also suggested I hire Baker's gun again. But after the last outing with Baker's gun I was not so keen. Who could tell what might pop up out of the bush this time!

One day Oupa had come down to the dam and stood watching me for a while. "Keep it up," he growled. "Rome was not built in a day." Then he asked me to accompany him to the neighbouring farm, to meet one of his friends from MOTHS. This friend happened to be an estate agent and he was showing a potential buyer around the neighbouring farm that had been deserted for so long.

The two of us crossed the broken-down fence and walked over the old maize lands. Two cars were already parked in front of the ramshackled house and tumbled-down sheds. I had met Mr Thompson before. He shook Oupa by the hand, nodded to me and introduced us to a dark, squat, serious man named Carlos Manteiga, who shook my hand firmly, and looked me straight in the eye, making me feel very uncomfortable.

I then stood to one side listening to the three men. It was going to be a real nuisance having neighbours, as Majola and I regarded the farm as our hunting ground and knew every centimetre. I listened to Oupa as he seemed to know it all. He knew the soil types, water tables, rainfall and the cost of various services. I was amazed at all his knowledge and wondered how Hill Farm had got into such an economic mess.

"I have an uncle in Durban, who will be helping me financially," explained Manteiga, starting to make notes on a small pad. "He owns two vegetable shops in Durban and one in Pietermaritzburg. I will grow vegetables and he will sell them."

The thought crossed my mind that maybe I could grow something and he could sell it for me. That was, if he bought the farm. I would have to get a move on with my dam. I pondered my problems as I listened with half an ear to the three men talking business.

Finally, the meeting was over and Oupa and I walked back across the dry fields. It was hot and still. What surprised me most was that Oupa was puffing and taking long deep breaths, like a man completely out of condition.

"These foreigners," he grumbled between gasps, "are getting in everywhere and seem to have all the money. That guy Manteiga comes from Mozambique. He is going to cause trouble amongst the local blacks when he brings Shangaan labour with him." He stopped in mid-stride to gasp for air. It was not actually surprising that Oupa was so out of condition. All he did was walk to the cow shed in the morning and deliver the milk. Then he'd return to sit next to the radio, move into the kitchen for lunch and afterwards back to his chair next to the radio. The walk across to the neighbouring farm had really shown him up. I found it also strange how Oupa had supported Mr Thompson's sales talk. In true Scots tradition he did very little for nothing. I wondered where the financial connection was between the two of them.

A week later I heard from Oupa that mister Manteiga had bought the neighbouring farm and would be moving in the next week. In the meantime, I had been trying to get hold of Baker to hire his rifle.

The holidays were now in full swing. I worked on the dam for a few hours every morning until it became too hot to work. Then I'd find Majola and we would sit around in the shade discussing this and that. The new neighbours were going to upset our hunting. The snake Majola had spoken of was in the bush not far from where I had shot the bushbuck, on the neighbouring farm.

One day, just after midday, we carefully crossed onto the neighbouring farm and went through the bush to where Majola said the snake lived. It was a small glade with a swampy bit in the middle. We settled in the shade and only spoke in whispers. He said the snake was big. He indicated with his stick and it was at least three times the length of his stick – roughly three metres.

We searched the area before us with our eyes. It was a funny, still place as there were no birds. Yet, I had counted about eleven bird nests in the trees. Insects buzzed around. Majola slept and snored softly. It was really very pleasant.

My eyes were never still. I searched the ground for a second time, and then moved my search into the trees. Opposite me was a mimosa tree with dry green leaves and heavy branches. Below it was a jumble of dry wood and small bushes. My eyes scanned the area a number of times. The snake could be anywhere. Time drifted by. Majola slept. I searched but got bored with the whole adventure of locating the big black mamba. I was about to wake Majola when I saw it. At first I was not sure, because I thought it was part of the mimosa tree, dappled grey with ageing green fungi on its skin which made it almost invisible. It had been there all the time, right in front of us. It was all of what Majola had said, easily three metres long. It lay dead still. If it knew we were there it was not showing it. I marvelled at its size and length, knowing only too well it was one of the most deadly snakes in Africa.

After a while I woke Majola. "Haw," he whispered. "It is magic, right in front of us."

Anything out of the ordinary became magic in the old black man's eyes. We left the snake's glade and headed for home. The reptile gave me the creeps. It was so evil, still, deadly and silent. Then, thinking about its appearance, it had probably eaten recently and was just basking on the branch letting its food digest. Had it been aware that we were present?

Majola interrupted my train of thought. "Mac when you shoot that one," referring to the snake, "you must hit it right here." Majola tapped the base of his skull. "We must not damage the head too much, the syngoma (witchdoctor) will pay good money."

"Yes" was all I managed to utter as we plodded along deep in our own thoughts. I was not that sure I was doing the right thing.

The next day I tried to contact Baker but he was away. The dam building went on painfully slowly. Early one morning I first heard, and then saw the tractors and bulldozers arrive at Manteiga's farm. Then, each day, engines started at sunrise and stopped at dusk. The bush was cleared, fields were ploughed and roads were put in. A large truck and numerous workmen arrived at the house and in a day it was transformed from a tumbled-down building into a white walled, red-roofed house. Two of Manteiga"s men started replacing the wire on the boundary fences.

One afternoon Carlos came across the boundary fence and inspected my dam building.

"You got quite a way to go," he said and then bent down and examined the soil. "It is a good clay soil and will make a fine dam wall."

"I hope to be nearly finished by Christmas," I said, but then almost immediately felt foolish. Deep down I doubted that I would ever finish the wall. The soil I moved seemed to go nowhere.

"You must keep it up Mac," he said sincerely. He asked after Oupa and then went off towards the house.

A water-boring truck had arrived, with its drill mounted high on its back, like a sort of rocket launcher. The machine had settled in the valley and proceeded to sink shafts deep into the earth in search of water. I watched from a distance, and started to feel very despondent. The transformation that was taking place next door was just money talking. Half of me said, "Give up the dam." The other half said, "You started it, keep going. It has to end sometime."

Then, one afternoon, I met two of Manteiga's labour fixing the boundary fence. They were surly looking men. I greeted them in Zulu. They seemed not to understand. I tried to start a conversation and found they spoke neither English nor Zulu. Then one tried to talk to me in Portuguese which I did not understand. This was the labour Manteiga had brought all the way from Mozambique to help him establish his new farm. To me it did not seem right as there were a lot of unemployed local men around.

That evening I told Majola about my meeting. "They are Shangaan dogs," he said. "They come from very far. Everyone's talking about them. We will have to be careful of them when there is a dark night."

I was always surprised at Majola's prejudice. I knew he thought nothing of the Xhosa and the Pondo tribes and regarded them as a type of traditional enemy.

Sunday was church, but this Sunday, after church, we had been invited to Manteiga's for a braai or barbecue. Oupa and Gran dressed in their Sunday-go-to-church clothes and I dressed in my school uniform. We bundled into the cab of the old Chev pickup and rattled into town. The service was long and meaningless in the airless old church and it was a relief when we all started to troop out into the hot, winter midday sun.

We arrived at Manteiga's to find he had prepared the 'braai' (barbecue) on the partially planted lawn under a syringa tree that supplied a little welcome shade. From close up the house looked really good. The lands around the house were neatly ploughed. Carlos said that we were welcome and that he was a very happy man as they had found water with the first shaft they had drilled and it was far more water than expected. It was enough water to irrigate a lot of land. I felt that twinge of jealousy again. The man was getting everything right. It seemed that all that counted was money.

He shook Oupa by the hand. "Mr Mac, if you had not spoken to me the day Thompson brought me round, I would never have bought this place," he said, and pumped Oupa's hand up and down. "This is," he waved his free hand, "just a little thank you."

I hung back, feeling completely out of place, and deeply jealous of the man's success. I knew that without money Hill Farm would never succeed.

Mrs Manteiga was short, dark and plump with two enormous dimples in the middle of her ample cheeks. She smiled happily as Gran introduced me to her. Her English was poor but understandable. Meat was already grilling on an open fire, giving off a fantastic aroma. A tray of drinks was brought out by the Zulu maid.

"Tell the girls to leave the record player and come and meet Mac," ordered Carlos.

The maid smiled knowingly and went off into the house. I had an uncomfortable feeling that I was being watched from the dark, shady windows of the house. It was confirmed when I heard a distant giggle. I was sure the girls had been peeping at me.

When they arrived, there were three of them. May was the youngest, Melanie was the next, probably thirteen or so, and Mia probably my age and by far the most attractive. They were all very similar to their mom, dark and pretty with dimples in their cheeks. The three were introduced to everyone. They giggled and smiled politely.

"Mia will be going to your school when it opens," said her mother. "What standard are you?"

"Seven," I said cautiously not wanting to get too involved.

"You will be in the same standard," said the woman with a pleasant smile. "She is very frightened of the new school. I hope you will keep an eye on her."

I said that I would. Mia smiled, showing off her dimples. She was really very pretty.

"Come with me," said Mia, "I want to show you the pony my dad bought me for my birthday."

I followed her and her two sisters around the sheds. I was relieved to be away from the adults. I also hoped Oupa was not going to make a spectacle of himself with Manteiga's booze.

I examined Mia out the corner of my eye. She was petite and very pretty with a dark complexion and long thick black hair hanging down her back. She had a surprisingly deep voice for such a small person. We came to a roughly built corral.

Mia leaned through the poles and called out, "Elvis, Elvis come boy!" and a black and white pony trotted across to the fence and nuzzled her through the rails. "I call him Elvis because of his mane. It's black like Elvis's hair," she explained. "I hope to join the pony club as he is brave and a good jumper."

I nodded knowingly; to buy, and to maintain a pony and join a pony club was an expensive business. I had seen a couple of pictures of Elvis Presley at school. I had also heard his songs on the radio. Other than that I knew very little about the singer. "He is a very handsome pony," I said, for want of anything else to say, as I patted his muzzle.

Strangely enough, I had never ridden a horse or pony. Although a number of years before I had ridden a donkey, it had been when Oupa had a bumper maize crop. The Africans from the nearby locations had used donkeys to transport the bags of maize. Whilst they waited for Oupa to sell them maize I had ridden a donkey around the farm, without a saddle or bridle, just a stick. It took a tap on the left to turn right and a tap on the right to turn left. They had been uncomfortable and tick-ridden. I grinned knowingly at the pony. Elvis would move a lot faster than a donkey and probably had reins and a saddle and I wondered if Mia would give me a go.

We four kids wandered back to the 'braai', only to find that Oupa was in full swing with a glass of brandy and Coke firmly grasped in his big hands, telling Carlos about the war, about ambushes and battles – his stories went on and on.

After we had eaten, the three girls and I left the adults and went into the lounge to listen to records. Mia had a collection of half a dozen Elvis Presley records. I listened in amazement as most of the songs I had never heard before. That afternoon I became a fan of Elvis.

Later that evening, when the brandy bottle was empty and we were feeling uncomfortably full, we rattled dangerously down the driveway back towards home. Gran and Mrs Manteiga had got on like a house on fire and I had to admit that Mia had been a pleasant surprise.

The school holidays came to an end and the long drag back to school started all over again. The rugby season was in full swing. All boys, unless they were exempt on medical grounds, had to play. However, I did not take part. This resulted in a letter to Oupa. I never found out what the contents of that letter were. Oupa had visited the headmaster Mr van der Walt. I had been left alone. I knew there was no money for kit, and the school bus left before rugby practice started. I would have to get a lift home with someone. No one had ever offered.

The Larsen brothers were the school's sporting heroes. They were big, muscular and blond – and the girls adored them, whilst the boys admired them. Wherever they went around the school they had their hangers on clinging to every word they said. Many of the gang even copied their hairstyles. Vinn Larsen, their father, owned an earth-moving business situated a few kilometres from Hill Farm. He was on all the school committees, supported the rugby team and always had a lot to say. Someone said that he and the headmaster had been seen going into the bar at the "Strong Man Inn". There were a lot of rumours about what went on in there. Often, when their mother was too busy to pick up the two boys in their red Mercedes sedan, they would travel in the school bus. I had very little to do with either of them and doubted that I would ever have a conversation with them.

Mia started school and we were in the same class and we often chatted at break. We got along extremely well. Once, she had come and sat next to me on the homebound journey, but this was frowned upon by the other students. There was an unwritten law, girls to the front and boys to the back of the bus.

I will never know where the problem started. It was a warm afternoon and school had broken up for the day. I stood in the shade waiting for the school bus. The other kids sat around on their school bags. It was unlike Chilli Pip to be late. Most days he would be waiting for us. As we waited, the two Larsen boys, accompanied by a gang of five, came ambling down the path. Obviously their mother was not picking them up today. One of the boys pointed towards me and the group swerved off their original course and headed straight for me.

"Why don't you play rugby?" asked the bigger of the two Larsens.

I was not expecting this. "I have no kit," I said feeling uncomfortable under the group's hostile stare. "Nor do I have money to buy any." There was a silence for a moment. There was a feeling of expectancy in the air.

"Are you chicken, like that pal of yours, Baker?" one of them sneered. I was taken aback. Baker was a fine track athlete. He had broken school records, and had been chosen for the interschool sports. Neither of the Larsens could beat him in a race. On the other hand Baker was no fighter and was useless at rugby. The Larsens had bullied Baker until his parents had seen the headmaster Mr van der Walt and the bullying had then stopped.

"No," I said swallowing hard, "I have not got a lift home either."

There was a giggle from one of the group. Expectations were high and there was a tension in the air that I had never experienced before.

"My dad, says old drunk Mackay won't last out till Christmas," sneered the smaller of the two Larsens.

I did not like the way the conversation was heading. Why bring Oupa into this? I shrugged and could not think of an answer. I did not want to fight and felt a tremor run down my spine. In the distance I heard the approaching bus.

"You're chicken!" the smaller Larsen sneered, thus getting a final word in.

I swallowed again. I truly did not know what to say. The bus rounded the corner and squeaked to a halt. Kids started to move towards it. The Larsen group broke up jostling for the front of the queue that was forming.

Standing in the queue a small hand grasped mine for a moment. Looking down I found Mia looking up at me.

"What did they want Mac? Are you okay?" she asked, concern written all over her pretty face.

I nodded dumbly. If there was another way home I would have taken it. She smiled, showing off her dimples.

"Just checking," she said softly and backed off.

Standing in the queue was the first time that I became aware that I was taller than the biggest Larsen, but very skinny and probably I was only half of his weight. I wondered what had brought on the verbal attack. They had not only had a go at Oupa, but at Baker too.

School continued, the full five days of the week. Then, on Saturday, I would spend a few hours on the dam wall. Sunday was church. Lunch was invariably roast chicken and whatever vegetables Gran could scratch up. I never told Oupa about the incident with the Larsens. Baker and I had a chat. He said the Larsens had left him alone since they'd been reported to the headmaster. Baker said he would hire me his rifle again if I came to get it. I still was not completely convinced that killing the big mamba was a good idea.

Every Friday Trinity School would hold assembly in the main hall. The whole school would attend. To be late meant a caning from Mr van der Walt. Everyone would file in and take a seat. Then the staff would come onto the stage and sit in a half-circle around the podium. There would be a slight wait. Mr van der Walt would enter, full of self-important dignity. Then everyone would stand until told to sit again. The assemblies were very boring, covering the introduction of new teachers, sport, the changing of classes and woe betide anyone not pulling his weight. He could easily be brought up before the whole school for an embarrassing tongue lashing.

I had managed to get a seat at the end of the row where I could see out of the window. Dlamini, one of Majola's relations, was painting white lines on the rugby field. The morning sun shimmered on the dewy wet grass. A large bluebottle fly was banging its head against the window pane trying to get out of the hall. I did not blame it as I longed to be outside. Suddenly cheer went up, bringing me back to earth. The two Larsen boys were on stage, both being presented with a certificate for having attended a rugby training camp. Finally they returned to their front row seats.

The headmaster continued his speech, half of which I had missed.

"On Saturday afternoon, at three sharp, I expect all of you to attend the match. This is a historic game. Trinity School plays against our biggest rivals, 'The College'." Another cheer went up. "Our team needs all your support. House leaders will lead you in the war cry as usual. There will be no leaving before the final whistle." Another cheer went up and Mr Wood, the team's trainer, smiled broadly and proudly. He stood up and invited the team up on the stage. Everyone clapped. I was not really interested but clapped anyway.

School broke up at 3pm and I wandered down to the bus stop, keeping a wary eye out for the Larsens and their gang. Thankfully they were nowhere to be seen. Chilli Pip was late again, and I stood in the shade. The younger kids had started a game of stingers, using a tennis ball. It was getting really rowdy. Then the bus arrived, and we clambered aboard. I looked back and my heart sank on seeing the Larsens and a couple of their followers come running out from the main building. Chilli Pip waited for them.

"Just making a few last minute adjustments to our game plan on Saturday," said the biggest of the two Larsens, as he pushed his way through the bus to a vacant seat three rows in front of me. Larsen and his gang were all in high spirits, joking loudly and telling the world what they were going to do to The College team. I sat and watched the traffic pass, hoping the Larsens would leave me alone.

We left town and were chugging along the main road. It was the way the boy in front of me behaved which made me sit up and take interest. He had stood up to see between the boys on the seat in front of him. Then, laughing quietly, he turned to his companion and I heard him say. "She is going to have trouble getting that lot out."

I stood up to see what was attracting their attention. I saw Larsen was leaning forward and was wrapping his chewed bubblegum around Mia's pony tail which hung down over the seat in front of him. As I watched she became aware of what he was doing, and she turned round, her face flushed.

"Keep your hands off me," her voice was deep and angry.

"You Porras are like a bunch of coolies. 'Look at my good quality cabbages and carrots'," he mocked loudly.

Mia pulled forward. Larsen pulled and stretched the bubblegum making a terrible mess. His gang laughed and jeered loudly.

"Leave the girl alone, Larsen," I uttered. I don't know who was more surprised. The voice seemed to come from nowhere. I was not even sure it was my voice or how I had got there. I was now standing over Larsen, who was still seated, but he was quick to respond. He kicked a few school bags out of the aisle and pulled himself to his feet.

"You like the little Indian girl?" he sneered. Then without warning he swung a punch at me. The big freckled fist skimmed across the top of my head. I was oblivious to all the shouts and jeers egging Larsen on. We were close, very close. I could smell his breath. It stank of bubblegum. My knee came up and he folded with a whoosh of escaping air and his mouth popped open in a gaping gasp. He toppled down amongst the cases and bags that littered the aisle with both hands clutching his groin.

It was all over in a second. I was panic-stricken for a moment. I knew my bus stop was nearby. I had to get off and away from what I had done. An unexpected heavy blow struck me hard on the back of my shoulder. Turning hurriedly round I found the second Larsen facing me. He was bigger and meaner than the first. His second punch thudded into my chest and sent me stumbling backwards but I still managed to maintain my footing. His face was red and his eyes filled with hate. I had seen him like this on the rugby field. He was rough and tough. He swung a punch again at me, so I ducked.

Oupa had, when drunk, boxed with me and shown me where to hit and kick. "Laddie," he had said, "hit a man on the nose. No one can see with tears in their eyes." Somewhere, deep in my subconscious, Oupa's words were there.

I slammed a straight left into Larsen's big face. Blood sprayed across the bus and the vocal supporters. Larsen made a choking sound and backed away. He held both his hands to his face trying to stop the blood flow. I now felt a desperate need to run, and raced blindly towards the exit.

Chilli Pip was waving his hands excitedly for me to get off. I jumped down into the dusty road. Mia followed me closely. She was a quite a sight, with bubblegum in her beautiful long dark hair. Her uniform was dishevelled and blood splattered. I stood there, my mind a blank. Then the shock of what I had just done hit me. The bus pulled away in a cloud of dust and black exhaust fumes. Baker dropped my bag from the window and gave me a thumbs-up with a cheerful grin. At least I had one supporter.

"You okay, Mac?" asked Mia, looking up at me with concern written all over her face.

My lips, arms, hands and legs started to shake uncontrollably. I walked carefully forward, picking up my bag.

"Let's go, Mac," said Mia taking my hand.

We walked for at least half the driveway hand in hand. I was only vaguely aware of her presence.

We stopped at the spot where she would cut across the fields to her house. I had stopped shaking and my mind was clearing a little. We stood hand in hand, and Mia looked up at me with concern on her face.

"I am going to tell my father what happened," she said softly.

I would also have to tell Oupa what had happened. The headmaster expelled pupils for brawling on the bus. Mia stood there, holding my hand. I felt slightly embarrassed, but there was no one to see or report on it.

"Mac," she said, and standing on tip toe, she kissed me full on the mouth. Her lips were soft like rose petals that were moist with dew. This was the third shock of the day. "Thanks. I am so very sorry," she whispered. Then she was gone, skipping across the dry old maize field. I stood there feeling like a real fool, watching the girl disappear into the hazy heat.

Oupa listened to my story without a word. When Gran tried to ask a question she was told to keep quiet. Oupa was silent for a long time. We three sat in the sitting room, a number of unlucky flies buzzing around the shut window. The cat yawned and stretched and then left the room.

"Those Larsen boys deserve all they got," he said finally. "But how are we going to handle it?" He rubbed his stubbly jaw.

"Oh my," said Gran wringing her hands. "This is terrible!"

"Go make a pot of tea," growled Oupa, and Gran left the room. "Van der Walt is a little trouble-maker," growled the old man. "I will sort the little Dutchman out." Then he fell silent, playing with his pipe.

Later that evening there was the sound of a car approaching and Stripe barked. Oupa rose and went outside. I peered through the window and recognised Manteiga's car. Then Carlos hopped out of the car and jogged quickly up the steps to where Oupa was waiting. The two men shook hands and he and Oupa walked towards the end of the veranda. Oupa's hand was resting on the short Portuguese's shoulder. I couldn't hear what was being said. The two men then entered the house.

"Thanks Mac, for looking after my little girl," Manteiga said shaking my hand firmly. "I am indebted to you. This is the second good turn your family have done for me."

I wondered about the first and then realised it was Oupa's sales talk that was being counted. I felt rather embarrassed, not knowing what to say. But I knew without any doubt that there was going to be trouble when Monday came. A caning was the least of my problems. I would probably be expelled from school. Sadly, there were only a few months until the end of the year exams.

The next day I busied myself with dam building. My thoughts kept on going back to the bus, the incident with the Larsens, my future at the school, and then the kiss. Although nearly seventeen years old I am a bit shy to admit that I had never been kissed by anyone other than Gran and a long-lost aunt who had visited us, never to be seen again. They had just been a peck. Mia's kiss had been so soft and caring and just thinking of it made me tingle right to the soles of my feet. I worked really hard to keep my mind occupied. Monday would be judgement day.

Sunday was the usual church, lunch and the old people going for a sleep. Later the phone rang. This was not usual, especially on a Sunday. Baker was on the line.

"Mac," he whispered, obviously not wanting anyone his side to hear. "Did you hear?"

"No, hear what?" I whispered back.

"Our school lost to The College. It was nearly a white-wash."
He hesitated.

I listened. This was not good news, I knew I would be blamed.

"I saw the two Larsens. One is walking very slowly using a stick.
The other has a bandage on his nose. You know it was broke?" he
giggled. "Are you there?" he enquired.

I nodded to myself and got that sinking feeling in my gut. "Yes I
am," I said. Baker was excited about the action. His enemies were out
of action, but I knew I was going to suffer the consequences. The
Larsen family were well in with van der Walt.

After the phone call, I sat on the top step trying to find reason,
and decide what I was going to do? Life had been very simple up to
now. Oupa and Gran had brought me up. I had been left as a baby
by one of Gran's hopeless daughters. She had gone off to Australia
never to be heard of or seen again. Gran said she had wiped her
hands of her. There had always been food to eat, but there had
always been a shortage of money as far back as I could remember. I
had my school uniform, school shoes, a battered khaki shirt and
shorts, and one threadbare jersey. That was my wardrobe. Around
the farm I went barefoot. My greatest possession was the BSA airgun.
I had a few rand hidden in the back of my cupboard that I had been
paid for shooting the bushbuck. I would save that for chickenwire to
fence off the veggie patch that I was planning.

A fence was essential against the buck, hare and bird population,
who would have a go at anything green. Poles were easy to find, I
could cut poles in the bush along the road. I had already selected a
number of young trees that would be suitable.

My greatest fear was that I would have to leave the farm to look
for work. On the other hand, if I worked hard at the dam and built
the wall high enough to hold sufficient water to last out the winter
and got vegetables into the ground, beans were a good proposition
for quick cash. Quicker cash would come in the form of the black
mamba. That was if I shot it. Majola said that the witchdoctor would
buy it for about forty rand. I had no doubt in my mind I was going
to be told to leave school. I wondered what would happen to the

Larsens. Would van der Walt have the guts to order them off the premises?

That Monday morning I had woken up to hear Oupa in the bathroom. He usually did not rise until nine. He was wiping shaving cream from his face as he eyed me in the mirror.

"I will be taking you to school today me boy. That van der Walt is not going to have everything his own way," he growled.

The next surprise was arriving at school to find Carlos and Mia waiting at the school gate. School had already started. Mia had had to have the bubblegum cut out of her hair. She looked even smaller and thinner with short cropped hair. We were all made to wait in the secretary's office. The secretary, a short plump woman, offered the two men tea, which they refused. She seemed slightly on edge and not her usual cheerful self.

I sat on the edge of the chair studying the school photographs that adorned the walls. Rugby photos covered the wall in front of me, cricket the other, and the third a mixture of tennis, hockey, and athletics. I was nervous as I had expected to go it alone. The presence of Oupa, Manteiga and Mia made me feel very uncomfortable and self-conscious.

After a short wait the secretary ushered us through into the headmaster's office. Oupa led the way. He was dressed in his Sunday-go-to-church clothes. He even had a soft felt hat. Van der Walt sat at his desk with his head bowed and was writing in a file. He waved the old man to a chair, which was the only one, and left the rest of us standing. I fidgeted and glanced at Mia, who was seriously staring in front of her.

Oupa crossed his legs and placed his hat on his lap. We waited. I don't know if van der Walt had expected us as a group. He had probably expected me to arrive at school alone. He could have called me to his office and given me my marching orders. Now, not only did he have Oupa, but Manteiga and his daughter were standing before him.

He sat back closing the file he had been working on. "Sorry to keep you all waiting," he said mildly. Before anyone could say anything he continued. "As you probably know we lost an important rugby match against The College. Our two main players were out of action. One happened to be the captain of the team. It was a very poor game and rather humiliating. Secondly, as you know, brawling on the school bus is forbidden and regarded in very poor light."

Manteiga tried to chip in, gesturing towards Mia, but van der Walt held up his hand.

"The school rules are very clear, any bullying must be brought to my attention. I, and I alone, will deal with it. As soon as the two Larsen boys recover from their injuries I personally will deal with them."

I knew then that he had everything worked out, I had been wrong to protect Mia. The other two boys were probably off sick and not around, and would only return when the dust had settled. Oupa tried to chip in but van der Walt cut him off.

"I have spoken to virtually everyone on the bus. It was clearly none of Mackay's business. It was up to you," and he pointed at Manteiga, "to report it to me, I would have sorted out the whole stupid business." Van der Walt sighed as if irritated by our inferior presence. Then he stared hard at me. "You, Mackay, I am asking you to pack up your desk and return whatever books you have loaned from the library."

Oupa tried to speak, but was cut off again.

"Miss Manteiga, you may return to your class," concluded van der Walt.

It was like a dismissal. Knowing now how van der Walt thought, I could see he was protecting and preserving what he regarded as the best for the school, the Larsens. We were low life, with no money and no future.

Oupa managed to get a word in, "What's going to happen to the Larsen boys?"

Van der Walt looked at Oupa as if he was plain stupid. "That, Mr Mackay, has nothing to do with you. It will be handled by the school, by me," he said bluntly.

I could see Oupa starting to boil, and his neck became very red around the tight collar.

Manteiga stepped forward, his face black with rage. "You, you," he stammered. "My daughter was assaulted and insulted by those two boys." He hesitated, as he searched for the right words. "She won't be coming back to your school and I will be reporting this to the education department – you are going to hear more about this."

Van der Walt sat back, with his fingers steepled before him. "Mr Manteiga, you do whatever you like," he sneered. "I think this meeting is over. And Mackay," he said indicating me. "I don't want you back on the school premises after today."

All I could do was nod. Then it happened. Manteiga and Mia were at the door and about to leave. I had begun to turn to leave. Oupa was boiling mad. He rose to his full height. Then his bear-like hand shot out, grabbing van der Walt by the throat, and in a flash Oupa punched van der Walt on the nose. He went over backwards, feet in the air and taking the chair with him. There was an almighty crash.

Oupa grinned at me, then he turned back to the headmaster. "And Van, you listen to me." He leant over the desk, towards the fallen headmaster. "Be careful what you do and say or the whole town will hear about you and Rosie, the coloured maid, at the Strong Man Inn." Oupa laughed casually.

Van der Walt's face was chalk white with blood pouring from his nostrils. He tried to rise.

Oupa threw a burly arm over my shoulder, "Let's go Mac, me boy. There's no way we are going to get a fair hearing here."

The days that followed passed slowly. I helped Majola with the cows. We hunted, set snares and I worked on the dam. I did not know what to do. My only hope of remaining on the farm was to get the dam completed. Some days I worked from early morning till late. The wall grew, but not fast enough.

I no longer had a painful back and my hands were as tough as leather. Before leaving school, life had not been very demanding but there had been new things to see and do every day. Now life was a bore and my future looked bleak. Who would employ someone who had been expelled from school? I would be in possession of the minimum school leaving certificate. I was also sure van der Walt would happily report negatively on my conduct. Days now were flying by and the dam, to be of any use, would have to go up another three or four feet. I also needed money to buy chickenwire to protect the vegetables that I planned to plant. Majola was still going on about the mamba and the money we could earn by shooting it and selling it to the witchdoctor.

According to Majola, Sunday was the best day to trespass on Manteiga's farm, because they did not work on Sundays and he said the Shangaan's were all drunk and asleep. I don't know how he knew all this but he seemed pretty sure of his facts.

Then, one Sunday afternoon, we climbed through the barbed wire boundary fence, and quickly entered the bush along the road, limiting our chance of detection by Manteiga's labour. It was warm and spring was upon us and a few of the blackwattles were covered in golden flowers. Everything was green and lush. Stripe was in a really good mood and sniffed around here and there. I had hired Baker's rifle, and bought twenty rounds. We ambled along, not in too much of a hurry. There were signs of duiker and hares. Majola stopped and wiggled into a thicket and then appeared a short while later with two wire snares.

"The Shangaan's are trespassing on our hunting," he said in disgust, waving the wire snares at me. "Those dogs must go back to where they belong in Mozambique! What do they want here?" He was angry and did not seem to see the point, which was that they were snaring on their employer's farm, where we should not be!

We ambled along past the spot where we had shot the bushbuck, and upset a couple of duiker, which bolted off through the thick undergrowth. We were very close to where we had seen the mamba. We walked cautiously through the dense bush. I had loaded Baker's rifle and carried it at port across my chest and ready. Even Stripe sensed we were after something and fell in at my heel. We approached slowly, examining every branch and each fallen log. The snake could be anywhere.

We were almost at the snake's glade when it happened. Looking back on the moment, I believe that reptile had been waiting in ambush. It happened so quickly. It was like a flash before my eyes. At the time I did not know where it came from, but it had to be the branches above Majola's head. Silver grey and blotched with green fungus and scales, its head the size of a man's hand, whipped by.

Majola let out a startled cry. I fell over backwards, knocking Stripe flying. I don't remember aiming or firing. The huge snake hung there, swinging from the branch above my head. I rolled away from it and then, regained my footing. I reloaded the single-shot weapon. Majola had struggled to his feet, walked about six paces and collapsed. I aimed at the coffin shaped head of the reptile. I saw a mark that could possibly have been a bullet wound but I was not sure.

The snake was acting lethargically, swaying from side to side in its upside down position. I fired again and saw the bullet strike. It released its grip of the branches, and hit the ground thrashing wildly. I knew it was dead, but it would take time for the three metres of coils to stop moving.

With a sudden shock Majola came to my mind. Had the snake bitten him? I dodged around the thrashing snake. Majola lay next to a thorn tree. I dropped down on my knees alongside him.

"Haw, Satan has bitten me Mac," whispered Majola. He took his hand away from his neck.

"Satan knew we were coming. He was waiting. Did you kill him?"

"Yes," I said, but a lump was forming in my throat.

"I will die very quickly. I am going to choke," he whispered, showing me his palm. There was a little blood on it. I could see the puncture wounds on his neck. With sickening shock I suddenly knew that there was nothing that I could do to help my friend.

"Don't leave me Mac," he whispered. "Listen to me please. Shortly I will not be able to speak. Above the door of my hut in the wall is a tin containing money. The money you will give to Dlamini, my brother, the one that works at the school. Tell him I wish to be buried at home in Zululand." Then he choked and his body went into spasms. "Tell him I died like a madoda [man], Mac. Now I see ngonyama, a lion Mac, he is an old male lion. Mac you and I will meet again." He laughed softly. "I am going to the N'kosi [god] now." His hand clung onto my hand, his whole body breaking into spasms, then violent convulsions. His breath came in short gasps. He choked horribly, and a shudder ran through his body and then he was gone.

I carefully unlocked his fingers, and laid his hands across his chest. The venom had taken less than five minutes to kill my friend. Majola was dead! I sat back on my haunches looking at my friend. His face was peaceful, his eyes shut, like he was resting, having his afternoon nap. I was mentally numb and my hands shook uncontrollably but I managed to force myself to think clearly.

Now I had to tell Oupa. He would call the police. The snake was still twitching, coiling up and then uncoiling itself. Stripe lay next to Majola, whining.

"Come Stripe," I said. My voice sounded very loud in the stillness of the undergrowth. Stripe growled but he did not move. Without warning I started to cry, I could not stop the tears. I went round the dead snake and ran from the bush and along the ploughed lands and through the new boundary fence. I did not care if anyone saw me.

Arriving at the house I found Oupa and Gran were having tea on the veranda. Out of breath, I told them what had happened.

"Where did you get the gun?" growled Oupa.

"I hired it from Baker – a school friend," I explained through hiccupping sobs.

"Put it away. If they ask, you shot it with your airgun," growled Oupa.

I did as he told me, whilst he went to the phone. I felt completely exhausted. Gran brought me a cup of sweet tea and fussed about me.

Sitting there in a daze the reality suddenly struck home. I would never hunt with Majola again, nor listen to his stories or share the badly cooked meat that we poached. Tears rolled down my cheeks. Why now? I kept on asking myself. Why now, when I needed my friend the most.

A while later the police arrived. I accompanied them to the bush on Manteiga's farm. We found Majola and Stripe laying side by side. Stripe was stroppy towards the two policemen when they wanted to move the body, and I had to grab him by the scruff of his neck to stop him biting them. They put Majola in a big, black plastic bag and loaded him into the van.

"The CID will come and see you tomorrow," said one officer, after taking my name. The two men then admired the snake that now lay still. I said I would walk home. They seemed happy enough about that and left. Stripe was sniffing around where Majola had lain and I put the snake in a bag and headed for home. Stripe refused to come.

Later that evening Oupa gave me a lift to Slang Spruit. A white person dare not enter the shantytown, especially on a Sunday. We parked on the outskirts and waited, watching for someone we knew. I watched the Africans passing by. Many rode bicycles, others walked. Eventually I saw a woman whom both Oupa and I knew. She had helped tend the maize fields many years before. I greeted her.

"Hallo, Mac, what brings you here?" she asked cheerfully as I approached her.

"Majola's dead, bitten by a mamba," I blurted out, feeling really bad.

She stopped and shook her head in disbelief. "I will tell his brother Dlamini," she said with tears in her eyes. "Did you kill the snake?"

I nodded, not trusting my voice.

The next day the detectives arrived and took a statement from me. They admired the snake and left.

Then, an hour or so later, Dlamini arrived in a battered van, driven by a flamboyantly dressed youngster. The three of us went to Majola's hut. I was surprised at how little he had. It seemed strange because I had spent many happy hours listening to his stories in the smoky interior. All he possessed was a battered overall, his old jersey, the boots I'd never seen him wear, an assegai and shield, a number of sticks of various shapes and sizes, an enamel mug and a pot and a plate. Nailed to the wall was the white skull of the bushbuck that I had shot, with a neat hole in the centre of the forehead. I asked if I could keep it. Dlamini agreed quietly. Dlamini broke open the mud wall above the door. In a cloud of dust a tin dropped to the ground.

"You will be my witness," said Dlamini. "We must count it." I was surprised. There was over a thousand rand in the tin. I had repeated to them all that Majola had said before he died.

"I will see that he is buried in Zululand," said Dlamini sadly. "Yebo, Majola was a good man, a madoda truly. He was a lion amongst men," said Dlamini sincerely.

Amongst the Zulu, being a madoda carried a lot of weight and was a title to be extremely proud of. I was also very aware that to these men lions carried certain mystical powers.

As we walked back towards his van Dlamini asked. "The snake, where is it?"

I pointed towards a vacant shed.

"If you give it to me I will see you get a good price for it," he said.

The damned snake had killed the only friend I had. Now I was busy making a deal with it. It just did not seem right. Sadly I collected the snake, still in the bag, and loaded it onto Dlamini's van.

Two days later a picinini arrived at the house on a bicycle carrying a cheap blue envelope with "Mr Mac" written on the front in pencil.

"It's from Dlamini," he said and then asked for a drink of water. I directed him to the tap on the side of the house. In the envelope I found a hundred and fifty rand. There would be more than enough to buy wire for the fence. The picinini returned, greeted me and left. I sat on the step in the shade. It was a small fortune, a terrific start in the right direction. I felt an unsettling unexplainable sense of guilt. I would rather have Majola around than this money. Deep inside me there was an emptiness growing, which I now fought desperately to control.

After Majola's death life became harder on Hill Farm. I took over Majola's duties, but Oupa did not pay me. I received a box of pellets now and again, when he remembered. At six in the morning I brought the cows into the cow shed. They were easy and knew their places. I would put the chains around their necks. Then I milked them by hand as we did not have a milking machine. There were only five that were in milk, and on a good day they supplied about forty litres.

At about eight I had finished milking and put the cows out to graze, I then went in for breakfast. Oupa would take the milk to a shop on the outskirts of Slang Spruit. Then he would return to his chair and the radio. I would go to the dam and work until lunchtime. It never seemed to end. Barrow load after barrow load just disappeared into the wall. It was during the afternoons that I really missed Majola and the stories that he told, while sitting in his smoky hut chewing on the stringy poached meat. My life had changed dramatically.

Lunch was always served at the kitchen table and varied from reasonably good to very poor, depending on what time of the month it was. That was if there was any money or not. We would all listen to the news on Springbok Radio and always in silence. Oupa, for some unknown reason, did not wish to miss one word.

Today it seemed to revolve around the Congo.

"A very volatile situation is developing in the Belgian Congo, Police and troops have been deployed to various strategic spots within the country trying to prevent total civil war. There have been suggestions from the Political and Tribal council that mercenaries may again be employed to assist the regular UN, Police and Army," said the announcer.

"Man," said Oupa, "I wish I was a few years younger. There are plenty of perks on those types of campaigns."

I was not really listening as I'd finished my meal and wanted to be excused from the table, but dared not move until the news had come to an end.

It was Friday afternoon and we were going to slaughter chickens. Oupa had a MOTHS meeting in the evening and Gran was going to make chicken curry for the members. I think they all took turns in supplying a meal. Oupa could not catch the chickens as he was too old and slow. Stripe and I would do the dirty work of catching the chickens and then I'd decapitate them and let them bleed. A drum of water was placed over an open fire. Oupa, sat on a kitchen chair with an apron over his lap and would take the bled chicken from me and would pluck it and gut it. The intestines were placed in a plastic bucket, along with the feet and head, and set aside to be sold at the shop at Slang Spruit.

"The Congo is a great place," said Oupa out of the blue while removing the chicken intestines. "Long ago I spent a few months on a diamond mine out there. There is beautiful soil up there, red and rich, and plenty of timber. I believe they are now growing coffee and hemp and whoever is involved is making big money. You know that the Belgians pulled out a few years ago leaving the country to the blacks. They can't agree on anything, so bang, they start a war. Old tribal enemies and greed cause most of it." He shook his head sadly. "Same thing would happen here if it was not for us whites."

I knew Oupa had fixed ideas about many things. Because the whites beat the blacks in war then they were in charge, and were entitled to the spoils of war. If the black man was strong enough and beat the white man then they were entitled to the spoils of war. That was why the white man was now in charge in this country as they had won the war.

It all sounded too simple. I remembered Majola telling me that in 1879 the English army, without cause, had just marched into the kingdom of Zululand and taken control for their Queen. The Zulus had fought bravely and killed many of the English soldiers but had lost in the end. I had just shrugged it off and let it be.

When Oupa was finished with the chickens I took the dressed chickens up the steps to Gran who already had a huge pot boiling, giving off a mouth-watering spicy aroma. I knew only too well what I would be eating tonight.

I returned to Oupa, who was preparing to re-enter the house. He pointed with his knife.

"Look who's coming," he said with a wink.

In the distance a black and white pony was trotting across the fields. Then it suddenly dawned on me. Mia was back for the weekend! She now went to school near Durban and only came home at weekends. I left Oupa and I walked towards her. She smiled and waved from a distance. Boy did she look beautiful!

"Hi, Mac!" she called and smiled cheerfully as she dismounted. She was slightly breathless with a sheen of sweat on her brow. I found it funny how easily I'd forgotten just how pretty she was.

"It's my birthday. Do you want to come over tonight?" she asked. Before I could say anything she continued. "It will be great, as a few of my cousins will be visiting. I would like you to meet them."

This spoilt it a bit. I would rather be just with Mia and her sisters. "Great," I said, and found myself hoping that she was not going to offer me a ride on her pony. Elvis looked rather high spirited and was shaking his head up and down as if keen to get going. Mia led

Elvis and turned to the dam. It looked very small after the many days I had spent sweating and moving earth.

"How much higher do you have to go?" she asked seriously. She dropped the reins, and went to sit on an old dry log. I seated myself beside her.

"A metre," I said still not knowing if it would be high enough. The dam had to hold enough water to last out a winter.

"You need to plant a tree or two for shade," she said. "A willow tree would look nice. One there and one there," she pointed.

I had never thought of trees. And I realised that just two trees would not use up too much of the precious water and would make the barren valley look alive.

"I wish there was a way to quicken it up," I said hopefully, thinking that she might say something to her dad, as I knew the bulldozer was still on their farm clearing bush. When Mia said nothing, I continued. "I need money, say about a thousand or two, then I could really get going," I said and pointed out to Mia where I wanted to start a garden, and where I would plant grass. She listened intently. We sat in silence for a time enjoying each other's company. A heron landed gracefully next to the trickle of water and proceeded to dart a frog and gulp it down.

After a while she said she had lots to do before her guests arrived and we walked over to where Elvis was waiting patiently.

"Leg up?" she said giving me her dimpled smile. I made a cup of my hand and helped her into the saddle. She was surprisingly light. "I'll see you tonight," she called over her shoulder as she trotted away.

I remained at the dam deep in thought. I would have to buy her a present and I also needed a pair of jeans for going out. I had better use some of the money hidden in my cupboard. There was more than enough to buy the wire that I needed. The money gave me a sense of security and possession, although a small amount of cash by other people's standards it was the most money I had ever had.

I returned home and, after explaining to Oupa that I had been invited to a birthday party, he was quite happy to drive me to Parook's shop. Parook sold everything, from car parts to shoes. Oupa remained in the pickup and I entered the cool pleasant-smelling shop and explained to Mrs Parook that I needed a present for Mia's birthday. Then, after looking around, I settled for a box of chocolates. Mrs Parook went to the back of the shop to gift wrap it and I examined the clothing department and bought a pair of jeans with brass studs, similar to those I had seen Elvis Presley wearing in one of the pictures.

Oupa was going to MOTHS this evening and Gran was going to a friend. Instead of me staying at home and listening to the radio I was going out. It was completely new to me.

That evening, dressed in my brand new jeans, I walked across the old maize lands and climbed through the boundary fence. There were a number of cars parked outside Manteiga's house. I always felt uncomfortable around strangers. As I approached I could hear loud laughter and music. I reached the door and stood self-consciously in the brightly lit doorway, clutching my wrapped box of chocolates, feeling completely out of place. I could see that the room was full of adults. Many of them were dancing and others standing around in groups talking, all with glasses in their hands.

I felt that I really should not have been there. No one had seen me. I could slip off and give Mia her present tomorrow. I'd say Oupa had demanded I stay at home at the last minute because they were going out. But I knew she would ask why had I not phoned? I had no answer. I was just about to creep off when Mrs Manteiga spotted me.

"Mac, Mac!" she called wading through the guests, a glass of red wine in her hand.

I stopped and turned towards her, smiling as best I could.

"Come along. Let me introduce you," she called merrily. Then, to my embarrassment, she placed a chubby arm around my shoulders and guided me into the room. I was introduced. My hand was pumped up and down by a dozen different people. Afterwards I could not remember one name. Everyone seemed to have heard about the fight on the bus. An old boy with a fine grey beard was already drunk, punched playfully at my jaw. "You got a good punch boy," he said.

I just smiled and ducked.

Mrs Manteiga led me through to a side room where there were at least twenty kids of various ages. The record player pounded out the music. A huge chocolate cake was in the place of honour in the middle of the table together with Coke, Fanta, sweets and biscuits. What a feast! Mia broke away from the group of older kids. Her mom left, shutting the door.

"Mac, you made it." Mia made it sound as if I had travelled from afar and not from just about a half a kilometre across the old maize lands and the newly ploughed land of Manteiga. Everyone was looking at me as I handed her the present.

"Ooh thanks!" she cried. Then, to make things worse, she rose onto her toes and kissed me on the cheek. I felt myself going red. She then led me across the room to her group and introduced me. Two seconds after the introduction their names were completely forgotten. I smiled and tried to revel in being the man of the moment, the chap who saved Mia from the Larsens, as well as the victim who was expelled from school for doing the deed. After all that, I was the one with a pretty poor future.

The rock'n'roll music was playing loudly, and the smaller kids were bopping around. I had no idea how to dance. Hopefully no one would ask me – or was it I who should ask? I had no intention of asking anyone.

One of the boys about my age with a girl in a checked dress and white bobby socks, poured me a Coke. Grinning he handed it to me. "The whole town's talking about you!" he shouted above the noise. "I go to The College. We would never have won the game if the two Larsens were there. They are killers."

I agreed with him, feeling very much out of place. I was dressed oddly amongst all the rest. The boy talking to me had a black and silver cowboy shirt, black jeans and a thick studded belt and high-heeled-boots. The others were dressed in their best. I had on a white school shirt rolled up above my wrists. I was wearing my new jeans that looked too new, and my old school shoes. I felt really shoddy. Mia hung around my elbow making small talk.

The chap that went to The College, whose name turned out to be Rodney something or other, was talkative. He seemed to have heard it all. Van der Walt was a drunken pig, and was known to frequent the Strong Man Inn with Larsen senior.

I was wishing the evening was over. Mia brought me a huge slice of chocolate cake. Then May wanted to dance. I said I was eating. After that I made sure I had a glass or cake in my hand at all times.

After what seemed to be forever, people started leaving. They were waving and shouting above the music, collecting their kids, hugging and kissing Mia. Everyone seemed very jolly. Outside car engines were roaring, lights flashing, hooters blaring, and people calling goodbyes as the guests headed back to town. It was time for me to go. Carlos stopped me and asked me to wait a while. Mia giggled and dragged me in to the party room. It was now empty and looked like a bomb had hit it. She went over to the record player, and shuffled through the records. Louis Armstrong's 'Blueberry Hill' rumbled through the room.

"Now, Mac," she whispered, "come and dance with me." I had not a clue. She giggled and wrapped her arms about me. I never knew such a small person could be so soft and warm. The heat seemed to ooze from her, and away we went. After a short while I got the knack of the beat and managed to shuffle along.

"Mac." She was on tip-toe again, and placed a firm long wet kiss on my lips. "Thanks for the present."

I was stunned and I missed a step and almost tripped over the party debris. Then the music ended.

"Dad wants to see you," said Mia knowingly, as if it was a sort of family plot, and I was the victim.

Just then Carlos came through the door with a glass in his hand and led me through into his office. It was cluttered and smelt strongly of tobacco.

What was happening now? Had I done or said something wrong? This was the first thing that came to mind.

"Mac, I have an offer to make you," Carlos said, lighting a cigarette. "I need an assistant. I was wondering if you would be interested."

A job was what I needed. I was going to say yes. He stopped me before I could open my mouth.

"Think about it, and we can talk tomorrow evening. You come across at about six," he said.

I was all of a sudden thrilled and excited. I would not have to leave Hill Farm or Oupa and Gran. Carlos smiled as he rose and walked with me to the door where we stopped.

"In the beginning, the money won't be too good but as we develop, it will improve," he promised.

I walked across the dark fields towards Hill Farm as if I was on the moon. First, I find myself in love with Mia, and then I was offered a job. What more could I want? I would see Mia every weekend. I even did a few hops practising my newly learnt dance steps.

I collapsed into bed. Mia, beautiful Mia, filled my head. Second, came the job. The salary was not important, as long as it was reasonable. I could continue with my dam, veggie patch, green grass and cows. I was content and very excited with the new prospect.

That night I had the strangest of dreams, of dust and wind blowing across a plain with gaunt thorn bushes that looked dead. Majola was there, his moth-eaten jersey flapping around his lanky frame. He vanished in the dust. An old scarred-faced male lion appeared out of the dust, then it too passed from my field of vision.

I woke up sweating and went and stood out on the step in my underpants, watching the first rays of sun poke between the distant black hills. The air was ice cold and it made me numb. I had to remind myself time and time again that Majola, my friend and my teacher was dead and gone, buried in Zululand and I would never see him again.

That morning Oupa sat at the breakfast table with a thumping hangover. His face was red and blue veins stood out around his nose and on his forehead. His boozy breath could be smelt three metres away. Gran took no notice of him and went about putting breakfast together.

I had done my morning chores and the milk was ready for Oupa to deliver to the shop. I wanted to tell them about Manteiga's offer. I was excited about the prospect, but realised that now was not the right time. Lunch-time would be far better.

"You take the pickup and deliver the milk," growled Oupa rising unsteadily from the table. He had only partly eaten his breakfast. He walked unsteadily towards his room.

"Men!" snorted Gran and scooped up the plates and went into the kitchen, where I could hear her banging things around.

Oupa seldom let me drive. He always said I would break the pickup. I could never work out what I did wrong. I chugged off carefully, quite at home behind the wheel, though I did not possess a licence.

The morning dragged. My head was full of figures. How much would Manteiga pay? Thirty or forty a week? I doubted it would be less than thirty rand. I could save half, buy some decent clothes and save for a car or possibly a motorbike. I could also invest in the farm. I had to stop myself. Thirty rand was not much and would not go very far.

Later, I pushed my fourteenth barrow-load of hard, yellow soil onto the wall, and tipped it. I stood looking, but not seeing and I wiped sweat from my face. We had not gone to church for obvious reasons. I also doubted we were going to get much for Sunday dinner with Gran in her mood.

I went and sat on the same dry log that Mia and I had sat on. A light breeze was drying the sweat on my face and body. I decided that it would look very nice with two willow trees on the bank of the dam. The green willows would very much transform the drab valley and with the green kukui pastures extending behind and my veggie patch to the right. In my mind's eye it would look very prosperous. I sat there and dreamed for a long time.

When I arrived back at the house for lunch Oupa was up and about and looking much better. Gran still had the sulks, but was in the kitchen and by the smell of it, we were going to get stew for lunch. I would wait until we were at the dinner table. Then I would tell them about Manteiga's offer.

Gran came into the dining room with two bowls, one containing stew and the other rice. She plonked them down on the table, and seated herself. Oupa took his position, said grace and then dished up. No one spoke. Oupa switched on the radio for the midday news.

"This is Springbok Radio," said the announcer. But I busied myself with the stew, not listening, and keen to tell them about Manteiga's offer. I sensed that something seemed to be worrying Gran. It was just the way she held herself. She was used to Oupa's binges and they should not have worried her.

"Ah," said Oupa bringing me back to earth. "Listen to this."

The news continued. "The decision has been made again by the acting government and tribal council, to recruit more mercenaries to assist the peace-keeping forces in the Belgian Congo." The announcer rattled on about the economy, peaceful coexistence and the United Nations. I really was not listening.

"Ah," said Oupa again.

Gran was looking at him with a fixed stare. "You're not going to send him there," she said loudly. Usually there was dead silence during the news.

"It will be his decision," responded Oupa.

I had an idea I was involved.

"Mac," said Oupa cautiously, as if expecting Gran to stop him, "last night at my meeting I met a chap called van Rensburg who was recruiting for just that in the Congo." He waved his fork at the radio. Gran stormed out frightening the cat. Oupa watched her go.

"They need men for a six-month contract, four hundred rand a month and, when completed, a bonus of three hundred." He stopped, letting the words sink in, as he spooned food into his mouth. "All found and if my arithmetic is good, that is two thousand four hundred, plus three. That's good money."

I was stunned. In six months away I could earn enough money to get the dam done, plant up my veggie patch and buy a cow or two of my own. My mind was racing. If I worked for Manteiga at thirty rand a week and if I saved every cent, I could not make anything near to what Oupa was talking about. Then the thought hit me. What about Mia? I would lose her. There were serious doubts all of a sudden.

Oupa was watching me. "Then there are also extras," he said. "There are diamonds and various precious stones in that country and, if the Europeans run, there will be things left behind, such as watches, rings and other things of value. Men might die in the fighting and there could be gold teeth." He laughed harshly at some bygone memory.

I had never thought of this, nor did I fancy the idea of robbing the dead or pulling out dead men's teeth. I knew that where there was war there would be death. But for some unknown reason I felt that I could not die. I sat and listened, any thought of food forgotten.

"You have to make a decision quickly," said Oupa. "I will have to contact van Rensburg and get organised. I don't do much these days but I could, using your money hire a number of labourers and finish the dam, do the veggie patch and build things such as the fence. So when you return, the dam will be full of water and the veggie patch secure with a strong fence."

What an idea, I thought. After all the days of pushing the heavy barrows, Oupa would supervise the labour and finish off what I had started. It was then and there that I agreed. What an opportunity! I now had a chance to get Hill Farm going again. All my dreams could come true. I would have to talk to Mia, to convince her that I was doing the right thing and persuade her to wait for me, as six months was not such a long time.

Chapter 3

It was freezing cold and near midnight. My threadbare jersey helped very little, as the small private airport buildings were not heated. The men all huddled together on the hard wooden benches. There were probably fifty of us and most were really rough-looking characters.

I had left home after half a dozen painful inoculations and a two-week wait. Mia had listened to me, tears in those big brown eyes. She had kissed me and said she would wait and write. She had also given me a photo of herself. On the back she had written, "Look after yourself, love Mia." I was thrilled, but in many ways wishing I had not signed up.

I had discussed my situation with Carlos Manteiga, who had agreed, saying it was a chance I was taking but if it paid off and if I was careful, he was sure I would survive and make a go of Hill Farm. All the farm needed was a bit of capital, then he had added that he could not have paid me more than thirty rand a week.

Gran had cried and argued with Oupa that I could be killed or wounded or even crippled for the rest of my life and he would have it on his conscience for ever for sending me to a stupid black man's war. The argument had raged for days.

On the other hand Oupa seemed to get a new lease of life. He accompanied me to the dam, where we sat on the log and discussed all the possibilities. He seemed to like all my ideas and added a few of his own. The money I earned would be paid into his bank account and he would employ two men. They would finish the dam in about ten hard days if he supervised them. Then he would have to hire a tractor to plough up the veggie patch and pasture area. He knew where he could get kukui grass runners for nothing. He would take the hired help there to dig them up and then replant them at the dam. Then, by using water from the dam to water them, they'd be given a good start. Then he would start on the veggie patch, using new fencing wire. They would cut the poles in the bush at the edge of the road. It all sounded fantastic and very easy. It also really pleased and encouraged me to see that Oupa was taking such an enormous interest.

I had travelled overnight by train to Germiston on the ticket supplied by my new employers. The men in my second-class compartment had taken no notice of me as they drank and played cards late into the night. At about midnight a fight had broken out in the compartment next door and everyone had crowded into the narrow passage. A big brawny man with smouldering eyes was brutally smashing a smaller man to pulp. A number of the spectators cheered him on while others just stood silently by. The ticket inspector had arrived and the fight had stopped. The almost crippled smaller man had left the train at the next station. I think it was Ladysmith. I had returned to my compartment feeling very uncertain about the company I was in. The fight had been completely one-sided and many of the blows delivered were unnecessarily vicious. Was this a portent of the conflict to come?

We had been collected from the station by bus and then were left at the airport. The bus driver had told us to wait. The sandwiches Gran had packed had long been eaten. There was a Greek cafe over the road that did a roaring trade as the day dragged by and we all became bored and hungry. No one seemed to know what was going on. At about six the airport offices had closed leaving the waiting room open. The card game that was started had eventually died. The big man with the smouldering eyes seemed to be the leader. I heard him being called Maritz by one of the men.

I sat, freezing, on the hard wooden bench. I no longer wanted to be here amongst these hard men. I longed for Gran, Oupa and even for Stripe and my room and my bed. But I knew there was no way back other than by completing the contract.

The man sitting next to me had fallen asleep with his head lolling on his chest and a battered suitcase at his feet. He stank of sweat and liquor. The man opposite me was short and blond and very well built. He wore glasses and was inclined to keep polishing the lenses every now and again. He introduced himself as Max Roux from Johannesburg. After an awkward introduction he remained silent.

It must have been about one in the morning when a car swung into the parking area. This made the men wake up and there was an air of expectancy in the cold room. Two men entered the building. Both looked like businessmen and were dressed in dark suits and carrying briefcases. They set about arranging themselves at a table.

"Right, listen here," said the first man. "When we call your names, come forward. We want all your identification documents for safe keeping. We will place you in two groups, so stay in those groups."

They started calling out names. Soon I was called. The two men were expressionless. On taking my papers they handed me a blue identity card. I returned to my seat.

A while later the sound of approaching aeroplane engines filled the building. Lights suddenly came on outside. Two twin engine aeroplanes taxied noisily in front of the airport buildings. Doors opened on the side of the fuselage and steps were rolled into place by two men in white overalls.

"They are Dakotas. We are at last on our way," Roux said excitedly.

I had heard Oupa talk of these aircraft with affection. He would be pleased to hear I had flown in one. We went onto the apron in our groups and climbed the steps. I was very tired, not having slept properly for what seemed like a very long time. All of a sudden all thought of sleep was gone. There was a general air of excitement amongst the men. Roux was standing next to me and was visibly shaking, but then it might have been the cold.

As the aircraft raced down the lit runway, I felt a type of relief, sadness and excitement all rolled into one. Here I was at last, on my way to earn a fortune; money that would set me up for the rest of my life. I had visions of marrying Mia, building a big house and having a prize dairy herd that I would show at the Royal Agriculture show in

Pietermaritzburg. Then the wheels of the aircraft lifted off the ground and we were airborne.

The lights in the crowded passenger compartment were dim. The big man, Maritz, who was sitting on the aisle, stood up. He leant across to the man next to him, a small man with a grey moustache and said, "You don't mind pal? I want to sit next to the window." The smaller man obviously was not keen on moving or changing places with him but did so reluctantly.

The plane droned on into the night. Men slept. Others sat and stared blindly in front of them. Silence prevailed for a long time. Roux sat next to a small port-hole. Leaning across I could see out. The earth below was covered with a black blanket. Occasionally there was a bright pin-prick of light in the seemingly endless black world below. I cat-napped. I was also over-excited and woke at the slightest sound or movement.

Time crawled by on the seemingly never-ending flight. Roux's movement woke me up. "Northern Rhodesia," said Roux. "It has to be. Below us is an airfield. I can see runway lights. We're going to land."

There was a distinct change in the engine note, as the pilot eased the aircraft down on to the runway. The plane was refuelled but no one was allowed off the aeroplane. Then we were on our way again. Stiffness set in. Men complained of cramp, and we watched as the sun rose. We now could see the second aircraft drifting along on our left. Below us, the earth was covered with fluffy cloud. Above, the sky was beautifully sunny and deep blue.

There was a water container on the aircraft but it had long since been emptied. There was no food. We roared on and on. It seemed endless. As the sun rose higher in the sky it became warm in the cabin. Men stripped down to their vests and sat sweating. It was extremely uncomfortable.

It was close to noon when the note in the engines changed and we began to circle over what looked like a town. It was hot and very hazy. There were broad tree-lined streets, and a very wide green river reflecting the sun. Two large steam boats or paddle steamers could be seen pumping out white clouds of smoke. One of the men said that it was the Congo river. There seemed to be very few cars and fewer people on the roads. The airport buildings came into view, with a cement runway shimmering in the heat. The buildings looked battered and poorly kept. A couple of large hangars appeared with numerous aircraft of many colours and descriptions. We hit the runway bouncing. The interior squeaking alarmingly with the strain put on it. We were down at last.

The doors were opened and steps fell into place. The heat was unbelievable. It was like opening the doors of a furnace. The men gasped and perspired as they collected their possessions. Then we began to shuffle slowly along the aisle towards the exit.

"Come along ladies!" a voice roared.

The men jumped nervously and I struggled to my feet. This was something else, the unexpected. We had been told we would be given basic training at Stanleyville, and that upon completion we would be guarding a sawmill. Presumably this was Stanleyville. That was all we had been told.

"Move your bloody feet!" roared the same voice. There was an unsettling authoritativeness in it, bordering on madness.

I nearly went tumbling down the steep step. By grabbing Roux I saved myself from falling.

"Fall in, fall in!" screamed the Sergeant Major. He was a block of a man with a tomato red face and a Hitler-type moustache. It was either high blood pressure or too much hard liquor. Later, we found it to be the latter.

Hanging onto my bag I hit the cement runway and fell into a ragged line of men. Roux gasped for air, the perspiration pouring down his face. To one side stood a drab army truck with its engine idling.

"Right ladies!" screamed the madman. "Place your belongings in the truck. Then return to this very spot. Move, move!" he screamed at us. We all ran, every one of us. We tossed our possessions into the back of the truck and ran back to fall into a rough formation. The sun beat down on us mercilessly. We stood panting and sweating and waited for the last man to come to a standstill.

"Did you have a good trip?" He actually appeared to laugh. The crack below his moustache, that was his mouth seemed to twitch. "So ladies, we are going to march to your new quarters. Then we are going to run, and so we will separate the boys from the girls."

We staggered off in unco-ordinated stiff movements. Many of the men like myself hadn't a clue about marching. The Sergeant Major climbed on to the back of the truck and watched our attempt at marching. The truck pulled slowly away at walking speed. We followed the truck across the cement apron and out into a broad tree-lined road. He remained balanced there shouting abuse. One of the men started to sing out left, right, left, right. I think it was Maritz. We marched along, getting our step right. There were not many people around. The black people I saw seemed blacker than their brothers down south.

"Double march!" our tormentor screamed. "Run, you silly bastards, run!"

We could hardly keep rank. A thin wiry man in front of me suddenly started to hobble, and left the line of sweating, cursing men. He staggered to the sidewalk, and fell onto a grassy strip. We passed on. What happened to him, I never found out.

Roux was at my elbow. "Oh my God, they're trying to kill us," he whined, but he kept on running.

We went steadily down the shimmering road, the midday sun beating down mercilessly. The humidity was terrific, burning right to the bottom of my lungs. We passed through two huge steel gates and into a courtyard where we were ordered to halt. We stood swaying and sweating, and many of us on the verge of collapsing.

"You signed on the dotted line," said our tormentor. "I am talking to you lot, do you hear!" he shouted. "Answer me! The answer, ladies is: 'Yes Sergeant Major!'" he screamed. "Answer me!"

I will never forget that red smirking face. We all tried, shouting "Yes Sergeant Major", again and again. Eventually he was satisfied. We stood there panting.

"I will kill the bastard," said one of the men behind me. I think it was Maritz. He seemed to be taking a prominent role in our little adventure.

"You ladies have been given to me to train and teach the art of war in this God-damned country." His voice lowered to almost normal. "If you don't listen to me, you will die, and even if you do listen you will still die." He laughed, walking slowly before us, his swagger stick under his arm.

"Right, the worst killer is disease, which the water carries. Typhoid, bilharzia and a dozen others the white man has never heard of. You will use the pills given to you. You will boil the water. Trust no water. The insects. Malarial mosquitoes will probably kill a few of you fools." He spat on the cement. "Never forget to take your pills. Snakes– too many to count, they're all poisonous. If the mamba bites you, it takes twenty minutes and you're dead. The hospitals here are ill-equipped, and the medics are useless." He turned at the end of the line of panting men. "Don't get sick" he warned. "As for the women," he laughed. "You lot that think they are cheap. They carry diseases that there is no cure for, and you will die." He slapped the side of his leg with his stick and seemed to change tack.

"Thieves, there must be one or two of you here. Raise your hands." No one did.

He smirked at us. "Queers. I hate queers, and child molesters." He moved along the line and came to stop in front of the nervous little man with a moustache that Maritz had ordered out of the window seat.

"Are you queer, madam?" he asked the small, grey-moustached man.

"No, Sergeant Major," he stammered.

"Then what are you?"

The man was obviously uncomfortable, could only open and shut his mouth. No sound came. "I was a teacher," he managed to stammer.

Sergeant Major smirked and walked on. My mouth was dry and I was really thirsty. He stopped in front of me and I could smell his rancid breath and body odour.

"You ran away from home son?" he asked in a soft voice.

"No, Sergeant Major," I managed to get out. To my relief he turned away.

"You like black women?" he snarled at Maritz.

"No, Sergeant Major!" shouted Maritz.

"Then tell me why there are so many little yellow bastards around South Africa?"

"I don't know, Sergeant Major!" shouted Maritz.

The Sergeant Major turned and faced the men. "Right, amongst you fifty men there are no thieves, no queers, no child molesters, no runaways, no lovers of black women. You all have completed your national service and passed a stringent medical and are a 100 per cent fit."

He strutted up and down in front of us, his steel-shod boots ringing on the cement. "My last warning is this. Do nothing to end up in this country's prisons. Do not pick up a rock. It can turn to diamonds or emeralds. Do not help yourselves to local women, because as white men you will never come out of prison alive." He smirked at us, tapping his leg with his stick.

"You fools have just had your first lecture on survival in the Congo." He stood and glared at us.

We sweated, dying for a drink.

"Fall into a single line. Lunch will be served and then you will receive your kit." He pointed towards a double door that stood partly open. Then he turned and walked away.

The kit was handed out by two black orderlies. The bush hats were one size and the khaki overalls were all one size. Socks and boots offered a choice of two sizes. Raincape, haversack, webbing, ammo pouches. Then came the khaki shirts and shorts, sleeping bags, mosquito nets and bug repellent, water bottles and purification pills. Rifles were the 7.62 Fabrique Nationale (FN). I caressed the weapon and I formed an attachment to it within seconds of receiving it, along with half a dozen empty magazines and a bayonet. We all staggered away towards a hall that was to be our sleeping quarters. The Sergeant Major was walking at our side, silent for a change.

The lunch had consisted of cold ham, baked beans and potatoes. It had been sufficient. The jugs of orange juice had gone down faster than the kitchen staff could replenish them.

That afternoon we were shown how to strip and clean the weapon. It was pleasant in the high ceilinged hall with the beds neatly lined up. Our kit was piled on top. We were all dead tired, some more than others. Brains worked slowly and fingers were clumsy with the new equipment.

At seven we were marched back to the dining hall. Stew was splashed into plates and the men ate silently. Then we went back to the hall.

"Six hundred hours, ladies," sneered our tormentor. "It'll be a little cooler then and we will separate the men from the boys." He turned and was gone into the deepening darkness.

I went over to my bed, piled high with my allotted kit. I wished I was back on the farm, away from these men, and away from the humidity and heat. I was dead tired. I thought of Mia. What was I doing here? I was, by far, the youngest amongst this group of men. Mr van Rensburg had told me when I had signed the forms if anyone asked how old I was, to say I was eighteen. No one had asked or appeared to care.

I hung up the mosquito net and packed my kit under my bed. Roux was on one side. The man who said he was a teacher was on the other. Roux was looking very unhappy. Teacher appeared to be having trouble making up his mind how to pack his kit under his bed and he kept on rearranging things.

Roux turned to me. "You hit the showers first. I will keep an eye on your kit. When you return, you will do the same for me."

Teacher heard him. "Will you watch mine?" he asked cautiously.

Roux nodded and stretched out on his bed. I could not believe it. We had just been warned about stealing, and here we were taking precautions against our fellow soldiers. Taking my towel I headed for the showers and Teacher followed.

I woke in the early hours. It was very hot and I could hear mosquitoes buzzing around outside the net. The hall was dead quiet. I crawled out of the mosquito net and padded barefoot to the ablution block. The lights had been left on, although the globes were yellow. There were gatherings of moths either flapping around or hanging on the wall and ceiling. I have never seen such an assortment of colours. I returned to bed still feeling very weary.

"Move you lazy bunch, move!" Suddenly I was shocked awake. It felt as if I had just returned from the toilet and had just put my head on the pillow.

"Five minutes and I want you outside, and fallen in. Move!" the Sergeant Major screamed. He was dressed in white PT shirt and shorts and white running shoes. One of the men, who was obviously a heavy sleeper, had not moved. The Sergeant Major came quickly down the line of beds, his shoes squeaking on the cement floor. With a crash he tipped the bed over. Its occupant went tumbling out hitting the floor with a solid thud.

"Move!" screamed the Sergeant Major.

It seemed funny. The fallen man had not moved. I laced my boots and watched. The fallen man was lying at an awkward angle. Our tormentor went round the bed and crouched down. Then he casually tossed the corner of the blanket over the man's head.

"He's dead," he said in a sober voice.

I got the first feeling of uneasiness. Were our lives really worth so little?

"There are forty-eight of you left. Fall in. Move ladies. Move!" shouted the Sergeant Major. We fell in outside the hall. The Sergeant Major went off towards one of the buildings and in a short while returned. Then we were on our way.

"Left, right, left, right!" he shouted. Then we started to run, along the deserted tree-lined roads, past the deep green Congo river, past the university and ferry station. Then on we went towards the airport. Then back we came. Men sweated and gasped for breath. It was easily six thirty by now. The humidity was horrific but we kept up a steady pace. The gates to our quarters were visible five hundred metres away with the two black sentries leaning against the wall. We were brought to a sweating, gasping halt. The Sergeant Major must have been fitter than he looked. He was sweating but not puffing like most of the men.

"You unfit ladies! You're a bloody useless lot! In ten days you will be in the battlefield. The unfit die like that fool in the barracks.

Unfit I say. Unfit to serve, unfit to earn the lovely money offered by de Bruins Timbers. Unfit I say!" He walked amongst us, looking disgustedly at each man.

"Who will be next?" He was obviously referring to the man who had died last night. "When I blow my whistle you fools will run, run like you have never run before! Imagine that one of those black buggers is after you with a spear!" He laughed sadistically.

A figure dressed in khaki appeared at the gate, and stood next to the two black sentries. He raised his arm and let it drop. The Sergeant Major blew his whistle and we were running. I passed a few men, then a few more. Suddenly I found myself with just Maritz pounding along ahead of me. I was running hard, my boots heavy, my shirt flapping as I passed him in full flight. Maritz gasped something that I did not catch. I went through the gate and passed the short, khaki-uniformed man and the two shiny black sentries. Into the hall I ran, quickly grabbing my towel. I would be first in the shower. I noticed that the dead man had been removed, the bed stripped and his kit removed. It was as if he had never been there.

The days passed quickly and I lost count. Our days started at six and finished after dark. We were all exhausted and often too tired to eat our evening meal. Roux moaned a lot, although he and Teacher seemed to get along quite well.

The small, thin man who had been at the gate turned out to be Lieutenant Muller, our commander. He was a German, always dressed in perfectly ironed khakis, pith helmet and polished brown leather leggings. He occasionally appeared and watched but said nothing and then disappeared into one of the houses in the compound.

We had been in the compound for eight days now, yet it seemed like forever. I had managed to write to Mia and Gran, placing both letters in the same envelope, hoping I could trust Gran not to read my letter to Mia.

I was starting to feel like a real soldier. We had been to the shooting range and, after a few faults, I had mastered the FN assault rifle and scored well. The peep sights were great. However, the

Browning machine-gun had been a completely new experience. It was brutal, filling me with a new sense of power.

Another two men had dropped out, one with stomach trouble, and the other's knee cartilage had packed up. This brought our numbers down to forty-six. The Sergeant Major had quietened down a lot, becoming less abusive and saying he could do nothing with a bunch of tramps and drunks.

Late on our second to last afternoon, we were marched into the dining hall. A blackboard stood there with a rough map drawn on it. The chairs and benches had been placed in a half circle. We took our places and waited. It was a relief just to sit around and do nothing. Then there was the sound of the Sergeant Major's steel-shod-boots crashing across the yard and into the building. Muller accompanied him.

"Attention!" he screamed. We shot up as one. "All men present Lieutenant." He threw the little man a parade ground salute. Muller touched his hat, smiling his acknowledgement.

Muller removed his pith helmet and placed it on the nearby table. He had one of those faces that did not give away his age. He could be twenty-five or fifty-five. He was short with blond hair and a permanent yellow type of tan. He hitched his rump onto the corner of the table. There was something dangerous about this man and it was not just his calm, professional casualness.

"You men have been assigned to my command." His English was perfect though with a clipped accent. "I have watched you and Sergeant Major Ross has discussed each and every one of you with me. I am inclined to agree with him. You are hopeless, a bunch of drunks! I have complained to headquarters, and they will take it up with the recruiting agency." Then he stopped talking and looked around. There was going to be no praise from this man.

"Tomorrow we pack, and we'll be moving by air to Djolu. Then we'll continue on by road to Villa Vista, the mill we will be guarding." He rose from his perch and pointed to a round spot on the map. "The Maringa river." He said it as if we all should know the name already. "There are two main tribes in that region: the Mongu and the Teng. The Teng," he shrugged his thin shoulders, "are the problem. They're a secretive, primitive tribe living in the rainforest, living by hunting and gathering roots and nuts. They do not communicate with anyone and are never seen. Their weapons of choice are poisoned arrows, for which there is no antidote, as well as hardwood spears and knives. For the past few months they have been threatening the employees at the sawmill, and the different felling gangs. The mill must be kept running at all costs. They have killed no one, and the occasional threat has been very vague." He shrugged again. "But if the Mongu and the Teng were to join forces there would be a problem. They're demanding that all whites and foreign blacks leave their sacred hunting area. But that is impossible." He tapped the blackboard with a piece of chalk looking around at us. "There are nearly two thousand people working at the mill, so you can imagine the size of the operation. Sections of you men will accompany the felling gangs into the jungle. Others will guard the mill to prevent possible sabotage and intimidation. There is also a small mine to the north that is currently in negotiations with de Bruins. They may need a section of you men there." He drew a line on the blackboard with crosses along it indicating a railway line. "Further downstream from the mill is a waterfall. Timber is transported to the head of the waterfall by barge. It is offloaded onto a train and then moved further to the Congo river where it is offloaded again and shipped downstream and from there to the four corners of the world. The waterfall and railhead are a hundred or so kilometres from Villa Vista sawmill. One section will be permanently stationed there. Your employer is de Bruins Timbers. Their head office is in Belgium, but with branches in France." He toyed with the chalk. "Hopefully the Teng will continue to behave, and we can finish our contract in peace, because if there is an uprising, from what I saw of your shooting abilities, I think the Teng will make mincemeat out of you." Muller retrieved his hat and without a word he stalked out.

It was only later that we realised what he meant by mincemeat. The Teng were cannibals!

"Little Nazi!" muttered Maritz who was sitting behind me.

"Bloody Hun!" hissed someone else.

"Right you bunch. You all heard what the Lieutenant said," snarled the Sergeant Major. "He's not impressed." He stood there smirking and extracted a notebook from his breast pocket. He started reading out names. Maritz and another big man, Rocky Stone, were promoted, amongst others, to Corporals. Then they were assigned men. My heart sank. "Mackay, Roux, Wilmot, Carr, Potter. What the hell is this? P...P?" and he pointed to a big, completely bald man whom I had noticed around. He was Polish or from one of those east European countries. We six were assigned to Maritz's section.

Maritz appeared to have had military experience and had tried to show off his skills but had quickly been put in his place by Ross. I would rather have been in another section, maybe with Rocky Stone. He appeared to be a more pleasant character than Maritz.

The Sergeant Major finished. "There will be no bum chums, no changing what has been ordered!" He smirked, and left us to digest the latest bit of information.

That night there was a tension in the hall that had not been there before. We were let off early, just after six.

Maritz and a number of his followers roved restlessly around the hall.

"Let's hit the town, or at least find a drink," said Maritz. Maritz went off towards the kitchen.

There had been no talk of passes. The sentries would not let us out. The only part of Stanleyville we had seen was when arriving by air, and our daily run along the river and through the park finished with a mad dash for the gate, which I had won every time.

"You know," said Teacher joining Roux and myself. "This is a funny set-up. Ten days training and we have seen no other soldiers except the sentries, the cook and kitchen staff; no other officers other than Ross and Muller. Not that Ross is not on the ball, but hell we are literally being thrown in at the deep end!"

Roux shuffled nervously around on his bed. "If they had told me about poisonous arrows and spears I would never have signed up. Anything could happen," he said with a sigh.

"I think we are being used," replied Teacher quietly.

Maritz re-appeared at the main door. "I've made a plan," he said to no one in particular. He made his way towards his bed in the corner where there always seemed to be a card game in progress.

"Loosen up!" shouted the Sergeant Major from the door. In his hand he carried a bundle of letters. My heart gave a huge leap. Mia might have written. Then he started bellowing names. The men bolted down the corridor between the beds to collect their mail.

"Mackay!" I was on my feet running. It was from Gran. I felt the envelope. There was another letter inside. I returned to my bed and sat and read. Gran's letter said that everything was fine. Oupa had hired a relation of Majola's to milk the cows and do odd jobs around the farm. As soon as the money arrived Oupa would start on the dam. They'd had a little rain and one of the cows had calved. And, of course, I was to look after myself.

A number of the men who had not received mail had returned to the card game at the end of the hall. Roux was sitting crying after reading his letter. Teacher looked bleak, and appeared to be taking a very long time to read two pages.

I had not opened Mia's letter. It made me nervous. I took a deep breath and tore the envelope open. Three pages of neat up and down writing, with a lavender smell to the pages. I was thrilled she still loved me, and was keenly counting the days to my return. I was completely absorbed, so I failed to notice the men leaving for the dining hall. Now alone I read the letter over and over again. It was fantastic to be loved and missed so much!

That night Maritz started a fight with Rocky. The two biggest men in the unit, slugging each other around the hall. However, they could not get the better of one another.

"You bloody English!" snarled Maritz as the two locked together yet again. Maritz was trying to knee Rocky in the groin but hopelessly missing. A few of the men cheered Maritz on and others cheered Rocky. At one stage a scuffle broke out between the spectators.

Then the two men went down amongst the beds, gouging and butting. Maritz was on top at that stage trying to choke Rocky. There was pushing amongst the spectators and Sergeant Major Ross appeared at the front of the crowd. He closed in quickly and chopped Maritz on the neck with the side of his hand and Maritz fell over, stunned. Rocky scrambled to his feet looking shocked.

"Right, ladies!" screeched the Sergeant Major. "Pack! Pack every damned thing you have in your kit bags!" He bent and sniffed at Maritz who was still on the floor recovering. "Local hooch! You think you can bullshit me? Five minutes. Fall in every one of you!"

He went off into the dark yard followed by the two black sentries who had been standing by the door with their rifles at the ready. They actually looked as if they would have used them.

"Oh hell," groaned Roux, "What now? We were not to blame."

"We're all in this together," said Teacher sadly, struggling to sling his pack across his back.

I remained silent. It was our last day, the first time we had got off reasonably early but it had been spoilt. We all knew Ross was going to make us suffer. We were jammed into the back of an army truck and roared out of town along a poorly lit and badly constructed road, past the airport and on and on. It seemed forever.

Eventually the truck stopped. "Get down and fall in!" bellowed Sergeant Major Ross. "So you bastards want to mess with discipline. You want to spoil my evening?"

We had been divided into two platoons and we stood as such. "Stone fall out. You're in charge of 'A' platoon. You arrive at base as one. If a man falls you carry him. Arrive short and you will return on foot to find him." He was raging. "That goes for you too Maritz. 'A' platoon away you go!" They set off at a steady jog.

"B" platoon – Maritz's – waited. Time ticked by and mosquitoes buzzed around.

"Right," snarled Ross "Forward march." We set off. It was a long way but surprisingly no one complained. We trudged along with our heavy loads. It was two in the morning when we all reached our billet. We were all completely shattered, our feet blistered and backs aching.

The next day could have been really interesting, except everyone was exhausted and bad tempered. The long walk had knocked it out of us all. We were screamed out of the hall at four, then fed and watered, and moved in trucks to the airport, where we were left sitting for an hour. Neither Maritz nor Rocky had apologised for causing the trouble the night before. Teacher said Maritz had been drinking with Potter and a number of men. Maritz had called Rocky a piece of Durban trash or something to that effect and that had been enough to start the fight.

We sat and sweated amongst our kit. The Sergeant Major had arrived, accompanied by Muller. Both were looking cool and in full control. A yellow twin-engine Transal transport plane came lumbering across from the hangar and we were loaded into it, then we sat on the floor amongst our kit. There were no windows, no seats or safety belts. The cargo door shut. Engines roared, vibrating throughout the aircraft, and we were away. The aircraft felt grossly over-loaded and really awkward in the air.

Roux, who sat next to me, was shaking with fear. "Oh god," he whispered. "There are no windows. This is against the law. They are not allowed to transport us like this, we are not cargo."

"Shut up," snarled Maritz who had heard him.

There were a lot of other funny nervous comments that did not go down well with most of the men.

We landed at an airport that was more like a field with a windsock that hung limply in the listless air. That was all we saw of Djolu. Three drab, jungle-green Ford four-ton trucks stood waiting. We were hustled aboard. The trucks were rigged out with steel deck and with uprights. Thick planks had been bolted to the uprights forming a protective wall and there was a pipe frame over the top which was covered by a taut green sail. A Browning machine-gun under dust covers hung on its pylon above the cab.

"The planks and sail are to protect you lot from the poisonous arrows," said Maritz with an unpleasant smile and showing off a broken tooth. "You assholes had better keep wide awake if you want to see home again!"

He seemed to get great pleasure out of bullying. None of us liked his attitude or the way he gave orders, but there was nothing we could say or do.

The trucks left in convoy. Dense jungle lined the dead straight road. In the beginning the road was good but it steadily deteriorated.

Deep furrows filled with green slimy water made up long sections of the road. After a long slow grind we turned off the main road. Now and again we could see the river through the trees. On the sandbanks basked groups of huge crocodiles. The truck ploughed on, swaying from side to side. The men in the back held on for dear life. I found that Teacher was a wealth of information. He knew the names of most of the trees and many of the numerous birds we saw. Maritz was in the front in the passenger seat, and was gratefully out of our way.

Pole and Potter had said very little. Potter was a lanky individual, deeply tanned, with a face like a horse. He was the one who had been identified as a drunk. The Pole seemed to be one of those big quiet types. He had claimed one of the back corners of the truck and was hanging on doggedly. Carr was about thirty with a sallow complexion and long untidy black hair, but seemed a pleasant character, happily speaking and joking with everyone.

It was late afternoon when the truck broke from the jungle. The river was on our right. The road followed the riverbank and in the distance the sawmill appeared with white smoke billowing into the blue heavens. Small patches of crops were growing on the side of the road. A large number of dilapidated mud huts made up what had to be the labourer dwellings. Naked children ran out waving and smiling and we waved back. A line of women walking along the road with bundles of wood on their heads stopped and waved. It was nice to be so pleasantly welcomed.

Then we came to rows of neat white-washed cottages, with bougainvillea and other exotic plants growing in their gardens. A red and white painted school building appeared, and nearby what looked like a clinic.

The mill was not as big as we had expected. It was built of planks and corrugated iron. Saws could be heard screaming above the truck's engine. Workmen stopped their work to wave. There was a jetty built of poles and planks sticking out into the river. A rusty old tug stood at its moorings, as well as number of barges in various stages of disrepair. It looked very tranquil and picturesque at six o'clock in the evening.

The truck swung into what had once been the base of the Royal Belgium Police, who had guarded the mill until recently. The buildings were prefabricated and painted battleship grey, with insect screens on the windows and doors. Fires burnt under forty-four-gallon drums that provided hot water. The security fence was missing in places. The cook, a large black man with a huge grin on his face, stood in the kitchen door watching us. This was going to be home for the next five and a half months.

The trucks pulled up in line. Maritz jumped down and jogged towards Muller who was beckoning him. I don't know what was said but when he came back his face as black as thunder.

"You guys," referring to his section, "stay put. You will sleep in the back of the truck. We will be stationed at the railhead."

"Looks like Maritz has made himself really popular," whispered Carr with a wink. "And we are going to go down with the arrogant bastard?" He laughed softly. Carr somehow saw a funny side to our situation. Everyone set about organising their mosquito nets and bedding and I knew it was going to be a very uncomfortable night.

Chapter 4

The night at Villa Vista was far from quiet. The mill's saws stopped work at ten. We could hear the workmen leaving, calling to one another. The generator that supplied electricity thumped away continuously. The sawmill was lit up throughout the night, obviously for security reasons.

Morning came far too quickly. The cook arrived and set about banging his pots and pans. His portable radio was blaring out the local music. We groaned and started to rise. I noticed Rocky Stone and Maritz having a brief confrontation at the ablution block, but they stopped at the approach of Sergeant Major Ross.

Breakfast was served under Ross's supervision. Then we loaded the truck with provisions, ammunition and tents. Maritz was called aside and given a map and instructions. He came back pumped up with self-importance.

"We going to the railhead," he said loudly, as if we did not know already. "You lot had better keep wide awake. You all know why we are here. It's to give these bloody Kaffirs hell! Just you keep that in mind." He had not noticed Muller approaching. Seeing him at the last moment he came to attention, obviously not realising he had antagonised the Lieutenant.

Muller stopped a few metres away. Muller's voice was quiet but with a dangerous cutting edge and loud enough for everyone to hear. "Maritz, you bloody South Africans are all the same. You are now in a foreign country. You and all these men will be working with black elements of the local police force, and I will not have you or anyone else referring to black people as Kaffirs or insulting them in any way. Do you understand?"

Maritz had gone red, but I doubt it was with embarrassment, more like rage at being corrected in front of all the men. "Yes sir," he blurted out. Everyone was standing around watching in silence.

"This goes for everyone." Muller continued, "If any of you cause any sort of racial conflict, you will be dealt with in the harshest of manners by me. If you have any sort of rank I will remove it. I will make your lives so unpleasant you will wish you were dead." He stood there in the boiling sun, neat and polished. Maritz looked huge against him.

"Secondly, if I am personally insulted by anyone of you drunks, such as being called a Nazi or a Hun, I will personally beat the shit out of you. Do you all hear me?"

Maritz had turned an even deeper shade of red. The man must have very sharp ears to have heard that comment. Either that or someone had told him.

"Yes sir!" came the chorus.

We left Villa Vista on a hundred and fifty kilometre journey by road. It would have been seventy five or so by river. Fortunately Maritz was out of the way lounging and smoking in the passenger seat. Potter had become the official driver. The rest of us hung on in the back of the truck, peering out from under the canvas canopy. The road was not bad until we had gone about a third of the way. Then it started to deteriorate. There were potholes filled with water and deep slime filled the furrows, but still we ploughed along. The jungle closed in around us. In many places the road was so narrow that the jungle brushed against the sides of the truck. We bounced and swerved and skidded along.

About midday we entered a black muddy chute, sliding sideways and then straightening out. Huge trees with a mess of monkey ropes and creepers formed an impenetrable wall on either side of the road. Then we got stuck. The truck revved, its wheels spinning and sending black oily mud flying. Potter cut the engine and jumped from the cab. We watched him from the back. Maritz stepped carefully down to avoid muddying his boots, and went over to the verge.

"Right, everyone out. Pole you and Carr cut a number of poles. Mac, you, Teacher, Potter and Roux start digging," ordered Maritz.

We stripped down to our shorts. The mud was black like thick oil and it stank. The truck sat on its axle in the mud. It looked like an impossible task. We dug and sweated. The bugs stung and we yelped. After two hours of digging, swearing and sweating, we were just preparing to move when Teacher called us together.

"Let me take a snap," said Teacher rummaging amongst his kit and appearing with a camera.

Maritz sat in the shade smoking. "You some sort of bloody tourist?" he sneered.

Teacher snapped him sitting alone on the verge. "One for the album," he laughed. Then we all posed, covered in black mud brandishing our knives and spades.

We were all aboard and the engine roared. We bounced out of the muddy trench and continued towards the railhead. An hour later we were stuck again, but dug ourselves out. The day was almost over when we finally seemed to burst from the jungle.

It was like a massive anticlimax. Potter stopped the truck and we gazed at the railhead. About a hundred dilapidated mud huts appeared with a red rusting corrugated iron shop decorated by a lopsided Coca-Cola sign. The arm of a crane poked out above the village, identifying what must be the harbour. The police station stood to one side and consisted of prefabricated buildings, with white paint peeling from the walls. An unidentifiable flag drooped from the flagpole out front. There was a rusting security fence surrounding the buildings. A football field separated the police station from the village. Pools of stagnant water glistened in the late afternoon light. The jungle formed a green claustrophobic wall around the settlement. Thunder rumbled in the distance.

"Oh my god," whispered Teacher. "Are we expected to stay here for six months?"

No one else spoke. We just stared in shocked amazement. The truck lurched forward going towards the police station.

Potter pulled up in front of the police station and revved the engine. The front door of the station opened and a short squat man appeared. He was shirtless and looked as if he had just woken up. He yawned, showing an array of yellow teeth under a moth-eaten moustache. His paunch protruded alarmingly and was covered with a mat of thick black hair. He waved a podgy hand and pointed.

"You can camp over there!" he called. He indicated a clearing beneath some trees about twenty-five metres from the station. The clearing backed onto the jungle. "I have been expectancy of you guys. Got stuck, huh! When you set up, come over to the station fir a welcoming."

Carr laughed out loud. "What a place! That policeman looks like a Mexican chicken thief. All he needs is a sombrero."

None of us seemed able to catch on to Carr's sense of humour.

Maritz had no intention of doing anything. He sat back, aggressively ordering everyone around. "Do this. Do that! Put that there! Move this." He claimed a tent to himself. Potter said he would sleep in the cab of the truck, which made a bit more space in the second tent. When everything was as Maritz fancied it, he ordered Teacher to guard the camp. The rest of us trooped over to see what the welcome was all about.

"I am Perry Hough, and I am in charge around here." The policeman smiled, showing off his yellow fangs. His accent was very strong but understandable. He handed out cold beers. "Meet Thomas. Gendarme Thomas is my valued assistant." He waved a hand towards a black giant of a man who was tending the fire, as the beautiful aroma of grilling meat wafted across to where we were all sitting at a makeshift table.

Hough dropped his voice, "Thomas speaks good English. He is not from here, but he and I have been together for a long time. He is easily upset. Please be very careful. I do not want him upset in any way." Hough looked around as if realising that someone was missing. "Who is missing?" he asked.

Maritz glanced around. "I left a man at the camp to guard it," he said, looking uneasy.

Perry Hough smiled, "You bring your weapons. No one, but no one, steals around the railhead. No one. You may call him."

Teacher duly arrived and was handed a beer by the big African policeman.

"Your job is to support me," said Hough, lighting a cigarette. "I told headquarters it was not necessary, but they insisted." He shrugged his shoulders. "The Teng have been around for a long time. Every now and again they make threats and everyone runs or gets nervous." He sipped his beer. "I have been in this region for fifteen years. Next year my contract expires and I return home to Belgium and a pension. I have seen only one Teng in all my years. The Teng live deep in the jungle hunting and foraging for food. They live by a very strong, how would you say? Religious conduct."

"Tribal law or code," offered Teacher.

"Ah yes, code," continued Hough. "It is very strict; no intermarrying with other tribes. No associating with white people. At times they may do certain things like pick certain fruit and hunt certain animals." He sipped more beer, obviously enjoying having strangers around him. "Their closest relations are the Mongu who are their brother tribe. Often the Teng are called Mongu Teng. The Mongu are employed throughout the region, going to school and attending church, but I believe just below the surface the two tribes could easily join forces. I also believe they share the same witchdoctors." He took a long drag on his cigarette, stubbed it out, and then finished his beer. Thomas, who was doing the cooking, looked up and in a few moments appeared with a tray of frosted beers.

I watched the big African with interest. He was a giant of a man, all of two metres tall with massive shoulders. His upper arms were as thick as my thigh. He served us and returned to his cooking, a beer bottle almost invisible in his big hand.

Hough droned on. "The Teng use poisonous arrows and spears that are made of hardwood. The poison has no cure. One dies in a short time," stated Hough bluntly.

"How far can they shoot?" asked Teacher. Maritz stared at him but Teacher took no notice.

"Probably twenty metres accurately," said Hough, taking a lit cigarette offered by Maritz.

"Thanks," he said with one of his unpleasant smiles. "The thing the Teng do, you understand, is this. When they kill the enemy, they open his gut, allowing the spirit to leave, and if they think the man is a great warrior they will not open his gut but they'll take him away and eat him."

"Cannibalism?" asked Teacher a little apprehensively.

"Ah yes, cannibalism!" said Hough.

I caught Maritz's look again. He did not like Teacher asking questions or helping Hough out with his English, which he spoke very well.

"Are there only two of you policemen here?" asked Teacher, swigging his beer.

"Yes, there are three of us altogether. The other man is named Ray. He is not to be trusted with liquor or women or gambling. He was sent here for punishment. He is kept to look after the station's radio and do other work around here. He speaks no English. I wish he would leave but he has a short time before being pensioned off. I have given him a hard time but he still refuses to leave." He shrugged. "The man has about nine months to go," he said finally.

We all sat in silence. Hough and Maritz were smoking and sipping their beers. Potter had long finished his and was waiting for the next round. Birds called to one another in the nearby jungle and an unknown creature screeched alarmingly.

Hough unfolded a map and spread it out on the table, using empty beer bottles to pin the corners down. "We are here," he stated. "One hundred and fifty kilometres from Villa Vista. From here east, it's about a hundred and twenty to the main road, south to Bombimba, north to St Patrick's Mission." He pointed with a stubby finger. "Here is Crossways School, a crossing of roads. To the west is the river. The road is closed and the pontoon was washed away years ago. The mine across the river is also closed. If you go east, one reaches the main road to Djolu and on to Stanleyville. There are a number of estates along here." He pointed to black spots on the eastern side of the road. "The Estate managers are okay. They are very hospitable and do their own law and order." Hough smiled to himself, and Thomas appeared with more beer. "If there are any questions please ask." We sat for a moment. "Not too many people, how would one say, yes?" Hough hesitated.

"Sparsely populated," corrected Teacher automatically.

I sat and wondered what Hough and Thomas had done to end up out here. The thing that kept on amazing me was the distance and vastness. At home I had looked up the Congo in Oupa's AA atlas. The atlas had given the wrong impression. I doubted anything could prepare one for the shear vastness, and distance or even the road conditions. The roads between Djolu, Villa Vista, the railhead, Crossways and St Patrick's Mission were not even on the map!

Thomas appeared out of the oncoming gloom with a tray of delicious-smelling grilled meat. Hough produced a number of green litre bottles, saying it was his favourite wine and that his mother sent him a case every month.

Potter was in his element, but the rest of us were a bit more cautious. The wine was semi-sweet and appeared to be dangerously tasty. I refused the wine and sipped my beer and chewed on my steak and watched the men.

It did not take long, for the wine must have been really potent. Potter was staggeringly drunk and nearly fell into the red hot coals. Carr was trying to tell jokes but kept on forgetting the punch line. Roux was saying how proud he was to be here protecting the minority. Then he started to compare the situation with his forefathers armed with muzzle loader rifles fighting the Zulus at Blood river. Maritz and Hough sat drinking and smoking in the dark shadows.

It was time for me to go. I finished my beer, thanked the policeman for his hospitality and returned to camp. Pole and Teacher soon joined me, but they had little to say.

The morning arrived with sudden brightness, intense heat and biting flies. I rose early. Potter lay in the dust next to the truck. The door of the truck was wide open. He obviously had not made it up the step into the cab. I stirred the coals of the fire and put the kettle on to boil, and went across to the police station to use the ablutions.

Carr was there lodged between the wall and the toilet bowl. He was snoring loudly. It had been quite a night for those two. I wondered how Maritz had fared.

The men started to wake up. There was no hurry. Teacher lay under his mosquito net and wrote a letter. Pole wandered off towards the station with his towel and soap. Maritz appeared, grimaced in the harsh light and, after two cups of black coffee, he looked a lot better.

"Right, you lot. We are going down to the harbour to watch the tug from Villa Vista arrive. Make sure you have webbing and rifles. It will be like a show of force, just to let these villagers know we are here to protect them," snarled Maritz.

I wondered where he had got that brilliant idea from. Every villager for kilometres around would know of our presence by now. We all trooped down to the harbour wall, in some sort of formation and sat around waiting for the tug to arrive. A wood-burning train came puffing out of the jungle wall, rattling along its rusting tracks onto the harbour wall pulling a dozen flat wagons. It came to a stop at the buffers and blasted its whistle and let off a cloud of steam.

I noticed two little black boys fishing further down the harbour wall. I wandered over to watch them and was surprised to see their catch of three nice-sized river bream. Using sign language I found out I could buy hooks and line from the village shop. This would be one way to pass the time and keep me out of the rest of the section's way.

Leaving the rest of the men, I walked through the village to the shop. It was dark and dingy and stank of booze and cheap tobacco. A large black woman grinned at me from behind the counter, showing off two missing front teeth.

She introduced herself. "Me, I am Miriam. You want cold Coke or Beer. I sell everything."

I bet she did! I bought Coke, a roll of line and a number of hooks, and returned to the rest of the men.

Maritz stared at me from bloodshot eyes. "Where have you been? You keep away from those black bitches, you'll get a nasty disease!" he snarled.

I kept quiet, not wanting to upset Maritz. Just then the distant blast of a ship's siren echoed across the water. The mobile crane that ran along the docks started up with a cloud of diesel fumes and clashing of gears.

The tug we had seen the previous day appeared around the distant bend in the river. It was towing three barges. The barges were piled high with big logs and planks. The tug crept slowly in and manoeuvred its way alongside the harbour wall and was secured. The crane started to unload the timber onto the waiting flat wagons. After almost three hours of shunting and whistle blowing the train puffed away, straining under its heavy load, back the way it had come, back into the black wall of jungle. The village settled down and returned to its peaceful existence.

The routine was set. The tug and train would arrive each day. The load would be noisily transferred and then the village would become quiet again. The next week drifted by peacefully. Every day I fished and caught a number of bream and an eel that had wrecked my line. Even Maritz seemed to have been lulled into some sort of harmony and let us be.

Each evening Maritz, Potter and Carr would leave for the shop and come back at an unearthly hour, drunk as lords. Potter seldom made the front of the truck and passed out under the stars, to be ravaged by mosquitoes. The step up to the cab appeared to be just too much for him in his inebriated state. Carr, on the other hand, would tumble into the tent and pass out either on top of one of us or on the floor. Maritz would suddenly decide to wake-up some unfortunate person up in order to make him coffee. This became a regular pattern.

One night Maritz followed his usual pattern. He stood swaying, his thumbs hooked into his webbing belt.

"Coffee!" he snarled. No one responded. He came over to where Teacher was fast asleep under his mosquito net. Using his knife he slashed the net open. With a startled cry Teacher jumped to his feet. Maritz punched him and Teacher fell back, unconscious. And so life continued. Hough drifted in and out but demanded very little of us.

Early one evening, Hough arrived at our camp, with two bottles of wine grasped in his podgy hands. "I have come to visit you guys," he announced, smiling happily. "Tomorrow we are going on patrol, to visit a felling gang. It is important. Have you guys got mugs?" He opened one of the bottles and poured. Potter was the first one there, his mug at the ready.

"It is quiet all around. Nothing is happening, as I predicted. All the fuss about unrest is just rumours. The company is wasting its money with you guys," he said as he sipped his wine. He had obviously interrupted Maritz's visit to the shop with Potter and Carr. I wondered if he had done it on purpose. I was starting to think that there was more to the ugly little policeman than met the eye.

Shortly after finishing his wine, he slouched off into the dark, back to his station, his message delivered. The three drunks left for the shop. The rest of us sat around the dying fire. Pole sat staring into the flames. Teacher was writing. Roux was trying to read in the poor lamplight. I sat and dozed.

"This is a photo of my wife," said Teacher out of the blue. He handed a snap to Pole.

"She is nice," said Pole. "Have you got kids?"

Teacher shook his head looking sad.

Pole rummaged in his kit and produced a photo. "My wife, and three kids," he said proudly. "They are in Cape Town waiting for me. I will take the money we get paid and start a fast food cafe. You know, hot dogs, hamburgers and chips."

Roux was now listening, and produced his wallet that contained a photo. "That's my, wife Sue and my daughter Mary," he said handing it to Teacher.

I felt as if this was a type of men's bonding thing going on, a "you show me yours and I'll show you mine" kind of thing. Teacher's wife was rather thin with black-rimmed spectacles. The Pole's wife was a fat, jovial-looking woman with three chubby kids. Roux's wife was blond and heavily made up with a very sulky mouth. The little girl she was holding in her arms appeared to be looking away into the distance.

"This is my girl, Mia," I said, handing the photo of Mia around. I felt she was far prettier than any of the other women I had managed to examine in the poor light.

"She is very pretty!" said Teacher softly, handing the photo on.

I must admit I felt rather proud of her.

Roux leant forward peering at each of us in turn. "I need a couple of thousand to get out of debt, and back on my feet, but if I knew we were going to be involved with poisonous arrows, and bloody mosquitoes," he said and slapped at his legs, "I would never have come. You know they lied, hey didn't they?"

We all murmured our agreement, but knew all too well that there was no way out now.

Oddly enough, that night I never heard the three drunks return to camp.

Hough and Thomas arrived early the next morning at our camp in their police Jeep.

"You must just follow me and try and not get stuck," said Hough grinning through his moustache.

Maritz looked rough, and Potter was sweating profusely, Carr was as white as a sheet. We left in convoy, following the main road towards Villa Vista. Hough appeared to know the way as the Jeep turned off the main road and entered a dark jungle track that wound between the big trees and there were signs that a bulldozer had worked there recently. The truck skidded and lurched, into one muddy furrow, and then bounced into the next. The track seemed to go on and on. We hung on for dear life. Insects and flies stung us even through our thick khaki clothing. Others seemed to concentrate around our eyes and ears making life even more unpleasant.

It was nearly midday when we arrived at what turned out to be one the many felling gang's camp. This consisted of a number of roughly built huts. Mud was everywhere. A battered Ford tractor was bogged down in thick mud. Around us numerous selected giant trees had been felled and had been sawn into lengths for easy loading. We all looked out from under our canopy in amazement. Had we come all this way for this?

A large blue-black lady and a dozen big-eyed, half-naked children stood and squatted around a big black three-legged pot that was simmering over an open fire. The lady smiled her greeting at Hough and Thomas. Hough stepped carefully out of his Jeep avoiding the mud as much as possible. We climbed down to stretch our legs. In the distance there was the continuous scream of chainsaws and the sound of trees falling.

These were the people, the felling gangs who entered the jungle in search of the valuable hardwoods. Out of curiosity I went over and peered into the pot. Two large monkeys were on the boil. I did not say it, but they looked very much like the smaller black kids who squatted around the pot waiting for lunch. They might have been cooking their own.

The woman sent one of the older children, off at a run. She had lots to say in the local dialect. Thomas joined in laughing, and Hough walked a short distance away and lit a cigarette. A while later a big pot-bellied black man arrived; he was dressed in a battered red overall. He had a sawn-off shotgun pushed through his belt. He greeted Hough and Thomas. The conversation that took place was never translated for us. After about half an hour, we left, skidding and swaying down the muddy track, back the way we had come.

That night I sat with a needle and thread, using one of the spare mosquito nets to make a hood. It was not unlike a beekeeper's hood. It would at least protect my eyes, nose and ears. Teacher tried to bribe me into making him one, but I told him to make his own.

Maritz sat next to the paraffin lamp and read an out of date newspaper. Roux had already gone to bed. There was a general atmosphere of tiredness around the camp.

"Tomorrow," said Maritz, "we're going to do a roadblock, so you bunch had better look sharp!"

There was a groan from Roux, aptly expressing what we all felt. It seemed such a waste of time as nothing was going on. A roadblock? No one travelled these back roads, other than Hough's Jeep and the timber tractors, which made a terrible mess of the roads. We had seen no other vehicles at all since our arrival.

The following day we left early, and this time only Thomas accompanied us. We bounced and skidded along the track through the thick dark jungle. Teacher and I tried to spot birds that we would look up later in the birdbook which Teacher had borrowed from Hough. It was more than a hundred kilometres to the junction of the two roads. We soon got stuck but eventually dug ourselves out. Just after midday we arrived at the junction. We all collapsed at the side of the road, seeking whatever shade we could find. A flight of hornbills, on seeing us, screamed their displeasure, cackling noisily, then they flew away.

There was no sign of traffic. The road was no different to the one we had travelled on all morning, with furrows and potholes full of repulsive green stagnant water. It was lined with thick, evil-smelling jungle. Mosquitoes and other stinging insects plagued us continuously. Thomas said the bus would be along soon so we sat and waited, but time dragged.

Eventually the bus arrived, but African time, three hours late! Thomas flagged it down.

Maritz climbed down from the cab. "Right you bunch of assholes. Let's do it properly!" Maritz barked at us. "Pole, you man the Browning! Carr, you second him! Mac, you and Roux back up the policeman! Teacher and Potter, get down on the other side of the bus to see no one jumps off."

The bus had squeaked to a stop. It was really crowded. The sign said it could carry sixty people but it probably carried double that. The people that did not fit inside sat on the roof amongst the luggage. Thomas climbed the steps, ordering the occupants out into the road. There was a lot of mumbling and shouting which stopped when Pole cocked the Browning.

Passengers tumbled out and stood in a rough line. Thomas's attitude had changed. He joked and chatted with the women, children and the old men who made up the passengers. Then he checked through the baggage and ordered the passengers back on board. A woman passenger handed over a bunch of ripe bananas which Thomas said was a present, as there was no room in the bus. The bus pulled away and the passengers waved with broad smiles on their shiny black faces.

Thomas stood and watched them leave, his hand half raised in greeting. Then he turned and spoke urgently to Maritz. "It is bad. Something is wrong. Only, women, children and old men are travelling. They are running. You see many carrying pots and other things from their homes." He wiped his face on a red handkerchief.

"If the Mongu join their brothers the Teng, there will be big trouble. We may go now."

The return trip seemed a lot shorter, maybe because Potter managed not to get stuck. Finally the truck burst from the jungle moving at about twenty kilometres an hour, and turned across the football field towards the police station.

I noticed two timber tractors and trailers were parked in front of the station, with people's belongings piled high on the trailers. Potter parked the truck and we all wandered across to have a look at what was going on.

Hough met us, his face serious. "The Teng have appeared," he said worriedly. "Look!" He led the way around the one tractor to where a body lay on the ground. It was covered with a multi-coloured blanket. He drew the blanket back. Before us lay the felling foreman we had travelled so far to see the previous day. A short shaft of what could only be called a puny little arrow with two red feathers, stuck out from the base of his skull.

"This man did not suffer. He probably died within seconds," said Hough covering the dead man again.

We stood around for a while and then returned to our camp.

"They are starting the killing!" said Roux his face sternly set. "We could be next, you know? They could creep up and 'Zap', stick one of those arrows in one of us!" His voice changed. It was now high pitched and anxious. "They lied to us when we were recruited! They didn't tell us about this! The food is shocking, the jungle full of cannibals!"

"Shut up or I'll shut you up," snarled Maritz.

Roux walked slowly away from us towards the tent. We all sat in silence. It was very true what he had said. None of us had known what we were letting ourselves in for when we had signed on the dotted line.

That night it was very quiet. The drunks did not go out. Potter took himself off early into the cab of the truck. I was sure that he had a bottle hidden in there somewhere.

During the last week I had noticed that Maritz had been watching the tug arrive each day. He would go off to the edge of the village to a spot that gave him a good view of its approach. Using binoculars, he would study the passengers. This morning at about ten, he had gone off on his usual patrol.

We were all sitting around the camp when we heard the tug hooting in the distance, and a short while later Maritz appeared running. Long before he was at the camp he was shouting orders.

"Mac, sort my tent out – make it snappy! Pole, take the Browning – I want it spotless! The camp is to be in order. Chop, chop!" He raced into the camp, changing from the shorts he was wearing to his khakis. He splashed water into a basin and hurriedly started to shave. We all rushed around getting things organised. We guessed that Muller was on the tug. Maritz had said it took forty minutes to dock. Then Muller would take five to ten minutes to reach the camp. I was surprised at how Maritz valued his rank and being stationed at the railhead. He also prided himself with the log he kept –only he wrote in it.

Later, as calculated, Muller appeared, carrying a bag across his shoulders, holster on his hip, his khakis immaculate. His boots were so shiny that you could see your face in them. We were sitting cleaning our rifles as he arrived. Maritz ordered us to our feet and saluted the German. Muller looked around the neat orderly camp. All of us were dressed in shorts, socks and boots, very orderly indeed. He returned Maritz's salute, checked the log and signed it. Teacher offered him a mug of coffee, which he accepted. I felt a tingle of excitement as he removed a bundle of mail from his bag and placed it on the table.

"Your camp looks good," he said sipping the coffee. "Things are changing very quickly, not only around here but in the tribal and political circles of this country. You had better keep wide awake! Anything could happen." He stood looking around the camp. "Tomorrow the tug will bring a bale of empty sacks. Full them with sand and build walls around your tents. They could provide possible protection." Then he and Maritz went off towards the police station.

"Would you believe that!" exclaimed Roux. "Sandbags! What's the use of sandbags? We need a wall between us and the bloody jungle!"

Teacher had attacked the bundle of mail. I stood expectantly by, as names were called, but I received nothing. I stood dumbstruck, searching for a reason.

Teacher saw my dismay and smiled understandingly. "They may have missed the post Mac. You will get two letters next time, you'll see," he said reassuringly.

I stood there feeling foolish and rejected. Everyone else had received letters, except Potter who never received anything anyway and didn't seem to expect one either.

A couple of hours later Maritz returned after he had accompanied Muller back to the tug. He took his two letters and went off to his tent. The other men had gone off in different directions, needing privacy to read. Roux had cocooned himself in his mosquito net. Pole lay blissfully on his stretcher reading. Teacher had gone to the ablution block. I did not see Carr leave. Potter was fiddling under the bonnet of the truck. I felt totally left out. I knew there was probably a good reason, and it was probably correct what Teacher had said.

Taking my fishing pole I went down to the harbour. The day was tranquil. The river water was sparkling green. Two large crocodiles lay with jaws agape on the sandbank and numerous wading birds patrolled the shallows. I baited up and dropped my line in. It was very deep below the wall. I sat with my back against a bollard, dreaming of the farm, Mia, Gran, Oupa, my dam, kukui pastures and Jersey cows.

Suddenly it struck! I was almost taken by surprise. The river bream put up a terrific fight, and I fought back. All other thoughts were gone from my head. After a great battle, I landed a bream weighing about two kilograms. One of the little black boys who had been watching me came over with a grin on his face, indicating he would clean it for me if I gave him a little of the flesh. It was agreed. The afternoon was drifting by in peace and tranquillity after all!

As the shadows were starting to lengthen, Teacher appeared and made his way slowly down to the harbour wall and sat near me. "It's beautiful!" was all he said.

I often wondered about Teacher. He looked like a teacher, not very tall and slightly built, with intelligent but gentle eyes, which matched his short, greying hair and a bushy moustache. He claimed to have taught geography and was by far more intelligent than anyone in the unit. He had never told us his reasons for being here. I had come because of the farm. Roux because of debt, and Pole wanted to start a fast food business. I wondered about Carr, Maritz and Potter. They all had problems, but had good reasons. But what was Teacher? There was the "queer" thing that everyone seemed to bring up, but to me, he looked, behaved and spoke no different to anyone else. He was just far more knowledgeable than any of us. That was very obvious.

The sun was setting, as I packed up, and we headed back to camp.

That night Maritz, Potter and Carr went on the booze. At two in the morning they arrived back in camp. Maritz was at his meanest.

"Coffee!" he roared into the darkness. He was standing there swaying in the flickering firelight.

"Come on you bunch of queers, kaffir-lovers, move your asses."

I was closest to the door of the tent. I untangled myself and made for the kettle, which already contained coffee. It just needed to be heated up. I placed it on the red-hot coals and added sugar and condensed milk to Maritz's mug.

In the darkness Potter was trying to negotiate the step up into the truck. He lost his footing and hit the ground with a thud. He stayed there, not moving. Carr had made it into the tent, tripped and fell. Then he started to puke. I was surprised at the speed at which Teacher and Pole appeared and dragged Carr, by the ankles, face down to one of the logs that we used as a seat and threw him over it. He stayed there.

"You Commie bastard! What the hell do you want in our company?" said Maritz aggressively pointing at Pole. Pole ignored him and returned into the tent. Watching Maritz, I became aware for the first time of the knife he carried up his sleeve. He gave me the impression that he was dying to use it. Then the coffee was ready. I handed him the mug and he staggered off towards his tent, mumbling to himself.

The next morning things around the camp suddenly changed with the arrival of Hough.

"We must make speed. Very quick!" Hough shouted. He appeared agitated and was sweating heavily. Thomas was at the wheel of the police Jeep waiting for us.

We were given five minutes, notice and had not been told what was happening. I doubted if Maritz even knew. We grabbed our webbing, ammunition and water bottles and clambered aboard. Potter looked like death, the mosquitoes had given him hell. He had bite marks all over his face and arms. Thinking about it, he had risen from his open-air bed to go straight behind the steering wheel of the truck. Maritz was no better off, and I almost felt sorry for Carr, who was white and shaky, hanging on to the side of the truck. I doubted if he had much more to bring up as he hung over the tailgate retching miserably.

We followed the racing Jeep, bouncing and swerving and skidding as branches and bushes whipped at the side of the vehicle. Surprisingly we did not get stuck, and reached the spot where we had held the roadblock after about three hours. Then we headed north. The road was a little better, passing through deserted and dilapidated villages with their banana patches and small plots of vegetables. Hough nearly missed the turning, as the Jeep broadsided dangerously and then entered a narrow lane, where a thoughtful person had put down a very long driveway of two cement strips. The Jeep had slowed down. The sun shone through the leafy canopy overhead and dappled the road before us. I felt the first sense of danger creeping up my spine.

The house, as it first appeared before us, was a picture to behold. It was built completely of corrugated iron and it was painted cream, with high eaves for coolness and a wide veranda with hanging baskets full of flowers of a million colours. Ferns and tree ferns were everywhere. The lawn was emerald green and bright. My senses told me all was not well. Then a faint smell of burning reached my nostrils.

We came to a squeaking halt at the entrance steps. The front door stood open, showing a dark interior. We stayed where we were, not knowing what to expect or what to do.

Maritz jumped down from the cab and spoke briefly to Hough. He then turned and bellowed.

"Pole, you and Carr set up the Browning. Mac, you and Roux get on the veranda. Teacher you and Potter go around the back. Be careful!" he warned.

Everyone hurried to obey, just as a large dog came staggering round the corner, with an arrow sticking from its rib cage. Without the least hesitation Maritz swung up his rifle and shot it. It collapsed, thrashing for a few moments before it died.

"Hate seeing animals suffer!" he commented, smiling cruelly.

I crouched amongst the array of ferns and flowers on the veranda. That had been a Teng arrow, similar to that which had killed the foreman. Roux crouched next to me, breathing heavily. There was an even stronger smell of burning here on the veranda.

We crouched and waited. Hough, Maritz and Thomas had entered the house. Thomas now returned, his boots ringing airily on the wooden floor boards. I noticed for the first time he carried a submachine-gun and ammunition pouches. He said nothing and took up position at the end of the veranda. Doves cooed in the trees, and a cuckoo sung out in the distance "Piet-my-vrou, Piet-my-vrou". We waited and sweated in silence.

Maritz appeared and lit a cigarette, drawing on it deeply. He looked pale. Hough arrived and went to the Jeep. There followed a lengthy radio conversation in French, which we did not understand. He shrugged and spread his hands in a hopeless gesture and signed off.

"Over there under that tree," he ordered.

Maritz turned to Pole. "Pole get the spade and dig a hole big enough for two people, there under that tree." Maritz pointed towards a shady mulberry tree. Hough returned into the house. Maritz appeared unwilling to follow Hough.

Pole took off his shirt and spat on the palms of his hands and started digging. We watched from the veranda. Maritz stood silently smoking. Time dragged and we sweated.

Then after a short time Hough reappeared. "Okay Maritz," he said.

Maritz grimaced, "Mac, Roux follow me," he ordered.

We followed him down the passageway, our boots echoing through the house. In the one room was broken furniture and numerous used shotgun shells scattered over the floor.

Maritz stopped out side a partly open door. "In there," he gestured. "Use the bedding to carry them."

I led the way, and stopped dead in my tracks. It was a terrible sight. The room was airy but the smell that I had been becoming steadily aware of, was now so strong that I struggled to breathe. A woman lay halfway across the bed, her eyes and mouth were full of white seething maggots. Her gut was split open and her intestines bulging with gases. Maggots seethed and overflowed onto the bedding. Rigor mortis had set in. Her body was rigid and her one forefinger pointed heavenwards.

Roux gave a cry and vomited up his breakfast, narrowly missing me.

"Get a move on!" shouted Maritz from behind the door.

Then I saw the second person, a naked man, who was slumped in the corner of the room. His intestines were spread across the floor and mat. Roux was crying. I went forward and grabbed the corner of the sheet and rolled the dead woman up in it. Roux was being sworn at and threatened by Maritz, but managed to get himself under control sufficiently to help me.

We dragged the woman down the passage and out into the fresh air, then bounced down the steps and dropped her into the hole Pole had dug. Moving the man was a lot harder. His stiff lifeless body was heavier and more awkward to move. His intestines had stuck to the floor. He fell off the mat as we tried to pull him along and emptied the seething contents of his belly on the passage floor. We left it there. Maritz did little, just smoked and shouted insults and instructions at us. We dragged him out and dumped him unceremoniously on top of the woman.

Hough stood next to the grave, his face bone white, a cigarette clamped in his jaws. He crossed himself. "Fill them in," he said in a soft voice.

Clambering aboard the truck we were only too pleased to be leaving. Roux was in a sorry state, crying and shaking. The stink of death clung to my clothing. It stuck in my nostrils and would remain there for many days, no matter how often I washed.

The truck followed the Jeep down the driveway and onto the main road. We did not look at one another. We did not speak. Hough appeared to have slowed down, seemingly reluctant to let our truck out of his sights.

The first village we came to was deserted, and the occupants evidently had fled. The truck suddenly came to a skidding halt throwing Carr and Roux across the back. Looking through the slats, we could see why. The police Jeep had stopped and there were a number of large rocks blocking the road.

"Mac, Roux move those stones," ordered Maritz jumping from the cab.

I went to the rear of the truck and peered out. On my right was a banana plantation. On the left an open field with a water-filled furrow along side the road. If it were an ambush it would come from the banana plantation. I jumped down into the dust. Roux did not move. He just crouched at the tailgate, his face streaked with dirt and vomit and his eyes a little wild.

"Move your ass!" screamed Maritz, coming down the side of the truck.

"Why me? I moved the corpses!" whined Roux.

Maritz jumped onto the tow-hitch, and leaned over the tailgate. There was the sound of a blow and Roux came crashing down into the dusty road. I noticed that Maritz had his knife in his left hand and held it low. There was a crazy glint in those bloodshot eyes. I grabbed Roux by his webbing and half carried him down the side of the truck, away from Maritz. The rocks were not heavy and we cleared the road quickly. Then the truck pulled away, and we resumed our original positions.

"Look!" shouted Carr pointing back the way we had come. A column of black smoke was pushing up into the clear sky. "They're burning the house!"

As we headed for the railhead I thought about Maritz. He was going to kill one of us with that knife. If I had not dragged Roux away from him I was sure he would have used the knife on him.

After the murders of the estate manager and his wife, everyone was on edge. Maritz became more aggressive. No one said it but I was positive that the Teng warriors had been watching us at the scene of the murder. They had set fire to the house after we left to give us a sort of warning of what was to come.

The next day, the sacks Muller had promised, arrived on the tug and we spent the next two days filling them with sand and building low walls around our tents. They gave us a sense of being just that little bit more secure.

During the late afternoon I would go down to the harbour wall and fish. It did not matter if I caught anything or not. To be away from the tension in the camp was a small bonus. I was sitting there watching the green river push gently by, as two crocodiles basked on the sandbank and listened to the continuous bird calls as the afternoon sun started slipping away. It was peace but in a crazy setting.

One afternoon Miriam came sauntering along the harbour wall. The thin cotton dress she wore hid little with the sun shining behind her. Her hair had been plaited with green and yellow beads inserted in the braids. She was not as black as the other Africans in the area. Her skin had an oily, yellow quality and there were signs of pock marks on her cheeks. She came on towards me making me feel rather uncomfortable. I recalled how Maritz had made a mockery of me the time I had gone to the shop to buy the line and hooks. She settled herself on a low pile of lumber with a friendly smile.

"You not come to my shop. Don't like beer, gambling, other things?" she asked waving her hands and showing chipped red nail varnish.

I shrugged. "I don't drink," I said, not wanting to have this conversation. If Maritz saw me talking to the woman, he would definitely make something of it, considering the mood he had been in over the last week. On the other hand, he and the other two drunks were frequenting the shop nearly every night. That appeared to be all right by Maritz's standards.

"Maritzie is a rubbish man," she said bluntly. "He buys beer on the book and only pays half. Says he will burn my shop if I don't supply the beer." She clasped her hands before her, with her eyes full of anguish. "I spent my life on the river, and I know men, but he is the worst!"

"Yes," I agreed. Maritz certainly had a way with people.

"You not telling him, hey?" she said cautiously.

I shook my head wondering where this conversation was heading.

"You like Maritzie?" she asked slyly.

"No," I said without hesitation.

She gave a brilliant smile. She had found someone on her side. She dropped her voice. "You know Annie? She loves Maritzie. He says he is taking her back to South Africa when he leaves. He make her his queen."

I looked up in shocked amazement.

"She very stupid. We all know white man cannot marry a black woman down there. It is against the law." Miriam smiled broadly and continued in a whisper. "Every night Maritzie visits her at about ten, then he comes back to my shop to gamble and drink. There are no law in Congo about such things. You come to my shop?"

I was trying not to laugh as this was really quite something. Of all people Maritz carrying on with a black woman. She obviously realised that I found the whole thing funny. Miriam smiled happily. I did not know what Annie looked like, but there were quite a few painted black women who hung around the shop plying their trade.

"Ah, Annie she comes," Miriam pointed using her head.

I looked down the harbour. I could not believe my eyes. There was a rainbow-covered, blue black mountain of a Negro woman coming along the dock. She was using a stick to keep her balance and help herself along.

Miriam smiled, "Maritzie bought her that dress of many colours from my shop."

I gawked in complete amazement. She drew level with us and stopped resting on her stick and smiled pleasantly.

"You catch fish soldier?" she asked in a husky voice.

I shook my head not trusting my voice, for I longed to roar with laughter.

"You catch a big'un, I buy okay?"

I nodded and smiled, imagining Maritz and the massive black lady together. Miriam rose from her seat, greeted me farewell and the two women slowly walked off towards the shop. I sat there stunned. Maritz of all people! I laughed and laughed until tears rolled down my cheeks. I knew that I would have to keep this information to myself for the time being.

That night the three drunks went on a binge. Only Maritz made it back to camp. He stood there swaying in his usual arrogant stance. I knew what to look for. The knife was there in his sleeve.

"Coffee, Mackay!" he snarled. He stood looking around and then shouted, "You useless bunch of assholes! Hey queer boy, seen any action lately?"

Like a fool Teacher answered him. "I am not queer." His voice was still slurred with sleep. It was enough. Maritz pounced. The knife flashed, opening the mosquito net followed by the thump of his fist connecting with some part of Teacher's body.

"Don't you answer back to me you miserable poofter!" he said backing off and rubbing his knuckles.

"Leave him alone!" said Pole. It was the first time he had stood up to Maritz. He had thrown his mosquito net aside and dressed only in a pair of shorts, he stood there large and white in the poor light.

Maritz backed off smiling. "Got teeth hey? You Commie bastard!" Then he turned and staggered off towards his tent, the coffee forgotten. Teacher crawled out of his mosquito net, wiping blood from his mouth. He came across and joined Pole and myself at the fire.

Pole shook his big head sadly. "It could be really nice here except for that man, always looking for trouble, always drunk," he said rubbing the sleep from his eyes.

I poured coffee into three mugs. It was just after two in the morning.

Chapter Four

I don't know when Potter and Carr arrived back at camp. The following morning they looked like death warmed up. Hough arrived at seven, saying he wanted us to set up a roadblock, to check the southbound bus.

After a slow uneventful trip we had arrived at the junction. Maritz had taken over the driving, having thrown Potter into the back where he bounced around and eventually he hung over the tailgate vomiting. Carr was not in a much better state.

We all sat around waiting for the bus to arrive. I had brought my writing pad and was writing to Mia telling her about the birds, the trees, the fish and the heat.

At about noon the sound of an approaching vehicle going north, got us all moving. Thomas stood in the middle of the road and waved a large grey Mercedes truck to a stop. Thomas smiled and saluted the driver, a dark-haired, very well built, smiling, young white man. Thomas was speaking French, which none of us understood. For something to do and out of curiosity I went around the truck and standing on one of the mud covered wheels I hoisted myself up to look in the back. There were a couple of wooden crates with red markings "Massey Ferguson" painted all over them. I dropped back to the road and rejoined the other men. Thomas had waved the truck on.

Turning back to us he explained. "Monsieur de Haas very nice man, lives with his brother at The Sweet Estate." That was it.

The bus arrived, late as usual. We followed our usual pattern of checking the over-loaded vehicle. Then we returned to the railhead.

For the whole day I played with the idea of telling everyone about Maritz, but then changed my mind. I would first like to see for myself. That afternoon, one of the black boys who frequented the harbour pointed out Annie's house to me. It was a square building, very neat, with a few wildflowers and surrounded by a fence to keep the chickens in the small yard. It looked a lot better than any of the other huts in the dilapidated village.

That night at about ten, I left camp to go towards the ablution block. As soon as I was out of sight I slipped away into the village and made my way to Annie's house. Squatting with my back to a mud wall of a nearby hut, I waited. Mosquitoes buzzed around, a radio played in the background, and a baby was crying loudly. I was just about to give up when a figure broke away from the dark village. The shadowy figure reached the gate, and opened it. Then a light was lit inside Annie's house. The door opened and Maritz stepped into the light. Then the door closed. I found myself grinning. "Wait until I tell Teacher this!" Teacher would be the right person to tell. He had suffered at Maritz's hands more than most.

The following day Sergeant Major Ross arrived on the tug. Maritz saw him coming and we were all organised and ready for inspection before he made it to the camp. We all stood in line while he prowled amongst us.

"Things are getting bad, my boys. No one knows who is in charge of this country, but we will continue. Around Villa Vista area there have been eight killings, six whites and two blacks. Guns have been used, Russian weapons. We found the empty casings. These buggers' shooting is as bad as yours. Our information is that the two tribes have joined together to rid the area of foreigners. People are fleeing." Ross abruptly stopped talking to us and he then ordered Maritz to go with him to the police station.

It was obvious that Ross had no intention of telling us more. Teacher grabbed the mail and started handing it out. Potter left us to go towards the truck – probably going for a quick drink.

I was thrilled! I received three letters with Gran's scrawly writing on the envelopes, but the best was Mia's lilac envelope enclosed. Taking my letters I headed for my hidey-hole in the jungle, just behind the camp. I sat on a log in the hot clearing. They asked about the biscuits, which again I had not received. It also appeared as if they had not received all the letters I had written and posted. I read the letters over and over again, drawing strength and comfort in the knowledge that Gran and Mia loved me and were concerned about my well being. Gran's letter told me that Oupa had started on the wall and things were going well. Had I received the fifty rand pocket money? Mia said that she loved me and was counting the days to my return.

This was great, I was smiling, happy again. In the distance the tug hooted to announce its departure.

On my return to the camp all was still. The men were engrossed in their mail. Teacher tossed me a brown envelope. "Pay," he said. It was my monthly allowance.

Late that evening I entered the ablution block. I could hear Maritz swearing viciously. Peering round the corner I saw that Maritz had Pole against the wall. His right hand was pinning him there by the throat, his left was holding his knife against the Pole's throat.

"You Commie bastard. Cross me again and I will kill you!" he was saying aggressively.

I slipped away unseen. Pole appeared a short while later dabbing a small nick on his throat. Maritz was out of order, but there was not much I could do. I could not understand why none of the older men seemed keen on reporting him to Ross or Muller.

Teacher sat and read an out of date *Business Times*. Breakfast had just been eaten. Maritz was quietly reading the sports section.

"Gold would be a good investment," said Teacher absent-mindedly.

"What about diamonds?" asked Carr.

"Yes, de Beers is up and looking good," said Teacher rustling the pages. "Keep out of timber. You can see what is happening here. They are stripping the jungle, moving as much as they can before the new government is elected, if it ever is." Teacher suddenly found he had an audience and he rose to the occasion. "de Bruins Timbers shares are probably worthless at the present time. The country is in turmoil. The new government will either tax the sawmill heavily or just take it over." Carr poured coffee for everyone. "They're trying very hard to make money for their shareholders. To keep the mill running they need security; that is us. We're cheap compared to what I have seen over the past months. Those big blocks of trees they've just squared off are mahogany, worth thousands! Villa Vista is not even taking the time to cut them into planks. They just square them off for easy loading. They will cut them into planks somewhere else in the world, probably a country that's more stable, with better workmen and a better political situation." He gulped coffee, not wanting to lose his audience. Even Maritz was listening intently.

"What do you think a load of timber is worth?" asked Carr.

Teacher shrugged, "At home a hardwood table and chairs are about five hundred rand, a desk of teak, six or eight hundred. Basically we are worth a few planks of hardwood!" and he chuckled at his humour. "Our stay probably cost de Bruins half a tug-load." Teacher grinned, "de Bruins could afford to pay us double and still walk away millionaires!"

Everyone had been intently listening to Teacher. We had not seen Hough approach. He had been standing listening too. When his presence was noticed, he chipped in. "de Bruins showed a profit of ten million three years ago, and I know the shares are now worthless. Take it from me!"

He had just confirmed what Teacher had been saying. Carr poured him a mug of coffee. The policeman sat down on one of the logs.

Hough cleared his throat. "I wish to get you guys up to date. The two murders we attended are typical Teng killings, except for one thing. The right ear cut off! Villa Vista's region has had six whites murdered. In each case all had right ears cut off. Two blacks were killed and just gutted." He slurped his coffee and continued. "Guns have now appeared. Russian SKS assault rifles. They have shot up a tractor and trailer but hit no one. They are poor shots. I doubt if it would be the Teng using the guns, most probably renegade Mongu." He sat still for a moment. Maritz lit two cigarettes and handed him one. Hough continued, "I think there must be witches involved here. But who? I do not know. The removal of ears has added almost a 'white man' involvement to it. I will keep on making enquiries and see what I can turn up." He rose, dusting off the seat of his trousers. "Tomorrow I wish you to take a written warning to all the Europeans in this area. I also know many will refuse to move. I will prepare the letters now. It is so I have it in black and white. You have far to go, so you will have to leave really early tomorrow morning."

We all knew about it. Far was not measured in kilometres but in the time it took to cover the ground in this country.

The truck rattled and banged, skidding in and out of the muddy furrows. Rain pelted down on the canvas canopy. We had left early, well before sun-up. It was not pleasant at the best of times. Potter was in fine form for he had not gone to the shop the night before. He had probably had a night-cap from his private stock instead. I had watched Maritz with interest. At about ten he had gone off towards the ablution block. He didn't return for over an hour.

At the first estate we arrived at, Thomas handed the manager the letter prepared by Hough and we continued on our way. We visited estate after estate. Most were ten or twenty kilometres off the main road.

At about two, we arrived at de Haas's estate called The Sweet. When de Haas came out of the house he was shirtless and I was surprised to see how well built he was. He obviously was a very strong man. I was also interested to see that he carried a pistol in his belt. He appeared pleased to see us and invited us in. His English was good with almost no accent. Maritz refused his offer politely, saying that we still had far to go. He asked us to hang on for a moment and went into the dark, drab house and then returned with a case of beer. We all thanked him and left. Beer was always welcome, especially if it were cold. The trouble was that as quick as you drank one you sweated it out almost immediately.

Back on the main road we continued north.

"It is Crossways," said Thomas pointing at the junction in the road. "That road," he said pointing west. "Swart's mine – that road is closed." He pointed east. "Stanleyville is that way. Here we go straight on, the next place is Crossways School then St Patrick's Mission – very good place. The nun's have done much for the Africans. There is a hospital, a school and a very nice church." He lapsed into silence. There was an unexplained concerned look on the big man's face.

The school appeared alongside the road. It was not much – two deserted classrooms, built with grey mud bricks, and a rotting corrugated iron roof. There was also a football field at the back. It was all dwarfed by the surrounding jungle.

After a while, Thomas continued. "The road to Swart's mine is no good. The boat to ferry cars was washed away two years ago. The mine was closed and the diamonds finished, all gone." He explained this by shrugging his huge shoulders. "There were students from an American university staying there recently. They were studying the plants and animals of the jungle. They have also left." He fell silent, and the truck skidded on and on along the seemingly endless road.

The road narrowed into a single rutted mud track. We slid down a muddy bank onto a bridge constructed of huge logs laid next to each other and then strapped with steel girders. We rattled across a deep black, fast-moving river with ferns and plants reaching right to the water's edge. Potter skidded the truck up the opposite bank. At one stage it did not feel like we were going to make it over the top. But at full power we lurched over the top of the bank and slid on and on down the narrow road.

St Patrick's village was probably the most organised place I had seen since coming to this country. Farmlands were laid out neatly with irrigation canals, which I thought seemed out of place, as there was not a shortage of water. There were men ploughing, using ox-drawn ploughs. They even stopped work to wave, dozens of school children waved, danced and smiled. Alongside the road, the huts appeared neater and well maintained. Many had been painted white and there were even houses with corrugated iron roofs. The whole area looked prosperous and very stable.

The mission was situated beyond the village on a low ridge. As our truck rattled up the narrow winding track, we saw a low stone wall which surrounded the mission with a large wrought iron gate and a sign saying "Welcome to St Patrick's". We swung through the gate into a large parking area marked out with white stones. Patients dressed in blue pyjamas sat around playing cards under shady trees. The mission buildings gave off a pretty pink glow in the bright sunlight. Then I realised that it had been built with red earth and then white-washed. The buildings were built in a U shape, with a large thatched church at the centre of the U. I estimated the church could hold probably five hundred or so worshippers. The buildings were all neatly thatched and looked clean and cool. We all looked around in amazement. It was serene and beautifully quiet. Maritz jumped down and accompanied Thomas towards the office block.

We all climbed down and spread ourselves around under the trees. We watched as Potter wandered off towards the church.

"Probably looking for a drink!" joked Carr.

We sat in silence, savouring the quiet peacefulness, knowing only too well what a long, uncomfortable trek it was going to be getting back to the railhead.

"Would you lads like a glass of lemon juice?" It was a woman's voice, with a beautiful lilt. An accent I had never heard before. We scrambled to our feet as one. A young nun stood there, her approach unseen. There was a slight smattering of freckles across her nose and slightly tilted beautiful grey eyes. Her accent was so soft and beautiful and her features so serene that even Teacher, who was by far the most talkative, was at a loss for words. She held out a tray. On it stood long, ice-frosted glasses. We stammered our thanks, and gawked at her as she seemed to drift away, gliding across the car park towards the buildings. My heart was pounding. She was, by far, the most beautiful woman I had ever seen. But then, I had not seen much of her. A habit covered her head and she wore a loose-fitting tropical smock that reached to her feet. But still, in my eyes, she was absolutely beautiful. We all sat in shocked amazement sipping iced juice.

"Have you ever seen such a beauty?" said Teacher in wonder

Potter reappeared ambling along and rejoined us. He took the glass of juice Carr had kept for him.

"Find a drink?" joked Carr smiling happily. "You had better share it with us before Maritz gets back."

Potter ignored the comment and climbed into the cab.

The trip back to the railhead was hell. It rained nearly all the way. We did not get stuck, but late that night we arrived, absolutely exhausted.

It didn't take long to get back into the usual routine, which contrasted so much with the tranquillity of our reception at the mission.

"Teacher! Coffee, beans and bread," snarled Maritz "and make it quick."

Teacher looked around vaguely and went about preparing the meagre meal.

Just then Hough appeared out of the gloom. He was really becoming a nuisance. When he arrived it seemed only to bring bad tidings. "You guys had better get some rest because I need a roadblock early tomorrow. All vehicles to be checked," he said.

We all looked at him in amazement. There was really nothing other than the bus that travelled these back roads.

Then, as an explanation, he continued. "The guns are getting into this region. It's not by river and it's not by air. That leaves the road." He turned abruptly and went back to the station.

"Hells, bells!" griped Roux. "This is getting bloody ridiculous!"

We all sat around the fire eating. No one was happy and everyone was dead tired.

Later that evening I noticed Maritz slip off into the darkness, going towards the ablution block and again he did not return for over an hour. I felt a certain amount of satisfaction at having something on him now, and I was going to share my information with Teacher.

A few nights later I got my chance. Teacher and I were alone round the fire.

"What? Repeat that," hissed Teacher aghast. "My god, he put himself in it. Do you know where that bastard comes from? Ermelo."

I shook my head, for the name meant little to me.

"The little town of Ermelo is in the Transvaal; it is the Afrikaner's stronghold. Church, rugby, 'braai vleis' and the police watch you like a hawk!" Teacher laughed softly, tears of mirth in his eyes.

I still did not catch on to what he'd said.

Teacher smiled evilly. "To be caught with a black woman in that area means the end. The bars won't have you on the premises. The church expels you, and no one will employ you. You're lower than the lowest." He laughed softly, tears running down his cheeks.

He seemed to find what I had told him very funny indeed.

"That is if you're caught." He hesitated, "But just say if photos of Maritz and Annie were to appear, at the Ermelo hotels, the police station, the church and rugby club."

I now caught on.

From that day Teacher was like a changed man. He smiled a lot to himself, and took his bird watching extremely seriously. When Maritz went off to the village alone, Teacher was not that far behind, with binoculars, camera and bird book in hand. I also kept on getting the impression that he wanted to talk to me, but he kept putting it off.

Hough was obsessed with roadblocks. There were days that went by when not even a pedestrian passed us waiting at the side of the road. We heard nothing from Villa Vista or Hough. Thomas no longer accompanied us.

Then one day de Haas came to a squeaking halt at our roadblock.

"How are you chaps?" he called, climbing from the cab and stretching. "The road seems to get worse and worse. Did you hear a couple of mines to the north have closed down for two months? They are waiting for this nonsense to come to an end."

We had not heard a thing.

"Here have a case of beer," he offered as he opened the passenger door. There were three cases on the floor. He handed the top one to the smiling Maritz.

"Thanks, always appreciated," smirked Maritz.

Whilst the men stood talking, I went round to the opposite side of the truck and hoisted myself up to peer into the partially covered back. There were four crates on the deck and all were marked in red paint "Massey Ferguson". I dropped back to earth and unseen by anyone rejoined the men just before de Haas left, honking his horn and waving. Maritz shared the beers out amongst us. We resumed our original positions, beers in hand.

That night, arriving back at the railhead, we had obviously had a visitor, probably Muller. A bundle of post lay on one of the stretchers. I'd received two envelopes with two letters in each. The light was fading and we piled wood on the fire.

Gran said Oupa had almost reached the top of the dam wall. She had not been well – and said it had been high blood pressure, but she was feeling a lot better now. Mia had visited her riding her pony and was enjoying school. There seemed to be a letter missing? This was really annoying when every letter was so important to me.

Teacher was sitting near me and leant across. "Mac, will you have a look at this," he said as he handed me a photograph. It was the one he had taken when we were on our way to the railhead. The photo was that of Maritz sitting on the edge of the road while he watched us dig the truck out of the mud.

"Look carefully," and he pointed with a grubby finger and moved the lantern closer. I turned the photo sideways to get more light. About two metres away from the prone Maritz stood a tall thin black man. He was resting on a spear and was standing on the very edge of the jungle. He looked very strange with swirls and a leafy look about his body.

"And there," whispered Teacher pointing. All I could see of the second warrior was his head and shoulders protruding out from the undergrowth. He also had the same leafy look of swirls and leaves about his shoulders.

"They were watching us dig the truck out," I said to Teacher quietly. "And no one saw them."

We realised now that these were our enemy, the Teng, the Spirit of the jungle. A shiver ran down my spine. They were practically invisible.

I found it rather frightening. If Teacher's wife had not examined the photo carefully and spotted the two warriors and sent the photo back to him, we would not have known they were there. Their camouflage was so good that even Maritz, sitting about two metres away from them, had not sensed their presence. He had not even smelt them.

I was beginning to think that the whole damned business was getting out of hand. It was really frightening to be up against an enemy we could not see. Surely the Teng were entitled to their forest. They were here first. They had always lived here, worrying no one and now their very existence was threatened. No wonder they were prepared to fight for what was theirs. We were wrong being here to fight for the timber company! I felt that it was grossly unfair.

Everyone was now examining Teacher's photo. Carr had produced a torch, and was grinning from ear to ear.

"How does a Teng camouflage himself?" asked Carr laughing, and answered himself. "He wears dark glasses. Have you ever seen a Teng wearing dark glasses?" He waited for a moment grinning. "No? Well it shows you how well camouflaged he is!" He broke down laughing at his own little joke.

There were a couple of nervous smiles. Roux had gone white and without a word slipped away onto his stretcher. Maritz went off to show Hough the photo and we settled down for the evening. It was rather unnerving to be up against an enemy so well adapted and camouflaged, fighting to protect their little bit of Africa.

Chapter 5

Life at the railhead had become boring, and the days dragged. For more than a month nothing had taken place. Maritz kept picking on Teacher, who kept on smiling his secret smile.

Pay arrived. Mail arrived. Maritz, Potter and Carr drank continuously. I fished and kept away from the camp as much as possible.

One morning Maritz smiled at us. This seemed completely out of character. We were lined up for a weapons' inspection. He said it kept us sharp. He had some crazy ideas. Teacher had not said anything more about any photographs of Maritz and Annie. He continued with his bird watching, camera, binoculars. Roux had become sullen and had developed a twitch in his right eye and ate very little.

Maritz finished his weapons' inspection. "Right, tomorrow, Potter, Mac, Teacher, Roux and Pole; you're going to Villa Vista. The truck needs servicing. Carr and I will guard the camp," he ordered.

"Why can't the truck be loaded on one of the empty barges?" asked Teacher.

Maritz looked at him blankly. "Show of strength, you stupid fool!" he snarled.

It was obvious he had not thought of it. It also sounded like he had been ordered to remain at the railhead. It would be pleasant not to have him with us.

The next day we left at first light. Teacher grabbed the passenger seat. It was not wise to sit three up front. The person in the middle had to sit with his legs apart around the gear lever. A sudden stop could inflict serious injuries.

There was almost a holiday air about us. To get away from the railhead for a day and see other members of the unit was a small bonus. The sun shone through the canopy and birds flapped across our path. Our orders were to get to Villa Vista by lunch, so the mechanics could work on the truck, and then we'd return the next day.

We were still only about twenty-five kilometres from the railhead when we got stuck. We dug and cursed and eventually, after about two hours, we got out of the muddy spot. It was well after four o'clock when we arrived at Villa Vista covered with thick, sticky, stinking mud.

Trucks were parked to one side of the compound. Muller appeared in the distance and then went into one of the buildings. Rocky Stone came across the muddy yard. He smiled cheerfully.

"Muller says that you're to sleep in the truck. The mechanic starts at seven sharp. See that you're there. Come across to the pub for a toot." He moved carefully across the muddy yard, trying to keep his feet clean, which was virtually impossible.

Potter led the way with a happy expression on his horse-like face. One of the prefabricated buildings had been turned into a mess. They were far more organised than our camp. There was a dartboard and a table tennis table. I stared in amazement and my heart gave a huge leap. On the wall was a telephone with a coin box. One of the men sat on a stool next to the phone. Tears were running down his cheeks.

"Yes mommy!" he wailed into the receiver, "Is daddy okay?"

When I got closer I realised that he was very drunk. He was swaying dangerously on the stool.

Rocky interrupted. "Have a cold one," he said, grinning while extracting beers from a paraffin fridge.

We took a beer each. I think Teacher, Roux, Pole and I were all thinking the same. I had a huge thrill of excitement. I would be talking, if at all possible to Mia and Gran. We would all be phoning home. After three months it was the first chance we had had to speak to our loved ones.

The conversation on the phone continued. "And how's Auntie Myrtle?" There was silence for a while.

"Can we use the phone?" asked Teacher, barely able to hide his excitement. Potter had already finished his beer and was standing by expectantly.

"Yep. As long as you've got enough cash, anything is possible," said Rocky with a grin.

Potter could not wait any longer and fished out his wallet. "The next one is on me," he said licking his lips.

Rocky beamed. "Where's that Maritz? We still have business to settle."

"Guarding the camp, with Carr," said Teacher watching the man on the phone.

Rocky had a far away look in his eyes. "You know, that stupid fool would not last a week here! We all work well together here, no shirkers and no bullshit. We have been split into three units. One unit is on a minute's notice, one guards the mill, and the other is on ten minute call. Muller and Ross have turned out to be pretty good chaps. Muller knows how to organise. Did you know he was an officer in the French Foreign Legion? They're a real tough bunch and probably the toughest fighting men in the world." He swigged his beer.

The conversation on the phone continued.

"He will finish in a moment," said Rocky seeing our anticipation.

A bell clanged outside, and the African cook entered with a huge pot smelling deliciously of curried meat. Then he returned with another smelling of piping hot potatoes.

"Chow's up," said Rocky. "Better help yourselves before the others get here!"

We were all hungry and got stuck in. The door opened and men trooped in. Some of them bought beers and soft drinks at the bar while watching us newcomers with interest. They settled at the long trestle table.

They were a desperate-looking bunch. Most of the men wore beards and others were half-shaven. Everyone wore grubby khakis. One of the men shouted at the man on the phone to give someone else a chance. Tearfully he climbed off the stool and collected his plate of curry. A lanky individual, known as Jerome, took his place quickly, taking no notice of our anticipation. Money rattled in the coin box.

The four of us from the railhead ate slowly, watching Jerome's every move. Each one of us was wishing he would just get a move on.

"I want a Durban number," he said into the receiver and gave the number to the operator and a few moments later said, "Hi, love is that you?" and then he turned his back to us. "And how's the car going?" There was a long pause. "When I get back I will buy a new one." There was another long pause. "Oh! Supper's the usual old crap, monkey curry."

I had finished my plate, thinking that it had been rather nice. Teacher had almost finished his plate. On hearing Jerome's comment, his eyes opened wide in shock and he made a grunting noise and ran for the door. Potter took no notice. Pole just shook his head and continued eating. Roux pushed his half-eaten plate aside. The men around us grinned. The amusement and anticipation on their faces should have been a warning to us of what was to come.

"We have it every Wednesday. You should see them being cooked. They look like human babies," said the soldier opposite me. The table erupted in a roar of laughter. The men were slapping each other on the back with tears of mirth running down their cheeks. It all felt surreal.

Jerome had replaced the receiver. "Who's next?" he asked.

Roux had jumped to his feet, sorting out the change from his wallet. His face flushed with excitement as he hurriedly positioned himself on the stool. He dialled and then listened. He dialled again with shaking hands.

"There's no answer," he said in a hurt voice.

"Put a couple of coins in," suggested one of the spectators, as the coins rattled in the box.

"No answer," said Roux again, looking sheepish.

"It's a one way phone," said Jerome smiling broadly and the men at the table roared with laughter at Roux's discomfort and obvious disappointment. Roux smiled sadly, tears sparkling in his eyes as he replaced the receiver slowly. My heart sank. I would not be speaking to the outside world tonight. It was just a cruel joke. There were no lines. The men at the sawmill had set us up. There was no way anyone could contact the outside world. The men at Villa Vista just made do with a lot of beer and a bit of imagination.

At seven the next morning the mill was a hive of activity. Barges were being loaded by the steam-driven crane that squeaked and strained under the weight of the huge squared-off timbers. All the time in the background the saws screamed deafeningly.

The mechanic, a large coloured chap, arrived and started work on our truck. Teacher stood around chatting to him. He eventually crossed to where we were all sitting in the shade.

"I need a donation. A fiver each will do the trick," he said.

Potter looked unhappily in his wallet, but the Pole did not move. No one wanted to part with money.

Teacher grinned, his eyes narrow slits. "You want to stay around here for an extra day? Come, hand it over." Money appeared like magic and Teacher went back to the mechanic.

A moment later Teacher returned smiling. "Now the truck has a major problem and will only be fixed late this afternoon. It will be far too late for us to leave today."

We all grinned happily. It was a small price to pay, and it was far more pleasant in Villa Vista than sitting around the railhead with Maritz worrying everyone. It was also nice to have a cook to prepare our food, and to be able to buy cold beer without having to go to Miriam's den.

That evening we had just finished our evening meal of fish and chips, which was nice and well prepared.

"Attention!" shouted Rocky. Everyone shot to their feet. Muller strutted in and looked around. He unrolled an enlarged photograph. It was Teacher's photo of Maritz and the Teng warrior. Muller stuck it on the notice board and stuck a piece of white tape across the top. "Our Enemy" was scrawled on it.

He smiled, "You men from the railhead keep quiet!" he instructed. Then he turned and strode away. Then all the men crowded around the photos.

"That's Maritz! Is he our enemy? He is not even carrying his rifle!" said one of the men and they all looked blindly at the photo.

Rocky Stone tapped the photo with his forefinger. "What do we want a photo of that stupid idiot in our mess for?"

No one had spotted the two Teng warriors, but then again the light was far from perfect. Teacher took a pen and pointed out the two warriors to the shocked men. It was now our turn to laugh as they gasped in amazement, followed by a lot of nervous glances. It really amazed me how the two warriors seemed almost invisible against the dark jungle wall.

The next morning we left in the freshly serviced truck. We were a few hours out of Villa Vista when Roux realised that he could not find his wallet. Then Teacher discovered his watch was missing! Roux jumped up and down angrily demanding we return and conduct a search. I had never seen him so agitated and aggressive. It was not the money that had made him so wild, but the fact that the only photo of his wife and daughter was in his wallet.

Whilst we had slept someone had obviously helped themselves. The warning of ending up in a black man's prison had no effect on the men at Villa Vista. We continued on to the railhead and managed to avoid getting stuck in the boggy stretches of road.

That night, as we settled back into the railhead camp, I noticed that there was tension between Maritz and Carr. At the time I did not know what had caused it.

The next morning Teacher had cooked breakfast and we were all lolling around drinking coffee and waiting for instructions from the police station. Carr suddenly struggled hurriedly to his feet, and without a word started walking towards the ablution block. His casual walk speeded up and the next moment he was running.

"I bet you two beers he won't make it," said Potter with a broad grin on his face.

"You're on! That oil is deadly. Enough to clean out an elephant!" said Maritz. Then he roared with laughter.

"He's not going to make it!" shouted Potter excitedly.

Carr braked, dropped his shorts five metres short of the door of the ablution block. Maritz gave a wolf whistle.

"That's two beers!" said Potter, with a satisfied look on his face.

The rest of us sat in silence. Maritz must have slipped a large dose of laxative into Carr's food. Now he and Potter were betting on the time that he would spend sitting on the toilet and how long would he last away from the toilet, before having to run for it again.

I personally think it was probably the worst day in Carr's life. No sooner had he returned to camp, than he was running again with Maritz and Potter betting beers on his progress.

Later, since we'd received no instructions from the police station, I took my fishing pole and headed for the harbour. The tug was due as usual at about eleven. I baited up and dropped my line in. This was where I could think. It had been a rotten trick Maritz had played on Carr, for to be ill in any way out here was one of our worst fears.

A while later Miriam appeared at the end of the harbour and came to sit near me. .

"Good morning," she said politely. "You no come to my shop?" I shook my head. "Lucky you not here yesterday night. Maritzie started a bloody fight. He stabbed two of my best customers; nearly beat the other fellow dead. Mean man that! He hit me with a stick. Look!" She hoisted up her skirt, showing me large black weals across her legs and naked buttocks.

"Other chap, Carr runs away. He hits no one. It's very bad for my business." She shrugged her heavy shoulders. "Dat Annie is a mad bitch, still running for Maritzie. She completely mad woman!" She shook her head sadly as if she had never seen anything like it before, which I doubted.

She looked around to make sure there was no one nearby. "You know the Teng are causing too much trouble. People are running away. You see many will go on the tug to Villa Vista. Then they catch the bus," and she waved her hand. "You know what the cause is? The bloody witch Gogo. She talk to the spirits and makes them angry. Then they come and we die."

I looked up, surprised at the information she was supplying. She hurriedly stood up adjusting her dress, and stalked off without a word.

At about eleven, the train puffed onto the harbour wall and then the tug arrived and the crane started offloading the timber. People from the village had congregated at the end of the harbour wall along with cardboard boxes and battered suitcases. There were also crates of chickens and a couple of pigs. Naked children with snotty noses hung onto their mothers and howled. A woman stood with a baby slung on her back. The baby began to cry until she hoisted one of her extended breasts over her shoulder hitting the unfortunate baby in the face. The baby greedily found the nipple and started suckling. Fascinated, I sat and watched. They were probably the first to leave. Others would surely follow. There was an almost tangible tension and fear in the air around the railhead. I could not quite place my finger on it. It was as if something sinister was about to take place.

Late that afternoon I arrived back at camp with a couple of fish, and took over the preparations for supper. It was hot and very still. There was no sign of Carr. Later, when I went to the ablution block, I found him stretched out on the concrete floor. He was as white as a sheet. When I spoke to him he could barely raise his head. I made him a mug of sweet black coffee and took it to him. I felt really sorry for him. He was like the rest of us, just trying to make some quick money.

The village was a lot quieter after the first exodus. We continued doing roadblocks and visiting the various estates. We never made it back to St Patrick's Mission. I often thought of the young nun who had brought us the iced juice. As far as we could hear there was nothing going on at Villa Vista, just an uneasy tension amongst the Africans. A number of the estates were manned by only a few labourers, while many of the white managers, their wives and children, had moved away for their own safety.

Post arrived with either Muller or Ross. A lot seemed to have gone astray. We all had letters go missing, and this just added to the general uneasiness and added unnecessary tension.

One steamy afternoon Teacher suggested that I should accompany him and Hough on a short patrol. I had little else to do and clambered aboard Hough's Jeep. We travelled down the road for a short distance and turned off down a narrow track towards the river.

"You don't tell no one about this bird business," said Hough. "It's like my pension. The money is banked for me in Europe. When I retire I will be okay." He stopped the Jeep and we jumped down, following him as he led the way down a narrow track.

Hough spoke to us as we walked along. "Many of the smaller birds bring in about five to ten dollars. The parrots are good. One brings in one hundred." He stopped and pointed. "I built the aviary."

I could see a partly visible netted construction that seemed to wind its way through the branches of the trees.

"It is good. The birds think they are at home in the jungle. I have two guys who work for me. They see that there is water and food and they trap them," said Hough.

He was obviously proud of his achievement. We came out in a small clearing where a dilapidated hut stood. Hough stopped with a concerned look on his face and then said, "There are not so many birds now!"

I had only seen a dozen or so brightly coloured birds in the aviary.

"How do you get them to the market?" asked Teacher.

"Ah, I have an arrangement with the train driver and with the captain of the boat on the Congo river and an agent in Brazzaville," said Hough looking around. He stood with his short legs slightly apart. "Something is wrong here!" he said nervously. Then he whistled softly and then again a bit louder. A scruffy African man appeared out of the jungle and hurried across to Hough. He was sweating badly, his eyes rolling. His fear was tangible. He spoke hurriedly to Hough in the local dialect. Hough removed his wallet and handed the man a wad of money while he questioned him briefly. Hough sighed and then he waved his hand in dismissal and the man hurried away and was swallowed up by the jungle.

Hough turned to us with a concerned expression on his face. "The Teng were here this morning. They told everyone to go. They are afraid and will not stay. That man's home is to the south; his brother has already gone. It looks like my bird business is finished," said Hough sadly. He went over to what turned out to be a well

119

hidden gate in the aviary and opened it, throwing it aside. "The birds must go back to their jungle" he said sadly, "just when things were going so well."

Hough suddenly looked around nervously and hurriedly loosened the catch on his holster. Teacher and I raised our weapons. But there was nothing to be seen. We followed him back to his Jeep. Drums beat in the distance, softly at first but then swelling to a solid thump, filling the jungle.

It was strange how I felt eyes piercing my back. The hair on the back of my neck tingled uncomfortably, and I broke out in an ice-cold sweat. But on looking back I could see no one. We climbed into the Jeep and roared off.

Hough wiped his sweating face with a clean white handkerchief. "I think they were watching us," he said softly.

I was sure he was right.

Chapter 6

Another week drifted peacefully by and then Muller arrived for his usual inspection. We were all prim and ready, with the camp tidied up and Maritz on his best behaviour. Muller dropped the mail on the table, and instructed Maritz and Potter to take the truck to the tug to collect a tin trunk that contained ammunition and to bring it back.

They roared off in a cloud of dust bouncing across the barren football field and disappeared into the village. Muller went off towards the police station. Teacher handed out the mail and this time Potter got a letter, his first. I took my one letter and went to sit by myself. I noticed Teacher copying addresses from the back of Maritz's envelopes. I smiled, for I knew Teacher was seeking revenge. He had not told me, but he must have managed to get a photo of Maritz and Annie together. If it was correct about what he had said, and if those photos were to circulate in Maritz's hometown, it would be the end of him. I felt almost sorry for the big man, as I knew it would definitely finish him off for good.

I remembered Oupa's threat to Mr van der Walt about the coloured maid Rosie at the Strong Man Inn. Nothing had ever come of Oupa punching van der Walt. That threat had obviously worked.

Gran's letter told of the work Oupa had been doing. The dam was complete so he was going to buy wire with my next pay cheque. I was really excited until I read Mia's letter. She loved me and was waiting for me, but Gran was not well and Oupa was drinking far too much, although she confirmed that the dam was looking good. Elvis had strained a fetlock. Her two sisters were teasing her about writing to

121

me but she did not care. School was okay, and Christmas was not that far away. Had I received her parcel? It was just another missing article. I sat back staring up into the leafy branches above my head. I was running out of things to say in my next letter home. I wished our time was up and we could leave this place. Christmas was definitely just round the corner, and I wondered what type of Christmas we were going to have here in this hell hole.

My thoughts were interrupted by the truck returning. Potter looked very concerned as he opened his first letter. He walked slowly away from us and towards the cab of the truck.

Later, Muller and Hough returned to the camp. Muller tossed Maritz the keys for the tin trunk saying, "Bring me a couple of grenades and a few flares." The instructions Muller gave us were short and to the point, "Mills bombs, pin, lever, detonator. Flares, point, trigger, fire."

Muller fired a flare over the village. Even in the daylight it was very impressive. Many of the villagers ran out into the open looking upwards at the spectacle.

"Do a few practice throws with the grenades to get the feel of them," ordered Muller.

Maritz set about instructing us how to bowl a grenade, as he obviously knew all about them. Muller left us and he went with Hough towards the station. They seemed to get on extremely well.

The days continued to drag by. I went fishing whenever I could. The afternoons always seemed to produce the best results. Otherwise I did what I was told and kept out of everyone's way.

One steamy afternoon Teacher arrived on the harbour wall. He walked aimlessly along, and he appeared really happy. I watched him. He was smiling to himself as he ambled towards me and came and sat next to me. For a couple of weeks now I had been getting the impression that Teacher wanted to talk to me, to confide in me.

He sat and fidgeted, and then blurted out. "My wife's pregnant. She was not going to tell me, thinking I would worry, but she could not help herself. She had to tell me." He sat there grinning, his eyes sparkling. "I had to tell someone. You can't believe how excited I am after all the years of trying for a baby. We had almost given up. Now

I just wish there was a way to get out of this place and go home right now, where I am needed." He sat on the harbour wall, kicking his legs like a school boy.

I smiled happily and patted him on the back. "Well done!" I said not knowing what else I could say to the little man.

That evening Hough arrived again with a couple of bottles of his favourite wine. After a while, when we had all taken a drop and in some case more than a drop, Hough remarked casually, as if it was the least important thing in the world. "You know, I think there is big trouble coming!" We all sat and waited. He drank a little and Maritz handed him a lit cigarette.

Then he continued. "There is too much tension amongst the Africans. I also think some of the Mongu have joined the Teng." He sat nodding his head. Carr added wood to the fire. "Assault rifles are also new to this region, especially Russian guns, and as for the ear business! Well, I just cannot get to the bottom of that!" Hough sat and rocked back and forth on the log.

"It's a white man thing, ears. Not significant to the Teng as far as I can establish." He mused in the firelight. "If they took a man's private parts it could mean something, but not just an ear." He shook his head, then he absently poured more wine into his mug. He handed the bottle to Teacher.

We were all very quiet. The arrival of the ammunition and grenades had taken us all by surprise. Things now were beginning to look very serious indeed.

"Do you think one of the great powers, like the Russians, could be involved?" asked Teacher.

"There are Americans, French, Belgians and Russians all snooping around," said Hough sipping his wine. "They all want a piece of the riches of this land but don't understand how complicated and dangerous it is mixing tribalism and western politics. Their agents destabilise a country then put their man in charge by giving him enough backing, arms, training, money and control. That makes him into a strong dictator. Then they expect favours, votes in certain areas, mining rights, or a stepping stone into another country. It is too much. It is easy to destabilise a region like this. Then it all spreads like a disease to the neighbouring areas."

Hough sipped his wine and smoked. Everyone was locked in his own train of thought. Mosquitoes buzzed around. The the fire crackled and threw ghostly shadows on the surroundings. Hough eventually bid us good night and headed off into the darkness towards the police station.

Without a word Maritz rose and went off to his tent. Since his food poisoning episode Carr was very quiet and no longer went drinking with Maritz and Potter. His joviality had left him. I did not blame him at all. He had been close to being really ill and to be sick here meant possible death. Carr had told me that he was still passing blood on odd occasions and did not know what to do. Since his letter Potter seemed like a worried man. He had said nothing but there was something missing from his usual behaviour. From the jungle behind us came constant squeaking, hooting calls and rustling that we had got used to. It was going to be an early night for me.

The next morning started peacefully enough until Hough arrived. "You must hurry," he said rushing into our camp. "My Jeep is not mechanically right. I will ride with you."

I had just served Maritz coffee in bed. The other men had risen and were standing around bleary eyed, with mugs of boiling hot coffee.

"Bring your food. We must go right now, Maritz," ordered Hough.

Maritz stood in the door of his tent in a pair of shorts. I thought he was going to tell Hough to go to hell. His top lip curled in a familiar snarl. "Get dressed. Move, you useless bunch!" He turned and went back into the tent.

We all scuttled to our tents and dressed, grabbed our ammunition belts and water bottles. I collected a couple of tins of corned beef and a pack of biscuits, and we were on our way. Hough had taken over the passenger seat and Maritz had climbed into the back of the truck.

It was still really early and the jungle was wet and dripping with moisture. The jungle fog hung motionless just off the ground. We raced along, bouncing down the road we had become so familiar with. On we raced. The kilometres passed as did the time. The heat of the day broke, and flies bit and stung. Then we cursed and sweated.

Upon reaching the main road we headed north, passing de Haas's 'The Sweet Estate'. About fifteen kilometres on we turned off into a narrow winding tunnel that went on and on. Fields of coffee trees appeared in neat rows. A house came up. It was a shabby, cement and corrugated iron structure. There was a yard with a few broken implements parked under a large tree. It looked quiet enough.

The truck came to a grinding halt. Maritz took charge. Although we had not been told what to expect, there was a certain atmosphere about the drab buildings that made us all nervous. Then the smell of burning came to my nostrils.

"Pole, man the machine-gun. You second him Carr. Mac, Roux get on the veranda!" ordered Maritz. Roux was slow to move; he received a hard kick to the chest and fell over the tailgate.

"Move when I tell you!" snarled Maritz.

Roux lay groaning in the dust. I reached the veranda and crouched down, rifle at the ready. Roux crawled painfully to his feet and joined me.

"Keep the engine running Potter!" bellowed Maritz. "Teacher, you follow me!"

Hough his pistol drawn, skipped from the cab onto the veranda and in through an open door.

Maritz and Teacher went off around the side of the house, weapons at the ready.

A short while later they returned and reported that all was clear. Teacher was white-faced, biting his bottom lip nervously as he crouched next to me. "They have been here," he whispered. "There are dead dogs with arrows in them. They have even killed the pigs and chickens."

Maritz went into the house in search of Hough. From within I could hear Hough and then Maritz coughing. Maritz threw one of the windows open and a cloud of smoke escaped. We waited. The smell of burning was now very strong. A frightening atmosphere hung over the whole deserted house.

"Mac, you and Roux come here!" called Maritz from inside. Roux hesitated then followed me. The passageway was smoky but not that bad and I could see all the debris of the attack, broken furniture and empty brass cartridge casings rattled under our feet. There was also the strong sweet and sour stench of death, and as we advanced it became so strong that it made me catch my breath. Maritz appeared out of the smoke, a rag tied across his nose.

The flames licked round the door and through the cracks in the floor. We peered into the kitchen. The ceiling was on fire and it seemed to extend itself as we entered the room. The house appeared ready to go up in one terrific blaze. The kitchen was in complete turmoil. There were pots and pans, broken china and cutlery scattered across the floor. The smell of death was even stronger here. We followed Maritz and dodged the burning pieces of ceiling that detached themselves from above our heads.

"In there, bring them out on the bedding and mat," gasped Maritz, pointing towards a door.

The smoke was choking me and my eyes were watering, almost blinding me. I shuffled cautiously into a small room. It had only a skylight. Obviously the defenders had gone in there as a last stand.

Crouching, I peered through the smoke. Hough was in the room with a handkerchief tied across his face. He waved me out but not before I had seen a naked man spreadeagled, guts open and bloody intestines spread across the smouldering floor like a macabre barbecue. A woman lay there, stripped naked, her snow-white flesh bloated and horrible in the poor light. Then the shock of a doll-like child that lay gutted in the corner. Not even children were spared. I looked hurriedly away, sickened at what I saw.

"Out, out! Let them burn in peace!" shouted Hough waving me away. I shuffled backward, bumping into Roux who was vomiting, crying and choking. I pushed him out into the wrecked kitchen with Hough following closely.

"Mac, get that extra diesel. We can at least let them burn properly!" shouted Maritz who was waiting for us in the kitchen. We four rushed down the passage and into the open gasping for air. I removed the jerry can of diesel from the truck and returned down the passage. Quickly I poured the contents of the can over the floor and bedding. It was a ghastly feeling being alone in the smoke-filled room with the corpses. Roughly twenty-four hours earlier they had probably been alive, talking, laughing and functioning as people. Now I was burning them, and it made me feel really ill.

I returned to the fresh air. The roof had started to burn with the flames shooting high into the sky. The heat was twisting and curling the corrugated iron. Potter moved the truck further away to a safer spot. Roux crouched at the tailgate his face stained with smoke, tears and vomit. He sat rocking back and forth. I suddenly remembered that he had a child of much the same age as the dead one we had just seen. I climbed aboard and took up my position in the right-hand corner. I was trying desperately to blank out what I had just seen. No one spoke. The house crackled and burnt. The black pungent smoke whirled around the yard. Something I had noticed was that there appeared to be no wind until there was smoke to blow around, and no rain when one needed it. After an hour we moved off, leaving the house a raging inferno.

That night Hough came across to our camp with bottles of wine under his arm. He sat down uninvited, slopped wine into mugs and took a long swig. We crowded around, helping ourselves to his bottles.

"Today things were really bad," said Hough. "The du Preez family were good friends of mine. Their other child is away at school. Poor little thing." He gazed around looking genuinely sorry. Maritz placed a lit cigarette in his hand. Hough smiled sadly, the shadows making a savage mask of what was already an ugly face.

"Thanks," he said. "Did you notice the ears were missing, right ears, and du Preez's gun is also gone. The cartridge casings I picked up were from a Russian weapon. It is the Teng and I am sure the Mongu are with them." He sat there nodding at his thoughts.

"Where's Roux?" he suddenly asked. We all looked around, none of us realising that he was not attending Hough's lecture. Teacher rose and went to the tent. He returned a short while later and nodded towards the tent. Roux was taking the latest murders extremely badly.

"We are going to do more roadblocks, but now we need to move up and down the main road, checking everyone you come across. Thomas knows what we are looking for," explained Hough.

A little while later Hough left for the station. Maritz went off into the dark, probably to visit Annie. Potter climbed into the cab of the truck, slamming the door behind him. Carr and Pole went into the tent and prepared for bed. I sat with Teacher next to the blazing fire looking into the flickering flames, which was very restful. The usual jungle noises continued behind the camp, but they seemed a lot louder than usual and added to the uncomfortable atmosphere.

The murders that had taken place were horrible. The smell and the maggots, the way the victims had been killed were all unbelievably savage. The stench of the smoke and death were entrenched in my nostrils. I had showered when we had returned to camp and spent an hour soaping myself. I had washed my clothes but the smell persisted. I sipped the last of Hough's wine. Teacher appeared to want to talk.

Eventually he whispered. "You know, I got a photo of Maritz and that black woman," he chuckled. "What a sight, like hippos on the job. They were in the banana plot. Can you believe it, in broad daylight!" He laughed delightedly.

It had to be a shocking snap that I would never see as there was nowhere to develop a film out here.

"You know, he is there now!" whispered Teacher.

The fire crackled and hissed. I did not really care what Maritz was doing, but one thing I was sure of, whatever might happened to him he deserved it.

That night I went to bed dreaming of corpses, white and rotting. Even the smell was there. I also dreamed of Mia, Oupa and Gran, and then the nun. Then there was dust and Majola appeared for a moment, but then vanished he was replaced by an old male lion that drifted by on the edge of my dream. I woke sweating, as the first grey light filtered through the morning mist.

By midday we were sitting alongside the main road watching and waiting. A tractor and trailer came rattling down the road. It was piled high with household belongings, and people were hanging onto every possible foot and handhold. It gave me the feeling there was more to come, more death, more burning. Again, I wished I was back on the farm. Even working for Carlos would have been better than this.

Every evening we returned to the railhead and left again early each morning. Muller arrived with the mail and little else. No one knew what was going on. According to Hough there was going to be an election, but he doubted if it would be a success, as there were too many tribes and tribal conflicts, and too many old scores to settle. Before we realised it another month had drifted by.

Roux was becoming a real problem. He spoke to no one and ate very little. One night, when we were preparing for bed, he suddenly sat upright, saying he wanted to go home. He started throwing his possessions into a kit bag. He had got as far as the door of the tent when Maritz confronted him.

"You're deserting! You useless bastard!" snarled Maritz. "You're as bad as the English – can't take it." His fist had smashed into Roux's jaw. Roux went down but was not unconscious. At one stage I thought he was going to go for his rifle. I watched Maritz. He had his knife in his hand, the blade running up the back of his wrist so it was almost invisible. Roux started to cry and just lay there in the dust. Maritz laughed harshly and walked away.

Teacher helped Roux to his feet and on to his stretcher and then turned to me. "Mac go and ask Potter for a bottle of that rot-gut he keeps," instructed Teacher.

I walked across the moonlit camp to the truck that was Potter's domain. I was surprised to see the cab light on. I tapped on the door and climbed onto the running board, and peered in. Potter was sitting in the corner with a book on his lap and half a bottle of clear liquid on the dashboard. I opened the door and was further surprised to see he was reading the Bible. He grinned drunkenly at me.

"Roux is having a bad turn. Have you got some of that booze to spare?" I asked. Potter just stared at me blankly and then very slowly he handed me the half-bottle. I left him there sitting with the Bible in his lap. He was the last person I thought would read the Bible, even in his drunken state.

Teacher made Roux knock back the half-bottle. He gasped breathlessly after each gulp. His eyes rolled back in his head and he slowly toppled back with a grunt. Teacher pulled the mosquito net over him and without a word he climbed onto his own stretcher.

Carr was in fine form the following day. He hung onto the side of the truck as we bounced and swerved along the jungle track. Every now again, he let forth a squeal, sounding like a distressed pig. "Potter slow down. You think you're taking pigs to market!" he shouted and squealed again. He had us all laughing. Even Roux smiled at his antics. He suddenly stopped his pig act, and then imitated a telephone ringing. He lifted an imaginary receiver to his ear, "Ah, Elke   Sommer, so nice to hear from you again," he said into his imaginary telephone. "When are we going to get together again? What, you don't know? Don't want to know me any more? Who? Say that again, Max Roux is your new heartthrob! I am really hurt! Anyway here he is." Carr handed the imaginary receiver to Roux. "For you old chap," he said, laughing loudly.

At first I thought Roux was not going to play along. His face lightened slightly as he caught on. "Hallo darling," he chimed into the receiver. "How are things? Not bad. See you tonight down at the Villa. Have a couple of bottles of bubbly on ice. I will be bringing a few of my friends. If you could organise dates we could have a party." Suddenly he was aware we were fooling. His face could be read like a book. Tears appeared in the corners of his eyes. He stopped his imaginary conversation abruptly and looked down at his feet.

"Max there's only about fifty days left," said Teacher crouching down next to Roux. "You must try and keep it together. We have to stick together otherwise none of us will make it."

Roux sat there with tears running down his cheeks. We all looked away, but we knew it was the only way that we would survive.

It was Friday and the bus would be coming. We were parked on the side of the road and we wrote letters and dozed. At about ten a thunderstorm that had been building up broke, drenching everything. Half an hour later all the rain had dried up and the humidity became suffocating.

Potter had left the cab and was sitting on a log, reading.

Maritz was restless, wandering around and annoying everyone. "You drunken bastard," he snarled at Potter. "You think reading the Bible will help you out of this bloody mess?"

Potter sat back with a half-smile on his horse-like face. "If I could just give booze up I might become a preacher," said Potter seriously.

Maritz roared with laughter, frightening a number of multi-coloured birds into flight. Potter shrugged and returned to his reading, ignoring Maritz. In the distance there was the throb of an approaching vehicle engine.

"Right you bunch. Look alive. A vehicle is coming," growled Maritz looking down the road.

We all took up our positions. A fully laden bus appeared in the distance. The bus driver knew the procedure and came to a stop in just the right position. Thomas ordered the passengers out. They mumbled amongst themselves but did what they were told. I noticed the driver nod to Thomas. Thomas was quick for his size. He raced up the steps and into the empty bus.

From where I was I could see him making his way down the aisle. The next thing I saw he was dragging out a lanky youth by the scruff of the neck. He bounced him down the steps and snapped on the handcuffs. There was a grin on his sweating black face. The bus reloaded and went on its way. The passengers smiled and waved as they passed us. No one seemed the least concerned that one of the passengers had been removed.

"He is the one we seek," said Thomas excitedly. "Maybe the key to many questions. We must return to the station as quick as possible."

We arrived at the railhead just after dark. Then the beating started. We could hear the swish of the sjambok (hippo-hide whip) and the slap as it connected. This was followed immediately by a high-pitched frightening human scream. I had never heard anything so terrible and soul destroying. I found it difficult to believe that a human could make such a terrible sound, that a man could inflict such terrible pain on another. For what?

We sat around the camp and tried to eat. My food had a bad taste to it, and the other men seemed to have lost their appetite. Only Maritz seemed to enjoy his meal, and also seemed to find the screaming amusing. The rest of us pushed our half-eaten plates of food aside. I think we felt very uncomfortable with the youth being tortured so near and we wished it would end.

Teacher was white and visibly shaken. He mumbled something about torture. Maritz slapped him viciously across the face, telling him to keep quiet, and that Hough knew what he was doing.

It was unsettling and it made me feel empty inside, almost dirty, and even sorry for the lanky black youth. The beating seemed to go on and on. And as the time passed the high-pitched desperate screams were getting weaker and weaker. Hough, Thomas and the other gendarme could be heard shouting at the unfortunate young man.

We could not go to bed with all that noise going on, although we were all dead tired. I felt restless, uncertain and frightened. I disliked Hough for what he was doing. How long could the beating go on for? Was Hough going to kill the youth? Roux had slipped off into the tent. The rest of us sat around the fire in dead silence.

The night seemed very long. Even the jungle was quieter than usual. At about midnight the police station was silent, and we could hear someone approaching the camp. Moments later Hough strode into the flickering firelight, with a couple of bottles of wine under his arm. He smiled. But the shadows on his face made him look like the devil himself.

"A drink gentlemen. Success at last." He said and handed the bottle to Potter, who started to pour. "That's the guy, we have been seeking – the key maybe. Tough yes, but they always talk in the end." He gulped his wine and looked round. Maritz was ready with a lit cigarette. I watched and noticed that there was a slight tremor in Hough's hands. "He has told us where to find two boxes of guns and ammunition. The one behind it all is the witchdoctor Gogo. She's a real bad woman, a Teng witch. I think that the Russians could be backing her, as only Russian weapons are being used. Gogo has been around for many years. There were rumours she had died, but she now has re-appeared. She is not only serving the Teng but the Mongu as well. Here we have the link between the Mongu and the Teng. The Teng, the Spirit of the jungle, the untameable!" He waved his mug towards the police station. "That youngster's mother is one of Gogo's group of lesser witches. She was trained by Gogo. She is also well known amongst the locals." He smiled and appeared proud of all his achievement. He dragged on his cigarette making the end glow in the dark. "As for the ear business!" he went on excitedly. "An exchange is made. One right ear of a white person for six rifles and ammunition."

We heard the police Jeep starting up at the station and the lights swung across the football field. Then red tail lights could be seen going towards the river.

"Going to feed the crocodiles!" said Hough grinning.

Teacher went bone white. Everyone fidgeted and was restless.

"We are going to leave at two this morning for the village in the east. It is far. This is where we will find the guns. There might be many armed men so we must take extra ammunition and food. We also need a bucket, a can of petrol or diesel and say twenty sticks. We will wrap lengths of cloth around them to make fireflares. When you have done all this you must rest. Today will be a very long day."

We nodded and fidgeted. Now it was all starting just when Teacher had begun counting the days to the end of our contract.

We left just after two in the morning with the police Jeep leading the way. Hough had his two gendarmes with him. Maritz was slouched in the passenger seat, smoking. It was far from cool. There was a clinging humidity in the air and it would probably rain before the sun rose, which would just add to the already sticky atmosphere. The truck bounced and skidded along in the dark, with the headlights casting shadows on the jungle walls. The numerous reflections from the eyes of nocturnal animals glowed in the pitch dark as we passed.

The road seemed endless and I prayed that we would not get stuck. To dig the truck out in the dark would have been a near impossible task. Leaving the main road, we passed through kilometres of coffee plantations. Eventually, the jungle started again and the Jeep stopped. Hough jumped out and came around to Maritz's side of the truck.

"We are very close. No noise and no lights, as we enter the village which is big. Three men will start setting fire to the huts on either side of the road. This will cause a diversion. It is obviously hostile, so we will judge and act according to our reception," he said with a flash of teeth.

The jungle along the path stank of wet rotting vegetation. The first faint greying of the coming of day filtered through the leafy canopy. The two vehicles crept forward. Maritz had taken over the machine-gun and removed its covers. The first huts of the village appeared. Teacher, Carr and Roux dropped onto the muddy track. They carried a bucket of petrol out of which poked thirty hand-made fireflares. Teacher lit a small lantern and walked slowly behind the truck. Carr lit a flare and tossed it onto the thatched roof of the first hut. It took a few moments for the fire to find its way through the top wet layer of thatch and into the drier one beneath and then it was burning. Then the next and the next burst into flame. Dogs started to bark and then people started shouting and screaming in terror. I crouched in the right-hand corner of the truck, peering out through the slats, my mind tired and blank.

The Jeep in front moved just as slowly, its tyres squelching in the soft muddy soil. The sunroof had been removed and Thomas's smooth dome-like head stuck out. The barrel of his submachine-gun glistened with a sinister sheen in the early morning light.

The doors of huts were flying open. Naked and half-naked panic-stricken people were screaming and running in every direction. From the corner of a hut a shot was fired at us. The bullet whistled over our heads.

"Bloody hell!" screamed Maritz.

Then the Browning started to fire. Maritz howled like a mad dog. People tumbled and fell over, a few rising again only to be struck by invisible forces and thrown into contortions.

A half-naked black woman was dragging a child by the arm, as she held another to her breast. She was running as best she could. She went somersaulting on crashing to the muddy earth. The child rose unsteadily but was hit in the back and went catapulting forward.

They lay still. I knew it was murder but there was absolutely nothing I could do.

I was in shock. People were being killed – murdered right before my eyes. It was happening in front of me. I could not stop it. I could not wake up from this shocking dream. It was real. I became conscious of being shot at, when splinters of wood stung my face. Before me in the path of the truck was a man wearing nothing but a loincloth. His rifle was raised, as he was working the bolt action frantically. In an incredulous haze I raised my rifle and fired a single shot. He went down. It was unbelievably easy. One moment he was alive, making a useless attempt at protecting his village and his people. Then he was dead. The truck passed over his body. Teacher threw his rifle into the back of the truck. We were suddenly at the outskirts of the village and Hough's jeep had stopped.

"Cessez le feu! Cease fire!" screamed Hough, as he jumped from the Jeep.

Potter had turned the truck to face the village, giving the Browning a good field of fire. Maritz swung the machine-gun to and fro on its pylon, looking for a target. He had a crazy glow in those smouldering eyes. A mangy dog staggered out from behind a hut. He fired, killing it.

Maritz turned facing us, his face flushed and eyes glowing with excitement. "Mac, you and Pole help the police. Teacher, you, Carr and Roux, take up position in those banana trees. Anything that moves, shoot!" he shouted.

The hut where we had stopped was at the end of the village near a cattle pen and a small stand of bananas. Thomas was opening the gate to the pen and chasing the cows out into the village. Pole, had grabbed a spade and joined Hough. I followed. Behind us the village was on fire and I could hear people screaming. Drums started beating and an out of tune trumpet belched forth in loud blasts. Every now and again we were shot at from the smoke. The marksman's aim was poor and usually too high.

Thomas was scratching around in the cattle pen. The next thing Pole was digging furiously. In minutes he had unearthed a green steel box, and then another. I crouched near the gate watching.

Hough was grinning as he smashed the lock. His smile was even broader as he held a rifle above his head.

"There are at least ten!" he shouted and smashed open the second box. "More!" he shouted, glancing around. "Mac check that hut!" He pointed at the hut which obviously belonged to the owner of the cattle pen.

I raced across the clearing, kicked the door open and plunged into the dingy interior, weapon in hand. It was empty except for a smouldering fire and a few blankets. The gunfire outside had increased. Maritz was returning fire. Drums thundered, the solid thump was penetrating into my head making me feel a little crazy. I ducked out of the low door and circled around the hut. I stopped, surprised by a pile of rough packing case planks that leaned against the mud wall. The planks had red writing on them. I crouched down trying to decipher the writing. After a moment I made out the words – "Massey Ferguson". Picking up one plank, I made a quick examination. There were scuffs of green paint on the inside. What had I discovered now?

"Hurry up Mac!" shouted Maritz urgently.

I sprinted to the truck with my find, one rough packing case plank. The Jeep was already moving away from us. I tossed the plank into the back and was hauled over the tailgate by Teacher and Carr. We were now returning back the way we had come.

Huts were burning, and pumping up white columns of smoke into the clear morning sky. Blood-splattered bodies lay in small pathetic heaps. The drums thundered. The trumpet honked alarmingly close. We crouched low as Maritz manned the Browning.

As we drew level with a larger heap of a dozen or so corpses, Maritz turned, with a smile on his flushed excited face. "Pole, man the machine-gun," he ordered and then banged on the roof of the cab. "Stop!" he bellowed. Potter stopped. Maritz jumped off the back of the truck.

"You bunch of English want souvenirs, come and get them. These bastards take our ears. We'll take theirs and we will see how quickly it will stop!" shouted Maritz.

Chapter Six

None of us moved. Teacher had turned white. Maritz was down amongst the dead, his knife already smeared with blood, a plastic bag hanging from his wrist. One body, not yet dead but probably seriously wounded, raised his head. Maritz kicked the man in the head then slashed open his throat and neatly lopped off his ear. I looked away for it was horrible, sickening and disgusting. Maritz looked like he was enjoying himself.

"He's mad," whispered Teacher hoarsely, "completely and utterly mad."

Potter leant from the cab. "Maritz, you had better hurry. Hough will be gone in a moment."

Maritz looked up from his bloody task, a grin on his sweating face with his eyes blazing. "Don't you want to join me!" he laughed loudly as he clambered over the tailgate, taking up his position behind the Browning again. "You bastards haven't got the guts to join me!" he shouted excitedly.

We all remained silent. He had a dozen or so ears in the plastic bag. My stomach heaved. It was bad enough killing these unfortunate people but to remove their ears as some sort of souvenir and to boast about it, that was unthinkable. Maritz was mad all right. What was he going to do with the human ears?

The truck caught up with the Jeep and we ploughed our way across the soft soil towards the jungle and the road out. The jungle closed around us and we entered an airless tunnel with the occasional patch of sky above us. Thank goodness it was over I thought.

Then, without warning, a trumpet blasted and arrows pelted down and guns were firing, bullets slapping into our plank protection. Maritz was swearing and was firing at an unseen enemy, raking the bush on either side of the road. I crouched in my corner and hung on.

Looking back, Roux was about two metres behind me. He was squatting down, his one hand through the slats holding on for dear life. Suddenly he withdrew his hand hurriedly, horror on his drawn face.

"I've been hit. Oh god!" he screamed, waving a bloody middle finger. Pole was the closest and quickest. He fell on Roux pinning him to the steel deck. Teacher whipped out his knife, went white, swallowed and handed it to me.

One blow from the razor-sharp blade and Roux's finger went rolling across the deck of the truck. There was a gush of blood. Roux passed out. Teacher wrapped a rough bandage round the stump. We left him there rolling unconsciously around the deck. What happened to the finger no one ever found out. It just disappeared.

After a time Roux came to and could no longer take the bouncing around the deck and staggered to his feet. His face was white and his eyes looked oddly bright. "Thanks, you guys. Maybe one day I can help you!" That was all he said.

Maritz was unaware of the life-saving drama taking place behind him. When told, he roared with laughter and said, "Lucky it was not his ding-a-ling. Then the silly bugger would have had a problem."

The truck left the village behind. We were all exhausted, but could not relax as we bounced along. Maritz resumed his seat in the front of the truck. Hough's Jeep left us behind.

I stood in my corner watching the road ahead. My thoughts were in a sick turmoil, for I knew that today I had taken the ultimate step. I had killed a man for money and I found myself asking the questions. Did the brave, foolhardy man have a wife and family? Who would now provide for them now that I had killed him. I tried to push the mental image of the lone man working the bolt action of his rifle away, but the image remained before my eyes for many days.

Later we stopped at the junction and brewed coffee and ate corned beef sandwiches. It was late afternoon when we reached the railhead. In our absence some post had arrived, but there was nothing for me. This was not unusual any more. The next post would produce three or four letters. Pole set about cooking supper. The rest of us waited our turn in the showers. Later in the evening Hough appeared from the police station with a bottle of wine. He seated himself on a log. Potter poured the wine into mugs.

"Sané," said Hough raising his mug. "Success, a total of twenty Russian SKS assault rifles and two thousand rounds of ammunition.

My commanding officer is pleased with the results. Lieutenant Muller wishes you all the best and says keep up the good work. By the way, that hunting rifle we picked up belonged to du Preez." He smiled happily and raised his mug.

Suddenly a thought struck me. I had forgotten all about the plank in the back of the truck. I went and fetched it. Hough and the others eyed me comically as I placed the plank before Hough like a sacred offering.

"I found this plank this morning,." I explained rather self-consciously. Everyone was silent listening to me.

"So what?" demanded Maritz.

"I've seen packing cases marked like this in the back of de Haas's truck." I explained hurriedly. "If you look here, and here, there are scuffs of green paint on the plank the same colour as the boxes that contained the guns."

Everyone was now examining the plank and the lantern was brought closer.

"You see the 'M' is the part of the word 'Massey Ferguson'. Further down the plank is 'G'."

"You think you're a bloody detective!" snarled Maritz nastily.

"I saw these types of boxes or crates in the back of de Haas's truck both times when we stopped him," I said defensively.

"How many boxes?" asked Hough, dragging on his cigarette.

"Four in all," I said looking around.

Maritz was scratching himself, staring hard at me. "Sounds like bloody rot to me. De Haas lives in the middle of the trouble. Why would he give them firearms?" he queried.

Hough toyed with his drink, ignoring Maritz. "I will make enquiries," he said slowly. "One never knows!" He sipped his drink thoughtfully. Hough changed tack. "Tomorrow I want you to go and collect old man Borg at Bongani village. Thomas knows the way. The old man is very stubborn and will not move. Maybe you will have to use force but he is to be brought back here," explained Hough preparing to leave us.

I found Maritz watching me thoughtfully. The gathering broke up. Maritz now approached me.

"Why didn't you tell me about those crates?" he snarled.

I shrugged. "At the time I did not think they were important."

Maritz sneered at me, "Who are you to think! You could have saved this whole sad situation."

I nodded and remained quiet. I'd wondered why he had not ordered a search of de Haas's truck. He was always quick to take the beers on offer.

I was on my way to the ablution block when I saw Maritz and Potter heading for the village. Surely they were both exhausted after the long day. I showered and went to bed.

The rest of the men were already in bed when I arrived. Roux was a still silent bundle under his net. Pole was already snoring softly. Teacher noisily killed a couple of giant mosquitoes that had managed to get inside his net.

"How the hell do Potter and you not get malaria? Half the time Potter can't make it into the cab and ends up sleeping on the ground," said Teacher speaking to Carr.

Carr laughed loudly. I listened with half an ear, for we all took pills regularly to prevent the mosquito-borne diseases.

"Well," said Carr, "the theory is that, if you drink enough, as Potter and Maritz do you've so much alcohol in your blood that the mozzies zap you only once. They get so pissed that they fly themselves dead against the nearest tree!" He roared with laughter.

I could not help but smile. Only Carr could think up an explanation like that. Potter got bitten virtually every night. He had big red lumps on the exposed parts of his body but within days they were gone. He would scratch and rub antiseptic ointment into the bites. Only once had a bite gone septic. I dozed off after the laugh.

Suddenly I was shocked awake. "Come you clever child, coffee!" I was shocked awake by the rasping slurred voice of Maritz. He was standing outside my mosquito net. I could smell the alcohol on his breath.

"Sure," I said coming fully awake and wriggling out of the mosquito net on the opposite side to him. I did not want him to split open the net with his ever handy knife. I shuffled out of the tent into the moonlit camp. The fire was still flickering. Maritz followed me. Potter was lying in the dirt after failing to negotiate the step into the truck.

"Coffee!" snarled Maritz swaying. "You think you can make a fool of me, hey boy?" he asked softly.

"No," I said shaking my head and placing the kettle on the fire.

"Then why did you not tell me about the wooden crates?" he demanded. Maritz was very drunk and looking for trouble.

"At the time I did not realise," I said cautiously.

I sensed that Maritz had it in for me. I also spotted the knife in his sleeve and kept the fire between him and me. The coffee was boiling, I carried the kettle over to the table, pouring a mug and adding condensed milk and sugar as Maritz liked it. I stepped around the fire handing Maritz the mug. He grinned drunkenly at me, and sipped the liquid. Then, with a startling shout, he flung the contents of the mug at me. If I had not been so alert, he would have hit me full in the face, most probably blinding me. As it was, the boiling liquid hit me on the shoulder of my heavy khaki shirt and splashed the side of my head. Pain shot through me.

"You trying to poison me boy?" roared Maritz.

I doubled up with pain, just as Maritz was closing in. Then something happened. At the time I was not aware of my actions. Later it all came back to me. My fist slammed into Maritz's groin. There was great whoosh of escaping air. His face went purple, almost black in the poor firelight, and his eyes bulged out like a bull frog. Then I made the mistake of my life. Instead of pressing home my advantage, I backed off.

With a blood-curdling scream he lunged at me. The knife missed my face by a fraction. Throwing myself to the ground I rolled under the truck and out the other side. Maritz was swearing. His cursing could probably be heard kilometres away as he shouted curses and threats into the night. I slipped away into the darkness.

I spent the night in the office at the police station. Before first light I crept out undetected by Hough or his staff.

I padded quietly into the still-sleeping camp, stirred the coals up and added wood. I had not slept particularly well. How was Maritz going to retaliate? He would, I was sure. The actions of the previous day had had a completely draining effect on me. Then, on top of that, Maritz's attack followed by the lack of a decent sleep had left me feeling physically and mentally exhausted.

Putting the porridge on to cook, I made myself a mug of coffee. What had happened last night was on my mind. No matter how many times I went over the incident, I could not find any way out. Maritz had it in for me. In turn I had retaliated. There was nothing else to it.

I also realised that previously, when finding myself in a tight situation, I had got the shakes. Last night I had not. My immediate reaction was to go blank but moments later I could recall my actions. This was a very different me.

I sat there thinking guiltily about the man I had killed as the sun crept over the trees. My thoughts turned to the little nun. Were the nuns at the mission not in danger? Surely they should abandon the mission and find safety further to the east, in Stanleyville or one of the other towns.

Teacher came out of the tent stretching and yawning. He wandered over to the fire and poured himself a mug of coffee. He enquired about the noise of the night before and about Maritz's performance. I explained what had happened.

He shook his head in disbelief. "That man's not going to forgive you, no matter what. Just be very careful," he cautioned and left me sitting there. He took his towel and soap and went off towards the ablution block.

The other men appeared one by one. Maritz was the last to rise, he shook his head groggily, his face looked puffy and tired and he helped himself to coffee. When he moved, he had a slight limp. He tasted the coffee and pulled a face and returned to his tent without a word. Far away, drums started to beat, softly at first but gradually building up to a solid thumping. Birds twittered and called to one another. Monkeys chattered deep in the undergrowth.

Half an hour later Maritz appeared outside his tent. He stared at me with bloodshot eyes, said nothing and headed for the shower.

About an hour later Thomas arrived and off we went. Potter and Maritz were looking the worse for wear. No one spoke. We just hung on for dear life as we passed down our usual route between the giant trees, slushing in and out of the green slimy water-filled furrows, bouncing over the hard dry sections of road.

We turned south at the junction. We had never been south before. The road actually seemed to improve and after a few kilometres we came to a stop on the edge of the village. It was a, village like them all, with battered thatched mud huts and small gardens with patches of banana trees, a corrugated iron shop, with its red paint pealing, and the inevitable Coca-Cola sign.

The air was dead still. A few chickens could be seen pecking at insects in the road. A dog dozed lazily against the wall. Then it rose and went from view behind the huts. There was no sign of human beings, no washing hanging out. No kids. I sensed the danger and knew that all was not well. Maritz climbed into the back, tossed his rifle onto a piece of canvas on the deck and took over the machine-gun. He had said nothing all morning.

Maritz tapped on the roof of the cab, and Potter started slowly forward. We were ready for trouble, crouching behind our plank protection. Thomas stood next to Maritz peering out from under the canopy.

"Stop outside the shop," Thomas called to Potter. "If the old man is still there the fridge will be working and the drinks will be cold."

We crept along. Nothing moved in the still, dead heat. We sweated. Nothing felt right. All of us were on edge.

Potter pulled up outside the shop and hooted. Silence! He hooted again. The door crashed open. Borg stood there, a filthy old man with stained grey beard reaching almost to his waist. His long-johns were grey with grime, a double-barrelled shotgun was held under his arm. He smiled showing an empty line of pink gums in the tangled mass of his beard.

Thomas jumped down and Maritz followed.

"Keep the engine ticking," ordered Maritz. "Pole, man the machine-gun!"

The rest of us climbed from the truck and entered the smelly little shop. A few tins of fish and other household goods were all that was on offer. The fridge worked and the Cokes were ice cold. We helped ourselves. The old man stood smiling. We did not understand his language.

On the other hand Thomas chatted away in the local dialect.

"He says he won't leave!" said Thomas.

Maritz grinned happily and, without hesitating, punched the old man squarely on the jaw. The filthy old man went down in a jumbled unconscious heap. Thomas snapped on the handcuffs and we carried him out to the truck. Maritz and Thomas followed carrying a couple of boxes of cheap gin, the cash box, a bundle of clothing and the shotgun. They threw the lot over the tailgate.

Carr gulped down the last of the Coke he had been drinking and tossed the bottle aside, rubbing his stomach and burping. I could see he was just about to make one of his wisecracks.

The silence was suddenly shattered by a volley of shots whistling over our heads, smacking into the shop wall. We dived for cover into the back of the truck. Pole opened up with short bursts.

Maritz climbed onto the roof of the cab. He stood there for a moment, ignoring the danger, and then jumped down. "They're trying to ambush us!" he gasped indignantly. "There are about thirty on the left amongst the huts." He clambered into the back of the truck, shouting instructions.

It did not seem to occur to him that we could just race away firing, since we had what we had come for.

"Pole, keep their heads down. We're going to have a go at them from behind. Potter, keep the engine running. Teacher, Carr, Mac, Roux, follow me!" As he spoke he tossed us grenades that he had taken from the tin trunk. There was that crazy glint in his smouldering eyes again.

We crashed through the shop. Rats scurried for cover. I kicked the back door open. Maritz took over the lead along a narrow track between the huts. A hut had caught fire and smoke was spreading through the village. The tracer that the Browning was firing had probably started it.

After a short distance Maritz stopped and turned to me. "Mac, you stay here. There are a few men in front of you," he whispered, his breath coming in short gasps. "Teacher, take the other side of this hut. When you hear my grenade explode, then throw yours."

Maritz, Roux, Teacher and Carr had gone on. I crouched down peering around the hut. At the time things were going so fast there was no time to be afraid. I flattened myself against the mud wall and crept forward. I peeped round the curved wall. A group of men dressed in vests and shorts, others naked to the waist and daubed with yellow war paint, crouched against the back wall of a hut. They were all armed with an assortment of weapons, spears, bows and a number of rifles. They were obviously waiting for the truck to pass. It was as Maritz had said – an ambush!

I extracted the pin of my grenade, carefully holding down the lever. To my left, a grenade exploded with a solid resounding thump. I tossed mine, high, aiming for the centre of the group of men. I stepped back against the wall. The earth-shuddering explosion seemed long in coming, but when it did I jumped involuntarily. I waited a few seconds, then crouching low I went round the hut firing. There was not much to fire at. The men lay scattered about, most were obviously dead. Others had horrific open bloody wounds. I fired single shots, counting each shot, killing the seriously wounded men. At that moment it just seemed the right thing to do. Smoke drifted across my vision. Unexpectedly two warriors burst out of the cloud of smoke brandishing spears. I fired and they went down. I had fired eighteen rounds from a magazine that carried twenty.

There was heavy firing to my left and someone was screaming in agony. The Browning was firing continuously. More huts had caught fire and were blazing furiously. Before me all was still, but my instinct caused me to look around.

Maritz stood there with a grin on his face and fire in his eyes. "Think you can hit me and get away with it sonny?" His voice sounded dangerously soft.

I could sense the danger radiating from him. I knew that I had two shots left. I had to turn and face him. As I was turning, I saw Maritz's face. It was aglow with hate. It was his eyes that got to me. They were crazy. His weapon came up pointing directly at me. He could not miss at this range. I saw his trigger finger take up the slack. I saw him

145

squeeze. I had to turn. Was I still turning or was I dead? The FN is a long weapon and it took time to turn and face him. I fired a single shot, feeling the recoil. Maritz went over backwards in an untidy sprawl hitting the ground with a thud. His chest was blown open by the angle of the bullet. There was a sudden gush of blood and he twitched a number of times and then lay still. I was gasping for breath. What had I done? I would have to run. I tried to gather my thoughts. He was going to kill me. His weapon had not fired. Why?

I went cautiously forward, as if expecting him to come alive again and jump up and attack me. I crouched down next to his body and picked up his weapon and pulled the sliding parts of his weapon back. I knew that the answer had to be his weapon. I peered into the chamber and I saw a crushed matchstick. Someone had jammed his weapon.

My mind was numb, struggling to cope with what I saw in front of me. I stood staring down at Maritz. Teacher, Roux and Carr came out of the smoke. Bullets were whining around us, smacking into the mud walls. Strange sounding voices were calling and shouting out all about us. The Browning was still firing. Drums thundered. I could not think. I was frozen to the spot. The four of us stood together looking at Maritz, seemingly oblivious of our surroundings.

It was Teacher who broke the spell. "Mac, watch out!" he shouted.

I stepped aside, my back to the wall of the hut. Teacher fired a short burst. Two painted warriors spun to the earth, where they thrashed around before they died. We stood in a frightened group for a moment. Roux's face was as white as a ghost. Carr was in shock, staring at Maritz. In death his face no longer had that surly aggressive expression.

"We must run!" shouted Teacher. "There are too many. Bring Maritz's rifle. Leave him. He's too heavy to carry."

We obeyed Teacher immediately. I picked up Maritz's weapon and followed the others between the huts. Then we were fighting for our lives. There was no professionalism in our method. Running from one hut to another, we were firing at anything that moved, using the thatch overhang to protect us from the falling arrows. Panting and sweating we rolled over the tailgate and collapsed on the deck of the truck. With a clash of gears it lurched forward. Pole was firing constantly, oblivious of the arrows, spears and bullets fired at him. He raked the side of the road. His legs were like two tree trunks firmly planted on the bouncing deck. The truck sped out of the village and joined the road.

I sat next to Teacher on the bouncing deck. I felt weak, frightened and confused. Teacher stretched across and took Maritz's weapon from me. He removed the magazine and peered into the chamber. No one was paying him any sort of attention. I saw Teacher insert his finger and remove the matchstick. I just looked away. I knew then that Teacher had jammed the weapon; he had saved my life. I took a long swig from my water bottle. My mind was still frozen with fright.

As we continued along the road Pole had opened the tin trunk and was handing out magazines. I had carried one hundred and twenty rounds. I still had half a magazine, ten rounds left. I was surprised my hands were not shaking as I automatically filled my ammunition pouches.

I sat there bouncing every now and then as we roared along. I was trying vainly to gather my thoughts. I decided that it would be best if I kept quiet. No one seemed to care what had happened to Maritz.

Pole eventually asked,. "What happened to Maritz?"

I remained silent, not trusting my voice.

Teacher came to the rescue. "He died," was all he said. That seemed sufficient. Pole shrugged and went back to watching the road ahead. No one else said a word. No one appeared to care.

It was during the late afternoon when we arrived back at the railhead. There was an almost a tangible tension hanging over the village. Groups of villagers hung around watching us. They were all openly carrying knives, spears and bows and arrows. There were no friendly waves or smiles any more.

Potter swung the truck into our camp, and hopped down.

He looked around surprised. "Did we leave Maritz behind?" he asked.

"He was too heavy to carry and they were trying to kill us, in case you hadn't noticed," said Teacher.

"He was dead?" asked Potter uncertainly.

Teacher just nodded. Potter swallowed, turned away and started counting bullet holes in the cab and engine compartment of the truck. He was trying to follow their route through the truck's body to make sure they had not caused any permanent damage.

Thomas had released old man Borg and escorted him to the police station. Roux was crouching down next to the almost dead fire, trying to blow life back into the coals.

Teacher stood watching the groups of villagers who were standing around. "I wonder what's going on down there?" he said, casually leaning against a tree. I saw Potter was ducking behind the door of the truck, drinking from a bottle of clear liquid. Pole had gone over to the police station to report to Hough. Suddenly drums started to beat in the distance. One of the groups of villagers started to shout and then chant. It was very unsettling.

After about an hour, Hough and the Pole returned to the camp. Hough's face was serious. "I have just spoken with Villa Vista on the radio. Pole is your new corporal. He has accepted the position."

Teacher was on his feet shaking Pole by the hand. One by one we congratulated him. Roux had appeared out of the gloom and was behaving very strangely. He was crouching down, his face white and contorted. We all turned to look at him.

"I'm going! Bugger the contract. They are liars. It will never stand up in court!" he sobbed swaying drunkenly.

He was being completely irrational. There would be no court, and we all knew there was no way out. We were trapped.

"Who's coming with me?" he asked and a shudder seemed to run through his body and he started crying.

Teacher went over to him, his voice gentle, as if talking to a child. "Roux, we have got to stand together to survive. Nothing could be worse than today and you did so well," said Teacher encouragingly. He turned to Potter. "Bring me that bottle of rot-gut." Potter obeyed without a word. Teacher took a sip and nearly choked, making his eyes water. He offered the bottle to Roux. Roux hesitated but then took it, swigging back a huge mouthful. His eyes grew wide and he coughed. Teacher patted him on the back. "Okay?" he said and allowed him take a few more swigs.

"Excuse me gentlemen," said Hough, chipping in and breaking the awkward mood of the moment. "There's now something else. It is a small matter of murder."

My blood ran cold. Had Pole reported me? Had he suspected that I killed Maritz? What was I to do? If the light had not been so bad I was sure Hough and the others would have seen the guilt on my face. I had the urge to run, but there was nowhere to run to.

Hough continued. "The whole village is up in arms. They want blood. The headman is the only one keeping the whole place together," said Hough looking around at us. "Annie was murdered last night. Her head was severed from her body and her right ear cut off. It was a clumsy attempt to imitate a Teng killing. Her body, judging by the drag marks which led to the river, is gone. Her head was placed in her pit toilet. There were boot prints. I took the liberty of checking Maritz's boots. There is mud and blood on his spare pair. I think it was a lover's quarrel." He tapped his cigarette. He was obviously aware of Annie and Maritz's affair. The other men seemed mildly surprised and amused at this information. "I told the villagers that Maritz was killed today. They do not believe me. They say we are hiding him. If we had his body it would close the case and satisfy the local natives."

We were all silent. Damn Maritz, I thought. Even when dead he still could not leave us in peace.

Then Hough continued. "Tomorrow you must return to the village and see if you can find Maritz's body. I doubt it will be there. He has probably been eaten already." He lit a cigarette, looking around at us all. "But you must try," he said. Finally, he turned and went off into the coming night.

I can honestly admit I have never been so relieved in my life. Yet I still had an empty feeling, tinged with deep fear. Did anyone suspect it was I who had killed Maritz? Teacher knew, but he was just as much a part of the killing as I was. I was sure he was not going to say anything. What was going to happen to us? Was Pole capable of controlling Potter and Carr? Teacher was backing Pole all the way.

Roux was on his way to a nervous breakdown. I would definitely back Pole. He was by far the most rational- minded and the strongest of our group.

Potter had gone off towards the truck. He now returned. He stood before us with his Bible in hand. I had a horrible feeling he had also lost his mind.

"Things have changed," he said. His long horse-like face was serious. "I am giving up drinking, and feel I should read to you. It's my new life. You know, fifteen bullets went through the cab. I have not got a scratch. It's a miracle." He shuffled through the pages, Carr added wood to the fire and the lantern was brought closer. Potter turned the Bible sideways to catch more of the poor light and then he started reading hesitantly, stumbling over the words. It was Psalm 23. I knew it off by heart. "The Lord is my shepherd." The men sat in silence. The fire was throwing shadows, and the jungle noises in the background were continuous. "And I will dwell in the house of the Lord for ever." Potter finished. He wiped his sweating forehead with the back of his hand.

We sat in silence. The last two days had been the most terrible and frightening days of my life.

That night Pole arranged us into watches, for neither he nor Hough trusted the villagers. Far away the drums were pounding, thunder grumbled deeply in the night and an owl hooted. God, how I longed for home, away from this madness!

The following day we left at first light. Potter was grey-faced, and had to swallow a few aspirin. Thomas did not accompany us as we knew the way, and Hough said he needed Thomas to help convince the villagers that Maritz had actually died. The truth was that he probably felt safer with the giant African around.

As we neared the junction and rounded a bend in the road, we saw a tree laid across our path. Potter stopped the truck and we examined the scene before us. Trees had fallen before. We would cut them in two and hitch the cable round them and drag them out of the way using the truck. This tree had a different look about it. The roots could not be seen. Potter edged the truck closer. Carr manned the Browning, and everyone was alert and ready to fire. When we were only a few metres away we could see the stump. It had been roughly cut, probably by an axe.

"Reverse!" shouted Pole. The truck reversed slowly. Nothing moved before us in the heat.

"Stop!" shouted Pole. He looked around at us licking his lips. "We're going to shoot up the bush on either side." We prepared our weapons. "Fire!" ordered Pole.

We raked the bush on either side of the road, empty casings rattled across the steel deck of the truck. After emptying two magazines we stopped and reloaded. The echo of the automatic firing died in the distance. All we had appeared to do was to frighten the birds.

Pole picked up the chainsaw. "Okay you all cover me," he ordered before he dropped over the tailgate into the mud. The chainsaw screamed as Pole set about cutting the fallen tree. He was obviously not prepared to order one of us into the open, and this made us respect him a little more. Crouching in the relative safety of the back of the truck I peered through the slats. There was no movement in the deep dark undergrowth. Roux seemed all right, crouched next to me. Pole had cut the tree in half and returned to attach the cable. Potter reversed with the wheels spinning. The tree parted sufficiently for us to get through.

The village where we had picked up old man Borg was all but gutted, leaving gaunt shells of huts. Many of the mud walls had collapsed and the thatched roofing was still smouldering. The shop was a heap of burnt wood and black twisted corrugated iron. Potter drove the truck as close as possible to the spot where Maritz had died. There was no sign of his body.

"Let's go home," said Pole.

Carr snorted, "I hope whoever ate that bastard has diarrhoea so bad that he never recovers." He said this with a surprising amount of aggression, obviously thinking of what Maritz had done to him.

Turning off the main road we came to where we had cut the tree in half. Potter stopped the truck suddenly, throwing us off balance in the back.

"Do you think you're driving pigs to market?" screamed Carr.

Pole was standing next to the Browning peering over the cab. "Oh my god," he groaned, "what next?"

I peered ahead and could see a round object on a stick. Then I realised what it was. It was hideous and at the same time frightening. My stomach heaved and my hands started to shake. Pole turned to us in a calm voice. "You stay in your positions. We're going to do the same as this morning, two magazines on automatic. Fire."

We raked the bush and undergrowth at the side of the road. Then Potter drove the truck slowly forward. "I'll get him!" shouted Potter from the cab. I was positioned in the front right-hand corner and saw it all. Potter stopped next to Maritz's head and opened the door. "Would you care for a lift Maritz, old chap?" Potter asked ever so politely.

"Stop acting the ape," said Pole shaking his head in disbelief.

Potter grabbed Maritz's by the hair and pulled his head off the spear on which it was impaled and lifted it into the cab. The engine roared as we pulled away.

Roux was white, his face contorted. "They cut his head off. They cut the Dutchman's head off!" Roux screamed in a high-pitched, frightened voice. He was hysterical. Teacher was trying to talk to Roux, to calm him down but he would not listen. His eyes rolled back in his head and he went into a type of fit, thrashing around on the floor of the truck.

We left him there. After a while he lay still, breathing heavily. Teacher watched Roux in silence. Pole stared ahead, his hand resting on the Browning. Carr faced away and said nothing. We were all deep in our own thoughts.

Arriving back at the railhead Hough came across to the camp with a sack to collect the head. It was a terrible sight, so bleak and bloodless in death. The eyes were wide open and the tongue slightly protruding through the lips. His right ear was missing, cut clean off. A Teng warrior would be rewarded with six Russian assault rifles for that ear. It was really horrific.

Teacher and Potter had gone off to the village and returned with a bottle of clear rot-gut. Roux was lying like a corpse in the tent.

Taking a mug of the clear liquid, Teacher went to sit next to him. Obviously his intention was to make him dead drunk.

We settled into our routine. Carr was cooking supper. Pole was busy cleaning the Browning. The village was quieter now. Obviously the viewing of Maritz's head had resolved the whole matter and the case was now, hopefully, closed and I would receive no further shocks.

Later Teacher appeared out of the dark, his face solemn. He placed the half-full bottle of rot-gut on the table and went to wash his hands. "There should be more of us here," said Teacher.

Pole shook his head, "I doubt they will send more men. Hough says there is a lot of trouble around Villa Vista. Nearly every day someone is murdered."

Pole helped himself to coffee, and sat looking into the flames. "We must stick together. The village is quiet, so they are obviously satisfied that Maritz is really dead. I have no sympathy for the man, no sorrow." He shrugged his big shoulders. "It was more of a shock seeing his head like that. I doubt I will ever forget it."

Potter muttered as he rose from the fire. "I am going to pack Maritz's belongings." He sauntered across to the dark tent and lit a lantern. His shadow could be seen stooping and moving around. "Will you look at this? It's bloody terrible!" called Potter.

What now? I thought. Nothing could be worse than Maritz's head.

Potter had opened the tent flap. "Look at this!" He held up a gold chain. A small brown object dangled from it. "It's an ear," he whispered. "It's fresh, maybe Annie's."

We stood in a group, staring transfixed at the ear that swung too and fro on the chain.

"I will give it to Hough," said Pole, taking it.

Carr was shaking his head, "I wonder if Maritz was completely all right in the head," said Carr sadly.

"He was mad," said Teacher. "Completely nuts! This place is enough to snap anyone."

We all returned to the fire.

I was no longer as confident as I had been that we were going to survive. We were now so few against the unknown. There were all sorts of things worrying me. One was that I had not received mail for the past three weeks. Then there was Maritz's death, as well as Roux routinely collapsing in fits and his general attitude. Potter was looking like death warmed up. It was probably alcohol withdrawal symptoms. The conditions were really to blame and they were taking their toll on everyone. Hough needed us to help him with his work. That was all. Villa Vista needed us to see that the timber was shipped out. No one really gave a damn whether we lived or died. I had a notion of us running, taking the truck and heading south. How far would we get? I doubted it would be very far. We were, effectively, trapped.

We sat in a silent uncertain group around the fire. Potter appeared out of the dark. He was as white as a sheet and sweat plastered his hair to his skull. His hands twitched and shook. He swallowed a couple of aspirin and then washed them down with black coffee. Without a word he went to bed. As I had suspected, his withdrawal symptoms had started.

The next morning I had slept late and when I rose Carr was already up and preparing the porridge. He began grinning cheerfully as I approached.

"I wonder what type of exciting day we're going to have in the tropics today?" he asked, stirring the pot.

Teacher joined us and poured coffee into the mugs. "It's getting worse. Listen to the drums," he murmured.

I became aware of the far-off throb. Funnily enough, only when someone mentioned them, did you listen and hear them. At times they seemed frighteningly close; at other times further away.

"What do you think they are saying?" I asked, knowing only too well that no white man understood them.

Carr gave an evil grin. "Had a beautiful roast – sorry you could not make it." He roared with laughter. "Gave us all stomach cramps and the shits." He laughed so much that tears rolled down his face and he had to sit down to stop himself falling.

Pole joined us smiling sadly. All the noise had woken Roux and he came to the entrance of the tent. He was pale and sweaty. Teacher handed him a mug of coffee. Roux stood awkwardly, holding the mug with two hands.

He took a few sips. "Sorry about yesterday, but I don't seem to be able to help myself. But I think I will be all right now," he stated uncertainly and look down at his feet.

Potter had not appeared. I went across to the truck and, standing on the running board, peered in. He was slumped in the corner asleep, his Bible open on his lap. I left him.

"Let's tidy up, Roux. You go have a shower and a shave and you will feel better," said Pole kindly. "Mac, get the breakfast things organised. Carr, you help." He hesitated for a moment. "I think Muller will arrive today."

He was correct about that. An hour later the tug could be heard arriving and a short while later Muller came walking up through the village. Pole lined us up and called us to attention.

"Beautiful day, is it not? I am sorry about Maritz but, from what I hear from Hough, he had a screw loose!" said Muller pushing his hat to the back of his head. "Fall out," he commanded. "And how about a mug of coffee?"

Carr obliged.

"Where's Potter?" asked Muller looking around.

"Not well, sir," said Pole, "but he will be okay."

Muller lit a cigarette and took a sip of his coffee, wearing a slight frown on his face. "You guys have done a good job up to now. Hough is pleased with your conduct. Teacher produced the first photo ever taken of the Teng. Mac has identified the route used to bring weapons into the area. The suspect is the chap de Haas and I believe that you all know him. You also saved old man Borg from certain death." He shrugged his narrow shoulders. The police Jeep started and came across towards the camp.

"I am going to accompany you and the police to pick up de Haas. He needs to be questioned," said Muller rising from his seat.

Hough stepped from the Jeep, and saluted Muller. Thomas was behind the wheel.

"You guys ready?" asked Hough with a smile.

We raced around, collecting our equipment. Pole helped Potter from the cab. He could barely walk and he helped him onto a stretcher in the tent. Potter was in no fit state to accompany us.

Roux was white and shaky. Up to now he had behaved reasonably well. Pole took up the position behind the machine-gun. Muller sat in the passenger seat and Carr drove.

We skidded past the spot where we had cut the tree in half and where we'd found Maritz's head. We reached the main road at about two. Hough stopped and came across to us.

"When we get close, we stop and approach on foot. If de Haas is not there, we'll withdraw and observe. When he returns, we pounce."

To me, it all sounded a little too easy.

The Jeep and the truck went on along the main road and turned off at the Sweet Estate sign. Halfway up the driveway the vehicles pulled off the road, amongst the rows of coffee trees, and we were soon hidden from view.

"Thomas and I will go in front," said Hough. "Then you all follow at a short distance."

As far as I could remember we were a long way from the estate house. We plodded along between the trees. There were signs that work had recently been done on the trees in the form of pruning the higher branches. In places weeds and grass had been slashed with a mechanical slasher. It had to be a near impossible job to keep the inner rows clear as everything grew very fast with the heat and the rain. After a long walk Hough indicated that we should stop. We all sat under the trees to wait. Hough and Thomas slipped away towards the house.

Time drifted slowly by and no one spoke. What was going on? My stomach rumbled loudly. It was now very close to five o'clock and I had left the tinned food on the truck. A dog barked in the distance and far away drums beat. Then Hough appeared sweating like a pig, his khaki shirt stuck to his body. Thomas followed with a young, slim black woman slung over his shoulder. She was unconscious.

"What is this?" asked Muller indicating the woman.

"She could be the answer to all the questions. She is a witch. We have recently questioned her brother," said Hough smiling through his tatty moustache. "We must hurry to the station so that I can question her properly." We all fell in behind Hough and Thomas and tramped back to the vehicles.

It was dark when we arrived at the station and we settled down to eat. No sooner had we started eating than the sound of Hough's interrogation began. At first there was the slap of the sjambok, then the high-pitched blood-curdling scream, followed by another slap of the vicious hippo-hide whip. It went on and on.

Teacher stopped eating and just sat there, staring blindly into the darkness. But the rest of us continued to eat as if nothing was taking place. Our collective response was a far cry from the time Hough had beaten the young black man to death a few months earlier.

"They are going to kill her," said Teacher in a pained voice.

"As long as she talks first, I could not care less!" said Carr helping himself to more beans.

"I agree with you!" said Roux.

Those were the first words he had uttered all day. I said nothing, but felt very little for the unfortunate woman, as I finished my meal.

Muller sat there smoking but made no comment. Eventually he leant forward. "Tomorrow I will be returning to Villa Vista. You guys will be okay. Just remember to back each other up at all times. Do not go alone. Always go in twos. Hopefully we will hear soon what the woman has to say. Maybe she can shed a little light on things. Hough says she is a witchdoctor working for de Haas. We should hear soon enough," said Muller helping himself to more coffee. We could still hear the smack followed by faint cries coming from the station.

"How did Hough know the woman was a witch?" asked Teacher. No one answered. No one knew. No one cared. Teacher got up and walked up and down. Eventually he came to a stop in front of Muller.

"Sir, are you going to let Hough kill that woman?" asked Teacher pleadingly.

Muller drew on his cigarette, making the end glow, and he took a while before he answered Teacher's question. "If Hough is right and the woman supplies information that will save our lives or other people's lives, then I say that is a good exchange. One person suffers and dies so that many can live."

Teacher turned away slowly and walked away towards the tent, a slightly built stooped little man. He was a man with a lot of feeling and far too intelligent and sensitive to be in this brutal situation. I think I agreed with Muller, although I did not like the idea of torturing or killing a suspect witch. I realised that it very was necessary for us to survive. Then, on the other hand, I could understand Hough's and Thomas's points of view. They could not let a crippled, broken person go free, back into the community where he or she could possibly bring criminal charges against them. It was just the simple principle, dead people tell no tales.

At midnight the police station was quiet and we all headed for bed. That night I lay for a long time, but sleep would not come. Mosquitoes buzzed around, attempting to find their way into my mosquito net. I probably knew more than most of our unit about African witchdoctors. The one called Gogo of the Congo Basin was probably not much different from the witch at Slang Spruit. Gogo would be more brutal because of her isolation and lack of the chance of being arrested for her brutal deeds. My old friend Majola had a typical African approach. He believed in the white man's God and once claimed to be a member of the 'Zion', a Christian religion popular amongst the Zulus in my home area. On the other hand if things went wrong, he would go to the witchdoctor. Once he had a headache for days and claimed that one of his enemies was trying to kill him. He had rushed off to the witchdoctor, Zondi, and had returned with a white powder in a twist of brown paper that he had been told to drink every morning. I swear it was ground up aspirin! He was also to wear a red scarf wrapped tightly round his head. The scarf had to be red, and it was bought in the witchdoctor's brother's shop. After two days Majola said the bad spirit had left, so had his headache and that the witchdoctor was a great man. I had to agree that the medicine had worked. Later I was told that the visit to the witchdoctor had cost thirty rand. No wonder Zondi owned two taxis and a car!

Zondi was a regarded as a valuable asset to the community. I had met him once and he had impressed me. He was a very alert and intelligent type of character. Witches in Africa were very secretive.

They employed apprentice witches to do a lot of their dirty work. They also had a vast knowledge of herbs, roots, the bark of trees and tree sap and other things, like snake poison and animal fats, they would even use certain human body parts for some of their cures.

The witchdoctors were known to solve all sorts of local problems, ranging from a woman being unfaithful to her husband, to head colds and impotency. One of the local white farmers had employed Zondi to prevent a stock theft. The thefts occurred once a month when one of the farmer's cows was slaughtered in the field. The meat was obviously moved by van. For a large fee Zondi was called in. He placed his magic potion known as "muti" around the field in which the cows grazed. The stock theft stopped.

A number of months later I had been chatting to a Zulu woman who helped out round the house. Somehow our conversation had got round to witchdoctor Zondi.

"Oh," she said, "I come from the same area as he does, near Escort." Escort was a short distance from Pietermaritzburg. "His family is very wealthy," she smiled happily. "They own a number of butcher shops."

I left it at that, not wanting to go any further with the conversation.

Gogo was probably in the same category, probably very clever and effective, having been brought up on all the customs and fears of the tribes she served. Death and manipulation meant nothing to her. I wondered why de Bruin's had not made contact with her? It could not have been all that difficult.

Muller left the following morning and promised to send more ammunition and rations. I had spoken to him and asked him if there was any way he could find out why Gran and Mia had not written. He had said that he would try and he took their addresses and phone numbers. I kept getting a sneaky feeling that all was not well on Hill Farm.

All that morning we watched the police station. Thomas was seen collecting a bucket of water from the ablution block. Later, Hough came and stood outside smoking. The second black gendarme, Ray appeared and then returned inside. Was the woman dead? Were they still torturing her?

In the end I took my fishing-pole and went to the harbour. There were six new crocodiles on the sandbank. The two old regulars were there with jaws agape. I baited up and dropped my line in. Far away the drums pounded. I sat there basking in the heat, with my rifle and webbing close at hand.

Uncertain thoughts were still drifting through my head. Had Hough and Thomas really known that the woman was a witch? They had appeared to know the whole family. How could they be so sure that she was involved with the Teng's demands and the violence, or did they not care. Where they just taking a gamble? Why would she be working for de Haas? She could not be a very good witch if she had to work for a white man. I knew witches were cunning. Perhaps the head witch, Gogo had placed her there to keep an eye on de Haas. It all became far too complicated.

A wagtail settled nearby and patrolled the harbour wall, pecking here and there. I sat and dozed and my mind wandered. What was to become of us? I might never see Mia again or I might never get home or get around to all the things that I had planned. Then my thoughts drifted to the little nun who had made an unbelievable impression on me. I wondered if she and the other nuns were safe? I reassured myself that they had been warned and they were in a big village with hundreds of men who would protect them if the Teng or their brothers decided to attack them. Or would they? My mind rambled on, thought after thought.

Miriam came sauntering down the harbour wall. "Hello, Mac," she said positioning her rear on a pile of lumber. "Maritz is gone. Annie is gone. Who's next?"

I found it a strangely sinister question.

"You hear the drums?" she asked.

I nodded, watching my fishing line.

"Business is bad. Why you and the other men not come to the shop for cold beer?"

I looked up at the serious-faced woman. "Everyone has stopped drinking. Potter is sick since he gave up. Carr, he no longer drinks since Maritz poisoned him. Pole, Roux, Teacher and I don't drink much, nor do we gamble," I added. The conversation died and we sat in silence for a while.

"Until you kill Gogo the witch, the Teng will not stop," she said and sighed as she rose from her seat. "But it is difficult, Gogo cannot die. Her magic is too strong." She glanced around and whispered. "There might be a white man paying her. Maybe the white man is her lover like Maritzie and Annie. Gogo loves things that are of great value; hippo teeth, stolen diamonds and money. She would know all about those things." She looked around, nervously licking her thick lips. She was about to move away. "Even to look upon her can make one dead," she warned. "You try get other chaps to come to shop, I will give you a free beer."

I nodded and grinned. She would not stop trying and she'd probably short-change one of the other customers to cover the cost of my free beer.

I packed up my gear and ambled back to camp empty handed. Everyone was relaxing. I took my towel and soap and headed for the shower. It was a beautifully warm, still evening, and almost airless. Smoke from the cooking fires hung in the still air above the village. I had that horrible sinking feeling in my gut, a sinister fear that seemed to grow with time and envelop the village and camp.

As I showered I wondered what had happened to the suspected witch? Had she talked? What had she said?

Chapter 7

"They don't tell us on purpose," said Teacher. "Look at this paper. It's three weeks old. They say there are going to be democratic elections in the Congo. They don't say when. Tshombe is all-powerful. Who do you think is going to look after him? The United States or the Russians? There's more to all this than meets the eye. It's a lot of bull!"

We sat around our cooking fire, listening to Teacher ranting.

"We don't even get told what's happening at Villa Vista. We're just fed just enough to keep us hanging on. You watch Muller or Ross. They only tell us so much. Hough is exactly the same, just so much."

He was right of course. Our little world at the railhead was like a dead end. Carr's portable radio did not have a long enough aerial to receive anything we could understand. There was just an African station that played the local music, which had a very good beat, but we had all just given up listening.

Hough had a radio that received the outside world's news, but he never ever invited us to listen. Since our arrival, we had been invited to the police station for the so-called welcome party, but we had never been invited to visit the police station again. Hough only ever came across to us with instructions or to pay a visit with a bottle of his favourite wine.

The tug hooted in the distance and there was the sound of the crane starting up at the harbour.

"Is everything in order?" asked Pole, glancing around the camp.

Since Maritz's departure we had got into a regular routine. Everyone had a job and did it. The camp remained in a reasonable state of tidiness. The atmosphere was far more relaxed than when Maritz was with us. Teacher had come out of himself and was everyone's friend. Potter had recovered from his withdrawal symptoms and was a different person, clear-eyed and with a better complexion. He now made it a habit to read us a scripture every Sunday. No one complained, but Roux was a big problem. Teacher called it depression, but we never knew what he was going to be like.

Carr still cracked his type of joke and we laughed, mainly at his response to his own humour. I was far happier with the company now, even though I had still not received a letter from home. It really worried me deeply. Everyone else got mail, except for Potter, who had only received one letter since coming here. I imagined all sorts of things, but why had Mia not written. Surely, with a few enquiries she could establish my address or ask Gran for my address. Her dad knew Mr Thompson, the estate agent. Surely he could get the address from Mr van Rensburg. They were all members of the MOTHS. I had a bad feeling that there was serious problem back home but there was no way to make contact.

That morning Sergeant Major Ross came striding up from the village, a bag over his shoulder. Pole called us into line and then to attention.

Ross grinned at us, "You ladies been behaving?" he asked, dropping the bag on the table. "Post," he said. Then he did a quick inspection of the camp, and finished by signing the log book. He moved out in front of us. "Christmas is just around the corner," he said, walking up and down. "In about five days, I would say." He was quiet for a while. He just stood there, a powerful red-faced, middle-aged man. Then he appeared unsure of what to say, which was not like him at all.

"The Teng don't know anything about Christmas. They don't particularly care, but we care. On the tug boat is a box of goodies I brought for you, and I can only wish you all the best." He smiled, pleased with himself, his red face beaming. He came forward and shook hands with each of us. "Lieutenant Muller asked me to convey to you all the best and hopefully we will have a quiet time over the festive season. Fall out, and I would like a cup of coffee." He went over to the fire and sat on a log.

I noticed Hough appear in the distance. He was walking quickly. At the edge of the camp he saluted Ross. He looked tired and flustered. "We have uncovered a serious problem," he said hurriedly, "I wish to send the men to St Patrick's Mission straight away." He waved his arm towards the station. "I have discovered a plot to massacre the nuns and destroy St Patrick's Mission station. It is very serious. The attack will start in only a day or so."

I got that sinking feeling in my gut. Would this blind, senseless, brutality never end? Could we, as a unit, survive more of this madness? Obviously the young witch had eventually talked. I wondered what was left of her after the three days of torture. Was she dead? I pushed the thought from my mind. What had happened to her actually did not matter. The young nun's serene face drifted before me. Surely the Mongu Teng would not attack a mission station. A tremor of fear ran down my spine as I reminded myself that anything could happen in this insane country.

Ross drained his coffee mug and looked up at Pole. "Okay, Pole, get the men sorted, but first Potter, go and get the box from the tug."

We all scuttled around collecting food and our equipment. Potter left in a cloud of dust for the harbour. We were ready to move out and stood around like old veterans who had done this so often. Thomas appeared with his submachine-gun slung over his shoulder, a bandoleer of ammunition pouches and a bedroll under his arm. Potter reappeared out of the village hooting furiously, causing chickens and dogs to scatter. We offloaded the cardboard box and Teacher peeped inside. Hough and Ross were standing to one side and were deep in conversation.

Soon we were all aboard. Hough came around to the back of the truck. "The information I have is that in the next few days the Mongu Teng will be attacking the Mission. God only knows what they hope to achieve by killing a few nuns. Furthermore, we know de Haas is the one supplying them with guns. He is also paying the witchdoctor Gogo. He has been the one who has caused this whole

165

problem. He may be involved in this attack, so do be very careful." The little policeman stood there perspiring profusely and looking up at us with his eyes screwed up, half closed against the light. "If you come across de Haas you have my permission to arrest him." He wiped the sweat from his brow. "You will probably get a bonus from de Bruins if you do." Then, addressing Pole and Thomas he continued. "The mission has a bus. The nuns will not be very willing to co-operate. You will have to force them onto the bus. You must escort them to St Martin's Mission at Djolu. I know it is a long hard road but it's for the best." He looked up at Thomas. "You know the mission at Djolu?" Thomas nodded. "Right away you go, at speed."

Potter climbed into the cab, slamming the door and revving the engine. Leaving now, at eleven, I knew it was going to be a long, hot and hard trek. St Patrick's was a long way away. Normally we would leave in the early hours of the morning. The truck would travel along at a speed ranging between ten and thirty kilometres an hour. On really good sections of road we speeded up to forty kilometres an hour. Then there was always the possibility of getting bogged down. I sighed and settled in my corner and prepared myself mentally for what was to come.

It was five days to Christmas. Teacher had peeped into the box brought by Ross and reported seeing tinned ham and turkey, potatoes and carrots, Christmas pudding and various bottles. It was funny how little things like the contents of that box meant so much to us all. Teacher was handing out the post. Roux was smiling. His wife had sent him a Christmas card, a new photo and a six-page letter. He carefully placed the photo in his breast pocket.

Teacher finished handing out the mail and looked up at me. "Sorry Mac there's nothing for you."

I remained silent and looked away, gazing outwards, blinking back my tears. I felt that Gran and Mia had deserted me, or that Mia had found a new boyfriend. Thoughts were jumbled inside my head. Surely she would have written to say something or even goodbye. But why had Gran not written? It was now a long time since I had received a letter from her too. Things must be seriously wrong back home. I looked back at the men engrossed in their mail. Teacher had received Christmas cards and letters. Carr's letter was at least twenty pages long. I wondered how anyone could write such a long letter. Pole had received hand-drawn cards from his children. Everyone seemed happy.

We roared along the narrow road, bouncing and skidding through muddy patches. On reaching the junction we turned north towards St Patrick's. We were making good time when the thunderstorm struck. Rain pelted down and lightning forked across the blue-black sky. The truck slowed almost to walking pace. Carr had braced himself in a corner and set about making us lunch – corned-beef and onion sandwiches. He claimed the onions would keep the mosquitoes away. He always had some funny ideas.

The rain stopped and we ploughed on. We passed Crossways School at about four, and then the road narrowed. The jungle scraped the sides of the truck as we forced our way through. We had now been on the road for five exhausting hours when Pole called a halt at the timber-built bridge.

We all dropped painfully to the ground. I hated to know what Potter felt like after wrestling with the steering wheel. Funnily enough I had never heard him complain. We threw a few dry sticks together and made a fire to boil water for coffee. The dark river rushed by, gurgling softly. The ferns and jungle grew right up to the water's edge and swayed back and forth.

Roughly an hour remained for us before we would reach St Patrick's Mission. The worst was behind us. We would spend the night at St Patrick's and then move on the next day. I stood stretching my tired muscles and looking at the dark river. There was a sudden sense of excitement as I thought of the beautiful little nun.

Then Teacher trespassed on my train of thought. "If we were to pot the ferns they would be worth a fortune in the outside world," he said, while examining the ferns that grew in a wet mossy hollow in the bank. We stood in a group listening to Teacher's impossible dream of quick cash.

I left the men and wandered across the bridge. They were massive logs that the constructors had dragged into position and strapped together with steel girders. There were no railings, nothing to prevent a truck or car or person falling into the swiftly flowing water. I peered into the deep dark water, wondering if there were fish. The river was one of the millions of tributaries to the Congo river. According to the map it passed a few kilometres behind Crossways School then wound this way and that and seemed to take a very long route to the main river.

The bank opposite was steep and muddy. I was surprised to see wheel tracks of a vehicle that had ploughed up and down the bank a number of times. I stood drinking my coffee and looking at the tyre skid marks. I climbed up to the top of the bank and looked back at our truck and the small knot of men below me, who were gathered around the fire. I was just about to turn back, when a thought struck me. Why had there been so many vehicles on the road? Judging by the tyre skid marks, at least eight vehicles had passed. The road levelled out at the top of the bank. I walked along examining the tracks. The tyre patterns were all the same. At least the ones I could see in the mud were. In many places the mud had been really churned up. In every case that I could see, the tyre pattern was identical and I decided that the same vehicle had been going back and forth. I was also sure it had been a large truck. Then it hit me. It was de Haas's Mercedes truck! I stood there staring at the tracks. What was he doing going back and forth? Surely he could not be directly involved? But then why not! He was the cause of the uprising. Was he transporting Mongu Teng to the mission? A sudden cold fear gripped me. I knew I was right. He had supplied the Teng with weapons. Why would he not transport them closer to the mission? Possibly we were going to be too late to save the nuns. The attack might have already started. I shouted for Pole to come and have a look.

He lumbered across the bridge, and clambered up the slippery road and joined me. "What's up Mac?" he asked.

I pointed out the tyre marks to him and told him of my thoughts. Pole squatted down and examined the tracks carefully.

Shaking his big head he looked up at me. "Mac you're right. They are the same pattern. We had better get a move on."

There was a sudden sense of urgency about the big man. We returned across the bridge with Pole shouting orders, telling the others about the tracks.

Moments later we were moving again, ploughing through the mud onto the bridge and up the slippery bank towards St Patrick's Mission. I could not bear the thought of the pretty young nun or any of the others being attacked by the marauding Mongu Teng. I knew how brutal they could be and their ways of killing their enemies. I hung onto the uprights, my legs braced to take the jarring and sliding. It was then that I felt for the first time a calm calculating sense. It was as if a great weight had been lifted from my shoulders. The enemy had tried to kill me but I had survived. I would not be dying here. I had become seasoned, hard-hearted and I searched for a word. I was dangerous!

Roux brought me back to earth, as he crouched next to me. "You know they are watching us," said Roux.

I looked into that sad strained face and shook my head. I had felt nothing. I was sure I would sense that similar presence I had felt at the aviary. I doubt if I would ever forget that feeling.

The road improved and Potter speeded up. The country started to change. The trees were not so tall. We passed through a few battered villages. They were all deserted which was a sure sign of trouble. Suddenly St Patrick's village was before us. It was ablaze with many of the thatched roofs on fire and a white cloud of smoke hanging in the still air. Potter slowed down and stopped. Pole climbed out of the cab and climbed into the back, taking over the Browning. We were all silent, peering at the devastation through the slats.

The truck lurched forward. What lay ahead? I did not know, but there was an icy dread in the pit of my stomach. Smoke from the burning huts hid the ridge where St Patrick's was situated. This, I knew, would hide our approach. The truck rumbled on past the farmland where previously men had ploughed with oxen, and on into the main street of the village, where the children had danced and waved to us before. The road led on to the mission.

Further on we came across numerous blood-red-splattered corpses that were strewn about, their intestines shining red and white in the late afternoon sunshine. Crows had already started feasting, flying up noisily as we approached, only to return to their grisly meal as soon as we passed by. A couple of dogs fought over a piece of meat and only separated when Potter nearly ran them over.

"Go, go!" shouted Pole. Potter put his foot down, bouncing over fresh corpses that could not be avoided. The Teng had been here all right. They had turned a peaceful village into a blazing inferno. It was utter carnage. Were we too late? The attack Hough had believed would only start in a few days had already started. I knew without any doubt that de Haas was involved. Why, what had he to gain?

We hit the steep section of road leading up to St Patrick's. It would have been an ideal spot for an ambush with low bushes right up to the road. Potter clashed the gears, and the wheels spun, making the truck buck forward.

The open steel entrance gate appeared out of the hanging smoke. When the smoke cleared the mission buildings were before us and they were mostly on fire. A number of the burning roofs had already completely collapsed. Flames licked out of the holes in the walls like long devil tongues capable of destroying anything.

Pole stood braced behind the machine-gun. His bush hat was pulled down low over his forehead. "We're going to stop. I will give you covering fire. Go down the left-hand side of the buildings and see if any nuns have survived!" Pole shouted, and then he banged on the roof of the cab. "Go left, go left!" he barked at Potter, who immediately responded by throwing the truck into a violent turn.

Without warning Pole started to fire. Three tattooed Teng warriors went spinning to the ground. It was the first real contact we had had with the true Teng. Their tall, lean, tattooed bodies gave a leafy mystical connection between jungle and man. The warriors had yellow paint, war paint, daubed on their bodies. Their brother tribe, the Mongu, were easily identified, for they wore European clothing but had also daubed themselves with yellow war paint.

There was a lot of movement in the smoke before us. A group of screaming men broke out from the smoke and ran blindly towards us. I saw one naked warrior smash a whit-clad patient over the head with a club. There were Teng, Mongu and patients all intermingled.

Pole fired and they went down in a bloody thrashing heap of bodies. There was no time to select targets.

"Go, go. Thomas you stay here!" Pole indicated his side. "Thomas watch our backs!" Pole's arms waved frantically, "You guys go, go left, go!" he shouted. Then he started to fire again, raking the area before us.

In a moment I jumped from the tailgate, followed closely by Roux, Carr and Teacher. It was only about fifty metres from the truck to the start of the buildings which would be where the offices were. The thatched roof was on fire. My mind was focused on the serene young nun as I raced ahead, my weapon held low and bayonet fixed. I jumped over a couple of corpses and flew onto the veranda. The machine-gun was firing in the background. I came to a stop next to a pillar and peered through the smoke.

The rest of the men joined me. Roux fired first, knocking over two patients but it could not be helped, for they had removed their pyjamas. If they had kept their clothes on it would have been a lot easier to identify them. The office to my left was on fire and I could see flames flickering through the window. The burning thatch above our heads would soon collapse inwards.

"Right, let's go," I said. Funnily enough, the men listened and we moved on forward but more cautiously, from pillar to pillar and doorway to doorway. We kept firing as we went. There was little to distinguish between the Mongu Teng and the patients. Often they were just a fast-moving shadow in the thick smoke.

I was starting to have horrible doubts. Were we too late to save the nuns? The mission had been overrun. What had happened to the nuns? Had they been butchered? If so, where were their bodies? I knew that all we could do was comply with orders and check the buildings. For a moment I had that hopeless feeling in the pit of my stomach and the little nun danced before my eyes. Then she was gone.

A Teng warrior armed with a spear burst out of the smoke directly in front of me. This brought me back to the present with a nasty shock. There was no time to think. I shot him through the chest. We plunged on through the pungent smoke, sweating, swearing and shouting encouragement to one another. More patients went down and several tattooed and painted Teng died as well. There was no one in the buildings we had passed. The smoke cleared for a moment and the kitchen was before us. It was the only building with a corrugated iron roof, and was the only building not on fire. We reached the corner in a mad rush.

Teacher peered through the window. "Look at the swine!" he screamed. Then, without hesitating, he crouched low below the window frames and rushed along towards the door, groping in his ammunition pouch for a grenade.

I peered through the grubby glass. Eight or nine Teng and Mongu armed with rifles were hammering on what looked like a freezer room door. I crouched and followed Teacher, who had stopped at the open door to prime the grenade. He looked at me for a moment and lobbed the grenade through the open door at the group of warriors. Then we took cover against the wall. Roux and Carr had joined us and were facing away from the kitchen and firing at any movement in the smoke. People were shouting and screaming around us. In the background the Browning was firing in short aggressive bursts. Inside the kitchen the grenade exploded with a violent shattering crunch blowing the windows out and covering us all in broken glass. Two seconds later we charged into the kitchen, sliding on the fresh blood and guts. The aluminium-topped tables and the tiled floor and walls were a blood-splattered mess. A wounded warrior raised his head. I shot him between his eyes and the back of his head blew out in a pink mist cloud. Teacher shot a second wounded warrior. We reached the door together.

"Open the bloody door!" screamed Teacher hammering with his rifle butt. I joined in shouting for them to come out. Hopefully the nuns were in the freezer room.

I looked back. Carr and Roux had positioned themselves at the door and were firing outward. On the tiled floor one blood-covered warrior suddenly came alive and lunged at Teacher. I shot him before he could cause any damage. Teacher had found what looked like an air vent, and he began shouting for the occupants to open up. They heard him at last and the door opened a crack. Then it opened fully, letting out a blast of cold air.

"Come, hurry!" I shouted, "We have a truck waiting!" The nuns started to file out. The women looked very frail and were shivering with cold and fear. Then I saw her, the young nun. I was relieved she was okay! Our eyes met for a brief second and she smiled. Not a big joyful smile, just a sad little twitch of the mouth, in a sort of recognition.

Teacher and I herded the thirty women across the kitchen to the door. Thomas burst out of the smoke a white-hot submachine-gun in his big hands. He turned and shot down two painted warriors that were following him. Then he hit a patient by mistake.

"We must hurry!" he shouted above the noise. "There are more Teng coming over the wall!"

Someone tugged at my sleeve. Surprised I looked down into a thin, wrinkled pixy face of a frail little old nun. "Our duty is to look after the injured. The people you have injured," she croaked.

I looked at her in complete amazement.

"God's work must be done!" she hissed, nodding her head vigorously and rolling her eyes. One of the other nuns came and guided her gently away from me.

Teacher took charge. "Carr, you look after the left side. Thomas, go in front. Roux, on the right! Mac and I will move between you. Forward!" he cried.

We trooped out into the billowing smoke, causing us to have only partial vision. Shadows flitted past, invisible and ghost-like in the swirling smoke. The Browning hammered away and all around us were horrible screams and shouts from the invisible enemy. Mongu Teng and the patients all got it. The younger nuns had taken charge of the elderly, and were hurrying them along. The old pixy nun tried to break away. She was wailing loudly about Satan. I wondered if she was mentally all right. One of the larger women latched on to her wrist and began dragging her along.

Bullets were whining around our heads. One of the nuns collapsed in a heap, the side of her head missing. We left her where she fell. Another nun received an arrow in the shoulder. We moved as quickly as possible down by the side of the church. Smoke and flames were everywhere. Two patients, who were lucky enough not to be shot by accident, sprinted by, one with an arrow protruding from his back. Another nun fell, then another.

The smoke cleared a little. The Browning could be heard firing close by. The truck appeared out of the smoke, parked slightly away from the church. Potter obviously saw us and came forward. The ugly muzzle of the machine-gun was poking out from under the canvas canopy.

Rushing out into the open, Carr jumped onto the tow-hitch, kicking the latches that secured the tailgate open. It opened with a crash. A number of the women clambered on to the deck. They turned round to help their comrades aboard. We were now being fired on from all sides. Bullets whipped around us. The little old pixy nun suddenly broke away with a startled yelp. She was surprisingly fast. Carr was closest and saw what had happened, and he was after her. He expertly rugby tackled her and slung her across his shoulder. He raced back and threw her bodily into the back of the truck. Another two nuns had gone down. I saw another with an arrow wound being dragged aboard.

Teacher, who was crouched to my right, suddenly jerked and rose to his full height and then staggered a few steps. Sensing danger I swung round without aiming and fired. A Teng warrior had risen from a heap of dead and was trying to place another arrow in his bow. As my bullets hit him he went down in a shower of blood and bone.

I turned back to Teacher. He was down on his haunches. Then he toppled slowly over. With horror I saw a short shaft of an arrow sticking out of his neck. He lay there breathing heavily. I crouched down next to the little man.

"Mac I have had it. In my kit is a letter to my wife. Post it for me." His head lolled to one side. "Mac, are you there?" I held his hand, as sadness and hopelessness intermingled washed over me and I knew there was nothing that I could do.

"Yes," I whispered, oblivious to what was going on around me. There was a movement next to me and the young nun came and crouched down next to us.

"The arrows are poisonous. There is no antidote," she said in a matter of fact way.

"Mac," whispered Teacher smiling. "I jammed Maritz's rifle, please don't leave me here."

The nun broke the spell. She half rose, pulling Teacher by the webbing. "Help me. We must hurry," she gasped trying to move Teacher.

The truck was loaded and waiting for us. Carr was shouting instructions. I hoisted Teacher's limp body over the tailgate. He was very light. Hands removed him from my grasp, and the young nun was hauled aboard by her arms. I vaulted onto the tow-hitch, and then propelled myself over the tailgate of the moving truck. I was a little crazy at that moment. I landed amongst the legs of the women.

Hurriedly I untangled myself and slapped a full magazine onto my rifle. The truck was moving and picking up speed. I was in a trance. Aim fire, aim fire! I don't think I had ever fired with such vengeance and hate. I was so angry, I did not miss. Teacher was either dead or very close.

The mission was out of sight as the truck raced through the gates. I clambered over the bodies spread out on the bouncing, heaving deck. Dead bodies lay bleak and uncovered. One of the women was thrashing around screaming in pain. Another with a bullet wound in the neck was spraying blood from a severed artery all over the place. When I found Teacher, the young nun was sitting on the floor with his head in her lap.

"He is dead," she whispered. I thought I saw tears in her eyes. I felt like crying too at the complete hopelessness of our situation. My eyes filled with tears and I stumbled away and took up my position next to Pole. Mentally I struggled to take it all in. Teacher was gone, dead. It was a similar feeling to what I had felt when Majola had died leaving a huge gap in my life. Suddenly I felt a terrific sense of loss and guilt. I realised that I could not remember when last I had thought of my old Zulu friend.

Potter was going far too fast down the winding road. The village below was covered in a blanket of smoke and here and there the bright glow of flames showed. Pole thumped on the roof of the cab, and then shouted to Potter to slow down. His actions probably saved our lives. As we rounded the last bend, a truck was in our path. I recognised that grey Mercedes. Potter swerved up the bank at the side of the road and the momentum swung us back onto the road. People were thrown recklessly about in the rear. A woman screamed horribly. I hung on. There behind the steering wheel of the Mercedes was de Haas. Our eyes met for a fleeting second. The back of the truck was bristling with armed Teng and Mongu warriors. Then we had passed them, bouncing and swerving as we went.

"Did you see that?" I shouted to Pole who just nodded his head, his face grim and eyes frightened.

Potter slowed down even more. The near miss had obviously shaken him, as he braked and tried to avoid running over the corpses that had been left scattered down the road. A woman was moaning in agony behind us. Others were sobbing, while another was praying loudly. We travelled on, back the way we had come and the jungle closed in around us.

The truck seemed to be having trouble. It would suddenly loose power and then surge forward. Potter stopped and jumped down. Opening the bonnet he peered inside the engine compartment.

"Pole, the engine is shot up. It's a miracle we have got this far!" shouted Potter. "I think we must keep going for as long as possible and put as much distance between us and the mission."

Pole agreed. There seemed to be a lot of miracles happening around us lately. With a cloud of dense blue oil-smelling smoke coming from the engine we carried on.

I looked back under the canvas roof. The young nun was still sitting with Teacher's head in her lap. Her eyes were shut and she radiated a tranquil peace. We had just fought for our lives, and rescued these women from certain death. There were dead and dying all around her but she had kept her composure. The old pixy nun kept on talking about doing God's work, and then started praying loudly. The bridge came up and we skidded down the bank, jerking and swaying up the opposite side. About a kilometre from Crossways School the truck jerked and shuddered to a halt. It revived for a moment, surged forward and then spluttered to a final stop.

Pole clambered down and joined Potter, who threw open the bonnet and peered in. Clouds of oily steam billowed out.

"It's stuffed. It's a miracle we got this far!" grunted Potter who wiped his hands on his pants.

Pole looked gloomy. "How far are we from that school?" he asked.

Potter scratched his head. "I would say a kilometre."

Pole looked around undecided. "If we stay here we will be dead. That is if they follow us. We need a place to hold out until help can arrive," said Pole nervously.

It made sense to me. The jungle encroached on the road and if the Teng were following or were around we did not stand a chance. Then it struck me. Pole and I had recognised de Haas and I was positive that he had recognised me, for our eyes had met. Then the question that really frightened me was: would he send the Teng and Mongu warriors after us so as to try and protect his identity?

"Right," said Pole rather loudly. "Carr, you and Roux dig a grave big enough for all the dead."

Carr dropped from the tailgate, taking up a spade and a pick. Roux followed and the two started to dig at the edge of the road. The soil was dark and rich with humus.

"Mac you get on top of the canopy and keep a good look out."

I did as I was told. Around us the jungle creatures were busy settling for the coming night. Birds flapped around and called to one another, unseen monkeys chattered deep in the undergrowth. Carr and Roux dug furiously and were already down to hip level. The dead were being removed from the back of the truck and placed in the shallow grave. Two black nuns had died from bullet wounds and another from an arrow. Another had bled to death from her throat wound. There were others but I had no idea what had killed them. Teacher's body was placed next to them in the grave.

The little old pixy nun was ranting on about Satan and God's work. I felt so bad about Teacher. I tried to look away and not watch. The nuns and the men crowded around the grave. Roux leant on his spade, tears pouring unashamedly down his face. One of the nuns appeared to be leading the burial service and was praying rather loudly.

Night was coming fast with long black shadows and birds' roosting calls. I crouched on top of the canopy. I could see that the praying women were beginning to agitate Pole. The whole burial ceremony was taking far too long. He wanted to get moving.

At last it was over and Carr and Roux hurriedly closed the grave. We then filled our ammunition pouches, stuck the thousand-footer flares through our belts, and packed what little food we had. One of the African nuns hoisted a jerry can of drinking water onto her head in true African fashion. Pole unclipped the Browning from its pylon, slung belts of ammunition around his shoulders and looked like an armoured knight of years gone by. I saw Thomas talking to Pole. Then Thomas dismantled his submachine-gun and tossed it, piece by piece, into the dense jungle. Clambering into the back he took possession of Teacher's FN and ammunition belts. He had used up his own supply of ammunition for his weapon.

As a group we marched off down the muddy road. Thunder rumbled across the sky. A large nun had taken the troublesome old one by the hand and was leading her along. It was a very strange procession. Without orders I had taken up position at the rear.

We were marching along making good time when without warning one of the nuns just in front of me staggered and then collapsed onto the side of the road. Only then did I realise that she had a bullet wound in her upper arm. Blood had seeped through the rough bandage and was running down her arm. Taking my water bottle I splashed water on her face. The young nun joined me. She crouched down and felt for the woman's pulse. "It can't be far now," she said in that beautiful accent.

I nodded and looked up to see the column was moving quickly away from us. I also knew that to be caught alone out here by the Teng meant certain death.

"You carry this," I said handing the young woman my rifle and haversack. It was heavy but not as heavy as the unconscious woman was.

I took a long look at the young nun. She was beautiful. Those eyes, steady, grey and slightly curved at the corners, looked almost cat-like. A wisp of sweat-soaked dark hair poked out from under her head gear. She did not complain but took my haversack, slinging it across her slender shoulders. Taking the rifle she hung it round her neck leaving both hands free. I hoisted the unconscious woman over my shoulder and set off after the swiftly vanishing group. As we walked along I watched the young woman trying to adjust her load. I had not been aware of her height until now. She was short and a lot thinner than my first impression; too thin I thought. I felt that I should at least try and start a conversation of sorts.

"What's your name?" I asked glancing around.

She looked at me, surprise on her face. "Sister Lily," was all she said rather abruptly.

"I am Mac Mackay." I said and we lapsed into silence, as we caught up with the rest of the group.

When we reached the school our relief was short-lived. The school had been burnt down and the corrugated iron roof had collapsed inwards. The school had consisted of two classrooms built of mud bricks. Much of the roofing still smouldered and everything was covered in grey-black ash.

It was roughly twenty-five metres from the road, through a rickety gate in a four-strand barbed wire fence, up a gravel path to the front door of the school. The burnt door still hung on its hinges. The dark holes in the wall represented the windows and gaped at us blindly. Darkness was almost upon us. The jungle behind us looked dark and forbidding.

Pole left us and went up the path and through the doorway. The nuns sat down exhausted in the muddy road. I placed the unconscious woman gently down next to them.

After a few minutes Pole returned, a troubled expression on his face. "We need cover," he said and pointed over his shoulder at the damaged building. "It's not good but it's the best we have at the moment. We need fire, food and to check all the dressings," ordered Pole. "I am sure help will come soon," he said, but I don't think he sounded at all sure of himself. "Ladies, the best place for you is under the partially collapsed roof where there is sufficient space." He looked around in the poor light. "Carr we need a few of those sheets of roofing to give us protection from the arrows, if we are attacked. The best would be in front of the doorway." He pointed over his shoulder. "Out at the back is a football field, easily two hundred metres to the jungle. I doubt they would attack us from there. If they come they will attack from over there." And he pointed east, directly in front of us. "It would only be a twenty- or thirty-metre charge across open ground." Pole stood there, big and nervous, shuffling his boots in the dust. "Right let's get going."

The women went up the path and into the building. Carr beckoned to Roux, who followed him into the ruined school. Two of the women were sent to collect firewood. Soon a fire was crackling inside the ruined building.

Potter, Thomas and I waited for Pole's instructions.

Thomas broke the silence. "The Teng, if they come, will come at first light. They do not fight in the dark." He held his head to one side. We all listened intently, as far away there was the thump of drums. Then I heard the drone of a distant vehicle engine approaching from the north, but as I listened the sound died. Then, moments later, it started again and faded into the distance. I knew, without doubt, that it was de Haas bringing the warriors closer to us and his intention was to silence us for ever. I looked at the others and I knew that they had also heard it. But no one said a single word.

The big nun appeared out of the gloom. "Grub's up," she called out. "It's not much but we will have to make the food last."

She was big all right. All of two metres tall, carrying quite a bit of excess weight, with a broad pleasant face. Her accent was similar, but not as strong as Lily's.

She stood for a moment and then continued. "I am Sister Susanna. We all would like to thank you for saving our lives."

Carr and Roux had appeared through the door carrying corrugated iron sheets and they stood and listened.

"I am in charge of the girls from St Patrick's, since Sister Pauline has gone a little batty." She stood there big and awkward. "Oh come on, come and eat."

She led the way into the charred and partly demolished building. A few of the roof beams still smouldered. We followed. Supper consisted of watered-down corned beef soup with biscuits. Pole handed Sister Susanna our first aid kit. She examined the contents by firelight.

"There's not much here," she eventually said. "But we will do our best."

After the meal we set about preparing our defences. We built a type of fortified wall with corrugated iron and soil that stuck out slightly in front of the building. This enabled us to see a fair distance down the road towards St Patrick's Mission and in the opposite direction until the road disappeared into the jungle, roughly two hundred metres away. The crossroad was out of our field of vision. We secured a few sheets of iron in a type of veranda, it sloped outwards to protect us from falling arrows and the elements.

We were all exhausted and had drawn lots as to who would stand guard. Unluckily I had drawn the two to four morning shift. We all settled down amongst the smouldering roof beams. Sleep would not come after all the excitement and horror of the day. I was surprised at Roux, for he was really behaving himself. Carr was out in the fortification. The Browning had been set up facing the jungle before us. We all carried flares and grenades and I was confident that we would be able to put up a good fight if attacked. I dozed off, waking with a start every now and then.

Suddenly I was shocked awake and my hand automatically grabbed my bayonet

"It's me," hissed Roux. "It's two, it's your watch."

Standing up groggily I crossed to the door. The moon was full and black wispy clouds appeared above the dark squeaking, pulsating jungle which was never quite still. A bushbaby (Lesser Galago) cried continually, sounding like a human baby, making my blood run cold. I stood behind the Browning machine-gun, watching the dark moon and the speckled black world before me. There was nothing but complete loneliness. We were isolated, hundreds of kilometres from anywhere or anyone. If we died it would not matter, and we would probably not even make the local newspaper back home. No one cared. It did not help my wishing to be back on the farm, or visiting Mia, or working until my back and arms ached. I let my mind wander over the day's occurrences. It was complete madness. We were here because of the greed of man. None of this need have happened. Maritz was dead. That I had killed him did not bother me any more. Teacher was dead. Was I next? Or Roux? Or Carr? What about Pole or Potter? We were not invincible, for we could all die like anyone else. Tears rolled down my cheeks. I doubted we would survive. How could they save us? The men from Villa Vista or Hough would not come in time. Hough did not have the backing to come immediately.

I was, all of a sudden, shocked back to the present. There was the rustle of clothes behind me. I spun round crouching low, my bayonet in my hand ready to kill.

"T'is I, Lily," the grey object whispered. "I brought you coffee for I could not sleep."

My whole body went limp. I had nearly attacked her. She approached and crouched down very close to me. With shaking hands I slipped the bayonet into its scabbard. She handed me a mug of warm coffee. I sipped it, holding the mug with two hands to stop my shaking hands from spilling it.

"Do you think they will attack us?" she asked in a soft lilting whisper.

"I don't know, but if they do we will have to stand and fight. We have nowhere to go and no other choice," I answered. Then I realised how silly it sounded. We were silent for a moment, not knowing what to say.

"What's your proper name? It can't be Mac," she asked.

"It's Donavan," I said softly.

"Ah, that's a nice name. It sounds so very honest," she whispered.

I was not sure if she should be out here with me but it was really nice having her company.

"I am Lily O'Hare and I come from Ireland," she whispered.

Someone hissed behind us and I looked back. The shadowy figure of a nun was standing in the doorway.

Lily turned back to me and touched me lightly on the arm. "I'd better go now," she sighed and she slipped away, ghost-like back into the smouldering ruin.

I sat there in the middle of a war. Mia was forgotten, Lily O'Hare had taken her place. I drank the rest of the coffee. I was in love again. Then the thought struck me. Nuns were not allowed to have relationships with men. They were not allowed to marry or have normal lives. So she came from Ireland, where the hell was that I wondered!? As far as I knew the Irish were a tribe in England like the Zulus in South Africa. I wished I had spent more time studying the map of the world. I felt completely thick and idiotic and wished Teacher was around to help.

Then I started to cry. We had buried Teacher with the dead women not ten hours ago. But Lily's presence did something for me. She had given me a stronger will to fight and survive.

Time seemed to creep by. Crazy, dangerous thoughts were spinning round in my head. When my watch was over, I returned silently into the building and woke Pole who was to take my place. I lay down in the dust to try and sleep and I must have drifted into sleep eventually.

Majola drifted by smiling, dead thorn trees then swirling dust hid him from me and for just a moment a male lion glared at me. I awoke with a shudder and looked around fearfully. It was dead still within the walls of the school.

I must have dozed off again and woke with a shock to find Carr crouching next to me. "Mac they are coming." He could not hide the tremor in his voice.

Sleep left me, and I was fully awake and I promptly broke out in a cold sweat. This was it. We were probably going to die today! Was there something I should be doing before dying? Thoughts raced through, my head. I sat there in the dust. One of the nuns came across and handed me a mug of weak coffee. I gulped it down, but there seemed no reason to rush.

Carr reappeared. "Get a move on. Pole wants you on the right."

I ignored him and collected my equipment and took up my position. Pole was crouched behind the Browning with Carr next to him. Roux, Potter and Thomas were on the left. Potter lay flat on the ground. Thomas sat with his back to the wall. Silently I took up my position on the right. The idea was that I would have a good field of fire along the south side of the building. I could see clearly for two hundred metres to where the road disappeared in to the jungle. Wisps of jungle fog drifted slowly through the still air like ghosts trying to escape from this hell. The jungle before us was deadly silent. The birds had not woken yet. Far away a jackal howled to the last of the stars. I sat there covered in a fine grey ash. I thought of Gran, Oupa, Mia, Carlos and Mrs Manteiga and then Majola. I smiled thinking of my old friend as he who had spoken of wars to me so very long ago. I wished he could see me now and wondered what advice he would give. He would probably say, "You cannot live forever so, if you must die, die like a madoda [man]." I grinned at the thought, and removed two grenades from my ammunition pouch and placed them in the dust beside me. Pole had placed a box of full magazines within easy reach. Slipping my bayonet from its scabbard I secured it. I was as ready as I would ever be to die as a madoda!

My movement seemed to have an effect on the others. Carr fidgeted for a moment then started to arrange himself in much the same way. This was followed by Potter and Thomas. Daylight was coming fast. The dull burning humidity returned with the coming dawn and the mist evaporated.

The drums started to beat ever so softly, building up to a crescendo. From the jungle directly opposite us there came a ghastly clicking noise. I looked around. Sister Susanna peeped round the corner of the doorway, her eyes puffy and red rimmed from the dust, her face and habit, streaked with grime. There was raw fear in her eyes.

The drum beats increased to deafening proportions, irritating me. We could not talk or communicate and I wished there was a way to block out the pounding. The clicking noise had also intensified, fitting insanely in with the thundering drum beats. The jungle across the road seemed to shake before our eyes as if blown by a strong wind. There was no wind, just the dead clammy humid heat. It was the start of madness.

A volley of shots broke the spell. Bullets whined around us slapping into the wall behind us and churning up the earth before our defence. Two bullets passed through the corrugated iron wall but caused no injuries.

"Steady, steady," said Pole in a gruff voice, pulling his bush hat well down on his forehead so just his eyes glowed in the shadow. His big shoulders were hunched over the machine-gun.

The drums stopped suddenly, and the silence was deafening for a second. The jungle broke apart. I gasped in amazement. It was both stunning and terrifying as a seething mass of glistening black bodies, daubed with yellow war paint, erupted from the green wall. At first I thought there were thousands but, in actual fact, there were probably only a few hundred. They charged straight at us. A dozen warriors ran ahead carrying rifles, they fired as they ran and their bullets whipped around us, while arrows pelted down on the roof.

"Fire!" shouted Pole, bringing us back to life. The Browning started to fire. Then we were all firing. Warriors fell and tumbled into heaps. The wounded rose and were shot down again. I had forgotten about the grenades and was firing on automatic, scything away at the sea of humanity.

"Grenades!" screamed Pole. "Grenades!"

I ripped the pin out of one and flung it into the seething mass just ten metres in front of me. Then I fell flat and snapped on a new magazine, not knowing if the one I had removed was full or empty.

The grenades crunched solidly before our defences. Dust and shrapnel, bits of human body parts and blood blew across us. Then we were up and firing again. The warriors were running away in blind panic, tripping over their fallen comrades. We fired and they died. As quickly as it had started, it ended. A terrifying hush fell over the battlefield. The dead and wounded lay strewn between the school and the jungle. One of the many wounded moved and was trying to rise and was shot mercilessly. Another with his half his stomach hanging out in bloody red coils rose to his feet only to fall over backwards and remain still. Yet another screamed in a high-pitched voice but a single shot stopped that.

What we did was against everything that I had been taught and everything that I had believed in. There was no sympathy and no mercy. We did not need orders but methodically killed any warrior who showed any sign of life. Eventually, after what seemed to be a very long time, silence hung over Crossways School.

A nun poked her head round the corner. "There is nothing at the back," she reported in a soft frightened voice. Pole acknowledged her and licked his dry lips. I groped for my water bottle.

The jungle before us was dead quiet, not even a bird call, just an airy terrifying silence that seemed to hang there.

Pole glanced my way, "Mac, about ten metres out, can you see the Russian rifle? The owner has an ammo pouch over his shoulder. We will cover you."

I nodded, for my brain was numbed by the attack. I would have probably done anything that Pole ordered without pause for thought. I removed my bayonet from my weapon.

"Fire," croaked Pole, and they raked the jungle opposite. I vaulted the barrier and snatched the rifle away from the dead hands. Using my bayonet I cut the bandoleer of ammunition away from its owner. Then I darted back and crouched behind the barrier.

Roux grinned and took the rifle off me. "First aid. There are a few still wriggling and I don't want to waste my ammo – might as well use theirs." I paid him no attention. Kneeling, he started shooting the remaining wounded that he alone seemed to see. A sudden lust to kill had appeared in his jumbled mind.

A number of nuns came to the doorway, peering out into the battle ground. Roux was still busy with his grisly, self-appointed task. Single shots whacked across the clearing.

"We wish to help the wounded," said one of the nuns. Then she saw what Roux was doing.

"You're killing all the wounded!" she cried in horror, her face showing her disbelief. "You cannot do it!"

Pole was on his feet in a flash, his big frame blocking the doorway. "Get back under the roof. They can come back anytime!" he shouted, pushing the surprised woman back out of sight and into the building.

I knew how the nuns probably felt about us killing the wounded but it could not be helped. There was no medical help out here and back at the mission kitchen three warriors whom we thought were dead had tried to make their last stand by attacking us. Teacher had died at the hands of a wounded Teng. It was all just part of this dirty business.

I quickly started to strip my weapon. Dirt had got into every cranny and the one thing I did not need was for it to jam if we were attacked again.

Roux squatted in the dust, his face twitching anxiously, his eyes bright with anticipation. The SKS assault rifle leaned against the wall. Nothing moved on the killing field before us.

The crows were first to arrive, cawing to each other. They were cautious at first, but got braver and braver. It was not a pretty sight to watch them, going first for dead men's eyes, then the softer parts of the bodies. A little later a few vultures arrived and sat in a tree opposite, to observe for a while before joining the feast.

There seemed to be a lot of noise coming from the nuns and I wondered what they were going on about, as it did not sound like they were praying. As the day dragged on it became terribly hot beneath the corrugated iron roof and we lay around sweating. Thomas looked like a comic book ghost, covered from head to foot in grey ash.

Pole busied himself checking the ammunition, his face serious and grey with fatigue and dirt. "If we are attacked again like that we won't have much ammo left," he said while he scratched in the dust with a stick.

"Lunch is ready," called Sister Susanna, coming to the doorway. "It's not much but we must be thankful."

Potter volunteered to remain as sentry. We all shuffled back through the door.

Two nuns were tending a pot over a small fire. They straightened up as we entered. Lily was one of them and she smiled sadly. "You lads had better eat and keep up your strength," she said, slopping a mass of braised steak, corned beef and soggy biscuits onto a plate for each of us. I had packed the tinned food and knew that there could not be much left. Rather guiltily I took the plate offered.

The little old pixy nun appeared from under the roof. She stared hard at us. "You are the devils," she hissed. "We are all going to die because of you. Even your colour has changed to one of death." One of the nuns gently pulled her away.

We probably did look like the dead, all grey with strained, tired expressions, our faces streaked with sweat and tears. Speaking for myself, I felt almost dead on my feet with exhaustion.

We all sat in the dust and ate. Then we washed it down with tepid water. I sat for a moment looking down at my feet. Then my gut heaved, as what I was looking at came into focus. A bloody part of a human eye socket and the dead angry eye stared up at me. Taking a deep breath and using the toe of my boot I pushed it under a piece of debris and out of sight. No one else appeared to have seen what I had done.

The meal finished, Carr stood there grinning from ear to ear. "That was delicious, thank you. I hope it was not our last meal," he said cheerfully.

I looked at him in astonishment. Was he also going mad? Roux shuffled uncomfortably in the dust. Pole scratched his head and looked concerned.

"Sister," Carr said with even a broader grin and an evil twinkle in his eye,. "Two Teng were eating one of our comrades. It was quite a feast. The one started at the top, as is the tradition, and the other at the bottom." We all sat there transfixed for no one knew what was coming next. "The Teng who was eating from the top says to the one eating from the leg end, 'How's it going down there?' The one at the bottom says, 'I am having a ball.' 'You're having a ball!' shouts his partner. 'You're eating too fast!'" Carr roared with laughter.

Pole shook his head in shocked amazement. How could anyone tell a bunch of nuns a joke like that! Sister Susanna's serious face suddenly cracked into a giggle and there were a few more snickers from under the roof. Roux had a stupid smile on his face. I think the funniest part was Carr rolling around laughing at his own joke. I joined in. Carr had an audience and I knew that he was not going to stop there.

"Have you heard this one?" He gasped between more of his crazy giggles. "Two dogs."

"Shut up," said Pole gruffly. For we all knew Carr's "two dog joke" and it was definitely not a joke to tell nuns! Carr stood there, an embarrassed look on his face. He looked like he was going to burst into tears. He turned and walked away and joined Potter on watch.

I watched him through the doorway and realised, for the first time, that Carr's jokes and behaviour were just part of a type of relief mechanism. If he had not distracted himself and the others present he would probably have gone the same way as Roux.

The day started to warm up. It was too hot to sleep. Swarms of black flies had arrived and covered everything. In the beginning we could smell the rotting flesh but we got used to the smell. More vultures and crows arrived, and started ripping at the decaying flesh and gorged themselves on the dead. A couple of jackals could also be seen lurking around the edges of the jungle.

The nuns were keeping the rear of the school under watch. Pole had organised us into watches. The sun beat down mercilessly. We lay in the dust and waited. Would help come? It had better come soon. Pole had said another attack like this morning and we would be out of ammunition. Food was also going to be a real problem and already I was beginning to feel hungry all the time.

It was about three when I heard the distant throb of the engine approaching from the south. I sat up listening.

"What is it?" asked Roux, also sitting up and peering over the barricade.

"Listen," I said. Pole was also listening. It took a good five minutes for them to hear it. Sister Susanna came to the door. She had also heard the distant vehicle.

"Thank God we are safe," she exclaimed clapping her hands. Then she rushed back to the other women.

"Do you think it's Villa Vista?" asked Carr, peering over the barricade.

"The timing is all wrong," replied Pole. "Maybe from Djolu, but I doubt Villa Vista. If they'd heard about St Patrick's, it would have been this morning, say about ten. They would only be getting to the railhead by this time and that is only if they have a good run. No I don't think it's from Villa Vista."

He looked puzzled as he went back into the school. The nuns' happy chatter died down.

Crows called and flapped amongst the bodies. Two vultures had a disagreement and started to fight, beating each other with their wings and trying to peck one another with their hooked beaks. The engine sounds grew louder and louder. By the sound there was definitely more than one truck or car. At one stage I thought I could hear the clatter of steel on steel. It was not loud enough to be a bulldozer but it sounded like a tracked vehicle. Possibly it could be the army, UN troops or possibly mercenaries from Katanga province, but it seemed too far west for any of them. "Something is wrong," declared Thomas peering over the barricade. "Who is this coming?" he asked no one in particular. Then he turned to Sister Susanna who was standing in the doorway. "Sister I think it would be wise if you and the other nuns stay quiet and out of sight."

She stepped back into the ruined building. All sense of a quick rescue was fast disappearing. Thomas came closer to the Pole and crouched down next to the machine-gun.

"I will watch through the holes." He indicated a couple of bullet holes in the corrugated iron. Obviously he did not want to show himself to those approaching.

We waited nervously. The vehicles or vehicle was travelling very slowly. The engine sounds got closer and closer. We were all tense and sweating profusely in the grey ash, the heat and the flies. The sound disturbed the crows and vultures and they flew up into the branches where they sat watching. The noise was very loud. We could now clearly hear an engine roar with a loud metallic, clanking sound.

When the vehicle appeared, at first there was a huge sense of relief, but this soon changed. It was a green military half-track armoured vehicle, not unlike the ones I had seen in war books on the Second World War. It was splattered with mud and a limp flag was hanging from what must be a radio antenna. On the back was a heavy machine-gun with a steel shield. A black soldier sat on the metal seat attached to the weapon with a litre bottle of beer in his hand. A second man appeared to be cranking the weapon around to face the school. Then a third man came into view. He stood up on the passenger seat, sporting sunglasses, a maroon beret and neat jungle fatigues. Binoculars hung around his neck. He looked very professional. It had to be the local army.

"Thank goodness!" breathed Pole, about to rise.

"Wait!" hissed Thomas urgently.

The half-track vehicle was moving very slowly. It sounded as if the exhaust had broken and the noise it made was deafening. Then the reason slowly materialised. The half-track was pulling a trailer. That sudden gut-wrenching fear was there again, for on the trailer were thirty or forty men all sitting around on what looked like a red lounge suite and an assortment of garden furniture. They were all drinking from bottles. Many wore steel helmets and camouflage fatigues, while others wore bits and pieces of various uniforms. One soldier, who stood out, wore a bright red dressing gown. They were all armed with an assortment of weapons. None of the passengers appeared interested in the scene of carnage before them. The vehicle crept slowly forward, the tracks grating and clanking loudly, churning through muddy patches.

Then a second trailer slowly appeared. It was heaped with various belongings. On top of everything was a white enamel bath tub. At the back of the second trailer sat a dozen women and children who peered around the side at the school.

A shiver ran up my spine. I could feel the danger. These were not government soldiers. The ones at the barracks in Stanleyville that we had seen were a well-disciplined, neat and well-organised troops. These were riff raff. They were probably bandits and army deserters who, as they went along, were robbing and looting whoever and whatever they came across. The whole convoy, or what one would call a half-track pulling two trailers, had now appeared and was moving steadily along the road towards us.

I wondered what they thought of the scene before them, a burnt-out school, a hundred or so rotting corpses and a couple of white soldiers hiding behind a flimsy barricade.

The half-track came closer and closer, squelching over a number of corpses that had died in the road. It came to a squeaking halt before us. The engine note died to a steady muffled beat. The heavy machine-gun was pointed directly at us. It was a terrifying spectacle just twenty-five metres from us. We did not have an answer to that weapon. It would probably be capable of blowing the school apart and we were also outnumbered by the bandits.

Pole crouched next to the Browning with Thomas lying next to him watching through the bullet holes.

"You had better ask those thieving deserters what they want. The one with the sunglasses is a known officer," whispered Thomas.

Pole cleared his throat as he rose from behind the Browning. He tried to smile and be casual but I could see his legs shaking. "Do you speak English?" he called loudly.

"Sunglasses" was standing on the seat, surveying the scene. He smiled casually, his white teeth flashing. "I am an educated fellow. Are you from Villa Vista?" he asked in perfect English.

"That's right," said Pole. "We were ambushed by the Teng." He waved his hand north, down the road towards St Patrick's. "We had to abandon our truck near the bridge."

Sunglasses smiled again. "Have you fellows not been to St Patrick's mission hospital? I have a few wounded chaps needing treatment. Morphine, and maybe other drugs." He smiled again, "You kill plenty of these Teng fellows," he said pointing towards the dead warriors.

"We never got there, to the hospital," lied Pole. "But a platoon of men from Villa Vista will be getting here tonight."

Sunglasses smiled his casual smile, which was starting to annoy me now.

"Ah, reinforcements !" he said loudly.

Pole nodded his head in agreement. Then he said softly. "Mac if we start shooting, take the driver out first."

Thomas had picked up one of the grenades and was weighing it in his big pink palm.

"I will throw this at the tractor," he whispered, obviously referring to the half-track.

There seemed to be a meeting going on between Sunglasses and the man behind the machine gun. The men on the trailer had picked up their weapons, but had not been told what to do and appeared drunk. A few men now stood surveying the scene. There was a dangerous, electric air about the situation we now found ourselves in. We waited sweating in the heat.

Sunglasses completed his discussion with the man behind the machine-gun and had just turned back to us. At the worst possible moment a frail voice called out, "Satan is coming. May the Lord have mercy!" The cry was cut off in mid-sentence.

Sunglasses smiled broadly. "You lied to me soldier. That was one of those bitches in white."

Pole remained calm. I could see the perspiration running down his back and down his legs.

"So what has it to do with you? We have no war with you," retorted Pole.

Sunglasses smiled. "We require their help, antibiotics and morphine. Their operating theatre will save my men's lives. You hand them over to me. I give you my word no harm will come to them."

What was Pole going to do? To hand any of the nuns over to these men would mean rape and eventually death. I thought of Lily in the hands of these men who had no respect for anyone, not even themselves, and a shudder ran through me.

Sunglasses continued speaking like a man used to giving orders. "I am going to give you five. You talk to the ladies in white. Say they must come with me. I take them and leave you fellows safe. No shooting no killing, nothing."

Thomas was shaking his head, looking up at Pole. "You cannot believe him. They are bandits wanting to steal the drugs from the mission. They will kill the nuns if we give them over. We are going to fight," he whispered. "If the nuns must die, we must also die. We have no choice in the matter," he said softly.

We were all silent for a moment.

Carr broke the silence. "Can't live for ever can we? Can't hand those women over to those black bastards."

Roux was visibly shaking, his eyes rolling and he licked his lips but said nothing.

Potter smiled sadly. "The Lord is my shepherd," he said simply.

I shrugged. "We have no choice but to fight," I croaked. My mouth was bone dry. I turned back to my peephole in the barricade. If this was how my life would end, so be it. Everything seemed to have been be such a waste of time. There were also so many things I was going to leave undone. Possibly I would die next to Lily. A sense of calm came across me. I knew I was not going to die and nor was Lily. It was not my time to die. I would fight and survive, no matter what the odds were.

"Soldier your time is up. What are you doing?" called Sunglasses. The bandits were preparing to have a go at us.

I went over my plan of attack in my mind. I could already see Sunglasses through my peep sights. One shot for him, the next for the driver of the half-track. The driver could not move, boxed in behind the steering wheel. I knew I could do it. It was like shooting rats off the rafters.

"I will go. It might save everyone's lives," said a woman's voice behind us. Looking round I saw Sister Susanna standing in the doorway, her face and uniform in a complete mess. "I will go alone," she said in a calm clear voice. "It will save all your lives." Pole turned to face her.

"That's right lady and bring the rest with you!" called Sunglasses smiling.

As I watched his followers smiled, relaxing a little. I was surprised it was Potter who shot to his feet. I thought he was going to hit sister Susanna. "We're all in this together. You're not going to sacrifice yourself. Get out of sight and see someone is watching our backs," he spat at her.

At first I thought she was going to refuse. Potter looked amazingly aggressive, standing before her blocking the doorway. She obeyed meekly enough, going back behind the wall.

"Are they coming?" asked Sunglasses. The smile was no longer there. His men were now itching to get started. They had all armed themselves and appeared to be pretty confident. One big gangly chap with a light machine-gun stood balanced on the trailer scratching his crotch. I placed him as number three on my hit list.

The blood-curdling scream came from nowhere. The scream was so terrifyingly high-pitched and horrible, that it made the hair stand up on the back of my neck. The best way to describe the picture before us was an optical illusion. The bandits behaved as if bees had attacked them. They were all screaming in terror, running blindly in all directions. As they ran and stumbled they pulled at the short shafts of arrows sticking from their bodies. We did not wait for orders but shot them down.

I fired a single shot. The driver of the half-track smashed back against his steel housing, bone and blood flying. The half-track, obviously still in gear, lurched forward with a terrific noise. Its tracks were churning and throwing up mud and human remains. Suddenly it broke free from its trailers and swung sharply towards the school. Then, with a loud metallic clank, it shed its left-hand track. Still at full throttle it spun to the right, ploughing up the soft earth and corpses around it. Finally, it came to a grinding halt with its nose against a big tree, its engine roaring and single track spinning madly throwing up clods of mud.

The world before us was full of screaming, thrashing, crying men, women and children.

"Fire!" shouted Pole. The bandits never fired a shot. I saw Sunglasses take a bullet high in his shoulder and my bullet took off the top of his head in a shower of bone and brains. Turning back to the thrashing dying bandits, I pumped shot after shot into anyone moving. It was a type of madness of the moment that said that nothing before us should live. A woman who had been taking refuge under the rear trailer suddenly broke cover. The Browning stuttered once and she was thrown violently to her knees and she then fell slowly forward, flat onto her face.

A child's voice screamed in terror and fought its way clear of the body that had trapped it. A small naked black boy stood for a moment, then with a sad little cry started to run back down the muddy road.

"Come here!" shouted Pole. Thomas joined in, calling him in the local dialect. The boy looked back with sheer horror on his face and ran even faster. The jungle closed on him and he vanished from our view.

"Poor little shit. Where the hell is he going?" asked Potter of no one.

We all knew that the first deserted estate was well over twenty kilometres past the junction in the roads.

A deadly, frightening hush covered Crossways School. The half-track had cut out. A cloud of blue diesel smoke drifted lazily across the scene before us. The air was full of the smell of gun smoke.

We had not reckoned with the Mongu Teng. They had ordered all foreign tribes from their jungle.

Chapter 8

We sat in a silent group trying to draw confidence from one another.

"It's not right how the Teng are being so persistent. They are not war-like people. Their actions are out of character. It's as if they wish to die," said Thomas. "For sure, they are out there watching us. They could leave us alone or block the road further away and set up ambushes. We would eventually have to come out. But no, they do the unthinkable. They attack us head on." He nodded his big sweating head. "Many of them die. I suspect the witch Gogo and de Haas have something to do with this business." He waved his arm in a hopeless gesture. "She must have made them a promise of good things in the other world, if killed fighting. Witches are really great liars."

"Do you think they will attack again?" asked Pole scratching his armpit.

"I do not know," said Thomas, "but I'm sure that when it gets dark they will return to their lodges, which are possibly situated very near. At night they believe they must sleep in a place where they are free from the evil spirits of the jungle." Thomas looked at us, "I think when it is dark it will be good for us to run. There is a fishing village that I know of not too far from here. There will be pirogues, fishing boats. We will take them and go downstream to Swart's mine. If we are lucky, the scientists studying the jungle might have left food. The mine is two days' walk from Villa Vista." He sat there, deep in thought.

"Why don't we just continue with the river to the Congo river?" I asked. To me it would be simple just to sail on till we reached the main river and possibly safety.

Thomas shook his head. "That river is too bad. There are waterfalls below Swart's, as well as hippos and many crocodiles. Better we go to the mine. Maybe we will be lucky," he said finally.

We sat around as the nuns handed out weak coffee and biscuits. Pole went off to have a conversation in private with Sister Susanna. The light was fading. Roux was out in front with the Browning.

Roux's high-pitched scream was almost indistinguishable from the sounds of the jungle creatures. We grabbed our weapons and plunged through the doorway. The Browning was firing. The Teng were very close, and arrows pelted down on the corrugated iron roof. A volley of rifle shots kicked up dirt and smacked into the walls around us. Roux was screaming and swinging the machine-gun from side to side in a blind panic. Pole pushed him violently aside and took his position.

Potter stood firing on automatic, oblivious of being out in the open. He was shouting. "As we walk through the valley of the shadow of death!" Astonishingly, he was reciting Psalm twenty-three as he fired, raking the mass before him. "We will fear no evil!" he shouted.

"Grenades!" screamed Pole.

Out of the corner of my eye I saw an arrow hit Carr in the shoulder. The arrow had bounced off the corrugated iron barricade. It could not have gone in very deep as he was able to pulled it loose. He quickly examined the point. It looked so puny. Then he emptied his weapon into the mass before him and looked at me. His eyes were large and frightened. His action had already become jerky. He threw his rifle down, scooped up two grenades, ripped their pins out with his teeth and with a howl and screaming like a madman he jumped the barricade. Carr ran in amongst the attacking Teng. Their ranks parted for him and closed around him. There were two crunching earth shuddering explosions. Bodies and body parts were blown around, shrapnel whistled over our heads. Dirt, blood and body parts slapped against our flimsy defences.

"Grenades!" shouted Pole, bringing us back to life. We lobbed our grenades and fell flat. They exploded frighteningly close by, covering us with soil, blood and pieces of human flesh. A moment later we were back up and firing again. Suddenly darkness was upon us. Pole fired a flare. The phosphorus glow turned the heaving retreating mass before us into a seething yellow and black beast. The warriors were fleeing and we were firing and shouting.

Then there was a hush, so quiet that it was terrifying. It was broken by a sickening moan and a horrible drawn-out scream. Roux took up the SKS rifle. He fired another flare and began putting the wounded out of their misery. The drums started to beat softly building steadily up to a solid thump that penetrated deep into my mind. We did not speak of Carr. He had chosen his way out, rather than to die slowly and painfully from the poisonous arrow.

Pole was checking the ammunition, talking to himself. "One belt of fifty rounds for the Browning. What have you got left?" he asked.

Potter checked his pouches. "Two and a half," he reported.

"Mac?" I had three magazines, Roux two and Thomas one and a half. There were three grenades and half a dozen flares. I could see Pole looking out into the killing field. There would be guns and ammunition out there, but we dared not go out.

The last attack had come unannounced by drum beat or the clicking sound. Could Thomas be wrong about the Teng fighting at night? They could be just waiting for one of us to break cover.

Out on the dark battlefield a jackal yelped and an animal growled menacingly. Unseen animals gnawed noisily at one of the corpses. I could imagine the little meat-eating jungle creatures coming from kilometres around to do their share of the cleaning up at Crossways School.

"At about ten we will move," said Pole quietly. "I wish to break a hole in the wall at the back. We will leave that way. I also think we are due for a thunderstorm."

He was right. The action had made us blind and deaf to everything else around us. In the distance the sky was illuminated every now and again and there was the faint rumble of thunder. Pole was silent for a long time, as we sat in a silent exhausted group.

Pole sighed, "I am very sorry about Teacher and Carr. Neither of them deserved to die like they did." He lapsed into silence, having said it all. The thunder rumbled a little closer.

Thunder crashed and the wind whipped the branches into a frenzy. It was pitch dark, lit occasionally by a blinding flash of lightning. We crouched next to the back wall of the school as one by one the nuns came through the hole we had made. The rain, big stinging drops, slapped against my hot, filthy, skin and although I carried a rain cape I did not use it.

Thomas led the way and Pole followed. He had removed the firing pin from the Browning. He now carried his FN. The football field was sodden under foot. I noticed the nuns had joined hands so as not to get lost in the dark. I was surprised at how few there were left. We had started with thirty of them. Now they were down to fifteen.

We were relying on the noise of the thunderstorm to cover our departure, whilst the rain would also cover our tracks. Our line moved slowly across the football field to the edge of the jungle and then headed north, following the jungle wall.

After a search Thomas seemed to find what he had been looking for. He found a narrow, dark tunnel leading into the jungle. We followed, slipping and sliding and tripping over roots and fallen branches. I had taken up my position at the rear. Dark shapes before me tumbled and fell, gasping and grunting with the effort of being pulled back on to their feet by their companions. The rain pelted down through the branches. The wind moaned in the treetops. We had been walking for half an hour but it seemed much longer when at last the column before me stopped. I walked into the back of the last nun.

"What's it?" I asked. She said something I could not understand because of the noise. I crept forward up the line, as lightning flickered through the trees. Before me was a wind-swept banana patch from which a few thatched roofs poked out. Then the lightning was gone.

"Mac," whispered Pole from the dark. "The village is before us. We have got to check no one is at home."

"Oh my god!" a woman's voice, cried out almost hysterical with fear. "It's creeping up my leg!" This was much too loud. The rain had slowed to a gentle drizzle, frogs and crickets croaked and chirped.

"Stand still girl" said Sister Susanna. A torch flashed in the pitch darkness. Dark shapes crowded around and there was the sound of a wet cloth being removed.

"Have you lads got a dry fag?" called Sister Susanna again. There was the shape of Potter, and a match flared. Potter backed off.

"Got the bloody swine," said Sister Susanna sounding satisfied. "He's the biggest one I have ever seen."

Pole had come closer to the huddle of women, his voice quiet. "Would you lot mind not making so much noise. The Teng could be here."

"Leeches, big blood sucking leeches!" said Sister Susanna. She said it as if they were the only problem we had.

Pole returned back to where we crouched, now waiting for the next flash of lightning. The storm was moving away. The thunder was getting fainter and the rain had almost stopped. There was the damp earthy smell of the nearby river. No sound came from the direction of the huts.

"Let's use the torch," said Potter. "If anyone was here they would have heard us by now."

He went back to the nuns and could be heard mumbling, and then soon returned with the nuns' torch. We crept cautiously forward, checking the village, but the occupants had long gone. Pulled up on the riverbank just outside the last hut were three dugout canoes. They were easily big enough to transport all of us. The dark, whispering river was at the edge of the torchlight and red crocodile eyes glowed at us from the dark, gloomy water. We huddled into one of the larger huts and sat around the walls, waiting for daylight. I was exhausted and everyone else was too.

First light had us out examining the dugouts.

"I can't swim," groaned Roux.

Pole heard and added "Neither can I, but we're not going to!"

Thomas seemed to a have a good knowledge of the rough-made craft. "I will take ten of the women in that big one. They can help by paddling a little, the current should take us easily all the way," said Thomas, his face showing his concern as he examined each dugout in turn.

The rain had washed most of the dust and dirt off us. All that remained was the dirt ingrained in the folds of our skin. My clothing was really grubby and was now almost dry on my body.

It was a sad sight, as the longest canoe was pulled up into the shallows, and one by one the nuns clambered into the unsteady craft, sitting down on the flat bottom. The paddles were taken up and the canoe wobbled dangerously as Thomas pushed off.

"Watch it, watch it!" said Sister Susanna as they dipped their paddles into the swift-flowing water and glided away.

Looking around I saw Lily standing by, awaiting her turn to board the next narrow craft. She was going to travel in our canoe. I felt an overwhelming need to protect her, and she in turn seemed to respond to my need.

We were about to push off when Potter stopped us. He clambered out and dragged the third dugout into the water and pushed it out into the stream and away it drifted on the current. Then he again took up his position in our wobbly craft.

If we had not been in such a predicament it would have been a memory to cherish. The river, deep, dark and green, pushed us silently along. Birds and monkeys called, hooted and chattered continuously. A flock of weaver birds had set up a colony on a small island and were jabbering noisily away as they constructed their snake-proof, hanging nests. Lichen, creepers and ferns hung down and grew right to the water's edge. Huge roots protruded like hundreds of snakes from the dark muddy crevasses amongst the foliage. Occasionally we could see Thomas's dugout gliding along ahead of us. There were no easy landing places along the bank.

There were many smaller streams entering the green water, and one of the bigger ones had pushed up a small sandbank. Half a dozen crocodiles of various sizes dozed in the early morning sun. If only I'd had a camera, what pictures I could have taken! The dugout glided along, leaving a faint ripple on the mirror-like surface.

Chapter Eight

An hour passed and then another. It was hot on the water and the sun's reflection dazzled us, causing us to shade our eyes. A large sandbank fringed by tall reeds came up on our right. Just beyond it Thomas's dugout was already up on the narrow beach. We saw a broken-down jetty and signs that there had once been a road right up to the water's edge.

"Look at that," said Potter pointing to our left, where there was another dilapidated jetty and behind it a shell house built of cement. There were creepers and trees growing out of the empty windows and any crack they could find. A larger tree grew from within, pushing up through the rotting corrugated iron roof. It must have been a terrific place to stay once upon a time, when the ferry was fully operational. I could imagine green lawns right down to the river's edge. It must have been fantastic for fishing and a peaceful and tranquil life.

We applied ourselves to the paddles, and beached the dugout. The women had formed a small group on the beach. Potter and I pushed the dugouts into the river and watched them drift slowly away.

"It's about half an hour's walk to the mine camp," said Thomas, as we set off along what must once have been a busy, well-maintained road in its day. But in time the jungle had encroached on the hard gravel surface and in time would reclaim it completely. Deep potholes filled with water and in places the water had eroded and opened up small gullies.

Potter and I walked ahead of the others. Potter was humming a hymn. I knew the tune but not the name. A troop of monkeys surprised by us took off, trapezing through the branches barking and chattering as they went.

"Would you eat a monkey?" Potter asked. Then he pointed to a big male.

I grinned, thinking of Villa Vista and their curried monkey. My mouth watered, but it all seemed so long ago now.

"Have we not already eaten one of them?" I said. I felt as if I had not eaten for weeks.

Potter was silent for a moment. "They were just having us on, weren't they," he eventually said.

I could feel his uneasiness. I just laughed. I actually could not care less. If there had been a way other than shooting the monkey out of the tree I would have done it right then. But a shot would have brought the Teng down onto us like a swarm of wasps.

The first sign that we were getting close to our goal was a small village of tumble-down mud huts, probably where the labour force had lived. There followed a more robust shed with part of its roof missing. Then there was rusting steel winding gear, and a covered pit. An overgrown village of prefabricated houses of various sizes came into view and parrots broke from cover, screaming their alarm. They had been attacking a small stand of fruit trees. Peering through the dirty windows we found that the houses were all empty. One had the feeling that they had not been lived in for a very long time. We followed the line of houses. One had been burnt down. Ironically, they were all locked.

Thomas had joined us. "That is the house where the people who were studying lived." He pointed to a house set slightly back from the rest. It had a nice wide veranda. The door was locked and the curtains were drawn.

I smashed the door open with the butt of my rifle, and walked into a stuffy, dusty, hot, airless, house with a bare, plank-floored passage. There was furniture, and the kitchen had a huge black, wood-burning stove. The pantry was on the right.

"Praise the lord. At last we will eat!" exclaimed Potter peering into the pantry. I peered over his shoulder, feeling a sudden relief at what I saw. The shelves were packed with tinned food, tinned meat, vegetables, peaches, tea, coffee and sugar.

Sister Susanna joined us and was visibly pleased. "Right boys, let us get in there, and we will have grub organised in a jiffy."

We backed off politely.

Back on the veranda, we all sat around waiting. Lily and the injured nun that I had carried appeared down the road. They were walking very slowly. I felt a twinge of guilt at not having kept an eye on her. The woman with the arm wound looked very pale and drawn and was sweating heavily. Her arm, if not looked after properly, could easily become septic. I went down the road to meet them.

For something to say, I said "There's food!"

"Pity there's not a decent medical kit," said Lily worriedly, as she glanced at her labouring companion. It made me realise how concerned she was about the other nun's condition. I kept quiet and walked with them, hoping there would be no more deaths or mishaps.

Later, after our meal, Potter burped and rubbed his stomach. "That was good. I almost feel human," he said.

We were all feeling content and reasonably safe for the first time in a long while and we lounged about on the veranda. What a feast we had just eaten of braised steak and onions, potatoes, peas and carrots followed by tinned peaches and Ideal milk and coffee. Wow, it had been really great!

The women had taken over the house and we had moved onto the veranda.

"Thomas says it is two days' walk to Villa Vista from here," said Pole, as if looking for volunteers.

We all remained quiet, basking in the contentment of a full belly.

"I am worried about the nun with the injured arm," said Pole. "That arm looks infected."

We sat in silence for a while. Potter's head lolled on his chest for a moment. Then he grunted and shook himself awake.

"We need two of you men to walk to Villa Vista," said Pole.

No one volunteered.

Thomas stood up, leant on the veranda rail and said thoughtfully, "I will have to be one, I have travelled the road before. There are many turnings going off to felling gang camps, and the occasional diggings. It will be difficult even for me to know the road." Thomas stood looking into the distance.

"We'll draw lots," said Potter. "That will be fair."

Everyone agreed. Pole took out a box of matches and wandered around the veranda arranging them in his hand. "Whoever gets the shortest match walks with Thomas tomorrow morning early," he announced.

We all knew it was going to be a long, hot, dangerous walk but equally we all knew it had to be done.

I had been watching Roux. His face was contorted and his eye twitched. He could not sit still for a moment. Pole returned from the end of the veranda and Potter drew first. He sighed with relief. Roux drew next and openly grinned. It was now between Pole and myself. I drew the match and as I touched it I knew it would be me.

Two days' walk! Two long, hot, hard days. I sat and fidgeted with my stump of a match.

"Bad luck," said Potter. Roux got up and walked away towards the deserted houses, ignoring everyone.

Far away thunder rumbled threateningly. Birds squawked and chattered. We were all very tired and stretched out on the hard wooden planks to try to get some much needed sleep.

However, the rest we needed was short-lived.

"Come and have a look at this!" called Roux, as he came stamping up the wooden steps. He sounded excited. "I've found a car in one of the garages."

He had us all instantly awake. It was now raining softly. Sleepy-eyed, we followed him through the rain. Anything was better than the walk that lay ahead for Thomas and me. My hopes were high as he led the way to the garages belonging to one of the end houses.

It was a Mercedes Sedan with one flat tyre, parked in a dusty, rat-smelling garage. Potter grinned happily as he propped up the bonnet, and peered into the engine compartment.

"Oil and water is okay, but no battery." He went around to the trunk. "No spare wheel," he announced sadly. After rummaging around he called out "A tool kit!" and rattled a bag. Then he shuffled around to the petrol tank and he snapped the cap off. Pole handed him a long reed which he'd picked up from outside the door, Potter inserted the reed into the petrol tank. "Looks like half a tank," he reported excitedly. "This machine could save our lives if we could get it going," he said.

"Why would anyone leave a car out here?" asked Roux.

No one could answer that. Potter said he wanted to examine the car properly and we left him to it. We all went off to search the remaining garages for anything that might help.

The rain had stopped and the sun blazed down. There was no sign of the nuns. They were probably catching up on sleep. Roux and I had wandered from building to building but found that there was nothing that would help us. I noticed a half-eaten paw paw, that the birds had left and I climbed the tree and picked it. Then Roux and I sat on the steps of one of the houses and I divided the fruit between us.

From where we sat we could see the scientist's house. All of a sudden the nuns appeared on the veranda. They looked desperate. There was something frantic about their hurried searching movements. They split up into two and spread out in a search pattern. Lily and one of the other nuns came towards us.

"What's up now?" sighed Roux. "Those bloody women are a real nuisance. It's just one problem after another, and we have to put up with their whining and inability to keep up. We should have forced them to go with the bandits," said Roux.

I was surprised at Roux's attitude. "You would never have forgiven yourself," I said quietly. Roux shrugged and looked away, his face a twitching mask.

As Lily approached, she called out, "Have you seen Sister Pauline?" She was referring to the old pixy nun.

I shook my head. "No!" I shouted.

Pole and Thomas went and joined them. Pole called to us, "Mac, you two look around the labourers' village and the mine. If you see anything call us!" We acknowledged him and set off.

Just past the labourers' huts, I found a faint footprint in the mud. It was heading back towards the river crossing where we had arrived with the dugouts that morning. Lily and another nun joined us. We stood around examining the track.

"It's her footprint," I said finally.

Lily sent her companion back to report to the rest of our group. Roux, Lily and I walked along the road back the way we had come. Here and there we came across a more visible footprint. The woman was obviously going back towards the beach. The little old pixy nun had been a nuisance right from the beginning. Instead of this we could be all resting or trying to get the car going, but we plodded along in silence, with the sun blazing down and the jungle heaving noisily around us. I found myself wishing Roux was not there as I was a little self-conscious chatting to Lily with someone else present.

The tracks led on, reaching the narrow strip of sand where the footprints were much clearer and they went, without hesitation, straight into the water. We just stood there, staring at the green river, so dangerous yet so quiet, as it pushed gently by.

"She's gone," I said. "There are crocodiles." I pointed to the sandbank with reeds. Two large crocodiles and a number of smaller ones basked in the sun. The peaceful picture before us was actually death camouflaged in many forms. Lily stood there dumb struck. Roux's agitation and fear was obvious. His hands were never still as he fidgeted with his rifle and his eyes blinked and face twitched continuously.

"We had better be going back," said Lily, a quiver in her voice. Roux had already turned and was walking away. All of a suddenly all the crocodiles on the sandbank slithered hurriedly into the water as if disturbed.

I stopped and looked back and saw to my amazement a movement on the sandbank, or was it beyond. I hissed a warning. Lily, Roux and I ran for a small stand of tree ferns and plunged in amongst the wet fronds. From our hiding place we watched with fear and horror as on the water from behind the reeds that grew on the sandbank a dugout canoe appeared. It was far longer than the one Thomas and the nuns had travelled in that morning. Mongu Teng warriors sat in silence. Just the soft grunt of the paddlers was all that could be heard as they pushed the canoe smoothly along. It resembled a sort of spiked creature. It bristled with spears and rifles. The warriors' black bodies and yellow war paint shone brightly in the sunlight and their leaf-like tattooed bodies were a frightening reminder of the danger.

"Oh my god!" whispered Roux.

I glanced at him crouching behind me. Roux's eyes began to roll. His face was contorted and white with fright. I turned back to the river. My mind was working in a blur. They would see our footprints on the beach. They would investigate and then follow us to the village. That would be the end. As a group, we were low on ammunition. We could not fight the Teng in the jungle, nor could we hold off an attack on the house. It became very clear we had to act at once and I realised it was up to us. The river was on our side, for Africans were usually very poor swimmers. I looked around to instruct Roux but he was nowhere to be seen. He'd probably gone to a better vantage point, with a better range of fire. Lily crouched next to the thick stem of a tree fern. Her face had gone white and her grey eyes looked terrified. With or without Roux I would have to act. I turned back and counted. There were fifteen warriors in the canoe. Were there more following? I did not know. I hoped Roux would back me up. We could not afford to let them put a foot on dry land.

A guttural cry came from one of the warriors in front of the canoe. The canoe altered direction towards us and the narrow beach. I then knew without doubt that they had seen our tracks in the soft beach sand. I slipped the only grenade I had from one of my ammunition pouches and checked my weapon. I knew I was taking on a dangerous enemy. They were men that were prepared to die for their beliefs, men that were prepared to charge head-on at an automatic weapon. How many warriors would a 7.62mm bullet go through? All this bounced around my brain as I tried desperately to organise my thoughts.

I aimed carefully at the centre of the front warrior's chest. My finger took up the slack of the trigger. Everything else was blank. I fired and felt the recoil, aimed and fired again and again. The result was pandemonium. The canoe overturned spilling its human load. I raced onto the beach and tossed the grenade into the middle of the churning mass of humanity. Then I crouched down to steady myself as I selected my target. The grenade submerged in the water then exploded with a dull whoosh. Bloody bodies were thrown about. Men screamed and gurgled horribly and the water turned crimson. I could not miss at fifteen metres.

The last of the echoes of gunfire died away. It was eerie. An unnatural silence seemed to close in around us. I stood there with the sun beating down on my back. Before me the river current pushed the overturned canoe away. The dark swirls of blood dispersed, and the bodies drifted sluggishly away on the current. Then they sank below the surface, one by one. Then there was nothing. It was now as it had been when we'd arrived. Lily came up quietly behind me and came to stand at my side. Her face was white and tense. She said nothing. Her presence gave me a comforting reassurance. I doubt that, had she spoken, I would have been able to answer. A crocodile passed by with just its eyes above the water. Then it disappeared below the surface looking for a meal. A fish eagle called twice.

I stood there for a long, long time, Lily's silent presence seemed to help me recover.

"We should be going," said Lily softly at last bringing me back to earth. "There was only one canoe." Then, as an afterthought, she added, "Thank God."

I stood there hearing her words but not responding. Fifteen Teng had died. It was not fair, for it was their jungle. They were being manipulated just as we were. Then Roux came to mind. He had not stood by me. The swine had run out on Lily and I. He had left us when I had needed his backing. I left the beach on wobbly legs and in a state of mild shock.

Lily walked next to me. She was crying and between her sobs she said. "It's not what I have always been taught, but here in Africa it's so different, so cruel, so dangerous." I placed a protective arm over her shoulder. She did not try to remove it.

We walked on slowly and in silence. I was recovering fast. Roux? How was I going to handle him? It was pointless trying to beat him up. It would be best to tell Pole. They would take away his bonus and possibly transfer him to Villa Vista.

Lily had stopped crying and stooped to wash her face in a rain water puddle. I stood waiting. The undergrowth on the side of the road was young and dense. The sun was reflected off a shiny object among the foliage. I hissed a warning. Then crouching low I pulled

Lily by the hand to the side of the road. All my senses were alert. God, would this madness never stop? After a few moments I sensed it was not an enemy trap. But what was catching the sun? Cautiously I crept off the road and into the lush jungle, weaving my way between the vines and creepers as always, alert for snakes. Lily refused to wait on the road and followed closely in my tracks.

There, before us, stood a rusting Peugeot car. I had seen the reflection of its rear wind-shield. There were two bullet holes through the rear wind-shield, both in line with the driver. It had obviously been there for a very long time. I forced my way around the side of the vehicle, cutting back the encroaching undergrowth. The driver's side door stood open, and creepers had entered the vehicle. A green snake appeared from beneath the car and quickly slid away into the undergrowth. I stood and watched as it made its escape.

"It gives me the creeps," whispered Lily.

Then I nearly stepped on a skeleton that lay half out of the driver's seat. Small creatures had been making a meal of the poor chap, who was partially covered with leaves and other jungle debris. I crouched and peered into the car to see a large rat scuttle away with a lot of rustling. The seat had been ripped and torn. Rat droppings and the stink of rat urine were everywhere and especially strong inside the car.

The key was still in the ignition. I turned it and was amazed to see the weak red ignition light came on. I switched it off immediately. A live battery was what we needed. "Look, did you see that? A battery with a bit of juice."

"Who is he?" asked Lily and she pointed at the corpse.

I shrugged, for I was not really interested. The battery was all-important. I checked the glove compartment and found a rusty automatic pistol with six shots in its magazine. Rats had chewed up what could have been the car's manual. I crawled out of the interior. Lily backed off to give me more space. My foot brushed against the dead man, disturbing a dull yellow object. Crouching down, I examined the skeleton's neck. Then scratching with the point of my bayonet I uncovered a heavy yellow chain that poured out between the bones, followed by a large pendant of the same yellow metal, and what appeared to be eleven diamonds and a large ruby in the centre. I squatted down and looked in amazement at the beautiful pendant.

"Is it real? Is it not gold, diamonds and a ruby?" whispered Lily, her face flushed and shining with sweat. Her grey eyes were sparkling. "It is real treasure!" she breathed.

I removed the pendant from the corpse and we carefully wound our way back to the road. I washed the pendant in a pool of rainwater. It was beautifully designed.

"It must be worth a real fortune!" said Lily a little louder than I felt was necessary.

A thought struck me. If it was worth a lot of money, how was I going to get it out of this land without being caught? There had been rumours that the police would be checking our possessions and doing body searches when we left and I could not take that chance. I would surely die in a Congolese prison. The owner was dead, whoever he was, so it was not really theft or robbery. I stood there trying to take in this new discovery.

Lily was smiling and holding the pendant to her chest. "Does it not look grand? It might be worth a fortune," she smiled. Then her face became serious. "Mac, I am not a proper nun. I have not taken my vows and I doubt I ever will. I have not told anyone but you of this. I came here as a volunteer, a novice, because I was interested and because I am a trained nurse. The mission valued my experience, but for me it has been an adventure in darkest Africa that has turned into a nightmare. After all that has happened, when I return home, which will be soon," she stopped for a moment to swallow nervously. "I am going to resign. Actually I should have been home yesterday. Do you realise it's just two days to Christmas?"

I stood there dumbfounded. Lily was looking up and down the road as if expecting a search party. I doubted anyone would come.

"Why are you going to resign?" I asked cautiously. Was this not a trick on her part to get her hands on the gold and diamond pendant? Did she know something I did not about gold and diamonds?

She blushed visibly. "Are you stupid? Can't you feel it? You and I are meant to be together." She smiled and looked me in the eye and then hesitantly took my hand in hers. "I knew from that night at Crossways School, when I brought you coffee. Just you and I sitting out there and neither of us knowing what tomorrow would bring. Then, to top it all, Sister Susanna spying on me. I then realised that I could not ever be one of them." She giggled nervously, her grey eyes alive and sparkling and she released my hand.

I stood there on the jungle road desperately trying to find reason with what Lily had said. A thought struck me. "Lily," I said hesitantly and found that I liked saying her name. "First we have to get out of this mess before I can say anything. Would you be prepared to take the pendant out with you when you leave? You will have to give me your address so that when my contract is finished I can find you." I was suddenly excited, realising that our feelings were mutual and a fortune could be in our hands. "They would never search a nun," I said and all of a sudden very sure of myself.

She nodded blushing furiously. "If that's right, what would the risk be worth to me?" she asked smiling, red faced.

I thought for a moment that she was teasing me by making me bargain. "Twenty-five per cent," I said hoarsely.

"Make it thirty!" she said with a flash of her eyes and a wide smile.

"Deal!" I replied quickly. She thrust out her small hand and I noticed how she had chewed her fingernails down to the quick. We solemnly shook hands in the middle of the overgrown road.

She removed her habit. For the first time I saw the beautiful Lily O'Hare. She was thin, with short-cropped auburn hair, and from her ears hung small gold earrings in the shape of crosses. She had the most amazing steady grey eyes that were slightly tilted at the corners. She slipped the chain over her head and let the pendant drop down her front.

"It will be safe with me. Just make sure they don't kill you," she said smiling nervously and patting her chest. "As soon as I find a pen to write with I will give you my address." She hesitated, and touched my lips with her fingertips. "Now not another word about it, do you hear?"

As we walked along the road to the mine I found myself telling Lily about the farm, Oupa, Gran, and the cows, and how I was going to make my fortune with the money I had earned. I explained how guilty I felt about trespassing on the Teng's rights to posses their jungle. In the twenty minutes, walk I think I told her my life story.

As we approached the house, Pole appeared from behind the veranda wall. I had been right. They would never have risked coming out in search of us. I wondered what Roux had told them upon his return. Roux appeared, standing to one side, his face a white, twitching mask. I watched him out the corner of my eye, realising that the man could just snap at any moment.

I told Pole what had happened. Roux just stood there his eyes glazed and strange. I told Pole about the canoe and the encounter with the Teng, and about Roux running out on Lily and myself. Then I told him about the car battery with a little life still left in it.

The other men sat around listening to me. I did not like the way Roux held his rifle. From where I was I could see the safety catch was on safe. If he had placed it on fire I would have shot him. His face was a blank mask. He did not respond to Pole dressing him down. He just stood there with a faraway look on his face. Potter fidgeted, wanting to go and collect the battery, to see if the tyres would fit, and check if there was any petrol in the car.

The evening noises had begun and a purple haze hung over the village. After we had eaten our second meal of the day we set off lazily to collect the battery and any fuel we could extract from the car. Potter had found a piece of hose and a can to collect any petrol that could have remained in the tank. He also carried the tool kit.

We walked along in a group avoiding the puddles. I found the spot easily enough and we all trampled into the young vegetation. I forced open the bonnet of the car and quickly removed the battery whilst Thomas and Potter siphoned off the small amount of fuel that remained. No one took much notice of the corpse.

Eventually Thomas went over and scratched around the skeleton with a stick. "I wonder what happened here?" he said. "It looks like murder. I will take the car's registration number and see if I can make any sense out of it," he said.

I could not have cared less. It was just another dead body. Finding out who had killed the man and why, was the least of our worries. The moon filtered through the higher branches, lighting our way as we walked back to the mining village. The tyre was going to be the biggest problem because the Peugeot's tyre was the wrong size.

"If all else fails we should just let all the tyres down and travel on the rims," said Potter in desperation.

"The car in the jungle had all four wheels intact," I said. "But it would take days to cut it out of the jungle."

Pole went into the Mercedes garage with Potter at his side. I sat down with Thomas next to the door, hoping that the Mercedes would burst into life at the first turn of the ignition key. Potter and Pole fiddled noisily around under the bonnet.

"Right, give it a try," said Potter. Pole had positioned himself behind the wheel. The Mercedes started with a cloud of smoke and a clatter, then a loud clack-clack sound and a long drawn-out hiss and then it died. My heart sank. There was something seriously wrong with that car, which was probably the reason it had been left behind.

Potter regained his upright position, his face white in the poor light. He kicked the car viciously.

"The bloody engine is shot. That's why they left it here." He jumped up and down in anger.

Pole came out of the garage and joined Thomas and myself. "We are going to have to cut that Peugeot out of the bush. It's going to take at least a day and that will be a day too long. We don't know if it will run, but we must try and start it first to see." He sat there, while we waited for him to make a decision. "Mac, you and Thomas must leave early tomorrow. The nun with the arm wound is in a serious state and needs medical attention. If the car runs we will meet you along the road. There could be all sorts of obstacles, fallen trees and mud. On foot you might even beat us to Villa Vista."

We sat thinking for a moment. I wondered what had happened to Roux, for he had not joined us. No one seemed particularly interested and I let it be.

Later we trooped back down the road to the Peugeot, and into the jungle and replaced the battery. Fuel was poured into the tank and the carburettor was charged. Pole pulled the skeleton away into a thicket. The engine coughed once, spluttered and then died with a cloud of smoke. "There's still life in the battery," said Potter. "We dare not try again, but it does not sound too bad. It's going to be one hell of a job to cut it out." Then as an afterthought he added, "You know, it should push start."

It was nearly midnight when we returned to the mining village. Sister Susanna met us at the steps. "Roux has packed and gone. We could not stop him. He forced his way in and took a lot of food," she announced. She stood there, her face flushed in the lamplight. "He said we were all a bloody nuisance and his contract would not stand up in court. He sounded completely irrational."

We all stood there. Damn Roux. He had finally done what he had threatened to do at the railhead. We all knew that a man alone would die in the jungle. We had probably all thought of deserting but we were all locked in this world of big trees, death and disease. The only way to survive was to stick together, as Teacher had once said.

Pole just stood there shaking his head in disbelief. It was one less gun, one less fighting man. The car was going to take at least a day of hard chopping to move it, and even then there was no guarantee that it would start and be able to make the trip to Villa Vista.

Sister Susanna wanted to talk. She held her hands clasped before her. "Two of the girls have gone down with malaria," she blurted out looking uncomfortable. "There is not much in the medical kit. Sister Rose is delirious." She was referring to the nun with the arm wound. I knew then that we could not wait. Thomas and I would have to get to Villa Vista as quickly as possible.

"You chaps will leave early tomorrow," ordered Pole, indicating Thomas and myself. Pole excused us from guard duty, saying Potter and he would manage. I lay down on the plank floor to try and get some sleep. What had happened to Lily and her home address? I wondered briefly but then sleep hit me.

It was still dark when I woke to find Lily crouched down next to me with a jug of coffee and a packet of biscuits. "Coffee in bed, young man?" she said with a smile.

I could see Pole standing at the end of the veranda with a mug in his hands. Thomas was up sitting on his bedroll, a steaming mug held with both hands.

As Lily's back was to both of them, her hand squeezed mine. Then she handed me a piece of cardboard. "My address," she whispered. I placed it in my breast pocket and took the mug offered. "Meet me round the back in five minutes," whispered Lily and she was gone.

Soft rain was falling and a wispy ground mist played spirit games amongst the black bushes. The jungle was ghostly and silent. I crawled out of my rain cape, stretching myself. Pole ambled over and stood there, mug in hand. He seemed to want to talk but could not get it out. Thomas stood up and started belting on his equipment. We were ready to leave.

Excusing myself, I went round to the kitchen door. I stood in the darkness and waited. The door opened and Lily came out. She stood very close to me.

"Are you all right?" she whispered.

I said that I was.

"You had better place that address in this plastic bag, so that it does not get damaged." She handed me a small plastic bag. "Now you won't have any excuse for not arriving." Her hand rested on mine for a brief moment. "Good luck and may God be with you," and then she was gone.

I felt I should have reacted in some way, put my arms around her or hugged her and possibly kissed her. I stood in the rain feeling like a real oaf, wishing I had at least made an attempt.

Chapter 9

Thomas set a blistering pace. The sun beat down through the overhead canopy making the roadway into a hot airless tunnel. We literally raced along the narrow track, slipping and sliding while trying to avoid the bigger and deeper puddles, but it was almost impossible. Flies and bugs swarmed around us constantly stinging and annoying.

At about ten we passed through a deserted and dilapidated village. We stopped and rested for a while. We ate and drank and then moved on again. Neither Thomas nor I felt like talking so it was in silence that we travelled. We stopped again at midday to eat and rest. We had been walking for seven hours. A number of small trees had fallen across the track but none big enough to cause too much of a problem for a car or a truck. In the far distance drums tapped out their secret messages.

Thomas stopped and spoke for the first time. "We are going very well. We must be very close to halfway. I think, if I remember correctly, there is a big village ahead."

I swatted a fly that had just bitten me. I thought about Roux. Which way had he gone? We had seen no human tracks, just animals. It had rained last night and this would probably have obliterated his tracks if he had come this way. Then, on the other hand, Roux would have had very little choice of roads out of the mining village and it seemed probable that he would have had to use this one.

A while later we set off again. The road had dried considerably by this time and we increased our pace. We passed through the large village that Thomas had spoken about. Like all the villages it was deserted and decaying.

At about six o'clock, we came to a smaller, half-burnt-out village. We stopped and surveyed the scene of desolation before us. Thomas wiped his sweating face. He suggested we find a hut in the village, a hut that would be acceptable to spend the night in, for it would be nearly impossible and very dangerous to walk the road to Villa Vista in the dark. There were junctions leading to old felling camps and mines and roads that led nowhere. With these road conditions, one false step and either of us could break a leg or twist an ankle, thus rendering one of us useless.

We chose a sturdy hut with hardly any rat droppings, and we threw a few sticks together and started a fire to boil water, in order to refill our water bottles and to make coffee. I selected a tin of meat and sat eating, using my bayonet. I felt Thomas watching me.

"Why you come here to fight? At your age you should be at school? My eldest son is the same age as you and is studying and wants to be a doctor." Thomas's questions tumbled out of him. I chewed on my meat and then explained to Thomas my reasons. It was getting dark and all I could see of the big black man was a dark silhouette and his white teeth shining in the firelight.

"You know Mac, I think the Congo is in for a hard time; too many tribes, two hundred and fifty, maybe more. Some are strong and some are weak. The strong will kill the weak." He shook his big head, "I do not know, but at times I think I should leave and go back to my people in the east. Hough will retire soon. I should go also." He sighed as if he was having trouble making a decision. He continued, "Hough is a good man. He and I have made quite a lot of dollars with birds." He grinned, showing his white teeth in the flickering firelight. I had not realised he was also involved in the bird business. We were silent for a while.

"Maybe I should go home and start a shop and, like you, buy a herd of good cows. Cows are important to a man." He fell silent again.

In true African tradition, he understood how important cows were. Then his breathing changed. It sounded as if he had nodded off. I went outside to relieve myself. I stared up at the stars which peeped out from cotton wool clouds. It would probably rain before sunrise as it usually did.

I awoke from an exhausted sleep. Thomas was up and had started a fire. He looked over the flames at me.

"Today we will have to be very careful not to get lost. From here on there are many junctions," he said. I agreed, and started helping myself to coffee. Peering out of the door it was still pitch black. We ate while we packed our few possessions and as the first greyness of dawn seeped through the village we set off. My muscles were stiff and my legs painful but they soon warmed up. Once I got into my stride I felt very strangely confident that we would be in Villa Vista sometime today.

At about eleven we started to have trouble when the road split into three. We came to a stop. There were no signposts in that part of the world. We examined each road in turn. There were no human tracks or vehicle tracks to indicate recent passers-by. We stood there undecided, not knowing which road to take. All three seemed to go in more or less the right direction.

"Look," I said, "I hate doing this but the nuns are relying on us. We will have to separate. You take the top one." And I indicated the road on the right. "I will take the middle one." I did not like what we were doing at all, but under the circumstances, it could not be helped. "We're probably only twenty or so kilometres from Villa Vista. We should give ourselves six hours, then, if it is the wrong road, you have a sleep and then we can meet back here tomorrow. If you get to Villa Vista first then you will find me here on the way past or I will find you here at this junction."

Thomas looked doubtful but agreed. We were losing valuable time, but that could mean life or death for at least one of the nuns.

"If we both find nothing down the road we will meet back here and take the third road together," I said. I could think of nothing better and Thomas could not come up with a better suggestion.

With a lot of doubts I set off alone, moving as quickly as possible along the muddy track. My thoughts wandered to Oupa, Gran, Mia and the farm. Why had they not written for so long? I had a horrible feeling that there were serious problems at Hill Farm. Then I thought of Lily O'Hare and all other thoughts seemed to fade away. The pendant was real gold with genuine diamonds and a real ruby. It was hopefully worth a few thousand rand, enough to make the whole effort worthwhile.

Time ticked by and then a deserted village came up. I stopped on the outskirts; I felt no sense of danger. I passed through, keeping a wary eye open for tracks that would warn me of the presence of villagers or the Mongu Teng. There was nothing. I had now been walking for four hours since leaving the junction in the road.

Far away drums beat. Then they were drowned by the rumble of distant thunder. The thought struck me, tomorrow was Christmas Day! At five o'clock I stopped. This was definitely the wrong road. I had been walking fast for the last six hours and I had covered a vast distance, but to keep a check on the direction I was taking was difficult because the road changed direction continuously. I would go on until I found a suitable place to camp. The road wound between huge trees. The jungle had turned dark and sinister but had thinned out a lot. There were signs that a felling gang had operated ahead of me. But, judging by the tree stumps, the trees had been felled a long time ago. The jungle thinned out even more and I came upon a number of abandoned, roughly built huts with a heap of old cable and rusting saw blades. I stood there looking around in the poor light. I had never before witnessed the devastation caused by the felling gangs, nor had I somehow linked the huge squared off blocks of tree trunks that were unloaded and loaded at the railhead with the jungle. It now struck me that I had been hired to assist in the destruction of the world.

The valueless trees had been left standing, scattered like hundred-foot gaunt mourners watching over the graves of their neighbours. I walked on a little further into the man-made morass which seemed to go on and on. Heaps of dead branches and neatly cut stumps were divided by areas of dense undergrowth and were spread out before me in the poor light. The timber tractors tracks had cut deep furrows into the muddy earth, which were now filled with green slimy water. I knew that the furrows would be there for ever. I also knew that the magnificent tall trees would never grow back in my lifetime. I knew, without any doubt, that man should not be here.

I stopped and decided that there must be another road that would lead out of the tree graveyard. That road would lead to Villa Vista. But as I examined the network of tractor tracks around me and the vast darkening area before me, I knew that I would never be able to find the road in the time that I had allowed myself.

I stood there feeling very dejected, very lonely and quite sorry for myself in this vast sinister world. Sister Rose and the other two were relying on us to get help. It could mean life or death to them. Hopefully Thomas had taken the right road and I would meet him tomorrow as he accompanied the men from Villa Vista. I stood there feeling very tired with the dark African night suddenly upon me. I chose one of the huts, and made a small fire to cook on. Night birds called and a troop of nearby monkeys were having a noisy disagreement. My feet and legs ached. I dozed fitfully, waking every now and then. The night seemed to be endlessly filled with desperate and vivid dreams.

As the first morning light filtered through the jungle mist, I set off back the way I had come. It seemed easier now that I knew the road. I reached the junction at about ten, and found a comfortable spot to wait for Thomas and the Villa Vista trucks. There were no signs that they had passed already. It was Christmas day, but it felt no different to me. I made myself lunch and began to wonder where Thomas was. Time started to drag. Surely he must have made it through. If he had not, why had he not returned to the junction? The rescue party from Villa Vista should have been here by now!

After waiting for a while I looked down Thomas's road. There was no sign of Thomas. Neither was there the sound of approaching trucks. I thought that if I walked down his road I might possibly meet him. I did not want to take the third road alone, when maybe he had already reached Villa Vista. As the time crept by I became doubtful and unsure of what to do. I walked slowly down his road peering into the sun-dappled distance. I could see Thomas's boot tracks in the mud. I decided that I would give myself an hour and then return and take the third road alone.

I had probably walked about five kilometres, when warning signals clanged in my head. All was not right. I crept into the dense bush on the edge of the road peering ahead. The feeling persisted. A flight of brightly coloured parrots went squawking by. I crept carefully forward until I could see a straight section of the road. It was dappled with sunlight and was unnaturally still and quiet, as if all the jungle creatures had fled. I stood in the dark shadows looking ahead. There was nothing. No Thomas coming down the road, no sound of trucks approaching.

At first the thought did not seem that important. Here we were plodding around the jungle leaving trails of combat boots in the soft earth. The Teng could spot how many of us were around, just as I had been doing by following Thomas's spoor. If they saw a set of barefoot tracks they would think it was a tribesman passing to check on his or her village. I was used to walking barefoot, so I sat down and removed my boots and socks, and tied them to my kit. I set off again feeling rather more comfortable. I would walk a little longer before turning back and taking the third road.

The further I went along the road, the more sure I was that all was not well! I relied on my senses and kept to the very edge of the road attempting to leave as little spoor as possible. To have a meeting with the Teng in these conditions could only end in my death.

A half-hour crept by when, in the distance, there was an unidentifiable object that shimmered in the heat and shadows. I peered into the patchwork tunnel that covered the road. It seemed to shimmer just above the ground and I could not work out if it was moving or not. I cautiously crept forward every nerve in my body ready to react.

As I got closer I could smell it, the sour smell of death. But there was also another faint smell of burning on the still air. This was the smell I had first encountered at one of the estate houses. It was the smell of burning human flesh. I crouched and examined the strange form that seemed to hover in the centre of the road. The heat waves gave the object different forms. My curiosity forced me forward.

Then all before me was clear. Thomas was hanging there by his ankles. He was completely naked with a huge swarm of flies which had settled on him. His head was about a metre off the ground. His private parts were missing. Instead there was a gaping hole. Blood had run down over his torso and head forming a dark red covering, dripping into a jelly-like pool below him. His fingers were just touching the ground.

My immediate reaction was to run, but I forced myself to stay and look around. My senses also told me that there was no one around. I circled the big policeman slowly. There were numerous bare footprints in the soft soil with his boot prints clear amongst them. I went on a little further. There were tracks that showed he had passed and had been caught on his return. Obviously Villa Vista was not that way. I started to move back the way I had come. Drums started to pound frighteningly close. I walked cautiously away keeping a weary eye on my back trail.

The Teng had not gutted Thomas. They had not eaten him. Hough had once spoken about what the Teng did to a man's private parts but he had not continued with the reasoning behind it. The smell of burning was still strong in my nostrils. My every sense was alert and I had the horrible feeling that it could easily be me next.

I was in deep shadow when I stopped and checked my back trail once more. There was movement at the very edge of my vision. I crouched down, trying to force my eyes to focus through the pattern of shadows and heat waves. Then a lone, shadowy person materialised. He was coming down the centre of the road. My immediate thought was that the Teng were after me. There was no alternative but to fight. I plunged into the jungle, preparing my weapon and dropping flat amongst the low bushes and undergrowth. Above me hung huge masses of creepers, I burrowed in amongst a tangle. If the Teng wanted me they were going to have a fight on their hands. I waited, but my mind was tired and blank. If this was my time to die then let it be. I would not have been able to avoid it.

Looking back down the road there was a blur of shimmering heat waves and now more unidentifiable fast-moving dancing shadows appeared. Now, there was more than one man coming down the road. There were broken floating shadowy people following the first man. They seemed to falter then rush forward in waves of disjointed movement. Then Roux appeared out of the jigsaw. He was hatless and shirtless and his face a white, desperate contorted mess. I brought my rifle to my shoulder with a sort of relief. Then I realised that I would have to make a terrible choice. The Teng were not after me and probably did not know I was even there! I had very little ammunition, and certainly not enough to take on the band of figures in hot pursuit of the charging Roux.

As he got closer I could hear Roux gasping for breath and see his eyes crazy with fear. If I fired and gave my position away, what would happen to the nuns? It was possible that I would shoot two or three warriors in the road but the rest would escape into the jungle. Then they would hunt me down. It was the most terrible decision that I had ever had to make. I lowered my weapon. There was nothing I could do. Roux was going to die and there was nothing I could do to save him!

Roux was virtually level with me when the Teng overtook him. I bit my lip and closed my eyes and buried my face in the dirt. I heard the crack of a solid object striking Roux and there was a frail cry of agony. A second blow and a second agonised cry of complete terror; a cry of one knowing he was, by all means, a dead man. Then there was silence, followed by a burst of human voices. It was the chatter of a language I did not understand. Presumably they were congratulating one another after the chase.

I looked up at the Teng. About twenty tattooed, yellow-daubed warriors were standing around the body of Roux lying crumpled on the ground. I was very close. I could smell them. They smelt like stale mould. I lay there shaking with fear, biting my bottom lip to stop my teeth rattling. Sweat poured off me in rivers. I tried not to stare at the group of men, but found it impossible not to watch. They hitched Roux by his ankles and wrists to a pole. They lifted his swinging limp body between them and then went off back the way they had come. I lay there shaking long after they had gone. Tired and very sore, I crawled out of my hiding place and set off back the way I had come, but now at a steady run.

At the junction I made a rough sign with sticks pointing down the third road on the off-chance that Potter had managed to get the car going. Then I set off at a comfortable jog, controlling the mad urge to run faster and as far away from Thomas and Roux as possible. My bare feet gave off little puffs of dust on the dry sections of road while in other wetter spots I was almost ankle deep in mud. Far-off the drums thundered. The beat seemed to change direction. It was at times far away to the north, then very near me. It was actually too close for comfort.

I ran and ran, and as the sun crept away behind the trees, a small decaying village appeared through the trees. I approached cautiously. There was no one around. I was tired and confused. I had run so far. I had run for most of the day. Villa Vista should be very close but it was all so confusing. The road went this way and that making it impossible to judge distance or direction. There were the occasional roads branching off, and a few fallen trees, but I was positive I was on the main road. It was broader than the branch roads. In most cases the branch roads had started to be retaken by the forest.

I chose one of the better huts and set about boiling water to fill my empty water bottles. I could not have gone on, even if I had wanted to. I was exhausted, and my whole body ached. When I stood I was like a drunk wobbling around on rubber legs.

I sat with my back to the wall of the hut, eating from a tin, waiting for the water to boil and watching the birds settle for the night. It was the day after Christmas Day. What a way to have spent it! I felt very lonely and frightened. I kept on asking myself "Why me?" A couple of tears rolled down my hot cheeks. I tried not to think about Thomas and Roux but I could not help it. It had been a horrible way to die. Roux had been mad to walk out on us. I sat and dozed as mosquitoes buzzed around and night birds called. It was not yet dark. I sat there too tired to move. Villa Vista must be very close indeed. I would get there tomorrow.

I was dropping off to sleep still sitting up, when in the distance there came the sound of an engine. At first I thought I was dreaming. I sat bolt upright. Was I also going mad? The sound was a loud, solid beat and it was getting closer and closer. Collecting my few belongings, I hobbled painfully away from the hut to the roadside, knowing that I would have to be very careful. It could be that Potter had got the car started or it could be bandits.

I positioned myself just off the road, watching and waiting for the vehicle to appear. If it was an unknown vehicle I would hide and let it pass. Then the Peugeot burst out of the jungle. It was running lopsidedly and was covered in mud. The exhaust had broken and was making a terrific noise. A thrill ran up my spine. My tiredness evaporated. My walk was at last over.

Potter stopped, a grin on his face, "Want a lift pal?" he drawled, looking around as if expecting Thomas to appear. Sister Susanna sat next to him in the passenger seat, her face and clothing covered with mud. I peered into the back. Three exhausted, mud-covered women huddled there. There was no room for me.

"We guessed that we'd have a few more kilometres to go. Did the Teng steal your tongue, pal?" asked Potter, climbing out.

There was a large lump in my throat. "They killed Roux and they killed Thomas. They cut his privates off," I whispered.

Sister Susanna was close by and had obviously heard me. She opened the door and clambered out. "It's so barbaric!" she exclaimed and placed a large motherly arm around me. I wanted to cry and cuddle up to her. The rain started suddenly. Big silver drops pelted down as we all stood in the open not worrying about getting wet. "You will be all right now lad. It's not far to the mill," she said reassuringly and released me.

Potter was shaking his head and muttering, "Not nice, not nice," and he popped open the boot jamming it with a stick. "In you get Mac. It's third class but better than walking!"

I settled myself into the boot and with a clash of gears and a cloud of exhaust fumes we moved off, bouncing and skidding along. I hung on. It was uncomfortable but definitely better than walking. The women chosen to accompany Potter were the biggest and strongest of the group. Lily was not amongst them.

Then the car got stuck. The women and I pushed and shoved and after a back-breaking struggle, regained dry ground. The mud thrown up by the spinning wheels covered everyone.

Then on we went skidding along in the semi-dark. A tree had fallen across the road blocking our path, and we were out again. Sister Susanna began wielding an axe with expertise. The tree parted and on we went. Just as suddenly, we broke from the jungle onto a hard, well-worn road surface. Potter stopped, for it was now really dark. I climbed out of the boot.

Sister Susanna was examining the road. "It's the Villa Vista road," she exclaimed from the darkness. "The river is dead ahead, and I can hear the saws. The mill's just round the corner."

I went to the front of the car. Visibility was so bad that we could only see a few metres ahead. The car had no lights. Sister Susanna and I walked ahead with the car following us, chugging along noisily.

As we rounded a bend in the road we saw lights glowing dead ahead. I felt a funny little sense of relief and achievement. Seventy or so kilometres on foot! I had made it! I knew we would have to go back to get the others but first I had to sleep. I stumbled along with a jumble of thoughts in my tired mind.

"Hey you guys!" a loud harsh voice challenged us from the dark.

"It's me, Mac and Potter and some nuns!" I called hurriedly and excitedly. I had a sudden fear that some trigger-happy fool would shoot us up. Jerome appeared out of the dark, cool and gaunt, followed by another two men with their rifles at the ready.

We arrived at the compound. Muller, Ross and Rocky were there. Then the questions followed. How? How far? How many? I tried to answer them but was too tired for my mind and body were numb. Muller listened to all of our account of the last few days. I then collapsed onto a stretcher that had been pointed out to me and, within seconds, became dead to the world.

Out of nowhere a hand was shaking me awake. Surely it was not morning already. It felt as if I had just put my head down.

"Wakey wakey!" said a voice I recognised as Rocky Stone.

He was crouched down next to me with a mug of coffee in his hand. Potter was opposite sitting with his hands in his hair and a mug on the floor at his feet. It was still pitch dark outside.

"We're making an early start," said Stone, straightening up. "You guys had better come with us. There's chow in the mess if you're quick." He left us.

Potter scratched his stubbly chin. "Better have a shave and a wash." He pulled a handful of the ingrained mud from his hair and then seemed to change his mind as he made no move to go for his clean-up. I did not want to know what I looked like. I had dried mud on my face and clothing and I had past caring what I smelt like. Food was more important and to get back to the mine, back to Pole, Lily and the other nuns and pray the sick had survived.

Chapter 10

The trucks split up at the junction of the three roads. I accompanied what was called the burial party. No one gave me a choice. Sergeant Major Ross was in charge. Muller went with the second truck to Swart's mine.

Stopping the truck near to Thomas's suspended corpse we raked the jungle on either side of the road with automatic fire. It always amazed me how quickly a corpse started to decompose in the heat and humidity. Birds, insects and jungle creatures had already started on him. Thomas was a complete mess.

As usual, Ross was well organised and ordered a hole to be dug close to the rotting body. A piece of canvas was placed beneath Thomas. Jerome climbed onto Rocky's shoulders and cut the monkey-rope that secured Thomas's ankles. Thomas, with what seemed like a great sigh of relief, flopped down onto the canvas. We dragged him along and dropped him in the hole and quickly covered him with the soft, fresh earth. No one spoke and no one said a prayer. It all seemed so very wrong to me. Thomas had been a real solid character and a privilege to have known and worked beside; the type of person this God-forsaken country really needed.

The burial completed, I took up my weapon and walked down the road a little way. I remembered the smell of burning flesh and knew that I would have to investigate. As I moved off the road onto a dark dank narrow track I saw a large black scorpion scuttle away underneath a heap of dead branches. I gave it a chance to get away and then continued, peering into the dark shadowy jungle. Then I caught the faint smell of death in the still air.

"Take it easy pal!" called Rocky softly. "You don't want to end up the same way."

My senses told me there was no one around. There were no Teng. No sound of drums beating. The birds chattered and called to one another and monkeys screeched and barked. The men were following me, with their weapons at the ready.

The clearing that appeared was not very big. There were many naked footprints in the soft earth and signs that the Teng had been there. There was a type of rack made of sticks over a now dead fire. I knew this was where Roux had ended up. There was a strong smell of rotting flesh. I went cautiously forward. It might sound rather callous but the Teng had obviously regarded us as a worthy enemy to want to eat us, even Roux, of whom I could not think a worse example.

Rocky and a number of the men, joined me gaping and gagging. There was now an almost suffocating stench on the hot stagnant air.

"They ate Roux here!" I gasped, and neatly kicked a severed hand from the ashes of the fire. It was Roux's hand, the one with the missing middle finger. The finger I had cut off in the back of the truck to save his life. I had often wondered if he really had been hit by an arrow that day, or had it just been a sharp stick brushing against the side of the truck?

There were a number of pieces of clothing including Roux's wallet, which contained a picture of his wife and child, and a few bank notes. The Teng had no use for money. I searched around the clearing. Then, behind a bush, I found a pile of fly-covered bones. There were ribs, legs and an arm along with dried intestines. They did not all belong to Roux.

"They must have eaten two people here," I said poking the bones with a stick. "There are two sets of ribs."

Rocky peered over my shoulder and agreed with me. We would probably never know who the second person was. Ross arrived and insisted we bury the bits and pieces.

We returned to the junction to wait for Muller's party to return. I sat on a log in the shade. I kept on telling myself it could have been me, buried out here. I was no tougher and no better equipped to survive. Then I thought of Lily and I hoped to God she was safe and that the sick nuns would be all right. Jerome had started a card game in the back of the truck. Ross sat reading a novel. For us it was all in a day's work.

Late that afternoon Muller's truck appeared. We climbed aboard our own and prepared to follow. Lily hung out over the tailgate. She smiled and waved at us. Pole's moon-shaped head peered over her shoulder. Boy was it great to be alive! I had not seen Lily for a couple of days and I now realised how much I had missed her.

The trip back to the railhead was uneventful. The nuns were soon shipped off by de Bruins to Stanleyville. Our section was now down to three and we had been issued a new truck, which was rigged out with a Browning machine-gun, ammunition box, chainsaw, cables, jerry cans for water and fuel and rations.

Muller had praised us, saying we were great fighting men. It was a bit hard to take, as had we not fought, we would all have died. I doubted that our military ability or fighting skills were anything other than our desperate struggle for survival.

Back at the railhead Potter opened the box of Christmas food, while Pole started to sort out the different tins.

"Let's have ham, potatoes, baby carrots and peas. Shall we try and roast the potatoes?" said Pole smiling happily in anticipation.

We were going to have the meal which we had missed over Christmas. Hough arrived with two bottles of wine and a broad welcoming grin on his flat, evil face. He settled on a log, mug in hand. He shrugged his shoulders when Potter declined his wine and instead poured himself a mug of coffee. We sat around waiting for the policeman's usual lecture. Pole busied himself around the fire, his mug within easy reach.

Hough cleared his throat and spat into the flames. "I first want to wish you a Happy Christmas, and pray no one else will leave us," said Hough.

I found it rather a funny way to put it.

"Thomas is going to be missed by me and all the community. He was a great man and a good policeman. Let us drink to him," said Hough seriously.

"Thomas!" we all said in unison raising our mugs. Hough continued, "I have a little extra money I will send to his wife. She will also be getting his pension." We all drank again. "To Carr, Roux and Teacher. I wish them well wherever they may be. We drink to them," he said smiling like the devil. We raised our mugs, "Carr, Roux and Teacher," we repeated solemnly.

Hough smiled happily and, sipping his wine, looked around as if he had forgotten someone. Of course, it was his supplier of lit cigarettes. "Here's to Maritz."

We drank but no one said a word.

"Right, let me bring you guys up to date. I think de Haas still could be around. The witchdoctor Gogo is definitely still around. We have, how do you say, a recipe to start more trouble in this region. I have put out various feelers into the community and one of my senior officers has taken it upon himself to make enquiries about de Haas. We can only wait and see." He smiled happily, the flickering of the flames reflected on his face. "At the same time, we are short-staffed," and he shrugged, spreading his hands before him.

We sat in a silent group. Far away thunder rumbled. Potter shuffled his feet in the dust. Pole stirred a pot on the fire and then straightened up. It was funny how the man did not tan! He was still as white as the day we had arrived here. I just wished the whole, unfair business would come to an end and we could all go home.

Pole served our meal with great flourish. He carved the ham, dished up vegetables and served each of us in turn. The so-called roast potatoes turned out like soggy chips but the rest was great. Hough was offered a meal, but he refused. He seemed happy sitting, drinking and smoking, and watching us gorge ourselves. We ate in silence. I was thinking of the excitement of Christmas back home. There had always been cards and presents, always a roast turkey and all the trimmings. It was a time that I would always miss. It was a very special time of the year.

Pole broke the silence. "When this job is done, I never wish to see a gun again in my life. Too many terrible things have happened in the last months, too many innocent people have died and for what?" He answered his own question. "So that de Bruins can strip the jungle, so that men can lose their lives. None of us present here will ever forget this place and the men we have actually murdered. It is all wrong." He rose and walked away into the darkness.

Hough, Potter and myself remained silent. Pole had said it all in a few brief sentences. Hough excused himself and went off to the station. Potter and I just sat there in silence staring into the flickering flames.

From that day on the tug started to arrive twice a day, and the train ran continuously. Arc lights and a portable generator were placed on the dock. I fished, ate and slept. We never ventured far from the railhead.

One balmy afternoon Potter joined me at the harbour. "You see what they are doing?" he asked knowingly. "Politically, things are happening. De Bruins are shipping out as much lumber as quickly as possible, for time must be running out. The barges are over-loaded and the train is over-loaded. I just hope they don't forget to pay us!" and he laughed nervously.

Since Teacher's death we no longer received our out-of-date newspapers, which were the only link we had with the outside world. Amongst Teacher's kit I had found the letter addressed to his wife and had posted it. I still had not received any mail from home. Pole still received his letters regularly, and I had joined Potter in ignoring the arrival of the mail.

One evening, Pole was in a pretty good mood. He had received a late Christmas present, a box of biscuits, and had shared them with us. Hough appeared out of the darkness with a bottle of wine. He lit a cigarette and poured a mug of wine. "Tomorrow I wish to visit The Sweet, de Haas's estate.

"I have been there before, but I wish to have another look around. I also find it surprising that since you guys returned there have been no sightings or attacks here or at Villa Vista." He smiled happily. He was probably thinking of his bird business and the possibility of getting it going again. This was going to be the longest trip we had done since returning to the railhead.

235

The next day we left early. Potter drove, while Hough settled into the passenger seat. Pole and myself occupied the back where there seemed to be an awful lot of room. As we approached The Sweet Estate house, Pole arranged himself behind the machine-gun and I took up my usual position in the right-hand corner.

The house now had a dilapidated, abandoned air. The grass had grown long, and weeds were protruding from the gravel driveway. Pole remained at his post, and I dismounted to join Potter and Hough. The front door was locked. Hough pointed and Potter smashed it open with the butt of his FN.

Hough talked while looking around. "He lived here with his brother and sister-in-law until recently. Where have they gone? I don't know." His voice was echoing in the empty house. "But then again, were they his relations? I doubt it. I also do not think de Haas returned here after the attack on St Patrick's." Hough wandered down the sparsely furnished passage. "You guys just look around. Anything you see suspicious, call me. I will start in the office at the back of the house."

Our boots echoed through the building as we split up. I entered what must have been a very comfortable lounge and stood looking around. I found it rather strange that Hough had waited so long to visit and search the house. He had claimed to have visited the house before, but I had my doubts. How come the door was locked and we had to break in! Sometimes he seemed to operate in a confusing pattern, like sending us hurriedly off to St Patrick's to save the nuns. Surely it was his duty to accompany us, not send his deputy. He seemed to pick and choose without logic.

I stood in the centre of the lounge on a huge grey mat with little red flowers and I looked around. There were teak chairs covered in leather, a royal blue sofa and a number of old-looking pictures on the wall. One, the biggest picture, was of a huge bear with its arms spread wide and mouth open. Its teeth and tongue appeared to be dripping with blood. It was a funny picture to have in one's lounge. A drink cabinet was against the wall. I pulled the net curtains back to give more light to the room. We had not been told what to look for, only to search. I rolled the big mat back. There was nothing other than dust beneath it. I replaced it and went from chair to chair to sofa, but found nothing. The drink cabinet was locked. Using my bayonet I popped open the lock without causing too much damage to the woodwork. There was a fine collection of bottles but they meant little to me.

Potter joined me. "There's blow-all in the dining room," he said coming across to join me. "Well look at this." He picked up a bottle of clear liquid without a label, and he opened it. At first I thought he was going to knock it back but he just sniffed it. "That," he said with a grin, "is the genuine Russian vodka. Look." He capped it and turned the bottle upside down. On the bottom was writing of a type I had never seen before. It was imprinted in the glasswork. "That's Russian writing, and this is the real cheap stuff. I spent time on the boats travelling the east coast of Africa and we used to swap cigarettes with the Russian sailors for this booze." He deftly examined the other bottles and said they were all right. "I find it funny there is only one bottle. A person gets a taste for this muck. Let's look around. Maybe there's more."

We moved together through the house searching here and there. In the kitchen we found a half case of the same liquor and then outside in the garage we fond a couple of dozen empties. Potter grinned. "This guy has a real taste for this stuff. What did I tell you!"

We went back to see Hough and found him sitting with his feet up in de Haas's office, a cigarette clamped between his teeth. Papers were piled up around him. "Look at this." He pushed a pile of papers across to Potter and me. "They look like shipping orders, dates and place of arrival. If we check the dates on those papers I bet you we will find them pretty close to the date you guys stopped de Haas's truck at the roadblocks." He drew on his cigarette. The room was getting very smoky. "Note the Massey Ferguson parts for a sprayer, parts for a tractor, parts for a sprayer." Hough grinned happily. "Mac, pop round to the sheds to see what tractors de Haas has, and I will bet you a couple of beers there won't be a Massey Ferguson in the sheds. Look at their spraying equipment as well, whilst you're there." As I left, Potter started telling him about the Russian vodka.

I wandered around the yard. The sheds were all locked but the locks were no problem. There were no Massey Ferguson tractors or spraying equipment. I made my way back to Hough and Potter and reported what I had found.

Potter had got himself involved in the paperwork. I wandered aimlessly around the house and soon worked out which room was de Haas's. A few items of clothing hung in the cupboard. The bed had been made neatly with corners tucked in. The clothing was nothing special, khaki shirts, shorts and underwear. I stopped in surprise. There was similar writing on the labels of the underpants as on the vodka bottles. I dragged the bed away from the wall to see just dust and cobwebs. Under the mat there was nothing. I had a notion there might be secret panels and doors there, but there were none.

I took the underpants to Hough and, as he examined the labels, he looked concerned. "I think it's become obvious that de Haas is a Russian agent, and he is, most probably, the cause of all the trouble."

I left Hough and Potter in the smoke-filled room and went and joined Pole. I told him what we had found, but he only shrugged his big shoulders.

"You know the communists are evil. Me and my family ran from Poland but we were lucky. Many were not so lucky." He sat there looking into the distance. "Me, I was lucky. My mother taught me English. She was a good teacher and made me promise not to tell anyone she was doing that. No one knew she spoke English. My father might have known but no one else. She said it would help me." He smiled at the distant memory. "She was right," he concluded.

Just then Potter called from one of the windows. "Pole, Mac. We need your help."

Pole and I crossed to the house. Hough had found a safe. It had been hidden by a chest of drawers. The chest had been pushed aside, which was easy enough. The safe was cemented into the wall, and we all stood looking at it. It looked very strong.

"We're going to open that safe, you guys," said Hough positively. "If we can't open it we're taking it with us."

"There are hammers and chisels in one of the sheds," I volunteered. "I'll get them."

Pole swung at it with the four-pound hammer. The clash of steel meeting steel resounded throughout the house. When that didn't work we turned to the chisel. It made very little difference he caused hardly any damage to the black steel safe.

Pole stood back to examine it. He was shirtless and sweating profusely. He spat on his palms and swung the hammer. Sparks flew as the metals clashed together.

"It's no good. The bugger is not opening!" gasped Pole. Then he handed the hammer and chisel to Potter and he started on the cement work. This went a little better. He hammered away covering the room with white powdery cement. Time was passing and none of us wanted to be on the road in the dark.

"I say we stay here tonight, remove the safe and take it with us tomorrow," said Pole eventually. Hough agreed. Neither Potter nor I cared. There seemed to be a number of comfortable beds in the house. They were all we needed.

In the fading light I went for a wander around the house and sheds. The labourers' compound was only a short distance away. It was beautifully quiet. I plodded along, looking at this and that. It had to have been a very good life living out here. Fruit was plentiful and everything grew very quickly and easily. Labour would be cheap. Coffee and hemp were easy, manageable crops.

My thoughts drifted to Hill Farm and Oupa, Gran and Mia. What had happened to them? Then I thought of Lily and the pendant. Was it worth anything? This place in Ireland, where she lived, Wexeter, Plough Lane, sounded so unreal. Was she just having me on?

I wandered round the labourers' compound. The buildings were starting to fall down. The occupants had fled taking all their possessions. I was about to return to the others and was standing at the edge of the coffee plantation and saw to my right there was a small stand of sugar cane. Something was moving around breaking the stalks. Then I heard a grunt. It was a pig. I unslung my rifle, for it could be wild. I stood there watching. The sugar cane swayed and rustled and I saw the pig was heading straight for me. A piglet squealed. There were more. A pig with piglets had probably been left behind by the farm labour. Mother pig appeared large and black and round, in prime condition. Three little fellows followed her, running helter skelter across the yard. She took no notice of me and headed for one of the open huts. One little piglet hung back and stood facing me for a moment, eyeing me with its beady little eyes. Then, with a squeal, dashed after its mother. I laughed at the comical little fellow. I stopped abruptly, feeling rather foolish. It had been the first time I had laughed at anything for what seemed to be a very long time. I tramped back to the house.

Potter and Pole were still at it. Hough was boxing up the papers he had decided to remove and had opened one of de Haas's bottles of wine. The sun was setting when the safe eventually broke loose from the wall. It was rather heavy and it took three of us to carry it to the truck.

I was nominated as cook. We did not have much, just a few cans of food and coffee. We all sat around on the veranda eating. No one had much to say.

Hough eventually stretched and stubbed his cigarette out on the floor and stood up. "I will be hitting the bed," he said, leaving us as he entered the silent but airy house.

Potter waited for a while, then said, "Hough is a bit shook up about the Russian being here under his nose and not spotting him."

Pole burped, and finished his wine. "The Russian bear is a cunning, strong creature. When I was a child my father used to tell me stories about the bear's cunning and strength. 'Never trust a Russian!' he used to say. They are different, think differently and behave differently, and they always do the thing you least expect them to. They have one aim and that is to rule the world." Pole sighed and continued. "Both my parents died before we ran from Poland. I am thankful for that." We lapsed into a comfortable silence. In the last few hours I had learnt more about the Pole than I had in the last five months.

"You know," said Potter suddenly, "there are only ten days to go!"

The next morning we left The Sweet Estate and returned to the railhead. It had been a really restful night. For the first time in roughly five months we got to sleep in a proper bed, with sheets and pillows. We were all in very good form. Pole was singing to himself in Polish. Potter was driving extremely well, avoiding muddy patches and puddles when he could and racing through bogs. To get stuck meant a long delay with only four of us to dig the truck out.

After arriving back at the railhead Hough went off to the police station and we settled down to wait. The afternoon tug brought Jerome and cutting equipment. Jerome was a real cool customer. He sported a pencil-line moustache and was always neatly dressed. Today he wore a neck scarf tucked into his shirt, giving him a rather professional air. He greeted us casually as we loaded the gas bottles and cutting torch onto the truck drove to our camp.

Hough arrived shortly. "Can you open it?" he asked, indicating the safe.

Jerome examined the safe. "Piece of cake, just watch me," he said, slipping goggles over his eyes. He set about cutting off the hinges. Then he started on the lock. "Voilà!" he cried and stepped back as the door dropped into the dust. "Not much of a safe, was it now! Plenty of time to catch the tug back to civilisation," he joked.

Hough was into the safe like a fox-terrier after a rat. He placed his body in front of the open safe so that none of us could see what he was doing.

"Ah!" he said removing a file and a number of envelopes. There was also a large wad of money.

"That's Russian bucks, and that's dollars," said Jerome, trying to see round Hough.

Hough was moving quickly, placing the contents of the safe in a bag that he was carrying.

"Right," said Hough straightening up. "That's it. Thanks a lot Jerome."

Jerome beamed. "The pleasure is all mine!" he purred, giving off that superior air. "Could have popped that one with one hand tied behind my back." There was a slight hesitation. "How about a coffee before I board my boat?"

Pole set about pouring coffee for us all.

Hough stood up and slung the bag over his shoulder. "I will see you all later," he said walking away towards the station.

"Not going to share those dollars between us boys!" called Jerome smirking.

Hough was tense. He stopped and turned. "There will be no looting in this region. I will see you all later." Then he walked off towards the station.

"Cheeky little shit," sneered Jerome. "He is far too big for his boots. Fancy not sharing the loot between us. I won't open a safe for him again." Jerome made it sound as if Hough had committed a serious wrong.

Back on the tug, Jerome leant on the rail smoking and he gave us that superior smile. "Anyway, thanks for the coffee and we will see you chaps around. There are only nine days left."

Potter and I stood on the harbour wall watching the tug pull away, disturbing the mirror-like surface of the water with its wake cutting a dead straight line. Jerome remained standing at the stern rail, calm and collected with a cigarette hanging from the corner of his mouth.

Potter punched me on the arm. "I'll buy you a Coke."

The shop looked even more dingy than I remembered it. Miriam smiled, pottering around behind the counter. She looked doubtful when we ordered half a dozen bottles of Coke. She placed the bottles in a bag and took our money smiling.

"You see trouble finished. You hear no drums. Teng have gone back to their place," she said as she rattled the change around in the palm of her hand. "Gogo, she run away." She dropped her voice to a whisper. "Maybe she run. Too many Teng and Mongu have died. She might have a white man lover. She has gone with. Gone to a far-away land where we will never hear or see her again."

I often wondered about the bits of information that Miriam supplied. They were often very close to the truth. "We will be going soon," I said for want of something to say.

"The mill at Villa Vista will close. There will be no work. I am afraid soldiers of another tribe will come and destroy us. Destroy our country and our children. There is to be an election, but us black people do not understand elections. They who think of such things do not understand the likes of Gogo, and a witch's power." Miriam stopped talking, slightly out of breath.

"They do not understand!" she said sadly.

I knew she was telling the truth. Life was not fair.

Potter and I returned to camp in silence. What Miriam had said was sadly true. What was going to happen to this place, where witches and tribal rights and customs played such an important role in their daily living?

Hough, on seeing us, came across from the police station carrying his bag. He obviously had had no intention of showing Jerome what he had removed from the safe.

He emptied the bag on the table. Then he pointed to the contents. "The yellow file, I understand it is about company policy, nothing to interest us. There are a number of letters from the company's head office, covering coffee prices, fuel and the likes. A few hundred roubles, and a few thousand dollars in notes. Then there are two letters written in Russian. I do not understand Russian. There's one letter that looks like maybe a sister, or lover," and he pointed to a white envelope. "The other is more interesting. It has no post mark and looks official and was obviously delivered by hand." He smiled, bobbing his head as he appeared to enjoy the mystery.

Pole grunted, taking the official looking envelope. "I can read and write a little Russian, but I am not very good."

"Give it a try. It is better we keep it amongst ourselves for the time being, though," said Hough.

Pole went to the tent and returned with a writing pad and pen and then he settled himself on a log.

Potter and I lounged around quietly waiting. Hough had gone back to the station. I kept on thinking about those nine days – nine long days. I was going home! What would I find? I pushed the thought away. I would have to go to Ireland. How was I going to get to Ireland? Probably by boat if it was an island. Maybe by plane. And what would it cost? The thought crept in occasionally that Lily was a complete stranger. Had she known the value of the pendant and given me a false address? I doubted it, but when lying awake at two in the morning I was not so sure.

Later Hough arrived back at the camp with a bottle of wine, which he opened and poured into mugs. Then he lit a cigarette and sat down. Pole and I joined him.

After a time Pole sat back looking around at us. "I don't know how accurate I am, but what I have written is the best I can do," he said. Potter fetched the lantern and placed it closer. The lantern light was not particularly strong, but then Pole's writing was large.

"I will read the one I do not think is very important first. It is from Nikita to Paul. It reads, 'Mother has died in her sleep bless her. We all attend the burial. She has left you a vase and jewellery. I will keep it until you return.' There is a lot about mother's illness, about half a page. Then there is a bit about a holiday to the Black Sea. Then there is some sort of family talk about uncles and aunts."

"It could be code," said Potter, his eyes sparkling, searching for a mystery.

Pole shook his head and continued, "At the end there is a note that his promotion is due and hopefully he will receive it because he deserves it. She will be very proud. Signed off 'love Nikita Petrovitch'." Pole shrugged. "That's the best I can do," he said.

"So, de Haas's Russian name is Petrovitch!" said Potter, his eyes still dancing with excitement, looking for a spy story. No one commented.

"The next letter is more interesting. It is from someone whose signature I cannot read. It's just a squiggle. It has no date, no postage stamp, but he calls our de Haas 'Dear comrade Paul'. To me this letter has a hidden meaning but I could be wrong. It reads, 'Dear comrade Paul. Your success has amazed us, but there is a small section missing, the icing on the cake. Remember our lecture. The unexpected, unexplained, the western world cannot understand and will not be able to. The meeting has taken place and has been agreed. Pay less than originally expected say twenty-five thousand. The money will be transferred. If the situation and help improves, pay her a further twenty-five. Her assistance is of great value in the struggle. The other articles requested are en route and should arrive at B any day now. They must be collected immediately, knowing how untrustworthy the assistants are. Our carrier of messages, Gideon, will give you the other dates when you are to meet him. All of us are pleased with your success at entering the closed ground.'" Pole faltered. "The wording here is difficult to understand." He tapped his pen and had a drink.

We all sat spellbound, each of us trying to read between the lines, trying to understand what the writer was getting at. Each of us probably had his own interpretation.

"There is more," said Pole. "It goes on, 'The world around you is changing, hopefully to our leader's satisfaction. Your achievements are being noted high up. Once you have read this letter it should be destroyed. I thank you again for your efforts.'" Pole sat back, "Another interpreter might read this letter differently. My Russian is not that good."

"Ah," grunted Hough, his face excited. "I see truth coming at last to the surface." We all looked at him for an explanation. He puffed on his cigarette and then finished his wine. "De Haas. I suspect his real name is Petrovitch, which is a common Russian name. Nikita is probably a relation. His instructions come from downstream, and his seniors are pleased with his progress." Hough held up one finger in the fire light. "The controller, or whoever it is keeping an eye on Petrovitch is encouraging him. Pay her twenty-five whatever, then another twenty-five if the assistance is good. I suspect dollars. There were dollars in the safe." We all nodded. Hough must have counted them but he did not tell us how much was in the safe. "Gogo the witch is an intelligent woman. Many of these witches have attended European or mission schools and understand the value of money, especially such as dollars. They are manipulators with no regard to human life or wrong or right by our standards." He sighed, "Yes, I believe Petrovitch somehow contacted Gogo, and offered her money for her assistance. She has her followers, her lesser witches to assist. Look, we found one at The Sweet working for Petrovitch. She knew that the mission was to be attacked. Was she planted there at The Sweet to keep an eye on Petrovitch? Or was she a messenger?"

Hough poured more wine. The firelight was dancing, throwing long flickering shadows.

"Petrovitch would know about the tension between the Teng and the people at the sawmill. He would also know that, if he played things right, the Mongu would join their brothers the Teng. Gogo could place spells on the Teng and Mongu, promising them greatness in the Spirit world if they fell in with the plan. She got the money. Petrovitch achieved the destabilisation of the whole region. They could now place their man in charge of the region. His controller would be happy with him. His superiors in Russia would be pleased." Hough smiled and sipped his drink.

Potter tossed more wood on the fire and it blazed up.

"The letter talks about unknown, unexplained action that no one would understand. I think that would be the attack on St Patrick's Mission. Attacking a group of helpless women who are only doing good for the Africans of this region would cause a great many people to leave. That action has caused at least half a dozen missions to close down. The people at Villa Vista are very nervous and I believe that when you all go they will also close. A few of the smaller mines to the north have already shut down." Hough sighed and continued to sip his drink.

"If we were to go into the other regions," said Pole, "we would probably find another de Haas, another Petrovitch or agent of theirs doing the same thing. They wouldn't need to use witchdoctors, but by gathering groups of dissatisfied army officers, or police, or even labourers and forming cells, that would grow and cause havoc. Then when the country became completely ungovernable they could place their man in charge, supplying him with money, guns and other types of support, thus making him powerful. A strong dictator." Pole sat there, large and white, and looked into the fire. "Then why did Petrovitch not come back to The Sweet for the letters and money?" asked Pole looking at Hough.

Hough shrugged, dropping his voice. "You and Mac saw him transporting warriors at the mission and he obviously saw you and decided the game was up. Then, possibly, he realised the estate house was being watched. I placed gendarme Ray there with a rifle for a few days." He laughed softly, "I was looking for a short cut and promised him a large bonus if he shot de Haas for me. He is not a bad shot. I have warned the border posts and the police are watching out for him. He has not re-appeared but there are many ways out of this country."

Hearing all this I now understood part of Hough's reasoning. He had no intention of putting de Haas or Petrovitch before a court of law. As I knew so well, life was really cheap out here.

Hough grinned to himself. "We know the Mongu Teng warriors were rewarded with rifles for a white man's ear. The weapons were brought up the river to Bombimba as farming equipment. Petrovitch met the boat. I suspect it was the <u>Gideon</u>, a steamer that travels around a lot. The boat is also difficult to keep tabs on. You met Petrovitch coming from Bombimba carrying the guns." Hough dragged on his cigarette making the end glow in the dark. "The whole damned plan is now before us. We now know it all." Hough smiled cruelly. "I would love to question Gogo. She has been the cause of so much unnecessary death. Then I would like to...," and he stopped, laughing. His ugly face danced in the firelight. "Just shoot de Haas out of hand."

We all smiled and probably all felt the same way.

"Would Petrovitch be a member of the KGB?" asked Potter quietly.

I had never heard of the KGB and it obviously showed.

"Secret police and spying," said Pole. Then he continued. "Yes, he is behaving as one of them, the arrogant bastards."

It was late, the wine was finished and, with nine days to go, the answers to the last five and half months' questions had been given.

Hough stood up, dusting the seat of his trousers, a smile on his ugly flat face. "Tomorrow I will make various enquiries as soon as the shipping office opens. The *Gideon* is a regular visitor to Bombimba. We might take a drive and visit that little steamer. There is also an excellent hotel, and there is nothing going on around here." He waved his hand in a final gesture and left for the station.

Chapter 11

I really did not want to go to Bombimba. I felt safe here at the railhead and we did not know what was going on in the outside world. As far as we knew there could be a full-scale war there. The 'bandits' at Crossways School were proof of this. There were only eight days to go. I think Pole and Potter thought the same.

Hough obviously sensed our attitude. "It will be all right," he reassured us. "Nothing is going on down at Bombimba. I wish to interview the captain of the boat, that is all. He will know who accompanied the crates of guns, and about de Haas, I mean Petrovitch. He would never allow such stuff to be transported without a guard of some nature." He sat back smiling, sucking on his cigarette. We were silent while we finished our breakfast.

Hough tossed the dregs from his coffee into the fire and stood up. "I am taking a chance. There is possibly nothing to learn, but then I can at least say I tried." He hitched up his submachine-gun and tightened his ammunition belt. He seemed pleased with himself this morning. "We have plenty of time. The shipping office says the *Gideon* will only arrive about four," said Hough.

We tossed our equipment onto the truck and away we went. Hough was reclining once more in the passenger seat. Potter was singing a hymn at the top of his voice. At times I wondered if Potter had brain damage from all the liquor he had taken in.

It was two hundred and fifty kilometres by road to the village, which was situated on one of the tributaries of the Congo river. Once on the southbound road, the going improved and we hurtled along at a steady forty. Many of the villages we passed through had been burnt down. There were signs that there had been fighting. A few rotting corpses and bloated dead cows lay along the roadside. Crows and vultures were circling everywhere. As we got closer to Bombimba the situation seemed to improve. People came out to wave and kids danced on the side of the road. Men and women were labouring in their banana patches and vegetable gardens. Houses had corrugated iron roofing, a sure sign of prosperity and a sign we were back in civilisation.

The town was a lot bigger and different from what we expected. There was a shanty town on the edge and then it improved towards the centre, with brick buildings. Obviously, it had been recently attacked, for all the buildings were pockmarked by bullets. Probably the smartest-looking building in the town was the hotel 'Le Rouge' that looked as if it had also been shot up. The locals lounged around in doorways and a few greeted us with a smile and friendly waves.

The truck stopped in front of the police station and Hough called us together. He had an evil grin on his face. "I have not told the local gendarme that we are coming, in case he warns someone. We are going to visit him. Then I am going to get him to assist us when the *Gideon* arrives. You can see the docks from here." He pointed down the road. The road stopped at the river. "Tonight I am going to stand you guys a great meal at the hotel. The beds are clean and comfortable. We might call it a farewell gift. I have also a little surprise planned, but I will tell you later." His eyes sparkled and he was laughing, with his yellow teeth protruding through his tatty moustache.

The police station was a concrete building with steel bars on the windows. There were signs that it had also recently come under fire. Hough went inside and we loafed around outside.

After a while Potter jumped down off the truck and looked around. "Mac and I will go and see if there are any cold drinks at the hotel," he said and we wandered across the road, and into the cool rather smart interior.

"Bonjour Monsieur," came a musical greeting from a pretty half-caste girl behind the reception desk. Potter and I smiled happily.

"Do you speak any English?" I asked, feeling rather out of place in the rather smart foyer.

"Oui, I do a leetle," she lisped, "Can I be of' help?"

"Have you cold Coke?" I asked.

"Oui, monsieur, through that door is the bar. My 'usband is there. He will be of 'elp."

We went through the door she indicated. The bar had been only slightly damaged, a broken window, and a couple of bullet holes. A big fan pushed the hot air around. There was a long mahogany counter with many bottles on the shelves.

The husband, a large bearded man, sat reading a newspaper. He looked up and smiled. "You very welcome. Beer?" he asked.

I shook my head. "Cold Coke, say half a dozen bottles."

He busied himself behind the bar. "You all late for the fighting. By one day. A truckload of rebels, come shooting and killing. The gendarmes open fire, killing seven. The others run like hell. Me," and he patted himself on the chest, "I got two from the balcony." He laughed loudly. "They are worse than animals, really bastards, murdering and raping. Want everything for nothing, just kill and take. They got one hell of a shock, I am telling you," and he laughed again.

We agreed with him and said we would probably see him later. Then we took the bottles and returned to the truck. Hough had still not returned. We loafed around in the shade drinking our cold drinks.

It was about four when, in the distance, we heard the echo of a boat's siren. It echoed across the river into jungle and town. Many village people appeared out of the buildings, all carrying baskets of produce and live chickens, and what the locals called "bush meat". "Bush meat" could be anything from worms, to monkey or crocodile. The colourful procession of hawkers was laughing merrily and calling noisily to one another as they made their way towards the harbour.

Hough arrived with a tall, gaunt gendarme. He did not bother to introduce the man. Six black gendarmes appeared, all carrying submachine-guns and ammo pouches. They all looked half-drunk, and were laughing and talking amongst themselves and ignoring us completely. With a grinding of gears we headed for the harbour.

251

Potter parked the truck on the harbour wall and we watched the *Gideon* approach. It made a beautiful picture in the late afternoon sunlight. It was not a pretty boat. It had a rusted superstructure and a worn and battered smokestack. It towed a large barge that was crowded with passengers. A red and white cow stood on the barge, placidly chewing the cud. A couple of bagged pigs squealed as a passenger stumbled over them. Looking down from the harbour wall I was amazed to see two large crocodiles with mouths bound and securely tethered.

The *Gideon* was carefully docked and ropes were thrown down and the steamer and its barge were secured. Then Hough took charge. He ordered the villagers away from the edge of the dock, whilst his thin comrade stood with hands behind his back and said nothing.

"Pole!" called Hough. "You man the machine-gun, and make sure the people see it." Pole removed the cover and cocked the weapon, swinging it from side to side on its pylon. Surprised black faces peered at us from the deck of the *Gideon* and the barges. It must have been a rather unnerving sight, especially if you had a guilty conscience.

Hough, in the meantime, had lined the six gendarmes along the harbour wall. Then he came closer to the truck and in a hushed voice said. "Watch those gendarmes. They are drunk and will be looking for trouble." I noted that he did not say how to sort out any trouble if it did occur.

Silence hung over everything like a damp blanket, with just the soft throb of the *Gideon*'s engine and the soothing gurgle of the river. The passengers stood and waited. The villagers stood in silence to one side, peering at the *Gideon*.

Hough and his comrade strutted up and down the harbour wall. Then, when everything was to his liking, they marched up the gangplank. A large jet-black Negro met the two policemen and they disappeared into a cabin situated behind the bridge. We waited. Time dragged. The gendarmes on the wall started to fidget.

"How long are we gonna be sitting here?" bellowed a strong American accent.

Chapter Eleven

One of the gendarmes had quickly positioned himself on the gangplank and was preventing a large well-tanned white man, who was followed by a scrawny white woman, from coming ashore. The gendarme had taken a step back and cocked his weapon.

"You're gonna hear more about this. I'm an American citizen from the School of Botany. I am a friend!" drawled the loud threatening voice.

Pole nodded towards me. "Mac, tell that stupid fool to shut up and sit down. That policeman is going to shoot him!"

I dropped off the back of the truck and approached the American.

"Do you speak English?" he called and I nodded. The gendarme backed off even further, his weapon still pointing at the man's belly.

"Would you mind shutting up and sitting down. I don't think this is going to take too long!" I said quietly.

He looked at me with an amazed look on his face. "We have been already sitting here for half an hour. We're here to help. We study the fauna and flora at Swart's mine!" he shouted as if to tell all the on-lookers his important business.

I shook my head in disbelief. It sounded like no one had heard about the Teng uprising or the gangs of bandits and army deserters roving around.

"Just keep quiet and sit down, please!" I repeated, none too gently this time. The woman appeared nervous and moved back a few paces.

"I am John Rogers, junior professor!" he said importantly, as if that should have made all the difference.

I could feel the tension in the air. The gendarmes had been in action recently. They were drunk enough not to care. They wanted more action. The passengers on the boat were restless, not liking the position in which they found themselves. If anyone was going to start shooting they were also in the line of fire.

What were Hough and the other inspector up to? Why were they taking so long? Surely a few brief questions could have solved the whole situation.

A couple of the passengers were now standing closer. A middle-aged black man in a colourful shirt, pushed his way closer to Rogers and pointed at me.

"This is African democracy. The gun, it is the ruler. The white scum are brought in to persecute and kill the poor blacks," he sneered in very good English.

Rogers now had a supporter. He turned and nodded his head in agreement with the black man. Then he turned back to me. "We will see about this. You!" He was addressing me now. "Take me to your commanding officer."

I stared at the man. Could he not understand I had just saved his life? Could he not feel the tension in the air and the killing lust of the gendarmes? I carried my FN under my arm, holding the pistol grip. I took a pace closer. The black man in his coloured shirt obviously realised he had gone too far, and he backed off. Rogers stood there, his legs apart in an aggressive stance.

"I demand..." was as far as he got. I brought the barrel of my weapon up in a short, sharp swing, hitting him between the legs. He folded, his mouth open but no sound came. He sunk to his knees, face white and both hands clutched his groin. I stepped back and away. The woman, who had not spoken as yet, rushed forward and crouched next to him. The hatred in her eyes was directed at me. The gendarme, sweating profusely, nodded his head as if he agreed with my action. A tense stillness hung over the harbour and the air was thick with a sense of expectancy.

The tranquillity was suddenly shattered by a cold-blooded scream, followed by a number of resounding thumps from the captain's cabin where Hough and his comrade and the captain had gone. Then a steel door of the cabin flew back on its hinges with a crash and the man whom I believed to be the captain appeared stumbling drunkenly across the deck. He was huge against Hough and his skinny comrade. Blood poured from the captain's face. Obviously he had not been co-operating. Hough, who was grinning broadly, followed close behind the big man. He drew and reversed the pistol and slammed it into the big man's kidneys. The captain howled in agony. Then he fell forward, hanging onto the rail for support. The captain slowly raised an arm and pointed at the sea of faces in the barge. Hough was there at his elbow. His companion had his submachine-gun in hand and they looked down into the open barge.

Hough shouted an order in the local dialect. A well-built man in a red shirt broke from the crowded barge. There was desperation in the way he moved. He jumped onto the rail of the barge and then plunged into the river and started to swim away and towards the opposite bank with the current impeding his progress.

One of the gendarmes on the wall raised his weapon. Then he lowered it. The gendarmes on the wall were all laughing loudly and cheered the swimmer on. The passengers on the barge and boat were all mesmerised by the swimming man, who surged forward with short, strong strokes. The village people had shuffled forward like a wave to the very edge of the harbour wall for a better view. Hough was standing smoking with his partner and the captain lay slumped on the deck at his feet.

I knew what was going to happen but I could not look away. It happened amazingly quickly. A swirl of water, showing part of a crocodile's tail and then without a sound the swimming man was gone. The river drifted serenely by.

The show was over and the passengers were gathering their belongings. One of the women on the harbour was bargaining loudly. People were laughing and a baby howled. Whoever the man was, he had not been prepared to undergo Hough's questioning. He probably would have ended up in the river anyway. Life was really cheap out here.

Hough and the local inspector came off the boat to where I was standing. Hough smiled at the still-hunched Rogers. "Ah, Professor Rogers and Miss Sally. I did not think you would be back this way," he said smiling through his tatty moustache. "I am afraid this whole area is under a state of emergency. Tomorrow you will return downstream. You may stay in the hotel for the night. It is very comfortable and the food is good." Hough laughed and the local inspector nodded knowingly. "Your embassy has slipped up, not supplying you with the information," said Hough as a matter of fact.

"That man assaulted me!" complained Rogers in rather a high-pitched voice, pointing at me.

Hough nodded, "Oh non! You asked for it my man. This man saved your life. Come up to the hotel and I will buy you and your lady a drink."

That evening Hough had promised us a farewell meal. It was the best dinner I had ever had. For starters there was a river fish, with finely chopped lettuce and French dressing. The main course was a fine herb-filled duck, roast potatoes and well-prepared local cabbage. It was delicious. I felt as if I could just eat and eat. The dessert was simply vanilla ice cream. Perfect!

Ivor was the name of Hough's opposite number. He was in charge of the Bombimba police station, but I never did hear his surname.

Potter, Pole and I sat in the smoky bar gorging ourselves. Hough kept on filling our wine glasses but Potter stuck to soft drinks. Eventually, I was too full to move.

Potter grinned, "That is what I call good."

The pretty coloured girl, whose name was Eva, had started clearing away the piles of empty plates and wine bottles.

Professor Rogers and the woman were at a table in the far corner paying us no attention at all. The hotel owner came in and pulled a chair up to our table. Hough poured him a glass of wine.

"It's very good wine," he said sipping it and smacking his lips. "I am worried about the thieving rebels that came calling. Do you think I should send Eva to her mother?" asked the hotel owner.

Ivor sat smoking. He shrugged his shoulders and smiled at the girl removing the plates.

"My friend, your guess about what is going to happen to this wonderful country is as good as mine." He dragged on his cigarette and stubbed it out. "I personally think, if one leaves here there might be an even worse evil downstream. There are even more people who are politically active but around here we will be okay. There is trouble all over and members of the army are deserting and criminal gangs are every where. Katanga province is not a safe place and downstream there is major political unrest." He spread his hands in a final gesture. "All I say is if we stand together we should be all right." He nodded his head and looked at Hough as if wanting confirmation.

It was then that I noticed Professor Rogers and his partner taking an interest in the conversation. Rogers stood up, "May we join you?" he asked, speaking to no one in particular. He and the woman joined us pulling up their chairs.

"This independence business is nonsense," said Hough. "These people cannot rule themselves in a European type of parliament. It is just impossible."

Ivor nodded his head in agreement.

Professor Rogers threw back a drink and then said, "They will bring in the UN soldiers to sort any trouble out. There are talks being held at this very moment with politicians and tribal leaders. There are also a few other bright young African politicians who appear extremely hopeful." He stopped abruptly looking around at each of us. Then he continued. "Downstream there is a lot of talk and jostling for political power, but nothing violent. We thought it would be the same at the mine and Villa Vista."

Hough grunted like a pig. "You just wait and see. This place will turn into a blood bath. It has a history of brutality going way back. I have no faith in foreign troops. Tourists, that's what they are." Hough grinned evilly through the cigarette smoke and then continued. "Rogers, you be wise and do what I say. Tomorrow you go south, down the river, and catch the first plane out. This advice will save your lives." His eyes glittered in the semi-darkness. "Today you were nearly shot by one of the drunken good guys. You were lucky. Your American citizenship does not count out here. In a few days these guys will be going." And he indicated us. "There were seven of them to start with. They are now down to three. I have also lost one of my men. It does not look good. So you take my advice." He sat there nodding his head and playing with an unlit cigarette.

The party died after Hough's little lecture. Rogers said he would leave in the morning on the *Gideon*. Ivor left very unsteadily, with a cigarette jammed in the corner of his mouth and his submachine-gun slung over his shoulder.

Later I sat in a hot bath of soapsuds. I only now became aware of
how filthy I was. The grime seemed to come off in layers. What had
happened to Oupa, Gran and Mia? Why had they not written? I
would know in about nine to ten days' time. It was funny how Lily
had just taken over from Mia in my mind. I now found I thought of
her more and more. Was the pendant safe with her? Was everything
she told me the truth? I sat dozing, half-drunk and letting my mind
wander, the hot water soothed my weary bones.

Breakfast was a grand affair. Tables were laid with silver cutlery
and white china. The silver percolator gave off that fantastic aroma
of roasted coffee beans. There were piles of bacon and egg on shiny
clean plates, toast and marmalade. Rogers and his woman appeared
carrying their luggage, placing it on the floor near the door. They
greeted us and sat down at a table. I seemed to have been forgiven
by the professor.

"Before we leave," said Hough, "I wish to show you the work of a
friend of mine," and he smiled happily. "It's only a beautiful work of
art but well worth seeing."

We all nodded with our mouths full, and all as happy as we had
ever been on this nightmare trip.

Rogers and the woman boarded the Gideon which was going to
return downstream. The big black captain stood on the deck, his
head swathed in a bandage, but still going about his duties.

Hough took us along a narrow street near the river. "Here," he
said pushing open a gate in a wall. We all passed through and
entered an overgrown yard in which was a dilapidated house with a
broad shady veranda. We tramped up on to the veranda. On the
veranda of the house was a shelf. On the shelf were a few dozen wood
carvings of African men and women. Each was involved in a different
activity. One woman carried wood on her head and another a pot
and another was chopping wood. There was also a gendarme and a
warrior. Each had been carved in great detail and then polished until
the wood shone like glass.

"Ah, Perry, it is good to see you," said a deep voice from the dark
interior. An old black man with a beautiful white beard wheeled

himself out of the dim interior, sitting comfortably back in a wheel-chair. Hough smiled and the two men shook hands.

"My friends!" said Hough, introducing us each by name. The old man shook our hands.

"Alexis is the best carver on the river. He is a true artist," said Hough admiringly. "This is his work, people! He refuses to carve animals. Man is his work."

The old man laughed and clapped his hands in the traditional African way.

It took us some time but we each chose a carving. I chose a warrior holding a spear and Potter chose a man squatting down drinking from a beer pot. I though it out of place that he should choose that particular one, as it was while on this journey that he had managed to straighten out his drinking problem. Pole chose an African gendarme. We held our gifts admiring them.

Hough was happy. "I now wish to show you a secret place," said Hough. He looked around as if someone might have been watching. "Look, there is a secret hiding place between the legs." He turned my warrior over. "There!" he pointed with his stubby finger. It was a crack that seemed to widen internally. "Once a small article is placed inside it can be sealed with wax or even a nicely carved piece of wood."

The old man watched our surprise and laughed and clapped his hands. Hough paid him and we left.

Hough walked along between us. It was funny how we sort of belonged to one other, each part of a unit playing his part. I could never like Hough but he was an essential part. We had operated well together, and we were definitely not to be messed with.

"I have decided to give you guys another present. You remember the dollars we found in the safe. There were more at the back, but no one other than I saw them, so I took them. Some I will send to Thomas's widow. Some I will keep and some I will split between you guys." He grinned happily. "You guys were given a raw deal. This little money might sweeten it all a little," said Hough as he walked along, full of his own self-importance.

"Thanks," we said in unison, not daring to ask how much.

"It is nothing. How would you say, just spoils of war? If I handed it into police headquarters it would just go into someone else's pocket. When we get to the railhead you will give me your carvings, and your addresses. I will send each of you your carving and your little bonus. I do not think I will be staying much longer in this country, with all the talk of elections."

At last we reached and boarded the truck. I was looking forward to being back at the railhead. There was a new sense of urgency and I wanted to get out of this place as soon as possible. The trucks engine burst into life. Ivor waved us off from the police station. The hotel owner and his wife Eva waved and smiled as we passed. She was really pretty. We trundled down the dirt road towards the railhead.

It was fantastic to be clean and to have slept in a clean bed and to eat proper food off clean china plates. Once, the death of someone like the courier who had been eaten before our eyes would have worried me but I had already virtually forgotten about him. We had just seven days left.

Chapter 12

I sat in the back of the truck on my kit, dozing in the and letting my mind wander. It was funny how little things like knives and forks, clean linen and a bath had made life seem good again. I was comfortable and satisfied with life. The memory of roast duck and wine of the night before still made my mouth water. Rogers had been an arrogant fool. I wondered how a person who was obviously intelligent and well educated could be so stupid and blind to what was taking place around him. The woman had not opened her mouth all evening. She had just sat there sipping her wine and smoking.

As I mulled this over in my mind I decided that I would have a few ducks around my dam. Then I suddenly came back to earth. If there was a dam! What had happened was that I had been cut off from the outside world. No Christmas card or present, not even a letter. For nearly two months, none of the letters that I had written had been answered. The uncertainty was there again. Had Mia and Gran really deserted me?

It started to rain, drumming softly on the canvas canopy. Where there were holes in the canvas the rain leaked through. Pole stood with his back to me looking out into the rain. His legs were like tree trunks, standing firmly placed apart and braced.

We had passed through a burnt out village. The next village was old man Borg's. We were about fifty kilometres into the tropical jungle. From here the road would deteriorate. Hopefully we would not get stuck. I clambered to my feet, as the jolting and sliding was becoming too much for my backside and spine. It was far better to stand with legs acting as shock absorbers. I stumbled to my spot in the right-hand corner and peered out at the drab, dripping green jungle. The road was more like a muddy stream that entered dark tunnel then broke out into an open clearing, and the road changed direction continuously. In many places the road was wide where previous vehicles had got stuck and others had forged a new way around through the surrounding bush so as to avoid the bog. We still had about another two or three hours to drive to reach the railhead.

"What's this?" shouted Pole ripping the covers off the machine-gun and bringing me back to the present with a jolt.

"Feu! Feu! Feu! Fire Fire!" screamed Hough from the cab. Potter deftly changed gears, and the wheels were spinning.

We had entered one of those open places in the forest. Three trucks, or had it been the lead truck, were bogged down, holding up the rest. Behind the trucks there was a tractor and trailer and about fifty men covered in mud were struggling to push or pull the lead vehicle out. On the back of the lead vehicle was a heavy machine gun similar to the one the bandits had carried at Crossways School. The trailer, attached behind the tractor, had all sorts of odds and ends on it. A grand piano was balanced on top as well as chairs and tables and a bedstead, all loaded untidily. I took it all in a flash.

Pole swung the Browning in an arc, hammering out a deadly salvo. I saw a soldier trying to man the machine-gun being lifted by unseen hands and tossed aside. I flung myself to the tailgate and started to pluck grenades from a bag. We were close to the enemy, so close that I could see the whites of their eyes. The horror, the shock and the fear were etched clearly on their faces. A few of the men started reaching for their weapons, while others dived under the trucks desperately seeking cover. I lobbed a grenade into the back of the first truck, then one at a running group of men.

I flung grenades indiscriminately at the vehicles as fast as I could extract the pins. The grenades exploded in our wake with solid earth-shaking crunches and columns of mud and bloody bodies. There was no time to check what damage I had caused. I ducked as bullets smacked into the wooden sides of our truck. Suddenly we were gone into a dark slippery tunnel.

Pole was laughing and slapping himself on the leg. "That was a bit of a surprise!" he shouted excitedly.

Thinking back at the sudden thirty seconds of vicious action, I recalled the rattle of Hough's submachine-gun that was almost drowned by the thud, thud of the Browning and the crunch of grenades. I was all of a sudden afraid. There I was a few minutes earlier dreaming, unaware of my surroundings as I tried to relaxed and to find an answer to my personal problems. To relax now could mean death.

The truck skidded to a stop and Hough's head popped up over the tailgate. "Oh Non! Should we go back and give them another fright!" He shouted and laughed excitedly. "They did not know what hit them."

Potter joined us. We were all laughing and congratulating each other. At the time the quick flash of action seemed almost funny. It had got our adrenaline pumping. Even so, it had rattled our nerves. If the bandits had been more alert we could have easily ended up on the receiving end. We did not have the fire-power they had. It was probably their engine noise that had drowned the sound of our approach.

Still laughing and congratulating ourselves we skidded on down the muddy road and arrived at the railhead. It was funny how I felt secure in the tented camp with its sandbags, the battered police station and the sad excuse for a village nearby. Hough went off to the station saying he was going to warn Ivor. The rain had stopped and we sat around dreaming of roast duck, potatoes and wishing time would go faster.

"Hey guys. Post!" shouted Hough who stood at the edge of the station compound waving a small pile of letters. The post must have arrived with the tug. Pole set off to collect it. Potter and I did not receive post and did not even bother getting up.

Pole returned, smiling, "Mac here," and he tossed me a single white envelope.

My heart gave a huge leap, a letter after all this time! It was my first letter in months. Hurriedly, with mouth dry and hands shaking, I tore it open. Then I realised that the handwriting was not Gran's or Mia's and it slowly dawned on me that Lily had written it. Lily! With my heart pounding I moved away to the privacy of the tent. Lily had written! I was filled with a sense of great excitement.

After I had read the letter I sat there cocooned in my mosquito net. The letter was short and to the point. Lily had left the religious order and gone back to the hospital where she had worked before, in a place called Wexeter. She was enjoying her work and everything was all right. In the letter were directions from London and how to get to the place called Ireland, indicating railway stations, ferries, and then finally how to find her house. She could not wait to see me again. "Tons of love, Lily".

I sat there for a long time. Gran, Oupa and Mia had deserted me. Or had they? I still had my doubts, but they had been replaced by an angel.

Today, when we had thought the whole nightmare was over, we could have easily been killed by the bandits. It did not help to be lax, or think the whole episode was over until my feet touched South African soil once more.

Pole was cooking supper when I joined him and Potter. No one commented and no one asked about my letter. Everyone around the fire seemed engrossed in thoughts of his own.

Potter broke the silence. "It's decent of Hough to give us a present of those dollars. If I remember about six months ago, which is difficult," he laughed, "a dollar was worth about one rand sixty."

Pole looked up from the fire. "Every cent will help. It's good of him to be prepared to smuggle the money out in those carvings." He laughed, rubbing his ample belly. "What I would not do for a roast duck and a plate of those potatoes!"

That evening, as we three sat round the fire, there was a great feeling of togetherness. We, hopefully, were going to be the survivors, if nothing else happened.

I went to bed that night and lay awake for a long time. I was more than thrilled that Lily had written, but what had happened to Gran, Oupa and Mia? Thoughts drifted round in my head until the early hours. I woke, not having slept very well.

Potter was making breakfast, and Pole was returning from the ablution block. After tidying the camp I left Potter and Pole reading and went off to the harbour to do some fishing. I needed time to think. As I passed through the village I noticed many of the families had returned and were repairing their huts. They all seemed to be cheerful enough and called their greetings to me as I passed by. The tug would be along in an hour or so.

The next few days drifted by in peaceful bliss. Hough came across one evening with a bottle of wine. We sat around listening to him talk of political and tribal chaos, gangs of rebels and bandits consisting of army deserters and criminals all wanting a piece of the country and what was in it. He was seriously thinking of taking early retirement, saying he doubted that he could survive long after we left.

Later that evening he produced a notebook to take our addresses for him to post the carvings to us. I suddenly realised, like Potter, I did not have an address. I did not know if I had a home to go to, and it made me feel rather sad and dejected. Potter gave Hough Pole's address in Cape Town, saying he would go down there and start a new life. He still spoke of becoming a preacher. My thoughts drifted to Lily and I went to the tent to get her address.

Hough eyed me with a comical expression on his ugly face. "Mac, you're a smooth operator." The other men laughed, but I felt embarrassed nevertheless.

"Got yourself a nun?" roared Hough. Potter and Pole were also laughing. Hough shook his head with tears in his eyes and a grin on his face. "I have been here fifteen years, and all I have ever been told is what a bad guy I am, drinking and beating the crooks. I once shook Sister Pauline's hand, bless her." They all laughed. "You had better tell us how you did it." This was followed by another burst of laughter.

I sat there smiling, not minding that Hough was taking the mickey out of me. He still had not told us how much he was going to give us and none of us asked.

The last few days dragged by and we were all restless, loafing around the camp. Then the morning finally arrived. We were packed and ready to move out.

Hough came hurriedly across from the station. "News!" he called. "This will interest you guys." He stopped in front of us puffing on a cigarette. "Last night de Haas passed through the border at Bangui. He was still driving the Mercedes truck, but he has gone out of this land. The border post was not manned and he just drove straight through." He shrugged as if it was an acceptable occurrence. "There is something else. He was accompanied by a black woman and they were acting, how would you say, luvvy, duvvy." He laughed harshly. "Is it not strange?"

We all agreed with him. But all we wanted to do was to get out of this place as quickly and as soon possible.

I had often wondered about Miriam and how the titbits of information she offered turned out to be true. I suppose it was possible that de Haas might have had a relationship with an African witch-doctor. A woman with possibly twenty-five thousand dollars, and possibly educated in a European school. That was, if the woman was Gogo.

We all solemnly shook Hough's and gendarme Ray's hands and climbed aboard the truck for our last journey. The whole of the village stood in a group on the edge of the football field. Miriam, prominent in her many ways, was standing next to the headman.

Potter stopped next to the crowd of villagers. Miriam acted as the interpreter. "The chief," she referred to the headman, "wishes you all the best and thanks you for your protection. He also hopes you will come back and visit us one day."

He had to be joking, I thought, I never wanted to see this place again! The headman stood there in his vest and baggy khaki shorts, his mouth jabbering away.

Miriam continued with the interpretation. "He also wishes to give you a small present of wood from the jungle that has been made into men." Two sub-headman came forward, with three wooden carvings of what could only be Teng warriors. The swirls, imitating tattoos, were burnt into the hardwood. Each was different. One carried a club, one a spear and one a bow. They smiled proudly as they handed each of us one and shook our hands. We thanked them with lumps in our throats at this unexpected show of appreciation.

Then, with a blast of the horn, which resulted in the crowd cheering and clapping their hands, we pulled away. I felt a huge sense of relief. The whole adventure was at last coming to an end. I sat alone in the back of the truck, and watched the village swallowed up by the jungle. I made myself comfortable on one of the rolled up tents which would cushion the jolting, sliding ride that was ahead of us.

What was going to happen to the people at the railhead? If the sawmill closed there would be no tug with its barges, no felling gangs, no train and no reason for the train to travel to this secluded part of the world. Miriam would close her shop and move on. Hough spoke of leaving and retiring early, as he called it. The Teng would have their dark jungle world to themselves again. That was all that they had wanted anyway.

The same transport plane that had delivered us to Djolu removed us from the field that served as a runway. The men sat and lay on the cargo deck. Forty-six of us had originally arrived. There were thirty-one of us left. We did not speak of the missing men or of how they had died or what suffering they had endured.

To my way of thinking, Maritz had caused his own death. He had tried to be someone he was not. He wanted control and wanted to control by physical force and bullying those around him. He was even prepared to kill to maintain his control. He had a serious chip on his shoulder, probably a mental disorder.

I had often wondered about those first days when we had received our limited training, and how Sergeant Major Ross had asked him about black women, then how he had questioned Teacher about being a queer. Teacher had been a good friend and had done his share to keep us together during trying times. Carr had been all right, with his wisecracks. We had never discussed his death. He had made his own decision. He would have died from the poisonous arrow but had chosen a quicker route out of this life, by taking as many warriors with him as possible. He probably saved us from being overrun and slaughtered. Roux's face, as he ran from the Teng, would haunt me forever. I was now going to start a new life. I did not know what lay ahead for me and felt nervous and frightened at the prospect.

The plane banked, rocking over the hot air waves. Stanleyville would be below us. At Stanleyville airport we were told to dump our kit and change into civilian clothes. We changed on the runway, the heat waves shimmering around us. The cement apron was so hot that it scorched the soles of our feet. My jeans were so tight that they were uncomfortable, and my shirt popped across the shoulders. Thank goodness my shoes fitted. We were formed up, placing our few belongings at our feet and we stood sweating in the boiling heat. Muller and Ross, dressed in neat safari suits, stood relaxed before us.

Pole was on my right and Potter on my left.

"We had better stick together," whispered Potter. "There are a few hungry looking men around."

I had not thought of the danger of our present company. A couple of armed gendarmes and what must have been a customs officer appeared from the main building. They were taking their time.

Muller joined them. The customs officer started to check our belongings, then to body search each of us. He worked slowly, examining each article as if it possessed a fortune in contraband. An aircraft came noisily along the runway and stopped on the apron. Steps were wheeled into place.

"Hope that's our bird," said Potter fidgeting. "It's big enough for us all."

The customs officer eventually reached us. He poked around in our kit, searched us and examined the contents of our wallets. Then he saluted Muller and Ross and marched off. There was a general sigh of relief amongst the men. Everyone was keen to get going.

Muller and Ross saw us onboard. Ross stood there in the boiling heat, a squat red-faced man. "We will see you ladies in hell!" he roared.

We all jeered at him and he laughed, slapping himself on his leg with his stick. Even Muller was smiling. They were not accompanying us.

Chapter Twelve

The flight south was uneventful. The plane had far more room than the ones we had arrived in and seemed a lot quicker. In the early hours of the morning we landed at the private airport from where we had departed. It seemed like a lifetime ago.

Two suit-clad men were waiting for us in the waiting room. We handed in the blue identification cards and received our passports as well as other documents with our bonuses of three hundred rand. There were no stamps in our passports. Nothing to prove we had left and returned.

A bus idled outside, waiting for us.

"A few words gentlemen, before you leave," said one of the men. "We are still looking for a few men to return to the Congo in our next intake. Would any of you be interested?"

A loud jeer went up cutting him off.

He waited for silence and then continued. "As I was saying, pay, accommodation and food will be improving. There is a whole new commando unit being formed. You men can be proud of what you have achieved. You men have been part of the start of a new generation of soldiers that will join the ranks of the Wild Geese of Africa."

"Bullshit!" shouted Jerome, who was right in front of the group, and raising two fingers. "Let's get out of here!" he shouted. There was a chorus of agreement.

"Stick together!" urged Potter quietly and we did just that. The men eyed each other with greedy expressions on their unshaven faces.

"We get off at the first hotel we come to," whispered Pole.

At the first opportunity we took a room at a Holiday Inn, where we shaved, showered, had breakfast and a sleep. I tried to phone the farm, though fearful of what I would hear. All I got was a dead line. I then thought of phoning Mia but changed my mind. I would be home the following day.

I made enquiries about a train to Pietermaritzburg and managed to get a first class ticket on a train leaving at about eight that evening. I wanted to travel in comfort and arrive in style, even though there would not be anyone to meet me.

Later the three of us found a clothing shop, and I purchased new jeans, a shirt and shoes. Potter bought a charcoal suit, shirt and tie and he actually looked quite professional. A dog collar would have made him look like a preacher.

Pole was not interested in buying clothing and spent about an hour on the phone to his wife. Then he spent the rest of the day walking around with a fixed happy smile. Potter and he would be leaving the next day for Cape Town.

That evening Pole and Potter insisted on coming to see me off at the railway station. Tears were in Potter's eyes, as he blew his nose loudly. "Mac, you come and visit us in Cape Town," he said choking on the words and wiping his eyes. Then he blew his nose again. "I am going to start afresh." He stood back smiling sadly and then said softly. "I have wasted so much time."

Pole smiled, shaking my hand. Then he enveloped me in a bear-hug. "Mac, you come visit. Okay."

I had his address in my bag. I nodded, not trusting my own voice. I climbed up the steps as if in a trance. I still could not get over the fact that I was back and safe. I found my compartment, put my bag on the rack and opened the window, grinning foolishly at the men with whom I had shared the horrors and savagery of the last six months. The guard blew his whistle and the train started moving. I stood there with my hand raised long after Pole and Potter were out of sight.

Shutting the window I turned slowly and sat on the plush leather seat. Uncontrollable tears were pouring down my face. I just sat and sobbed and sobbed. All the horror, fear and uncertainty of the past months seemed to well up from with in me. It had to be a sort of relief mechanism. A long time later I dried my eyes and knew it was all over.

The other occupant of the compartment was a wiry little man dressed in an old suit. He told me he sold cutlery and was going to Durban. Then he left for the saloon.

The train travelled through the night. I went to bed. I slept reasonably well, keeping the farm, Oupa, Gran and Mia at the back of my mind.

Chapter Twelve

Coffee was served by the steward as we came out of the tunnel into the mist-covered valley where Pietermaritzburg lay. I was home. What was I going to find? I tried desperately to believe that there had been one big foul-up in the mail and that Oupa had completed the dam, planted grass and fenced the vegetable patch. But deep down I knew it could not be that simple.

I caught the municipal bus as far as it would take me. Then I walked down the road towards Hill Farm. It was a beautiful day. Doves cooed in the bush on the side of the road. I was surprised to hear a bushbuck ram bark up one of the valleys. They had never been known to come so close.

I reached the gate, which was shut, and stood looking up the long driveway lined with bluegum trees. One of the trees had recently been hit by lightning. It stood grey, gaunt and bare. Then I noticed a cardboard notice flapping in the morning breeze. I stood staring at the official-looking notice. My mind went blank. I could not believe what I saw. I stood for a long, long time. "Sale of Execution." I stared at it. It was dated the 18th February. It was ten days away. I stood there hopping up and down on one foot. What was I going to do? What was going on?

I walked up the driveway to the drab grey house. The grapevine looked really good, laden with grapes. No one had picked them. Gran always made grape jam. The questions raced around in my head. What had happened to Gran and Oupa? The screen door swung gently in the breeze. The back door was open. I walked into the most filthy kitchen that I had ever seen. The sink was piled high with unwashed plates. Empty tins lay on the floor. Beer cans lay scattered around and it stank of rotten booze and vomit. I stood there gawking. Someone moved around in the neighbouring room.

"Who's there?" came Oupa's slurred voice.

He shuffled into sight and stood there, staring wide-eyed at me. He was unshaven and filthy, his hair a tangled mess. His big frame had shrunk. From where I stood gaping, I could smell his unwashed body and the rancid stink of alcohol.

"Where the hell have you been, when we needed you?" he snarled.

"Where's Gran?" I stammered. Had Oupa gone mad, or lost his memory?

He stood staring at me. "She died, long time ago," he said slowly.

I stood there, tears forming. Was he lying?

"When?" I asked.

He looked vaguely at me. "Two... three months ago!" he said, coming closer, and he stared at me through bloodshot eyes. I stood my ground.

"Where have you been?" he asked again.

But I ignored the question. "What happened to all the money Oupa?" I asked hoarsely. I already knew.

He looked around vaguely. "It's gone. Had to save the farm."

I pushed past him into his room. It stank of every possible form of filth.

"You want to rob me, boy?" snarled the old man from the door.

I ignored him as I began rummaging through the filth. A rat scuttled for cover and cockroaches ducked between old clothing. I found Oupa's bank book and went onto the veranda, out of the filth and stench. With shaking hands I traced the transactions of the last six months. The money had been paid in on the second of every month. Oupa's pension was paid in on the fifteenth. There was nothing, just fifty cents in the book. I sat down and looked down the valley. There were the vacant cow sheds and the broken rusting tractor. There were no signs of animals or poultry. Oupa must have sold them all.

I had a horrible sick feeling in the pit of my stomach as I walked away from the house, drawn towards the dam. What Gran had written in one of her letters was that the dam had been completed. It all looked pathetically small. Murky yellow water had risen to a depth of about two metres. There were poles planted around what would have been the veggie patch. There were also signs that a tractor had ploughed where I wanted to plant kukui grass.

Gran had died. I stood numbed by the thought. Oupa had given up and gone on the drink, using my money and his war pension. But what had happened to Mia? I would really like to speak to her.

Possibly we could get together again. Then I realised that she only came home over weekends.

For six months I had risked death in that terrible place and all I had to show were a few hundred rand in my pocket. My dream of developing Hill Farm had vanished. The bank would sell Hill Farm on the eighteenth. What would happen to Oupa?

I sat on the log where Mia and I had once sat, and where Oupa and I had once sat and discussed the future of the farm so keenly. I knew it could have worked, if Gran had not died, if Oupa had held things together. If only!

I suddenly saw the neighbouring farm. It had been there in front of me all the time. Manteiga's land. I could see it from where I sat. It was green and lush, with sprinklers rotating and spraying a silver showers of water over the crops. I knew then that I would have to go to Ireland. A tremor ran through me. I needed to see Lily. Would Manteiga lend me money? Would Manteiga tell me what had happened to Hill Farm? I wondered where they had buried Gran. I would like to visit the grave. Time passed and I sat there in the sun, my mind a jumble of thoughts. Then a heron landed gracefully at the water's edge and started its never-ending intense search for food and I knew all was not hopeless!

The shadows were growing long when I eventually made up my mind. I climbed through the new barbed wire fence. I crossed a field of cabbages. The Manteiga's house looked good in the late afternoon light, with its white walls and red roof. Dogs barked at me, and two dogs bounded towards me. One was familiar. With a thrill, I recognised Stripe. He looked older and beaten up; one ear was torn as if he had been in a dogfight. But that attitude was still there as he snapped at my heels. I stood still, looking down at my old friend, and tears welled up in my eyes. "Stripe," I said bending down. He growled at me, then suddenly recognition was there in his eyes and he whined and sniffed at me, his tail wagging furiously. Then he jumped up into my arms. I carried Stripe, scratching his head with my free hand. Sadly, it looked like Stripe and I were going to be the only real survivors of Hill Farm.

I walked on towards the house, I would have to borrow enough money to get to Ireland and the only person I knew who had any was Carlos. Would he be prepared to lend me so much money? I had never borrowed anything from anyone before. I knew I was taking a chance in asking but I was desperate. How else would I get enough for an air ticket?

As I neared the house and shed, Carlos came out of the shed wiping his hands on a wad of waste. He looked up with a surprised expression on his face. Then he walked very quickly towards me. "Mac!" he shouted, far too loudly. "Mac, you're alive!" He shook me vigorously by the hand and slapped me on the shoulder. "Damn it man, the old man said you were dead." He stopped abruptly. "Gran died, you know?" I nodded. "I am sorry." He stood there, looking me up and down. Then he said, "Stripe arrived here one afternoon and he stayed. He is a bloody good dog." Carlos pointed at Stripe, who I still carried in my arms, and Stripe growled at him.

Carlos continued quickly. "You will forgive me but as your friend I must tell you all. Come, please." Carlos led the way into the house, calling to the maid to make tea. He told me about Oupa. He had worked hard in the beginning, employing two labourers and hiring a tractor. Gran had got sick. It was to do with her heart. She had died in hospital. Sadly, he had only learnt of it a week later, when she had already been buried. Oupa had been drinking and told him that I had died. They all had been very upset and Mia had been so upset she had left school and gone to stay with relations in Angola, where she had settled down nicely and was happy.

From that day the old man started drinking heavily, playing the horses and going missing for days at a time. Once he had asked him where he was getting all the money from, the old man had rudely told Manteiga to mind his own business. He had spoken of insurance. Tea had arrived and I became aware I had not eaten since breakfast, for my stomach was rumbling.

"Hill Farm will be sold by the bank on the eighteenth of this month," said Carlos sadly. "I will be hoping to buy it." He spread his hands in a gesture of despair. "My job offer still stands."

"I have a problem," I said cautiously. "A friend owes me a lot of money but lives in Ireland and I must collect it." I did not want to go into detail and thank goodness Carlos did not question me. "Oupa used all the money I earned," I said as an afterthought. Carlos knew that much already.

"How much?" asked Carlos without hesitation. I thought it would be about a thousand but really did not know.

"I need to buy a ticket to London, then across to Ireland," I said. Carlos was on his feet in a flash. "It is urgent Mac?"

"Yes, and it will be the only chance I will have to make something out of the last six months," I said.

Carlos left the door of his office open, the phone call was brief. "Yes, yes, London, okay." I heard him replace the receiver and heard him rummaging around in his office. Then he called out. "Mac, I can help you. No problem with that."

I stood in the middle of the lounge with a thousand rand in my hand. "I will pay you back with interest," I said, still in a state of mild surprise.

Carlos laughed. "No, Mac, I owe you. You pay back the money when you can. No interest. You are a friend of this family and will always be welcome."

It was a nice comfortable feeling being welcome and belonging to this close-knit family.

Outside it had got dark. Car lights lit up the house and yard. "It is my wife and kids," said Carlos rising and going to the door. I felt out of place, wanting to cut and run now that I had money in my pocket.

Moments later Mrs Manteiga came bubbling into the room with her shopping bags and the two sisters in tow. She stopped in mid-stride. "Goodness, a ghost!" she shouted hugging me.

The sisters crowded around. May giggled, "What's it like to be dead?" she asked holding my hand and looking up at me with wide eyes. "Mia's going to be real cross to hear you're still alive and well."

"Go get us a cold drink," said the mother, laughing and pushing the two giggling girls away.

"Mac you are to stay here tonight. That house is not fit for no one, other than drunks." She stood there ordering everyone around. Carlos had slipped away and into his office, but he now returned.

"Mac, I have spoken to Air Portugal. You must pay tomorrow and leave from Johannesburg. Your flight is in two days' time. I've told them it very was urgent." He smiled and winked, "I have connections you know."

The night I spent with the Manteiga's was really pleasant. Carlos was interested in the Congo, the soil, the diseases, the timber, the witches, as well as the little I knew about the politics and tribalism. I gave Carlos the carving of the Teng warrior, the one carved by the railhead sub-headman. Carlos placed it on the mantelpiece. Oddly they avoided any further questions I asked of Mia. Only to say, that she was happy and living with relatives in the city of Luanda in Angola. It was close to midnight when I eventually got to bed.

I woke in the early hours, not knowing where I was at first. I sat at the window watching the sun creep up over the far-off black hills. I would have to go back to Johannesburg from where my flight would leave. At least I was now headed in the right direction. And Oupa, what of him now? He had his war pension, and I presumed the MOTHS would look after him, as they always had. I did not want to see him again. I would rather remember him as a tough old Scott telling his war stories. I was going to miss Gran more than I liked to admit. She had always been so sensible and strong.

The next day, before taking me to the railway station, Carlos had taken me to the graveyard near the hospital where Gran had been buried. I stood there looking blankly at the small gravestone. Her name and dates were finely engraved on it. At least Oupa had got that right. For me there were no tears, just emptiness. Gran was gone. It was funny, for she had always seemed to be the stronger of the two old people. I stood with the morning sun burning down on me, my hands clasped but no prayer would come. Just that emptiness prevailed. "Gran," I said soberly, "thanks for everything. I should have listened to you and stayed." I turned and walked away. A little piece of me died that day.

Carlos had stood respectfully a short distance away. He now fell in alongside me as we walked away through the graveyard, with the white gravel pathway crunching loudly underfoot.

The flight from Johannesburg to London was long and cramped but at ten in the morning I found my way from Heathrow to Euston station by following Lily's instructions. At the railway station I bought a book on Ireland, not wanting to be caught out with zero knowledge of my destination.

The train passed through the shabby outskirts of London and into a green countryside dotted with farms and villages. I tried to read the book on Ireland but kept on nodding off to sleep, much to the amusement of an old man and lady who sat opposite.

"Where are you from my boy?" asked the old lady with a strong accent. "The sun has really got to you."

"Africa," I said bluntly and smiled back at her.

"South Africa where they treat the black people so badly?" asked the old man.

I nodded. "The very same," I said slowly.

"Shame on you!" said the old woman aghast.

I just smiled and remained quiet. If they only knew what I had just gone through, maybe they would possibly have had a different opinion. I dozed and woke again, then slept fitfully through the journey.

After another two-hour wait at Fishguard, the ferry departed. I crossed the Irish Sea in a half-asleep state. I had read most of the book on Ireland and hoped I was well prepared for what lay ahead, but I had my doubts.

Late that afternoon I arrived at Wexeter and received directions from an old man walking his dog. I walked quickly down Plough Lane, as a cold wind whipped the hedgerows and grass into a frenzy. There was a smattering of snow on the low hills. I strode along with my coat wrapped around me and my hands deep in my pockets. The end of my journey was close and an excitement I could not describe welled up inside me. I would be seeing Lily O'Hare.

There were many questions in my mind. Would she be different amongst her family and what type of greeting would I get? And what about the pendant? Although this was the real reason for being here, it had not really entered my head yet.

As I rounded the bend I saw the house. It was as Lily had described. The third house in a line of three tumbled-down houses. There was a neighbouring field with a herd of really nice-looking Friesian cows. The grass and hedges were ever so green. In the distance the wind whipped the grey sea and I could see a ship passing.

I strode confidently up to the door. The bell clanged deep in the building. I stood there waiting excitedly. Would Lily open the door? How would she greet me? These questions seemed very important to me. The door opened and a small wiry woman peered at me. She had the most beautiful grey eyes which were slightly tilted at the corners. She could only be Lily's mother.

"I am Donavan Mackay," I said putting out my hand.

She took my hand in both her hands, smiling at me and then, in that beautiful accent, she spoke. "Mac, she called you. You've come a mighty long way to see our Lily have you not? Come along in." She turned and led the way into the chaotic interior. "Lily is at work and will be along shortly." She pointed to a comfy-looking chair. "Be seated, I'll put the kettle on."

I sat back and glanced around the beautifully warm room. There was a log fire in the hearth and old family photos on the wall. I removed my coat. The chair was soft and I sunk back in it. There was the sound of the woman in the kitchen, with a cow mooing in the distance and snowflakes were beating against the window pane. I dozed. I was here at last. A great sense of peace and love for Lily flooded over me and I must have fallen asleep.

"Mac, oh Mac!" Lily squealed and brought me fully awake with a start. She tossed her jacket onto the back of a chair. I struggled to gain my footing. Lily threw her arms around my neck and we kissed for the first time. It was a very different kiss to Mia's. This was a solid, slapping kiss.

"I thought you were never coming," she purred as she pulled off her scarf. "I have terrific news!" She looked around as her mother entered, smiling and carrying a tray. Lily changed the subject, "How was your trip?"

"All right," I said, realising she did not want to talk in front of her mother.

Lily's mum had sat down at the table and poured tea into the mugs.

"When did you leave? How long did it take? Were Pole and Potter all right?" asked Lily hurriedly.

I laughed trying to answer all her questions as best I could.

"Pop and the boys will be home in an hour," said her mother, buttering the bread. "I am sure they will be keen to meet your friend from South Africa."

Lily smiled happily. "Sure," she said.

I sat in the warm comfort, drinking tea and eating bread and jam and making small talk.

"Did I tell you I have four brothers?" she asked.

She had not.

"They work at the harbour. They are fine chaps."

Her mother nodded as if agreeing. I sat there basking in the warmth and listening to Lily chattering away. Her accent was almost hypnotic and made me really sleepy. Then there was the sound of the front door banging and a blast of cold wind came down the passage. Pop appeared first, a broad-shouldered grey-haired man; he came into the room. He pumped my hand up and down, and thanked me for saving his only daughter from the savages. Then the three brothers entered, all of similar stature. They looked pleasant, broad-shouldered characters. They greeted me warmly.

"So you're the hot shot from Africa," joked one. "Hear you had quite a fight on your hands, what with poisonous arrows and cannibals. Thanks for looking after Lily."

I just smiled politely, not wanting to get involved with war stories. The conversation waned quickly and then tea was served. Pop and the three boys went off into another room to watch television. This was something I had never seen before as South Africa did not have television.

I sat and chatted to Lily and her mum, wishing the latter would leave so that Lily and I might discuss the pendant. Lily had not mentioned the woodcarving. I was not sure if she had received it. I was interested to know how much Hough had given me.

Lily saved the day at last. "Mac and I will wash up the tea things," she said. Then she was on her feet collecting the dirty cups and dishes. I joined her.

"How can you ask a visitor do such a thing?" complained her mother but did nothing to prevent me. Lily placed the plates in the sink and turned on the water. She turned to me placing her arms around my neck. "Guess how much the pendant is worth?" she asked with stars in her eyes.

I shrugged, not knowing what to guess.

"I took it to a jeweller in Dublin, who's a friend of the family. His name is O'Riley," said Lily.

"Two thousand," I said.

"He says it's from the seventeenth century and very old and valuable. He would not buy it. He said he could not give me a fair price." It was all coming out in little gasps of excitement. "Forty thousand. He says the diamonds are extremely valuable but the ruby is nothing special."

I stood there and time stood still. Lily just stood there in silence, with her arms locked round my neck and her body pressed against mine.

"Forty thousand pounds?" I said very slowly.

Lily started to hop up and down excitedly. "It's a fortune. No one must know. Especially none of my family," she whispered.

I stood there, completely struck dumb. It was a small fortune. I had lost the farm, lost Gran, Oupa and Mia, and even lost all the money I had been paid, but suddenly I had forty thousand pounds, minus Lily's share. I could have bought Hill Farm outright and I still could if I moved quickly. I stood there in the kitchen holding Lily tightly. The water from the sink was overflowing onto the floor. My mind was confused. I could sell the pendant, and go back and buy

Chapter Twelve

Hill Farm. Was this the answer to my problem, the pendant? We washed up the tea things, and I was in a kind of a trance when we returned to the lounge. The men could be heard cheering on a football game in the neighbouring room.

Lily's mom was asleep in the chair. Lily went off down the passage and returned with the carving of the warrior. "What are you doing?" she laughed, as I turned the carving upside down, examining its groin.

"Have you got a sharp knife?" I asked.

Lily opened a drawer and removed a carving knife, "Big enough?" she asked, giggling.

Taking the knife, I probed with the tip of the blade and dislodged the wax plug. Carefully I extracted a tightly folded wad of money.

"Wow! Money is popping out everywhere," she whispered her eyes bright. "How much is it?"

I set about counting.

"Five hundred dollars, and don't you dare ask where I got it. I am not going to tell you," I whispered.

Just then the men were returning into the room. I slipped the notes, unseen by them, into my pocket. Hough had done me well. There must have been a substantial amount in the safe for him to give money away like that. It was difficult to understand how the policeman's brain worked.

"I have been given an address in London where we can sell that pendant," said Lily quietly so the family could not hear. "On Thursday, Friday and Saturday I will be off duty so we can go together."

This arrangement did not give me much time to get back for the sale of the farm. I also agreed that we would travel together. I was not completely sure if she trusted me or not but I could understand why Lily wanted to come along to collect her share.

The next day I spent loafing around, mostly indoors. Outside it was very cold. I watched television for the first time in my life and sat glued to every programme, thinking that it was really interesting. In between I attempted to plan my future on Hill Farm.

Lily arrived home at about seven. She was flushed from the cold outside and full of excitement. "Why don't we leave now? We can be in London by the time the shops open."

I liked the idea. "The quicker the better," I said.

Pop and the boys had just arrived. "We could get Pop to take us to the ferry terminal," said Lily hurriedly, smiling at her father.

He nodded in agreement."Going sight-seeing, are you?" he queried and turned back to his newspaper.

Mum was pouring tea. Lily's brothers were joking about that evening's football game. I knew nothing about football. The room buzzed with a friendly and homely atmosphere.

The front door banged loudly and there was a shuffling noise in the passage. Pop looked up from the newspaper and shot to his feet. Three men crashed into the room, with pistols and revolvers in their hands. My mind froze.

"Put yànds where we can see them," snarled the one waving an ugly automatic pistol. He looked nervous and was sweating profusely as his black beady eyes darted around the room.

What now? This was a bit much, an armed robbery? I hoped Lily had the pendant well hidden. The three men did not look very professional, but I knew a nervous man with a gun was very dangerous.

Everyone in the room did what they were told. Mum O'Hare was shaking uncontrollably with fear.

"Check the rooms," snarled one and the other two men rushed to search the rest of the house. I could hear their thumping footsteps as they passed above us checking the upstairs rooms.

Soon they returned. "Nothing," said one. Then he went into the kitchen, only to return shrugging his shoulders.

What the hell were they looking for?

The man with the automatic pistol pointed it directly at Pop. "Where's that no good son of yours?" he snarled.

Mum started to rise, her face white as a sheet and she looked as if she was going to speak.

"Shut up woman," said Pop hoarsely. "He is not here, and we have not seen the lad."

The man with the automatic pistol waved it around dangerously. I braced myself expecting him to shoot. The atmosphere was electric.

"Who might you be?" snapped the man, pointing the pistol at me.

"He's a visitor. He's not from here," wailed Mum in distress.

"I am from Africa," I said, trying my best to remain calm.

He grunted and passed me over. "Now where is Tim?!" shouted the leader. "You tell that no good bastard to return what belongs to the cause, or Ireland will not be big enough for him to hide in. He thinks he can make a fool of us."

I watched the leader. He was perspiring heavily. His oily skin shone in the harsh light and his black eyes were wild and never still. He was winding himself up. The man was unstable and the way he waved the big calibre pistol around was outright dangerous.

"Do you hear O'Hare?" he snarled.

Pop nodded, "I hear you," he said, surprisingly calmly. He was standing to one side with his back to the wall.

"Do ya all hear me," he snarled, spit flying from his mouth.

My mind was racing. Who was Tim? Who where these ruffians?

The man with the pistol turned away, pushing the pistol through his belt. Then, spinning back on the ball of his foot, he slammed his fist hard into Pop's midriff. With a loud hiss of escaping air the old man folded up and dropped on to the floor. The three men were backing out of the room, their guns still drawn and pointing at us. A moment later the front door slammed and there was the sound of running feet.

The brothers helped Pop to a chair, and he recovered slowly.

"Tim has brought far too much trouble on this household," said Mum fussing around.

"How about a drop?" gasped the old man. A bottle of whiskey appeared, as if by magic. Glasses were placed on the table and even Mum had a large one.

I sipped my drink but my mind was racing waiting for an explanation. "Who's Tim?" I asked. I could see that there was going to be no explanation. I remember Lily saying that she had four brothers and I had only seen three.

Lily looked embarrassed. "It's not fair involving you in this lot," she said.

I shrugged. I did not say it but as soon as I had my share of the money I would be off. As much as I liked Lily this was a bit much.

"He is my younger brother. He got caught up with the IRA," explained Lily.

"The IRA?" I asked. I had never heard of them.

"The Irish Republican Army. It's illegal. He went to prison." She stopped abruptly.

Pop nodded as if giving her permission to continue. "He had only six months to go, but heaven help him, he escaped and is now on the run." She shrugged her narrow shoulders. "It's being very bad news down here. We have not seen or heard of him since. For all we know he could be out of the country. Why the IRA are after him we don't know. It looks as if he has been involved in another crime which we are unaware of."

We all sat around the table drinking. I did not like the strong spirit that was drunk neat and I was making heavy work of it.

Pop leaned forward and explained. "He was caught with a small amount of explosive. That was all." He made probably a serious crime sound unimportant. "It's that brother of mine Jim. He's bad news, always drunk and fighting and involved in shady deals. He was supposed to take care of the boy." The old man poured more liquor into his glass, ignoring everyone else.

The room was quiet except for the ticking of the clock on the wall. What a night it had turned out to be, I thought. I was shocked at the night's occurrence; men with guns in this so-called peaceful country. It was now far too late to leave. Lily was apologetic, saying we would leave first thing in the morning. I was still tired after my flight and the train journey and ferry crossing.

Later Lily accompanied me to my room then slipping her arms around me and giving me a hug. "It's going to be just fine Mac, just fine," she whispered as we kissed goodnight. I really hoped she was right as time was running out fast. I crawled under the duvet and slept like I had not slept for a long time.

Chapter Twelve

I awoke in the early hours to hear the wind howling around the building. I felt a new, deep warm feeling for Lily O'Hare. I was not sure if it was love, but it was certainly a feeling I'd never felt before for another human. She had been trustworthy and a real good friend. She had looked after my interests, our interests. She had been honest about her brother Tim. Why would someone break out of prison if they had only six months to go? The IRA sounded extremely dangerous. I wondered what the IRA were fighting for?

I lay there letting all the questions drift around in my head. If I told Lily about the farm, would she come back to Africa with me, I wondered? Maybe, after a while, we could marry. I lay dozing, thinking about my situation. I was too young to get married. Did I really want to tie myself down when there seemed so much still to do? I was nearly eighteen years old and in possession of a small fortune. I sat bolt upright in bed. What had I been thinking? The farm had been the centre of my life all along. I knew Hill Farm inside out. It was not a good farm, with poor soil and long droughts. The grazing was also poor.

As the faint morning light filtered through the curtains, I decided I was being a complete fool. Why spend good money on a rundown farm? With the new money I could buy a better farm, one with a greater carrying capacity, in a high rainfall area with better soil. I sat there with the duvet wrapped around my shoulders. I pulled the curtains back and peered out. The country was covered in a soft white blanket of snow. It was beautiful but freezing cold.

I sat there wrestling with my thoughts. I had doubts about my future. Did I really want to be a farmer, considering the long hours and back-breaking toil, sick cows and cows calving in the middle of the night, and trying to find a market to sell my produce. There seemed to be a never-ending list of things, which did not include the breaking of equipment and machinery, the cost of the repairs, as well as drought and disease. All my life, no matter how good the year had been, there had always been a shortage of ready cash.

By spending six months on a brutal operation, I had earned more money than Hill Farm had produced in years. There had been hard times, sad times, terrifying times and fearful memories but the big

285

thing was I had survived. I had become hard and dangerous, with little regard for human life. I had grown up. I sat there in the cold, watching the moonlight reflecting off the snow, a wonderland of beauty. What was it that I really wanted?

Chapter 13

I re-examined my early morning thoughts as we sailed across the Irish Sea. Lily sat silently next to me, leaving me to my thoughts. What was I going to do? Where was I to go? I was restless and undecided. I had been brought up on Hill Farm, which was a doubtful proposition and far from a success. It was a damned hard way to survive. I would be following in Oupa's footsteps. I would hopefully receive about twenty-eight thousand pounds for the pendant and there were roughly two rand to the pound. I would have fifty-six thousand rand. It was a lot of money.

As we boarded the train for London, we had the compartment to ourselves. Lily sat close to me. She seemed to want to talk but did not know how to start. She got up and went to sit directly opposite me, her hands clasped in her lap and looking me in the eye.

"Mac, what are you going to do with your share of the money?" I told her about the farm. It was not the first time she had heard about it.

Lily sat in silence for a long time. "That's your dream," she said and then took a deep breath. "Mac, I don't want to go back to Ireland. There is nothing for me there. I would like to go far away. We could find a small hotel or boarding house in a country where there is sunshine and blue skies. It would have to be in the right position and I would make a go of it." She stopped abruptly and started to wring her hands, then taking a deep breath. "I would like you to be my partner, sharing with you whatever we make. I have a reasonable understanding of business and about a year's experience. My aunt has a boarding house in Dublin and I have worked there." She stopped talking abruptly.

I sat staring at her. She was a small, beautiful woman with natural auburn hair that had grown a little since I had last seen her. Her small gold earrings caught the light. She was wearing a drab coat and worn jeans. She sat and bit her bottom lip nervously. Her grey eyes were wide with apprehension. She stared back at me.

"I know I am not putting this across very well, and it may sound like cheek but you and I are meant to be together." She blurted it out and shrugged her shoulders in a hopeless gesture. "I know farming is really hard work with little return. Even in Ireland many farmers go under every year. I could imagine farming in Africa is a lot harder than in Ireland." It was now coming out in a rush. There was desperation in her voice. "If we bought a hotel, we could build up a small quality business together. You can't lose money as the value of property always goes up and up. You would not have to stay if you wished to go off. All I ask for is a partner, even a silent partner, that I can rely on," she stopped talking abruptly.

This was a completely new idea. It was also the way she put it. I would not be tied down, but it would be an investment. But if so, where would I go and what would I do? Her desperation was getting to me. What she suggested also made a whole lot of sense. We were in much the same boat. A sudden fortune had landed upon us, a fortune neither of us had imagined possible. Now I really did not know what to do.

Here I sat, looking out of a carriage window, speeding through the English countryside. It was sleeting, the almost-formed snow was slapping onto the windowpane. The farmlands were spread out in neat squares with neat hedgerows. A farmer's Land Rover could be seen parked in a lane and the farmer was out there driving a herd of cows before him. It was not pleasant out in the open, for it was cold and wet. Farming, wherever one was, was definitely a hard life to choose. Then the picture was gone with the passing train. It was that picture that changed my mind. I decided there were definitely easier ways of making a living.

There was actually nothing for me to go back to South Africa for. Was farming just a dream? Gran was dead and Oupa was a drunk. Mia, sweet Mia, was away with relatives in Angola and there had been no talk of her returning home. The farm was to be sold to cover the old man's debts. It all blew through my head. Lily sat opposite me watching my every move.

"You're not going to run out on me as soon as we have the money, are you?" she eventually asked nervously.

I shook my head, although I had thought of leaving, as this Irish family was far too complicated.

"Mac, I don't want to go back to that old untidy house, and those noisy brothers of mine. There is no future for me there. I want to make a life of my own, with you preferably," Lily blurted out.

I looked up surprised. Was this some sort of declaration of love?

"Give me a day," I said. I needed time to digest what she had just said and to sort things out in my head. Lily rose from opposite me and came and sat very close to me again.

"That will be fair enough," she said with a sparkle in those steady grey eyes.

The address in London given by O'Riley was not that easy to find, even with the help of a map. We had probably walked past the grubby jeweller's shop half a dozen times before we found it! There was no display window, just burglar bars and a dirty window with the name "Cohen" painted on. It was positioned too high up so that we missed it each time we passed.

I rang the intercom. A guttural voice asked what I wanted.

"I am Mackay from Ireland. O'Riley of Dublin sent me," I said, not very clearly, into the little voice box.

"Aye, come right in," said the voice. The door clicked open and we entered the grubby little shop. Before us was a dusty display cabinet filled with watches, rings and necklaces. That was all the shop had in it.

Standing there in the shop I became nervous as I realised there was now no easy way out. The curtains at the back of the counter rustled and a short, fat little man entered. His smile showed missing teeth, but the smile never reached his piggy eyes.

"Have you the merchandise?" he asked in a hoarse whisper.

I nodded and pulled the pendant from my pocket. He smiled, and produced a set of scales from underneath the counter then he positioned a jeweller's glass in his eye.

"Not stolen?" he asked softly.

I shook my head. "No. It comes from Africa," I offered.

He weighed the necklace, then felt the weight, letting it slip gently through his fingers. I could see the greed and the absolute pleasure the little man felt while handling the article. He placed it deftly on the scales and then removed it. Then he placed the pendant on the counter and tapped a figure onto his calculator. Using the eyepiece he examined the stones closely, grunting each time as he changed position. Finally, he sat back, his face a mixture of emotions, but greed was the most obvious. "Ah, a most beautiful piece!" he breathed.

This was taking far too long for my liking and I could feel the nervous sweat running down my back. I presumed O'Riley had contacted the hard-eyed little man.

"Well," he said. "How much do you want for it?"

I looked at him and my surprise obviously showed. "Fifty thousand!" I said. Did the man really want to bargain?

"Sorry matey, I can only give you thirty. Take it or leave it!"

I shrugged and put my hand out. "Thanks, I will try somewhere else," I said hoarsely as my mouth had suddenly become dry.

He smiled a cold smile. I leant forward, reaching out for the pendant. I swear I saw a large head lice crawling on his bald patch.

"Let's call it thirty-five," he said very slowly.

I shrugged. "I've already had it valued. The jeweller could not come up with the money. That's why I am here. Say forty two and I will be happy," I said licking my lips.

He sat there, his hard eyes boring into me. I decided that the little crook was not that tough. It was just greed. He tapped his pen on the counter, watching me.

"All right matey! You can't say I didn't try." He coughed and removed a cheque book from under the counter and searched for a pen.

I had given this a bit of thought. "There's a Barclays' bank down the road on the corner. We'll do the transaction there," I said.

He gave me another cold-eyed smile. "Mind if I bring my brother-in-law along?" He did not trust us.

"Bring whoever you like," I retorted. I knew I could push it a bit, and I could feel the greed in the little man. He was hooked on that piece of jewellery.

Later I wondered how much he was going to make out of it. It had to be a great deal. The arrangement was simple. He gave us the cash, we banked it and we walked back to the shop with the jeweller's brother-in-law. The brother-in-law was all of six feet tall and built like a prize-fighter, but he did not speak. The little man took the pendant, plugged his eyepiece in and quickly examined the pendant again. The prize-fighter stood there with his arms folded and his legs apart.

"It was a pleasure to do business with you Mr Mackay," he smirked. "If you come across more items of such quality I would be pleased to do business with you again." He nodded to his brother-in-law who stepped aside and opened the door.

Lily and I stood there. She was holding my hand very tightly. We could not speak. We had money in our pockets, but the rest was in our own newly opened bank account. We were to collect our cheque books later. A sheet of newspaper, blown by the wind, wrapped itself around my leg. I just stood there. I was rich. We were rich! Lily was weeping quietly and groping for a tissue.

"Come, I will buy you a late lunch," she said, drying her eyes.

I followed her dumbly and we crossed the road to a restaurant.

I had eaten well, but I could not remember what I had eaten or what I had drunk. I stood on the steps of the restaurant as the world slowly returned to me. Red London buses, black cabs, drab people in drab clothing hustling past, rushing to who knows where or why. London held nothing for me. There wasn't anything to keep me here now. Now was the time for me to leave. I had completed my share of the bargain. I had paid Lily her share. I knew I would miss her.

Then a horrible thought struck me. Where would I go and what would I do? Half of me said "Go back and buy a farm in Africa or buy Hill Farm." The other half said, "What for?" What Lily had said on the train was very real and practical. Some farms made it, some did not. I stood there on the cold London street, pondering my predicament. I would have to pull myself together, but first I must go back to the bank to pay my debt to Carlos for I had his banking details and at the same time we could collect our cheque books.

Lily seemed to sense there was something going on in my head. She cuddled up close.

"Mac, let's do something crazy. Let's go to the Mediterranean where it's warm. We can easily afford it. We can fly there straight away. It's not that far. I only have to be back on Sunday."

Lily was desperate again. I could feel it. She was trying to keep me and kept on breaking in on my thoughts, preventing me from making my own decisions.

"We can swim in the sea, and there's sure to be sun," she added with a tired little smile. "Look there's a travel agent on the corner. Come on Mac, let's go!" she pleaded. Her eyes were excited and she was almost pulling me off my feet.

I would still have time if I changed my mind. "Indeed why not?" I said in a phoney English accent that was not very good, "And we will have a cracker of a time!" She laughed, looking up at me, relief showing in her lovely face.

We flew from London to Paris where we changed planes for Marseille. Lily had eventually run out of things to talk about. I leant back in the airline seat with my eyes shut, trying to give myself space to think. Things were happening far too fast. The return to the farm was no longer necessary. I did not have to go. I did not need the farm any more. The dream had died with Oupa. But what next? I had money. I could go back at anytime that I pleased. Lily spoke of a hotel or boarding house. Did I really want to invest my money in that type of business? In a couple of months I would be eighteen. I felt a lot older and more worldly. A beautiful woman was wanting to share her life with me, to become my lover and partner, and to be my business partner. I had been surprised when Lily had told me her age. She was almost four years older than me. She really did not look it.

There was also another problem that became apparent at the airports. I knew South Africans were not too popular amongst certain people because of the politics and the apartheid laws. I also knew I had only been allowed to visit the United Kingdom on a visa for six months. I could not stay, nor take up residence or work in the United Kingdom. I had brought up the subject with Lily but she had shrugged and said, "Let's wait until we get back".

I sat there dozing, letting it all sink in. I could see my South African passport was going to cause a lot of problems. In the meantime I was determined to enjoy my new-found love, my money and my freedom.

I dozed, letting my mind wander from option to option. A shadow drifted over me and I caught the strong smell of alcohol. Then a familiar clipped voice said, "How are you, Herr Mackay?"

I opened my eyes with a start. Lieutenant Muller stood in the aisle looking down at me. I grinned foolishly. What on earth was he doing here, I thought.

"Let me buy you a drink," said Muller, smiling and attracting a steward's attention to order drinks. Then he looked at Lily and I saw recognition in his eyes. Lily smiled and moved over to the vacant seat next to her. I also moved up leaving the aisle seat for Muller to sit in.

"The world is a small place," I said grinning at my ex-commanding officer.

"Too small," said Muller. Then he greeted Lily.

The steward arrived with our drinks and we toasted one another.

"So what are you up to?" asked Muller.

"Going to the 'Med' for a few days," I said casually, as if it was the most natural thing to do in the world.

"I am going to have two weeks of sun, do a little gambling and live the good life," said Muller. "After that I will be returning home – home as in the Foreign Legion. I was an officer before I left a year ago. Since returning from the Congo I have applied and have been accepted." Muller took a sip of his drink.

Lily leant forward, looking at Muller over the rim of her glass. Then she asked, "Have you any ideas how Mac could remain in Europe? It's his South African passport you know. The British won't let him stay for longer than six months on a tourist visa."

Muller looked into his glass like a fortune-teller searching for my destiny. Then he dropped his voice to a whisper. "The South Africans have caused their own problems, but I know a way. Mac is a natural soldier and an excellent marksman. So why not meet me at nine on Monday in two weeks' time in Marseille, outside the white gates to hell – and then he can sign a five-year contract to serve France. You will receive the best training in the world. Then, upon completion of this contract, he'll have a French passport and French citizenship. His troubles will be solved for good." Muller sighed, looking long and hard at me, and he took a long drink. Then he added, "Five years is not a long time. Take it from me."

"What about an Irishman? Would he be accepted?" asked Lily, watching Muller closely.

"As long as he can complete the basic training and swear that he will serve France. He would be accepted," said Muller.

Then Lily remained quiet. I knew what she was thinking of. It was a way out for her brother Tim O'Hare, an IRA man and a prison escapee.

I felt the first tremor of excitement, but there were a lot of doubts. "I don't speak French," I volunteered.

Muller shrugged. "Many of the recruits don't speak French or English but they get by."

I looked at Lily, who looked concerned and obviously had not expected Muller's response. Then I offered Muller another drink, which he refused politely.

He stood in the aisle smiling down at me. "I must return to my seat. Mac, I will see you at nine in the morning outside the white gates to hell. Ask any taxi driver and he will drop you there. Ciao, Mac, Miss Lily." Muller bowed his head and went off towards the rear of the plane.

When we disembarked at Marseille I looked for Muller but, funnily enough, he was nowhere to be seen.

Chapter Thirteen

The French village of St Nicholas was a sleepy little seaside holiday resort just off the beaten track. It was just after eight and I stood on the hotel balcony admiring the view. It was already pleasantly warm. The sea was a tranquil blue with the morning sun sparkling on the water. Sails of many colours were already dancing across the bay. A scattering of early risers were already on the beach and joggers were shuffling past on the road below.

Lily joined me, coming up from behind and wrapping her arms around me, and then she kissed the back of my neck, causing an exciting a thrill to run down my spine and into every corner of my body. Never in my life had I loved anyone like I loved the beautiful Lily O'Hare.

Chapter 14

On our last night at St Nicolas we sat at a pavement cafe drinking wine. The more time I spent with Lily the more I loved her. She was great company, intelligent and practical and completely trustworthy. I realised for the first time in my life I was with someone who loved me dearly, she also gave me direction and hope. Lily had thought ahead and done a lot of planning and I was part of her plan, her future. Her plan was to buy a hotel and work together to make it work. Then gradually doubts crept in. I was not sure if I could do it, or be completely committed. All Lily had asked for was my share of the money. She had said she wanted a partner, a silent partner.

The idea of joining a regular army did not at first appeal to me, but as the days passed, things began to fall together. I had just spent six months in hell, and I doubted if anything could be worse than that. I was not ready to settle down, with Lily or anyone else. The idea of serving the public, even if it was my own establishment, did not appeal to me. But then, I did not want to lose the woman of my dreams. If we were partners we would have a bond and a contract. Whatever happened she would not be able to just leave me nor I her. I could not obtain a British passport so I concluded a French passport was just as good. Five years was not a long time. I sat there, trying to rationalise it all in my mind. There would be leave and days off, I hoped. I believed the training camp would be near Marseilles. Just imagine if Lily could possibly find a hotel near the base. That, I decided, was wishful thinking.

A song from within the cafe whispered across the still air. It was a soft angelic voice singing, "Where have all the soldiers gone?" There was an interruption as people left the neighbouring table. "Gone to graveyards, every one." I listened spellbound.

Lily caught the mood and the words and she held my hand very tightly. Then she sang softly, "Where have all the young girls gone?" Where had they indeed? Where was I going? This was probably the more important question.

On the 2nd April 1964 I signed a contract committing myself for a period of five years to the French Foreign Legion. This was the beginning of a "Red Road" to who knows where.

I left Lily O'Hare in possession of my fortune and in search of what she called our "dream establishment". We were both fully aware that changes could take place in our relationship and in our business arrangements but at the time I was madly in love with Lily and trusted her and her judgement completely.